EDEN

by

Matthew C. Plourde

This is a work of fiction. Names, characters, places and events portrayed in this book are either products of the author's imagination or are used fictitiously. Any character resemblance to actual persons, living or dead, is entirely coincidental.

EDEN

Copyright © 2010 by Matthew C. Plourde

An "Eden Saga" novel by Matthew C. Plourde
http://matthewcplourde.wordpress.com/

Cover artwork by Axel Torvenius

ISBN: 1453847383

EAN-13: 9781453847381

First Edition: October 2010

For my wife, Bonnie… you just never stop believing in me!

Myth is more potent than history
- *The Storyteller's Creed*, Robert Fulghum

CHAPTER 1

Alexandra Contreras opened her eyes and winced at the sting of dust and smoke. Her ears focused on the crackle of something burning nearby. Smoldering rubber and twisted metal released their associated smells into the mangled section of the bus. She tasted blood in her mouth. Through the grogginess in her head, Alexandra wondered why she was lying in a sea of shattered glass on the inside roof of a wrecked bus.

Before she found any answers in her pounding skull, Alexandra heard a man yell nearby.

"Anybody okay in there?"

Unsure if the man was asking about her bus, Alexandra looked around. Nighttime darkness filled the vehicle. She remembered the bus only had a few people aboard when she left San Antonio. No, that wasn't right. She left San Antonio on a large commuter bus. This smaller bus left from Laredo *last* night. Or was it the night before? Alexandra wasn't sure. To stimulate some coherent thoughts, Alexandra shook her head and a lance of pain shot through her forehead and down her spine.

Trying to manage her throbbing head, Alexandra turned and saw another passenger through the dark strands of her bloodied hair. He was a middle-aged man lying on his back about four feet away. Alexandra forced a smile. "Are you all right?"

The man didn't answer. He didn't even blink. Alexandra felt a rush of nervousness and fear gather momentum at the bottom of her stomach. Sweat chilled her hands as she realized the man could be dead. When the emotions reached her throat, Alexandra decided to leave the wreckage as quickly as possible.

She crawled across the broken glass and debris to a nearby window, which seemed to be the best exit from the overturned vehicle. The torn metal of the roof ripped through her slacks and dug into her legs. Whimpering, Alexandra clenched her jaw and reached for the frame of the broken window. As her hand grasped the metal, a pair of boots stepped into view at her right. She couldn't make out any other details, as the only light came from nearby fires.

"Ahhh…" A Spanish accented voice came from the boots. "Somebody alive?"

The boots were joined by a knee and then by a toothless smile. Attached to the smile was a Mexican man - perhaps forty years old, Alexandra guessed. His face appeared bruised. As he focused on Alexandra, his glossy eyes widened.

"You look like you can fit outta the window," he said, after he smacked his lips and drew his sweaty forearm across his mouth. "Need help?"

"No. I can make it." Alexandra said as she felt some blood run down her chin.

The toothless face rose out of view and Alexandra focused on dragging herself through the narrow window. She ripped part of her suit jacket and blouse on the frame as she squeezed through, but the soft dirt was a welcome mattress compared to the roof of the bus. For a few moments, Alexandra was content to lay in the dirt and catch her breath. She looked to the sky, but the stars weren't shining. The unseasonably cold air irritated the scrapes and lacerations she received from the accident. Then, Alexandra wondered if there was an accident. She couldn't remember.

"You gonna be okay?" the toothless man said as he shuffled closer.

A voice in Alexandra's head urged her to get away from the bus and the toothless man. Her internal compass was usually correct in these things. She looked at him again. He appeared to be dressed in overalls, but almost everything else was indistinguishable in the darkness. Everything except those glossy eyes.

"Yeah, I'll be fine," she lied.

Alexandra balanced on her knee and, after a pause to contemplate where her heels had gone - she planted both feet on the soil. The ground was cool under her bare toes. The toothless man took another step forward and Alexandra flinched. Her reaction caused him to take two steps backwards.

"Thank you… for your help," Alexandra said as she ran her fingers across her many cuts and bruises to determine the severity of her wounds. She rotated her elbows and knees and felt everything was in working order.

Then, she forced a smile at the toothless man. His eyes bore into her like a searchlight. What did he want? Alarms blared in Alexandra's head and her heart shivered. Something wasn't *right* with this man.

"I... I have to go," Alexandra said, wishing her voice was steadier.

After looking into her eyes, he nodded and meandered away from the bus. Though still groggy and now shaking with fear, Alexandra examined her surroundings. The bus rested on its roof in the middle of the dirt street. Near the driver's window, Alexandra noticed a sign balanced on the window frame. "Candela" was chalked upon the sign's surface.

"Candela," Alexandra whispered. Now she remembered. She was headed to the house she inherited from her mother. Though her mother's death was over a year ago, the wounds were still as fresh as the ones Alexandra received from the accident. If Alexandra was indeed near Candela, in north-central Mexico, then she had far to go. Her mother's house – the house where she spent her childhood – was still several hundred miles to the south.

Where were the police? The thought popped into Alexandra's head as she limped to the entrance of a small café. True, the police coverage here was nothing like back in San Antonio, but Alexandra reasoned she was probably unconscious for a good chunk of time. Or maybe it was only a few moments of blackout. She wasn't sure. Trying to balance herself, Alexandra slumped against the arched doorway of the café. She looked inside, but saw only darkness. That wasn't right. Alexandra's internal clock told her it was still before midnight. The café should have been as mobbed as an electric bug-zapper during a Texas summer sundown.

Alexandra scanned the length of the street to find most of the houses and establishments dark with inactivity. Smoke and light from a nearby bonfire framed a few buildings farther down the street. The closest street lamp was dead. Maybe the bus clipped the power but that didn't explain the lack of *movement*. Where were the people? Certainly, there should've been gawkers. A bus flipped over! People should've been everywhere, police included. Perhaps she wasn't unconscious for as long as she originally calculated.

Alexandra entered the café and utilized the glow from a nearby fire to find the light switch. It didn't work. Her eyes eventually adjusted to the dark, and a quick scan revealed a payphone at the rear of the cluttered dining room. Before she reached the phone, however, Alexandra heard scratching from the kitchen. She froze. The noise stopped for a second and was followed by the *clang* of a heavy pot striking the floor.

After the pot rattled to a halt, Alexandra called out, "Hello? I need to use the phone. My bus just –"

The door to the kitchen burst open before Alexandra could finish, and a large dog bounded into the room. Alexandra wasn't one to get startled easily, but she uttered a hoarse *yelp*. After vaulting a table, the dog halted in a hunched position and snarled as it focused on Alexandra. Light from the fire gave the creature's eyes and fur an orange glow.

Alexandra's legs were immobilized with fear, but her mind and senses raced. The dog wore a collar, so Alexandra ruled-out wolf or wild-dog. Most likely, the canine belonged to the café owner, and if Alexandra backed away, perhaps she could leave. Immediately, her legs were on the brink of collapse and her arms wouldn't respond.

Gathering her courage, Alexandra took a step backwards, toward the street. The dog mirrored her with a reverse step of its own and another snarl. Outside, a man screamed and the creature lifted its head to the noise. Alexandra decided to run for the door at that instant, but the dog was faster. It pounced on the table next to Alexandra, barked, and then leapt through an open window.

Alexandra grasped a table for support and released the breath she didn't realize she was holding. She took a few moments to gather her thoughts, but nothing made sense since she couldn't recall the accident. Her hair fell over her face and Alexandra ran a hand through the dark, blood-matted lengths. She traced a black strand down to her soiled blouse and ripped slacks. Cuts and bruises dotted her arms and exposed legs.

"What a mess," Alexandra whispered.

With another exhale, she pushed away from the table and walked to the phone. Like the lights, the phone was dead. That didn't make sense. Even if the power was out, the phones should still work. She wasn't an electrician, but the idea seemed reasonable. She tapped the hanger several times, but that accomplished nothing.

As she returned the receiver to the hook, she saw a shadow move across the far wall. Someone was at the door to the café.

Anxious from the incident with the dog, Alexandra crouched on one knee and peered towards the entrance from her spot in the back of the room. The toothless man appeared in the doorway, along with another man. Alexandra couldn't make out any of this new man's features, except that he was a good half-foot taller than his companion. They scanned the dining area and then turned back towards the street. What did they want?

After a few moments, Alexandra crept to a window. Heart pounding and half-expecting to be met by the face of that dog, she lifted her head to look at the street and the bus. Instead of the dog, she saw the toothless man and his friend loitering around the overturned bus. She watched as they took a few minutes to pick at the debris and then they shuffled back into the darkness.

Alexandra slumped against the wall and closed her chestnut eyes. Her cell phone was still in the bus – all she had to do was find it – if it survived the crash. After some relaxed breathing, Alexandra rose to her bare feet and glanced again down the street. When she was sure nobody was around, she departed the café and approached the bus. However, before she made the distance, she saw them. Several forms appeared from a ruined building and advanced upon her. Alexandra altered her course and hastened her pace down the street. Led by the toothless man, the small mob followed.

As Alexandra's heart quickened, so did her feet. She passed an intersection and risked a glance over her shoulder. The mob consisted of no more than ten men, covered in bruises and clothed in workman's overalls. Some of them carried rocks or crowbars, and all eyes stared blankly through her. The toothless man grinned when she looked his way, and the men broke into an all-out run.

This time, Alexandra's legs were ready. Five days a week at the gym were more than a match for the locals of northern Mexico. They couldn't keep pace. A minute later, Alexandra chanced another peek at her pursuers. The glance was enough for her to miss the depression in the road. With a gasp, she fell and twisted her ankle in the soft dirt at the bottom of the hole. She tumbled a full rotation and then came to a halt on the other side. Pain arced through her left ankle and Alexandra blinked back the tears as dust covered her like a blanket.

She commanded her muscles to function, but they didn't obey. The mob slowed and if the toothless man had teeth, Alexandra would've seen them from thirty feet away.

"Where's lady goin?" he asked, mouth open in a twisted grin.

As he advanced, Alexandra's mind wandered. The memory of a similar scenario demanded recognition. Several years ago, Alexandra was accosted by a group of men at the tram stop late one night. Bluffing, she told them she was a cop and she reached into her jacket. The men fled, not waiting to see if she pulled out a gun or a badge. After that encounter, she spent one night a week in a self-defense class. Though she never needed to use the techniques she learned on would-be muggers, some of the lessons were helpful in dealing with the over-thirty dating scene. Unfortunately, none of the men chasing her at the moment seemed interested in her phone number.

With the mob within fifteen feet, another figure appeared in Alexandra's field of vision. The mob halted when the stranger stepped into the depression between them and her. Alexandra didn't hesitate to test her ankle, but it failed and she fell back to the ground.

For the next several moments, Alexandra struggled to remain lucid through the pain. She felt her ankle swell and her knees burned from the fall. The stranger didn't move after taking position in the depression, and each member of the mob eyed him. Then, one of the men from the mob screamed and stumbled away. He was followed by several others and the mob was soon gone.

Alexandra had a handle on the pain by then. She managed to crawl a few feet to the side of the earthen road and her eyes remained locked on the stranger. He turned to look at her from beneath his hood. Through the darkness, Alexandra noticed he was taller than the other men, about the same height as her own five feet, ten inches. His face was shrouded and his hands seemed to be tightly wrapped with cloth. The remainder of his body was covered in tattered rags. Was he a beggar?

He took a step towards Alexandra and said in a raspy voice, "Please, come with me. I know someplace safe."

Though the voice was nothing more than a loud whisper, Alexandra sensed determination and strength behind it. However, she also felt uneasy in this stranger's presence, especially after the recent events.

"Stay right there," Alexandra said, ashamed at the quiver in her voice. "I just want to get my stuff from the bus and leave."

The stranger took another step forward.

"If I wanted to bring you harm, I would have done so by now." He looked at a nearby building and Alexandra heard some scuffling within. "This place is lost," he said. "We must not delay."

The stranger's voice carried an accent, but Alexandra couldn't place it. Another scream echoed to her ears and she closed her eyes. The fires. The dog. The mob. Now, the stranger. Alexandra felt overwhelmed. What was going on?

As if he read her mind, the stranger said in his whispered words, "I can promise you answers and safety... but, we must leave now."

Almost before he finished, Alexandra said, "I'm not sure I can walk. My ankle... I think I sprained it."

With a glace at her wounded ankle, the stranger said, "Put aside the pain and follow me. We don't have far to go."

Alexandra gritted her teeth as she rose. Her ankle protested, but she remained standing. The stranger seemed satisfied with her progress and turned to leave.

"Wait," Alexandra said as she took a tentative step forward. "Where are we going?"

Without looking back to her, the stranger said, "Not far, just up the hill."

Exasperated, Alexandra reached out and grabbed the stranger's arm. The skin was lean and hard underneath the rags. "I need my things from the bus," she said.

After glancing at her hand, the stranger tilted his head towards her. Light from a fire gave Alexandra a brief look at his features. Scar upon scar crisscrossed over his dark skin. However, the skin was so tightly drawn that it almost seemed smooth despite its imperfections. With a gasp, Alexandra released his arm and she retreated a step.

The stranger turned away and said, "I can retrieve your belongings once you are safe."

With a flare of light, the building behind Alexandra moaned and collapsed. Farther away, towards the bus, Alexandra heard a series of screams. She decided to leave the town, but how could she trust this stranger?

"You go ahead," Alexandra said. Her lungs burned from the layer smoke now settling in the street. "I'll find a safe place on my own." Though the stranger didn't trip Alexandra's internal alarms like the toothless man did, his visage frightened her.

With a sigh, the stranger turned to her and said, "There are things out here tonight that will look upon you as they would a meal - evil creatures who wish to do evil acts." He paused to survey the street. "I will protect you from them, but we must leave. Now!"

Alexandra's mind calculated every angle of her situation, and she arrived at one conclusion. She should follow the stranger. At least he hadn't chased her out of a café or down the street... yet.

"Fine," she said.

Without a word, Alexandra's new guide moved off the road and into the rocky badlands that surrounded the town. Alexandra's ankle screamed for rest, but the stranger didn't alter his pace. The pair ascended a small hill outside of town and aglow from the fires below, Alexandra saw a church.

CHAPTER 2

The stranger paused to give Alexandra's twisted ankle a break. Firelight from the town below outlined the brush, cacti, and stones that made up the small hill. A cool breeze carried billows of smoke to the area. Alexandra settled on the ground and leaned against a rock. As she gazed upon the tiny church, visions from her childhood untangled themselves from the recesses of her memory.

Young Alexandra decided church was a bore, but her mother brought her to service every Sunday. Alexandra knew the man at the pulpit was saying important things, but she wished to be free of that stone prison. Like robots, her pew-mates recited lines from a book or mouthed automated responses to the Padre. Where's the excitement in that? What's more, the crucifixes and clutter of Catholic decorations reminded Alexandra of her mother's bedroom – a place she avoided. When Alexandra was old enough, she left her home in Mexico to study in the United States.

Now, for the first time in many years, Alexandra found herself in front of a church. She tortured herself wondering what her mother would think of her godless life. The admonition tugged at the corner of her mouth and she felt her eyes begin to water. For what seemed like the hundredth time, she wondered if she was too selfish in her mother's final years. Alexandra's career and life in San Antonio commanded her time and energy. She hadn't visited Mexico in the past five years. When her mother died, Alexandra only sent flowers. Ashamed at how she abandoned her mother, she lowered her head and fought to keep the tears away.

"Can you continue?"

The stranger's raspy voice yanked Alexandra from her thoughts. She turned her swollen eyes to the stranger and wondered why she was with him. His unsettling visage flashed into her head for a moment sending a chill into her blood. She recalled his ashen flesh, which stretched across his bones like the skin of a drum. She wondered why the toothless man and his cronies ran from a beggar. Studying the stranger's movements, however, she reasoned this man was no beggar. Maybe a few hours ago she would have come to that conclusion, but the night's events jarred loose some of Alexandra's assumptions.

"Can you continue?" the stranger repeated.

Alexandra looked from the dark sky to her guide. Several tangles of dark hair fell over her face and she brushed them over her shoulder. With her other hand she wiped a few escaped tears from her cheeks. "You promised answers," she said with a quiver in her voice. "You can start by telling me who you are."

The stranger sighed. It was a strange noise somewhere between a whistle and a hiss.

"Once we are inside, you will have some answers," he said. "Come."

Without waiting for a response, he turned and stalked off towards the church.

Alexandra weighed her options. If she could navigate her way through the darkness, perhaps she could find some help in the town. However, she wasn't sure she could run on her ankle and it would probably come to that again. The stranger was correct – that town was dangerous. Her gut had led her here, so Alexandra decided to hold onto this life raft for now.

Most of the exterior stone walls were intact, but the inside of the church was trashed. Broken pews and debris littered the center of the one-room building. The stench of rotting daisies irritated Alexandra's sinuses as she entered. After a quick scan, the only visible religious artifact was a wooden crucifix on the wall behind what used to be the altar.

"How is your ankle?" the stranger asked as he emerged from the shadows near the altar.

Alexandra jumped and winced when she applied weight to her ankle. "Not good," she said as she ground her teeth to avoid crying. She slumped to the ground. Her slacks were ruined already, so she felt no regret when she tore them further to fashion a wrap for her wounded joint. For the first time that night, she noticed goose bumps on her bronze legs and arms. Her suit jacket provided little warmth.

"My things," she said. "You said you could get them for me."

"I did indeed," her companion whispered from the shadows.

Alexandra closed her eyes and rested her head against the cool wall. "Forget it… who knows where that mob is right now. Maybe in the morning we can…" She trailed off when she realized she was alone. With a sigh, she strained to stand and peer through the window. The small hill was devoid of any movement. The stranger was gone.

Moments later, Alexandra heard a woman's scream from the town below. Her heart kicked into a gallop and she looked around the small church for a place to hide, a weapon, *something*! In the end, she curled into a ball under a damaged pew and she cried. It was one of those purifying cries that went on for many minutes. Towards the end, she felt weak and her body shook with each intake of breath. After a few more moments, she let go.

She must have dozed off for a few minutes. Or maybe a few hours? She opened her eyes to find the familiar cry-crust deposited where her eyes met her nose. Since darkness still filled the church, she reasoned she couldn't have been asleep for too long. Her problems in San Antonio seemed somewhat trivial compared to her problems this night, and her crisis worsened when she heard booted feet approaching outside the church.

Where was the stranger? She opened her mouth to call out to him, but decided against the idea. Her heart leapt when she heard a *thump* against the far wall. She was certain more than one person was there! Who were they? Had the mob returned?

The *thump* was followed by another, though this one closer. Though the night was cold, sweat drenched her body. Her breath quickened and panic threatened to overtake her.

Alexandra attempted to calm her swirling emotions. Releasing a controlled exhale, she steadied her nerves and lifted her head, one inch at a time, until her eyes were clear to scan the room. The darkness parted as her eyes adjusted and the toothless man smiled back from the window.

Alexandra's scream died in her throat as she could only gape at the horrifying face in the window. She bolted to her feet and dashed towards the church doors. She was almost there when she heard two more *thumps* against the door and she stopped hard on her ankle, which twisted and yielded, sending pulses of pain through her body and dropping her to the ground. On the verge of hyperventilating, she scampered backwards against the wall and kept her eyes locked upon the door.

Wait, where was the toothless man?

Alexandra glanced at the window, and the toothless man was still there - grinning and motionless, as he had been moments ago. Was he alive... dead?

Something growled outside very near the wall she leaned against. Her eyes darted to all corners of the church. She scanned every possible entrance. When she looked again to the window where she saw the toothless man, he wasn't there.

"Crap..." she whispered, as she attempted to quell her thumping heart. She felt the wall for a handhold and found a section with a few missing bricks. Darkness still filled the church and the hill outside, but she ventured a peek through the hole. Until her eyes adjusted, there was nothing. Then, the landscape came into focus. The fires from the town still illuminated the hill and she recognized some familiar shapes, though only bushes and rocks. Abruptly, her view was obstructed for a moment as someone passed in front of the hole in the wall!

Ignoring the painful cry of protest from her injured ankle, Alexandra jumped to her feet. Before she reached the door, it swung open and the stranger appeared. He scanned the room and nodded to her.

"Wait here a moment," he said in his raspy voice as he closed the door, leaving her alone once more.

Alexandra sighed and looked from the empty window to the door and back again. If she was going to escape, now seemed like a good opportunity. Then she heard voices on the other side of the door. One voice was definitely that of her strange companion. The other was female, and they seemed to be arguing. Enough of this!

Alexandra run-limped to the door and opened it. The only person outside was the stranger. He turned to face her and grinned as he held out a duffel bag.

Glaring, she asked, "Who were you talking to?" Swallowed in darkness, the hilltop appeared empty save her companion, who dropped the duffel at Alexandra's feet.

"Are you hurt?"

"No," she lied. Though she wanted to say more, she couldn't find the strength. Maybe she was just hearing things? How could there be another person out there? Sighing, she dragged the duffel bag to a pew and kneeled.

The stranger seemed pleased with her answer. "I'm going to fortify this entry and the window," the stranger said as he lifted some wood and piled it near the entrance. "Try to get some rest."

Rest! Though Alexandra felt she would never be the same after the night's events, her wits and analytical mind kicked into motion.

"We can't stay here!" she told him as she rose to her feet.

Without turning from his work, the stranger said, "Yes, we can."

"We need to get to a phone… to a police station!" She threw her arms into the air. "Somewhere!"

"We won't find either of those things now."

"Have you even tried?" Alexandra asked. "I don't even know what I'm doing here… I can't wait here, I'm going to go find help."

The stranger dropped a piece of wood and faced her. Fists on his hips, he asked, "What more do you need to see tonight for you to trust me?"

"I don't even know you!"

"It's well that you don't," he said. "All you need to do is trust that I plan to keep you safe. I have proven that much."

Alexandra couldn't argue with that point. Still, there was something about her companion that wholly unsettled her. Until she could place the feeling, she decided she couldn't trust him.

"At least tell me your name…" she said, as she eased her way to the ground next to the duffel bag.

The stranger paused. Then, releasing his fists, he said, "Koneh."

Alexandra took the name and wondered at its origin. She glanced at the bag and said, "I'm Alexandra… and that's not mine."

With a shrug, Koneh said, "That's all there was. The bus was… picked pretty clean." Koneh resumed the construction of the barricade.

She knew before she finished with the zipper. This was a man's bag. Well, better than nothing! She ducked behind a pew and removed what was left of her slacks. The jeans she replaced them with were meant for a larger waist, but she secured them with her own belt.

She longed for one of her sports-bras as she removed her suit jacket and blouse. Instead, she settled for a white tank top, black long-sleeve shirt, and grey hooded sweatshirt. Unfortunately, the owner of the duffel didn't pack extra shoes - men! She doubled up on some white tube socks and was happy to cover her feet with *something*.

Once finished with her wardrobe change, Alexandra settled on her knees and was thankful none of her friends would see her like that. She must have looked like quite the fashion disaster. The elastic band that once held her hair in check was busted. To keep the waist long strands under control, Alexandra tied her dark hair into a knot.

Koneh finished with his makeshift barriers and walked around the pew to where she still rummaged though the remaining contents of the duffel. Alexandra smiled as she lifted a brown leather jacket and threaded her arms into the sleeves.

"Did you find adequate clothing?" he asked.

Without looking up, she said, "Yeah, it'll do for now."

"Good."

Koneh leaned against the pew and curled his left fist several times. The cloth wrappings around his arm appeared wet with some sort of dark liquid.

"Are you okay?" Alexandra asked.

After several moments, Koneh looked at her from under his hood, but he didn't respond.

She stared into his dark eyes. "Okay. We've made our introductions and I trust you enough to believe you don't want to hurt me." A shiver rattled its way through her body as she realized the night carried a chill normally reserved for rare winter evenings in central Mexico. "Tell me what's happening. What was wrong with those men?"

Thunder boomed in the distance. Koneh allowed the reverberations to subside before he began speaking in his raspy tones.

"Tell me Alexandra, do you believe in Heaven?" he asked as he crossed his arms. She thought she saw the glint of metal beneath his rags, but it was gone before she could get a clear look.

Alexandra blinked and remained speechless for several seconds. "Excuse me?" she said as she instinctively reached for the gold cross at her neck. More memories marched their way into Alexandra's consciousness.

She remembered Father Rodriguez asking her what she thought Heaven would be like. Beaming from ear to ear, a young Alexandra told the priest that Heaven was a dream of joy where she could be with her friends and Madre forever and ever.

Her next memory was one from young adulthood. Alexandra felt she could make more of her life in a city. She said she was leaving. Her mother gave her a golden cross and wished her only child joy and happiness. At the time, she pitied her mother for staying in impoverished Mexico. Alexandra thought her mother simple and unknowledgeable of the greater world. Maybe she should have pitied herself, as she now seemed lost in a situation where she believed her mother *would* know what to do.

Koneh waited for Alexandra to sort through her thoughts.

"Well," she said, "Mi madre… my mother…"

"Solon-om," Koneh uttered in a barely audible whisper as he bowed his head.

"What was that?"

He raised his head and again stared into her eyes with a terrifying intensity. Alexandra noticed his eyes were black-in-black. Was there anything *normal* about this man?

He responded, "My deepest respect to your departed madre…"

Alexandra's heart pounded several times before she asked, "How do you know about my mother?"

He loosened his gaze and said, "You failed to answer my simple question about Heaven, Alexandra. Do you need it rephrased?"

Was he… smiling? She couldn't quite make out the details of his scarred-smooth face, but she thought she saw the corner of his mouth curl into a grin. How could he joke after all that had happened?

"I understood your question, *Koneh*." She said, mocking his repartee. "No, I don't believe in Heaven. My mother was foolish to put her faith into something that isn't real. She's gone now and I never had the heart to tell her she was wasting her time."

Leaning back against the pew, Koneh whispered, "Real. It is a dangerous wall you scale to decide what is real for the rest of us. Through my travels, I have met many people who thought they knew truth." He paused and added some disdain to his words. "Fools, the whole lot of them."

"And you claim to be wise in the ways of *truth?*" She was intrigued by her new companion's unorthodox discussion style.

"The wise do not think they know truth. They teach others how to recognize it. However, I do not claim wisdom, nor the ability to teach... enough about me. You should get some rest. After the quake, and the mob... well, you look like hell."

Alexandra nodded her agreement. She *felt* like hell. Then, her mind caught up with the conversation and she said, "Wait a minute...what quake? You mean an earthquake?"

Koneh grinned again. This time she was sure of it. He whispered, "How do you think your bus came to be overturned?"

Alexandra felt the scrapes and bruises from the accident cry out for attention. It was as if they heard their name and jumped to be recognized. As hard as she tried, she couldn't remember what happened on that bus. Exasperated, she dropped her head into her arms and wished she was home - safe in her city apartment.

Almost to himself, Koneh whispered, "And I beheld when he had opened the sixth seal, and, lo, there was a great earthquake; and the sun became black..."

Alexandra shook her head when she recognized Koneh's words. She raised her eyes and said, "A few fires and a quake don't equal the Apocalypse."

With a sigh he said, "If you don't believe in Heaven, then it follows you claim *Revelations* is also an untruth. It is not *real* in your world."

"Yeah, that doesn't mean I'm not familiar with the passage you just recited."

Koneh pushed himself upright and looked down into her eyes again. Through his raspy voice, he said, "Well, the last days are not unfolding exactly as written, but make no mistake - Heaven and Hell have fallen to Earth."

"Fallen?" Alexandra was beyond confused.

"Yes. I intend to find out *why*... and you are going to help me."

CHAPTER 3

"Run that by me again. Heaven and Hell have… *fallen*?"

"Yes," Koneh said.

Alexandra didn't believe what she was hearing. A few days ago she was wrapping up the last of her cases in San Antonio. Her final act before vacation was to submit her portfolio to be considered for a judgeship.

The plan was simple, one week in Mexico to sell her late mother's house, and one week in the Caribbean to reward herself with some much needed personal time. Then, she could return to San Antonio and attack her career anew.

Instead of accomplishing that, Alexandra awoke in a bed of glass and blood. Men intent upon harming her chased her through the streets of a Mexican village. She found herself shoeless and exhausted in a crumbled church and her guide through all of this was a scarred man who spoke in whispers.

"Though," Koneh said, "I suppose you do not believe such a thing is possible?"

Recalling a phrase used by her first law school professor Alexandra said, "I accept it the same way I believe in life on other planets. I'll leave it out there as a possibility, but I'll never really *believe* it."

"Interesting. Flawed, but interesting."

"How is it flawed?" Alexandra closed her eyes and leaned her head against a pew. The night's events had left her drained.

"That is a question I should not have to answer for you," Koneh said as Alexandra heard him take a seat near the barricaded window. "Besides," he said, "we should stop talking so you can rest. We have far to go."

"How long did I sleep before?"

"I was only gone fifteen minutes. You should rest."

Alexandra wanted to ask more, but she already felt her thoughts defocusing and giving way to unsettling dreams. She glided across a blasted landscape. Debris and torn earth stretched to each horizon. The sky burned and the wind slashed through her as she stood atop a crumbled building. Below, in the rubble of a city square, a child sat upon a throne of gold. Angels with white wings attended him and armies of men marched in circles.

As if she was watching herself from outside her body, Alexandra raised her right arm. In her hand was a sword. Just then, an army of soldiers, demons, and angels rushed past her and attacked the square. Blood ran through the streets as Alexandra made her way to the throne. What was she doing? Moments later she reached the throne with the child upon it. She raised her sword and screamed in pain.

Then, she felt herself torn from that place and transported to the inside of a volcano. An old woman sat amongst the lava and smiled at her.

"You know what to do," the old woman said.

Alexandra found she could speak. "Where am I?" she asked.

"In the past," the old woman said as her manner grew grave.

"I don't understand."

"Understand?" the crone bellowed as she rose. Her white hair swirled around her head. "You are my instrument to use. Do not act as if we are equals! Do not think your soul pure!"

Searing air blasted Alexandra to the ground. Alexandra felt her flesh burn and she screamed.

Then, the heat was replaced by a cool breeze and Alexandra found herself on a grassy hill. On a stump sat the crone. She, somehow, looked even *older*.

"You have done well," the crone said with a smile. "The Earth is pleased..."

Alexandra approached and shook her head. She knew this was a dream and asked, "Who are you?"

Like before, the old woman's stare narrowed and sternness filled her voice, "Perhaps it is time for me to remove your taint as well..."

Alexandra awoke with a jolt and wiped some drool from the corner of her mouth. The interior of the small church came into focus as her eyes readjusted to the darkness. Through a hole in the roof, Alexandra could see the sky. Like in her dream, the sky was red and black. Alexandra rose to her feet and put weight on her injured ankle. Not bad, she thought.

"You slept a while."

Alexandra whirled to see Koneh sitting in the shadows near the altar. His black-in-black eyes stared through her.

"Shall we look outside upon what is left of our world?" he said as he gripped the altar and pulled himself upright.

All Alexandra could manage was a nod, as she was still clearing sleep's fog from her head. She stepped to the duffel bag and sifted through it again, this time looking for food. She found a few granola bars and thanked the owner of the bag as she unwrapped one.

"Want one?" she asked Koneh as he removed the barricade from the church door.

Koneh shook his head and resumed his work.

"More for me." Alexandra devoured another granola bar.

Finished with the barricade, Koneh paused before opening the door. He turned his head so Alexandra could only see one of his eyes peering at her from beneath his hood.

"Know this," he said. "The world beyond this door is not the same we both knew. We saw a glimpse of that last night, but I suspect much worse awaits us in the days and weeks to come. Whatever you see, whatever happens to you, whatever you are forced to do - know that *survival* is now your ultimate goal."

"Survival...?"

"The Earth and its denizens are our enemies... remember that." Koneh said as he turned and opened the door.

The small hilltop looked much as it did several hours ago with several notable changes. For starters, the town below was no longer burning. The area, however, retained its red glow thanks to the sky's unnatural coloring. Amongst the rocks and bushes rested new features on the ground - bodies.

Alexandra gasped, "Oh my God."

Koneh stepped outside and said, "I'm not certain we have the luxury of His protection anymore."

Alexandra followed her guide for a few steps and then stopped to look upon the church. The toothless man's corpse rested at the base of the window. A crimson halo of light surrounded what was left of the building. Beyond the church lay the scorched township. That was as far as Alexandra could see, as the sky shed little light upon the nearby countryside.

"What happened out here?" Alexandra asked. "These men…"

"Were destined for a fate such as this," Koneh said. "Do not fear sights like this one, as you will see much worse before our journey is done."

Alexandra glared at her companion. "A *journey*? Where do you think you're taking me?"

Koneh strode to the edge of the hilltop and scanned the horizon. His tattered clothing whipped and snapped as a draft swirled dust about his body. The wind subsided but never completely retreated from the area. While Alexandra waited for a response, she couldn't help but look at the bodies again. How could all this be real?

"There is another town to the east," Koneh said, as if he was reading the daily special off a menu.

Alexandra approached to better hear his raspy words. As she adjusted the duffel straps over her shoulders, she sighed. "You didn't answer my question… again."

"How is your Spanish?"

"What?" Alexandra threw her arms into the air.

"Our first destination should be a priest. I want to know what they know." Koneh turned his head to stare into Alexandra's eyes as he spoke. Alexandra found herself paralyzed as she gazed back. What was behind those black-in-black eyes? Before going too much farther, Alexandra decided she was going to find out.

"Does that answer your question?"

Alexandra scrutinized her companion and said, "Not entirely."

"What are you looking for?" Koneh asked as he crossed his arms. The dark stain from the night before simply joined the other marks and tears upon Koneh's arm wrappings. If his arms looked anything like his face, Alexandra understood why he bandaged them.

Alexandra broke his gaze and looked to the dark horizon. "Answers," she breathed.

For several minutes the pair seemed content to stand on the hillock and bury themselves in thought. Alexandra sorted through everything she saw and everything Koneh told her. Her lawyer's mind sorted the facts into one part of her brain and her assumptions into another section. While that simple logic trick processed, she closed her eyes.

The wind gained some intensity and she allowed her hair to become unraveled and whip around her body. Facts and assumptions - Alexandra sorted the lot of them until she opened her eyes. Like the *ding* of the microwave, she came to one resounding conclusion.

"It finally happened," she said, more to herself than her companion.

Koneh eased closer and said, "What happened?"

"Nuclear war."

With a sigh, Koneh shook his head.

Alexandra stepped in front of him and asserted her litigation voice. "Now hear me out," she said.

"Go ahead."

"Okay," she said, "look to the sky - you can't tell me that's natural. My mentor wrote a brief to Congress about the effects of a nuclear war. I read that brief."

"The sky is dark because of nuclear bombs?"

Alexandra nodded, "When a major volcano erupts, sunsets around the world are reddened for a time. In the late eighteen hundreds, a massive eruption caused red sunsets all over the world. The same thing happened at Hiroshima - darkened skies, red sunsets. Nuclear bombs release even more stuff into the atmosphere... the effects would be long-lasting and dramatic."

"Go on."

"Well, that's basically it." Alexandra curled her mouth into a frown. "Makes sense though... much more than what you propose."

With a huff that passed for a laugh, Koneh looked away.

"You don't agree?"

He shrugged and said, "I don't profess to know the truth of all that has happened."

Alexandra reined her hair into a more secure braid this time. While she weaved the strands into alignment, she wrestled with the notion of asking her companion about his scars. She reasoned Koneh must have been burned by exposure to nuclear fallout. After failing to find the proper phrasing for the sensitive question, Alexandra tucked the idea away for future contemplation.

"So," she said, "what's the plan? You mentioned a priest."

"Yes, a priest should know more of what has happened."

"I don't see how that's possible," Alexandra said as she adjusted the duffel bag on her shoulders again, "but I'm all for leaving this place."

Without responding, Koneh walked down the hill and into the scrubland. Alexandra took a few steps to test her ankle. She thought it felt improved. Still wary of her guide, she kept a good ten feet behind Koneh. If he insisted on keeping secrets, then she refused to trust him.

Alexandra guessed they walked for about ten total hours, with breaks scattered through the 'day', before Koneh stopped and gathered some sticks. Throughout their journey, the sky remained red and dark. The scrubland Alexandra remembered from her childhood teemed with life. Now, silence reigned as only the bushes and rocks watched over the barren expanse.

"You should sleep," Koneh said as he built a campfire.

With a shiver, Alexandra dropped her duffel, and then herself, to the ground. She drew her hood over her head as she watched Koneh. He went about his business like he'd done this many times before. In less than a minute a small fire was crackling and Koneh sat on the far side of it.

"I don't remember it ever getting this cold when I lived here," Alexandra said to break the silence.

Koneh prodded the fire but didn't respond.

"You don't talk much."

He stopped playing with the fire and locked eyes with her. "I do not waste words," he said.

Alexandra trembled as a shiver skipped down her spine. Turning away from Koneh's disturbing gaze, she said, "It's not a waste."

"As a lawyer, were you not taught the value of words?"

Alexandra stopped breathing and scanned her memory. "I never told you I was a lawyer," she said.

"You didn't have to. The way you carry yourself, the way you talk, your lack of a wedding band, the suit you were wearing - I knew it from the start."

Alexandra's voice rose. "Lack of a wedding band? You don't know anything about me!"

Koneh's shrug only fanned her anger.

"Well," she said as she forced composure into her voice, "I've made a few assumptions about you as well."

Koneh lifted the skin around where his right eyebrow used to be, but didn't respond.

Alexandra said, "You seem intelligent enough, and your English doesn't have a trace of Spanish in it. So, I'm guessing you came here from the United States. Perhaps as part of the failed oil rush a few years ago?"

Smiling, he waved his right hand and said, "Go on."

"Okay. You lost everything - like most did - and you turned to the Church to save you." Alexandra decided it was time to discover some of her companion's secrets. "When the bombs dropped, you were burned by the blast."

Koneh touched his face with one of his bandaged hands. For several moments, only the crackling fire spoke. Maybe it was too soon to talk about that?

"Yes, I have been burned," he whispered.

"I didn't mean to…" she said, biting her lip and unsure how to proceed.

After several moments of silence, Koneh cleared his throat. He walked to Alexandra and knelt at her feet. "Allow me to examine your ankle," he said.

Still feeling guilty, Alexandra didn't protest as Koneh unwrapped the torn cloth that served as her bandage. She watched as he manipulated the cloth and held her wounded foot with a surgeon's care. He pivoted her foot to test the range of motion. It didn't hurt as much as she expected.

"I'm sorry," she said as she reached out and touched his arm. "I shouldn't have mentioned the burns…"

When Koneh looked again into Alexandra's eyes, his edge was gone. Softness reigned in those two dark orbs and his mouth trembled. Eyes that were unreadable a day ago now bursted with emotion. He seemed on the verge of tears when he pulled himself together.

Koneh closed his eyes and whispered, "You take my pain away with the slightest touch."

Alexandra snapped her hand from his arm like she had touched a hot skillet. "What?"

As if waking from a dream, Koneh straightened himself and said, "I apologize." He hesitated before re-wrapping her ankle. "It has been a long road for me, one filled with pain and loss. Forgive me."

"Forgive you for what? Being creepy?" Alexandra prided herself on her ability to read people. Why couldn't she get an accurate picture of this man? Where was he from?

Koneh made a sound that she guessed to be a laugh. He said, "You're wittier than I expected."

"More assumptions…"

"Have you always been a fast healer?" he asked.

Shaking her head, Alexandra realized before she responded that he was right. "Yeah, I guess so" she said. "Though I never really thought about it before."

"Well, your ankle isn't broken, and you let me twist it father than I thought you would… I think you will be fine."

Koneh returned to the other side of the fire and leaned against a rock. Alexandra could no longer see his eyes, but she sensed he was watching her. To her surprise, she found her eyes lingering on him as well. A restrained tenderness hid beneath his scars. She couldn't deny her interest in discovering more about him.

Shaking her head, she rested against the duffel bag and closed her eyes. The day's journey caught up with her like her morning usually did before she had her nine o'clock coffee. She'd sell her diamond tennis bracelet for a cup of decent coffee. Alexandra opened one eye to admire the bracelet's sparkle in the firelight.

"Sorry mother," she whispered as memories of the day she bought the bracelet knocked on the door to her consciousness. Closing her eyes, she allowed the memories in and winced at the pain they now caused.

Five days after graduating from Cornell Law School, Alexandra packed her apartment. She had a job waiting in San Antonio and was departing Ithaca the next day. Chafed that her mother chose to remain in Mexico during the graduation ceremony, Alexandra purchased a diamond bracelet to reward herself and ease her pain. However, the jewels accomplished neither of those tasks.

Now, lying on the dirt of Mexico's back country, Alexandra's guilt overtook her exhaustion. The tears didn't come as hard as they did the day before, but Alexandra again cried herself to sleep. She dreamed of her childhood and of the happiness she forgot she enjoyed.

CHAPTER 4

Alexandra groaned in her sleep when she felt her mother shaking her awake. Sunday mornings were always the same. Who wakes up this early anyway? Her mind was made up - no church today. After all, she was fifteen years old, more than capable of making her own decisions about such things.

"No Madre… ten more minutes."

A man's whisper returned. "Alexandra, wake up!"

Ripped from her reverie, Alexandra's eyes shot open. She wasn't a child safe in her bed. Instead, her joints and muscles scolded her for making the dirt her home last night. She rubbed the crust from her eyes and pushed her hair aside. As she propped herself up on her elbow, the world came into focus. Koneh kneeled beside her.

"What time is it?" Alexandra asked as she rose to a sitting position.

"We must leave."

After yawning, Alexandra said, "Why?"

"I think we were followed," Koneh said as he rose and took a few steps away from her.

When Alexandra stood, her stomach and throat complained. Alexandra avoided the half-empty water bottle she found in the duffel bag the day before, but now she took it without reservation. The water was warm but welcome as it eased the pain in her throat.

"Followed by who?" Alexandra asked as she unwrapped a granola bar. Then, the reality of her terrifying flight from the mob resurfaced and her heart quickened. "You think…"

Koneh adjusted something under his tattered clothing. "We talk as we move," he said.

Alexandra grumbled as she lifted the duffel over her shoulders. "Do I have time to…"

"No," Koneh said as he jogged into the brush.

"Great."

Alexandra kept pace, but her ankle protested every foot-fall. The terrain offered no refuge, as the bushes hid divots and rocks. The red sky was selfish in the light it held from them. Several times, gusts of wind almost knocked her to the ground. In fact, the whole experience reminded Alexandra of the time she ran the Boston Marathon - take away the dirt, add rain, and one couldn't tell the difference.

After an hour, Koneh slowed to a walk and then stopped near a flat rock. Alexandra's heart felt as if it was going to burst.

"Rest," he said.

Recalling her marathon training, Alexandra circled the rock several times to calm her breathing. Her heart eased to a slow *thump*. Satisfied, she took a few swigs from the water bottle and then dropped to the ground.

"Don't get too comfortable."

Alexandra peered at Koneh from beneath her bangs. "Why did we just do that again?" she asked.

"I already answered that."

With a sigh, Alexandra closed her eyes and said, "Okay, who was following us… and why the rush?"

"If your enemies know where you are, be some place else."

"Enemies?" Alexandra opened her eyes and watched Koneh as he strode to the far side of the rock and scanned the horizon. He didn't look tired or even stressed.

"Remember when I told you the Earth and its denizens are our enemies?"

Alexandra nodded and waited for more. After a few moments, it was clear Koneh assumed he was finished.

"I hate when you do that," Alexandra said. "You didn't really answer me."

Koneh shrugged. "I am not here to answer your incessant questions."

"Why are you here then?" Alexandra asked. "I don't even know why I'm with you…"

Koneh grew serious and said, "Open your eyes, child! You have to steel yourself to your new life… quickly. This is not a dream that we can wake up from, and I hate to say it, but things are going to worsen before we can make them better."

Alexandra pulled her knees to her chest and processed Koneh's words. There was little she couldn't control in her adult life. School and work came easy to her. Alexandra graduated at the top of her class and had multiple career options open to her. The opportunity in San Antonio proved to be the best decision and she was on the fast track to a judgeship - which was what she ultimately wanted. Alexandra's promotion was a mere formality when she left for Mexico to settle her Mother's house and debts. Everything was under control and Alexandra had options.

Now, in this wasteland, Alexandra saw few options.

"So... what are our choices then?" she asked.

Koneh wrinkled his forehead, twisting his scars into a jagged pattern which cast shadows upon half of his face.

"There are two roads you can take, as far as I see it."

Alexandra stood and drew a deep breath. The dust and ash in the air filled her lungs, but she didn't cough. At that moment, she decided to hate this new world. Anger was effortless.

Koneh continued. "There's bound to be pockets of civilization here and there, some of them may even be large enough to build crude communities. In time, who knows what they can accomplish. Of course, I'm not convinced they will last long without the sun and fertile soil. It's possible you could find happiness in such a place."

"So that's one road?"

Koneh scanned the red-black sky for a few moments before answering. "Yes, that is one path you could follow."

Why was he looking to the sky? "And the other path?" Alexandra asked as she tried to catch his eye.

Koneh smiled as he turned from the sky to face her. "Acceptance."

Before Alexandra could respond, she felt a gust of wind and she heard - the flapping of wings? She looked to the sky and saw a winged woman descend to the Earth. Alexandra took a step backwards and fell to the ground.

The newcomer was clothed in a long white dress. Over the dress she wore a pitted golden breastplate that glinted from various spots under the rust. Light ashen skin extended up from the armor, over a long neck, and formed the most perfect face Alexandra had ever seen. Dark hair, much like Alexandra's, floated as if suspended from gravity and finally settled as the woman touched the ground with one toe.

The woman's black feathered wings scooped the air one last time before folding against her back and depositing their bearer firmly upon the earth. Alexandra could only gape at this woman, who stood a good six inches taller than herself.

Koneh smiled and said, "What? No questions, Alexandra?"

Alexandra had a million questions, but none of them possessed the courage to leap from her mouth.

The winged woman strode towards Alexandra and bowed. "I am Erzulie," she said as she smiled. "And it is my honor to serve you."

Erzulie's voice was melodious and pleasant, like a child who knew how to sing. As Alexandra fumbled for the proper words, Erzulie extended her hand. Dark tattoos twisted around her forearm and bicep. Alexandra also noticed a slender sword belted underneath her dress.

"Allow me to help you to your feet."

Still stunned, Alexandra grasped Erzulie's hand. With strength that belied her womanly frame, she lifted Alexandra to her feet.

Koneh approached the two women and asked, "What did you discover?"

Leaving her white-in-white eyes on Alexandra, Erzulie responded, "I count three distinct packs of hounds. One of them got close to you at the church. I dared not risk a closer glance to see who they serve. However, I do not think they are after you... yet."

"Why do you say that?" Koneh asked.

Alexandra felt like an intern at a meeting between two senior partners. Erzulie's eyes never strayed, and Alexandra felt uncomfortable under her stare. As the pair spoke, Alexandra found solace in the ground. It was a safe place to keep her eyes. She noticed Erzulie was barefoot. Around one ankle she wore a tarnished bracelet unlike anything Alexandra had ever seen. Alexandra wondered at the blue-black gem fitted into the metallic bands as her companions continued their conversation.

"Well," Erzulie said, "the hounds dragged off several women and infants - newborns. For the most part, they left the other people alone."

Koneh put a hand to his chin. "They don't know then. Good."

"Are you hurt?" Erzulie gasped as she dropped Alexandra's hand and cradled Koneh's bandaged forearm. Alexandra detected concern in Erzulie's voice and guessed these two had some sort of relationship.

"What are you?" Alexandra blurted. The words were instinctual, and Alexandra could no better control the weather at that point.

"She speaks! She does that often - and often it's a question." Koneh said as he took his arm back from Erzulie, but not before flashing a grin and nod in the newcomer's direction.

"How much does she know?" Erzulie asked.

"Not much. She's having a difficult time with acceptance."

"Do both of you have the same problem?" Alexandra mustered the strength to finally join the conversation. "What is she?" Alexandra pointed at the six and a half foot tall winged woman standing in front of her.

Koneh made a sweeping motion with his hand and said, "She wants to know. Tell her."

Erzulie took Alexandra's hands in her own and bowed.

"Without the fanfare, please," Koneh said.

After shooting Koneh a glare, Erzulie released Alexandra's hands and straightened. She put a hand to her chest and said, "I am Erzulie, Seraphim of the White Sacrament, Guardian of..."

Koneh cleared his throat with a grating cough. "She asked what you *are*, not what you *were*, my dear."

Erzulie sighed and said, "Removed from Grace, beyond forgiveness... I am a fallen angel."

"Angel..." Alexandra gasped.

"Do you not believe in angels?" Koneh said. "Well, you probably do now."

"I - I..." Alexandra couldn't find the correct words. She felt like a child who was just told about Santa Claus. Santa was real and as a child, Alexandra never had any doubt. "I don't know what to say."

"For everything, there is a first time," Koneh said. "However, back to the business at hand. Are we clear for now, Erzul?"

"We should head east to avoid the hounds," Erzulie responded, "There is a town… and a church. Perhaps we can find some food for Lex… Alexandra, that is."

"Why'd you call me that?" Alexandra asked. Nobody used that high school nickname with her anymore. How could Erzulie know it?

As if she never spoke, Koneh said, "And what of these women and infants the hounds are dragging off? Where are they taking them?"

"I only followed one such abduction. The woman was brought to a small army encamped to the north. I don't know who was in charge, but he examined her and then…" Erzulie glanced at Alexandra before continuing. "He left her at the mercy of his minions."

Koneh turned to Erzulie and looked into her eyes. "Erzul… you don't have to follow me this time…"

"Nonsense," Erzulie said.

"Its going to be dangerous and I cannot protect you both."

"Who says I need your protection?" Erzulie winked at Alexandra.

"Erzul…" Koneh's whisper trailed off into a non-audible breath.

The gravity of Alexandra's new world dropped on her shoulders like a wave crashing upon a rock. Alexandra had nobody. Her life was full of acquaintances, co-workers, and a handful of people who passed as friends. The thought of losing everything never carried much weight. Now that Alexandra could step back from her life and take a look at it, she realized she didn't have much to lose.

However, others in this world lost plenty. Alexandra assumed many lost their lives. As terrible as that was, the survivors are the ones who had to deal with that loss and the pain it carried. As Alexandra looked from Koneh to Erzulie, she realized how selfish she was. Others had to deal with this new reality just like she had to - and they had more at stake.

Life is *people*, not things and titles…

Alexandra could almost hear her mother's words reverberating through the years. Such a simple concept, yet it took Alexandra fifteen years to finally understand. Tears threatened to emerge in Alexandra's eyes as her heart reminded her how much she missed her mother. Years of denial and repression melted away the barriers Alexandra built around her feelings. There was no stopping the tears this time. Alexandra fell to her knees and put her face in her hands.

"Lex!" Erzulie rushed to Alexandra's side and put an arm over her shoulders.

"Is she okay?" Koneh asked.

Alexandra felt the cool steel of Erzulie's breastplate against her sweatshirt. "It's all right child," Erzulie hummed.

"We don't have time for this."

"Be still… she's been through much." Erzulie placed her other hand on Alexandra's arm. "Can you move?"

Alexandra wiped some of the tears from her cheeks and looked into the all-white eyes of the fallen angel. Compassion poured from every perfect line of Erzulie's face.

"Why?" was the only word Alexandra could manage.

"Shhhh… no more questions today."

"Why do you care what happens to me?" Alexandra sniffled.

Erzulie turned her head to Koneh who crossed his arms in response. They were holding something back, but Alexandra was too drained to fight with them. Instead, she squeezed Erzulie's ashen hand and rose from the ground.

"Never mind," Alexandra said. "Let's get to that town so we can find something to eat. I'm running low on energy."

"Good…" Koneh said. "Erzul - let us know if you see anything."

"Right." Erzulie glanced at Alexandra and said, "Can you continue?"

Alexandra nodded.

Erzulie spread her feathery wings and shot into the air. For a few moments, Alexandra watched the angel ascend until the dark sky swallowed her form.

"Where's she…" Alexandra realized she was talking to herself. Koneh was already twenty yards away and getting smaller.

Alexandra hustled to make up the distance and stayed behind Koneh. She looked to the sky many times over the six hour journey, but never saw the angel. The scrubland remained mostly unchanged throughout the trip, and the wind was their only companion. When they reached the town, Alexandra sighed.

"What were you expecting?" Koneh said as the two travelers sat atop a bluff which allowed them an unobstructed view of the blasted town.

"People... life... I don't know - something!"

"There are a few people alive down there."

The wind intensified as Erzulie descended from the darkness to join them on the bluff. Alexandra thought the fallen angel appeared strained. Perhaps flying was not as effortless as it looked.

"Okay, several things," Erzulie said in her melodious tones. "The town is in bad shape, but there are a few survivors, including a Catholic priest."

Koneh glanced at the ruined town and grinned.

Erzulie continued, "And the remains of a military outpost lay farther to the east. Not much was left, but I did find food."

"Who knows how much longer that can remain a secret," Koneh said. "Erzul - go back to that base and gather what you can. Alexandra and I will go talk with this priest. Meet on the far side of the town as soon as you are able."

Erzulie nodded and said, "Be safe." Then, the angel elevated into the sky and disappeared.

Koneh's eyes revealed some tenderness as he watched her ascend. When he realized Alexandra was watching him, Koneh turned serious.

"Stay behind me. We don't know what we're dealing with yet."

Alexandra frowned. "You have trust issues."

Koneh hesitated for a moment, and then descended the bluff. Alexandra's ankle protested every footfall upon the steep slope. Gritting her teeth, she endured the pain to keep pace with her companion. The sky seemed darker when they reached the bottom. She surmised the sun was going through its daily routine, unconcerned with the fate of the small blue planet.

"How's the ankle?" Koneh asked as he leaned against a rock.

"I'll make it. What about you?" Alexandra noticed Koneh's labored breathing. He seemed weary.

"Nothing I can't handle. You see the town?"

Alexandra glanced past Koneh and spied several campfires in the distance. Their light escaped from broken walls and windows to expose the settlement for what it truly was - a ruin.

"Not much left," Alexandra said as she returned her attention to her companion. "You sure you're all right?"

"As I said..." Koneh's voice trailed away as he cocked his ear to the sky. "Damn!"

Alexandra's inquiry died in her throat when she saw them. Ten men approached from the scrubland. One of them carried a shotgun.

Koneh sprang to action and maneuvered himself between the newcomers and Alexandra. As they approached, Alexandra noticed more weapons - knives, pipes and chains. These men appeared more determined than the toothless man and his gang.

"Give us the woman and we let you run for it, little man!" shouted the ruffian with the shotgun. His English suffered from a thick Mexican accent. They didn't slow their pace, and neither did Alexandra's heart. She was prepared to run.

"Pretend you never saw us," Koneh said, his voice no more than a hiss.

What was he doing? Alexandra turned to flee and knew she made a mistake. The man with the shotgun lifted the barrel. Thunder and smoke exploded from the weapon. Koneh took the brunt of the attack. He was propelled backwards as his chest erupted in a shower of torn cloth and dark liquid. It reminded Alexnadra of the surface of a pond splashed with handfuls of sand and rocks.

Koneh dropped to the earth and laid still. The echo and smoke from the shotgun filled the area. Alexandra hesitated and gasped. They were upon her.

CHAPTER 5

Their hands were everywhere. Alexandra couldn't muster the strength to fight, though she doubted she could stop all ten of them. She wondered if this was how her life was going to end. All the schooling and money she accumulated meant nothing at that moment, a lawless band of post-nuclear thugs sealed her fate.

The man who shot Koneh ripped her sweatshirt. He curled his mouth in displeasure as he noticed he still had several layers between his hands and their prize. Several of the man's buddies pinned Alexandra's arms and legs to the dirt. Even if she wanted to sneak a knee to someone's groin for good measure, she was firmly restrained.

The shotgun man was fumbling with Alexandra's jeans when he was yanked backwards as if he were tied to a rope. He landed on the ground, fifteen feet away. Alexandra found herself free and rolled to the side. There, standing when he should have been dead, was Koneh. He drew a *sword* from underneath his tattered clothing and glared at the other nine thugs.

"Leave or die," Koneh said.

Like a handful of marbles dumped on the kitchen floor, the group scattered. Most of them fled into the brush. Two thugs charged Koneh with their knives while a third went for the shotgun. Then, the shotgun man rose from where he was thrown and ran towards Alexandra.

Koneh's sword flashed twice as he sprinted between the two knife-carriers. Before their bodies hit the ground, Koneh threw his weapon in Alexandra's direction. She froze. Like a helicopter blade, the weapon whirled through the air with tremendous velocity. An instant later, the shotgun man lost his head as Koneh's sword *whooshed* past Alexandra. Blood sprayed Alexandra's face, neck, and clothing. After taking one additional step, the decapitated man tumbled into a bush. His head rolled out of sight.

Everything happened within several heartbeats, and Alexandra realized she was holding her breath. When she exhaled, she saw the last thug reload the shotgun and crack the barrel into alignment. However, Koneh was faster.

The shotgun roared an instant after Koneh grasped the barrel and pointed it to the sky. With his other arm, Koneh wrapped the man's neck in between his bicep and forearm. One violent snap later, it was over. Koneh dropped the lifeless body to the ground and scanned the area. The others were gone.

Alexandra curled into a ball on the ground and stared at nothing. The first human death she witnessed was the Texas State execution of mass-murderer John Drakes. Mr. Drakes was strapped to a chair and injected with a clear liquid. After several convulsions, his eyes rolled to a stop and he gazed right through her. That was enough to drive Alexandra to the bar that night and to therapy for months afterwards.

Like the execution experience, this one changed her. She didn't know how yet, but she couldn't form any coherent thoughts at that moment. The replay of the shotgun man's decapitation played over and over in her head. She felt as if she would never be rid of it.

A voice to her left whispered, "Is any of that blood yours?"

Alexandra's lower lip trembled. She didn't know. Wait. How was Koneh alive? Alexandra mustered the strength to look at Koneh's chest. It appeared the same as before - ragged cloth with mummy-like wrappings underneath. Though, the clothing was now stained and wet.

"We need to move," Koneh said gently. Was that compassion in his voice? "I'm going to help you to your feet now."

Alexandra nodded and steadied herself against Koneh's arm. The world around her spun, like she was standing at the center of a moving carousel. She put a hand to her forehead and groaned.

"I'm sorry," Koneh said when they were both on their feet.

Tilting her head, Alexandra wrinkled her brow in confusion.

"They should have never gotten that close to you," Koneh said.

Alexandra felt her senses returning to her. The carousel stopped and Alexandra pushed away from Koneh.

"You…" Alexandra said.

"Try not to speak."

"Those men…"

Alexandra's world refocused, but her thoughts still spun.

"Angels? You!" She pointed to Koneh's chest. "I can't take this anymore!" Alexandra lifted her hands and then dropped them to her side. She was on the verge of hyperventilation. Her heart threatened to race right out of her chest. Too much!

"Okay, just rest a moment. Collect yourself."

Alexandra shook her head. "I'm covered in blood... you're not dead. There's a decapitated body four feet from me. God knows where the head is. There're more bodies over there." Alexandra breath shortened and her volume increased. "I'm not collecting *anything* anytime soon!"

"Fair enough. Shall we continue to the town then?"

"Dammit! No!" Alexandra almost ripped her hair from her head as she pushed it from her face. "What the hell are you? Another fallen angel?"

Koneh drew his hood tight over his face as the breeze intensified. "Oh, I'm human like you," he said mysteriously.

"You and I," Alexandra shivered from the wind's chill and said, "are not alike. What are you?"

"I told you. I am human."

"You know what, Koneh? I'm done with twenty-questions. Dammit, you know what's going on!"

Koneh crossed his arms and said, "I explained the situation. It was you who refused to accept it."

"Fine!" Alexandra said. "Let's assume Heaven and Hell once existed and are now gone."

Koneh nodded.

"Then," she said, "what caused it, and what's going to happen to the world now?"

"Again, we went over this before. I do not know."

Alexandra's pulse slowed and her analytical mind took hold, like she was deep into a cross-examination. Control returned, and Alexandra composed a line of questions - like soldiers standing at attention.

Alexandra sent her first soldier into battle. "Okay, how do you know all of this?"

If Koneh didn't want to disclose everything, then she was going to trap him into telling her what she needed to know.

"You would not believe me if I told you."

"Do me a favor and try it out."

Now she was on the offensive. Alexandra decided she wasn't going anywhere until she was satisfied with information. If this was her new world and that meant discussions among dead bodies - so be it!

Koneh looked over his shoulder at the town and shifted his weight. Unyielding, Alexandra stood her ground and awaited Koneh's response. After a few moments of silence, Koneh looked into Alexandra's eyes and grinned.

He leaned close to her and said, "God warned me about the coming destruction."

Alexandra gasped. She hadn't expected that answer.

"Say again?"

"I warned you."

"But..." Alexandra fumbled with her words. "How?" The rest of her soldier-questions fled their posts like the air raid horn had just been sounded.

Koneh shrugged, "In a dream. Always in a dream."

"You talk to God often?"

"Only twice."

"And the other time?"

"I'm not ready to go into that with you." Koneh's grin twisted into a scowl.

"Fine." Alexandra felt she had no more information than when they started. Frustration threatened to overwhelm her. "We're not getting anywhere," she said.

"You do not believe me," Koneh said.

Alexandra opened her mouth to agree with her companion when she felt something in the back of her consciousness. It was the same feeling she experienced when she questioned witnesses and clients - the recognition of truth. She relied on that feeling and her peers recognized her uncanny talent at getting to the bottom of a person's testimony. Every angle she took led her back to the same place. Koneh thought he was telling the truth. The man must be crazy, Alexandra thought.

"All right," Alexandra said. "Tell me how you could survive what just happened to you. Are you wearing a bulletproof vest?"

Koneh again glanced over his shoulder to the town. Her questions seemed to make him uncomfortable. Perfect. That meant she was doing her job. Well, her former job, anyway.

"Listen," he said, "there are some things I'm not prepared to discuss with you quite yet. My past happens to be one of them."

"Well, I'm not going anywhere until you tell me."

"So you wish to wait here, for the remnants of that gang to return?" Koneh crossed his arms. "This is not the time to act the child."

"I just want some answers, Koneh."

"And I will give them to you," he said. "Just… not now. I simply cannot discuss this yet. Is it too much to ask of the man that saved your life - twice?"

"No," she said, the word grumbled from her throat. She felt like a selfish little girl. "And… I'd like to thank you for all that you have done so far."

"Never feel that you have to thank the likes of me," Koneh said.

Alexandra's stomach growled, her throat burned, and her body ached. Standing amidst the corpses, blood, and bushes grew less tasteful by the second. Alexandra removed her bomber jacket and tossed her ruined sweatshirt to the ground. After re-donning the jacket, Alexandra decided she could also use a change of clothes. Her jacket and dark shirt underneath offered little relief from the cold and her borrowed jeans were stained with a man's blood.

"Well, I'm ready to leave if you are," Alexandra said as she lifted the duffel bag and tested her ankle. Still some pain there.

"Listen," Koneh said after he stepped closer to Alexandra, "I know this is not easy for you. I'm not skilled in speeches or empathy, but I see the pain on your face."

Alexandra nodded, not exactly sure where he was going.

"Talk to Erzulie," he said. "She knows what to say in… well, in any situation." Koneh squeezed Alexandra's bicep and appeared as if he had more to say. However, he turned and took a step towards town.

His touch was less creepy than before and Alexandra felt excited by it. Like the 'bad boy' in school had just smiled at her in the hallway. Where were these feelings coming from? Her focus should be on surviving her new world, but she found her thoughts centering on Koneh time and again. His mystery intrigued her.

Alexandra followed by his side and asked, "So Erzulie was an angel?"

"That's right."

"What happened to her?" Alexandra felt like she was a child again, asking Father Rodriguez about heaven.

"She thought she fell in love with a human."

Puzzled, Alexandra asked, "*Thought* she fell in love?"

As they walked and talked, Alexandra noticed that the landscape had transformed more than she first realized. Everything was covered with a dark film of ash. She couldn't recall a time when the wind gusted as fierce and as cold as it now did. Even more out of place was the fact that the wind was the only sound beyond their voices. The buzz of life was gone.

"Well," Koneh said, "an angel does not possess a soul like you and me. So the best they can do is imitate human emotions."

"What does having a soul have to do with emotion?"

"Everything..."

Alexandra sighed. "That's not an answer."

Koneh stopped and smiled. His black-in-black eyes held her captive as his scars twisted around the corners of his mouth. Alexandra studied the lines and shape of his face for a moment. His jaw and brow formed hawk-like angles. He was definitely a handsome man at one time.

In his usual raspy voice, Koneh said, "If you seek details, you're going to have to ask the angel herself," and he continued towards town.

"An angel," Alexandra whispered. She shook her head in amazement at all she had witnessed over the past few days. Heaven and Hell... they were real after all. As a child they were easy to accept, as an adult she ignored them, and now Alexandra couldn't avoid the elephant in the room. At that moment, the world became a larger place for Alexandra Contreras.

Alexandra cultivated her musings as she kept pace with Koneh. Heaven and Hell – *real*? Though her analytical mind protested, Alexandra couldn't deny the tangibility of Erzulie and Koneh. The supernatural had become natural and Alexandra wondered what else this new world had to offer.

The wind shifted and brought the stink of something rotten to Alexandra's nostrils. In response, she switched to her mouth for air and closed her nose to the pungency.

"What's that?" Alexandra asked, almost shouting over the wind.

Barely audible, Koneh asked, "What?"

"That smell!"

Koneh stopped and lifted his nose to the air. After a few moments, he turned to Alexandra and shrugged.

"I don't smell anything."

"How could you not smell that?"

"I don't think..." Koneh paused as he looked into Alexandra's eyes. "I don't think I can do that anymore."

"Can't do what?"

"Smell."

Alexandra cocked her head to the side. A few days ago she would have pushed for an explanation, but instead she said, "Lucky you."

With a grin, Koneh resumed their march towards their destination. After another fifteen minutes of drudgery in the wasteland, they entered the outskirts of the town.

The area looked as if the Almighty Himself had lifted it into the air and tossed it back to the Earth. Only a few of the buildings managed to claw their way through the rubble to form familiar shapes, a few houses, a church, and a market. The path of destruction spilled into the scrubland to the east. Overturned rocks, bushes, and soil extended in a widening scar to the horizon. As the last hints of reddish light seeped through the clouds, Alexandra saw children playing amidst the ruins.

"Just stay close to me," Koneh said as he eyed the ruins.

Alexandra shifted the duffel bag from her right shoulder to her left. Her muscles reminded her that the bag was designed to be carried from one's car to a destination, not across miles of scrub.

"I'm right behind you," Alexandra said. "The sooner we find some food, the better…"

The pair reached the edge of the town proper and paused. Yellow firelight flickered from some nearby buildings, causing the shadows to dance. Alexandra realized the children she spied from a distance were now gone. Perhaps the stench drove them away. Before her, the fire-lit rubble town lay silent.

Alexandra opened her mouth to inquire about the delay when she noticed a group of men approaching. Some of them carried weapons. Alexandra feared the encounter at the bluff would replay itself here.

"Koneh..." she said, prepared to run.

"These men will not harm us. Look closely."

Alexandra squinted through the darkness and haze. Next to a man with a torch stood a priest, the white of his Roman collar shone like a beacon amongst the dingy crowd.

CHAPTER 6

The priest studied Alexandra and Koneh. Then, he asked, "¿Quienes son usted?"

Alexandra said, "?Nosotros hablamos ingles, si prefiere usted?"

"I do prefer English," the priest said. "However, we have little to offer if you are looking to steal from us."

The priest appeared to be in his fifties or early sixties. He reminded Alexandra of her first-year Tort Law professor - Irish-American, tall, gaunt, and wise in the eyes. Torchlight reflected off his mostly bald scalp and dust clung to his black vestments. Alexandra noted both confidence and fatigue in his voice. He had probably witnessed much over the past few days. Alexandra found comfort talking with someone who wasn't mysteriously scarred, an angel, or trying to kill her.

Alexandra said, "We only want a safe place to stay for the night. We won't be any trouble."

One of the rifle-carrying men scowled and leaned close to the priest. They whispered amongst themselves for a few moments. Most of the other men fingered their weapons or fidgeted with whatever was handy.

"We heard some gunshots a little while ago," the priest said. "Do you bring trouble here? If so, you are not welcome."

Alexandra didn't know how to answer the priest. She decided she would avoid the question. No need to draw more attention by recounting Koneh's fight against the shotgun man and his gang.

"We bring no trouble and we don't have any guns," Alexandra said.

Again, the group whispered amongst themselves. The priest ended the hushed discussion with a wave of his hand. He said, "We will not turn away anyone in need."

Alexandra smiled. "Thank you, Father."

"Richard Callahan." The priest returned Alexandra's smile.

Bringing her hand to her chest, she said, "Alexandra Contreras." She extended her other arm to her right and said, "And this is my guide - Koneh..." Alexandra realized that Koneh never provided a last name.

Koneh bowed his head. "Pleased to meet you, Father," he said.

"Koneh..." Father Callahan rolled the name around in his mouth. "That's a Hebrew name, right?"

Alexandra turned to Koneh and said, "Hebrew?"

"Not exactly," Koneh said. "May we enter?"

Despite her efforts, Alexandra couldn't unravel the mystery surrounding her companion. Alexandra originally thought Koneh was scarred from nuclear fallout, or radiation, or whatever happened when a human got too close to a mushroom cloud. However, her nuclear war theory was giving ground to a more supernatural one every moment she spent in this wasteland.

Koneh's secrecy annoyed her. He knew much more about what was going on, but he wouldn't share it. If Alexandra had him on the witness stand, the judge would instruct Koneh to answer Alexandra's questions. However, they were far removed from a courthouse, both in time and distance. Her life in San Antonio seemed like a blurry memory. The harshness of this new world demanded all her focus and energy.

"Very well then," Father Callahan said, seemingly disinterested in pursuing Koneh's name any further. "Follow me."

The other men eyed Alexandra and Koneh as they walked around the rubble to a clearing. Several fire filled barrels illuminated the area. Faces peered at the group from inside makeshift tents. Many more people lay on blankets on the ground. It reminded Alexandra of the homeless center she visited when she lived in Buffalo, though she only went there for directions.

The escort dissolved as men slumped to the ground on blankets or disappeared into their tents. Soon, only Father Callahan remained with the two newcomers.

"Forgive us," Father Callahan said. "We've had much trouble with looters and bandits of late, not to mention... well, the people are a bit anxious to be sure."

Koneh scanned the area and asked, "Where are all the women?"

Father Callahan's brown eyes watered as he blinked several times to keep tears from his face. "We can talk in the church. It's an easy climb."

Throughout the camp men cooked by the fires, loitered about the tents, or grumbled in their sleep. *Men*, but no women. Some of the men stared at Alexandra as she passed, a glint of hope in their eyes. Alexandra shuddered as she realized that something terrible must have happened to the women here.

"Maria!"

Alexandra turned and saw an older man limping towards her. Sighing, Alexandra wondered why all the crazy men in the world recently decided to gravitate towards her. It couldn't be her lack of perfume or deodorant. She now reeked of sweat, blood, and granola bars. Perhaps that was the exact combination of scents that attracted these freaks.

"Maria! ¿Donde tengale estado? Mi Maria querida!"

"Renaldo," Father Callahan said, "this is not Maria. No es Maria."

Renaldo reached for Alexandra and she stepped backwards in response. However, her retreat was unnecessary as Koneh grasped Renaldo's wrist and twisted. Renaldo dropped to his knees and sobbed.

"Maria... Maria..."

"That's enough, friend," Father Callahan said. "Let him go."

"Koneh... I'm fine." Alexandra touched her protector's shoulder.

Koneh looked at each of them in turn. His eyes narrowed. This man was a predator. Alexandra witnessed his lethality a few hours prior. For now, he was on her side, but what if circumstances changed? Was she really safe with such a dangerous individual? Alexandra wished she had answers to those questions.

Still sobbing, Renaldo fell to the dirt when Koneh released him. Without saying a word, Koneh climbed the small hill of rubble.

"Interesting friend you have there," Father Callahan said with raised eyebrows.

"Yeah," Alexandra said as she watched Koneh ascend. Alexandra wondered what the priest would think of her other friend – the one with wings.

"Like I said, it's not a rough climb. Dear Lord, are you hurt?" Father Callahan stared at her stomach, where her shirt was stained a shade darker by a brigand's blood. A few drops sunk into her oversize man-jeans as well, but those had dried.

Alexandra stretched her shirt to show the stain in the firelight. "This isn't mine." The image of her attacker's death flashed through her mind again. His life was over. Did he have children? Maybe family who cared for him? A wife? Alexandra closed her eyes. She despaired at the possibilities closed to those people through their deaths. Were their lives an equal trade for Alexandra's own life? Would it have come to that?

"Forgive me," Father Callahan said as he touched her shoulder. "I understand if you cannot talk about your loss just yet. It's a new world for us all." He squeezed her arm and climbed through the rubble towards the church.

Alexandra guessed the priest was more than empathizing with her own pain. Perhaps he lost someone special. Again, Alexandra was reminded of her empty life. These people lost families, friends, and homes. She decided her self-pity could be toned down a notch.

Alexandra glanced over her shoulder at the cluster of tents and people. Her eyes strayed to the ground where Renaldo, curled into a ball, shook from his sobs. She turned from the rubble hill and walked to him.

For her entire adult life, Alexandra believed monetary donations were the best way to help others in need. Her hands were never dirtied, in her mind. Now, however, she felt her heart shifting directions. Alexandra reached down and helped the stranger to his feet.

Renaldo's eyes, full of tears, thanked her. She smiled in return. After a few more sniffles, Renaldo limped towards a blanket. It was large enough for two.

"I hope you find your Maria," she whispered.

Despite the large hunks of uneven rock and pain in her ankle, the hill was a relatively easy climb for her. Though larger than the church she slept in a few nights ago, this church was in no better shape. She entered through a crumbled section of wall and found Koneh and Father Callahan talking in whispers.

"Anything I should know about?" she asked, though she was only half-joking. "Is my guide threatening you?"

Father Callahan released a nervous chuckle and motioned towards Koneh. "I was just asking him about his scars…"

Eyebrows raised, Alexandra looked at Koneh and asked, "And what did he tell you?"

"Not much…"

"Father Callahan has some food… warm food," Koneh said.

"Yes, I was heating some soup when you arrived. Would you like some?" Father Callahan said as he stepped out of the room.

The stench of the sulfur must have masked the soup's scent, but now Alexandra caught a whiff of the food.

"Yes!" Alexandra said. She heard the priest shuffle around in the other room. Exhausted, she dropped the duffel bag and then laid in a pew. The unforgiving wood creaked and provided little comfort. Alexandra was glad to be off her feet – feet covered only by soiled, layered tube-socks.

"So where are you headed?" Father Callahan asked as he carried two steaming bowls into the main section of the church. He rested one near Alexandra's head and then settled in the pew behind her to sip his own soup.

Alexandra dove into the rice soup. Though it was a bit bland compared to the Thai counterpart she was accustomed to eating at lunch, the meal warmed her belly.

At least it wasn't another granola bar.

As she enjoyed the soup, she allowed Koneh to answer the priest's questions. Of course, Alexandra doubted her companion would provide any actual answers. Let someone else feel the pain of talking to her guide.

"Tell me something, Father," Koneh said from the pew opposite Alexandra. Somehow she was stuck in the middle of the two men. "Have you had any visions? Has God spoken to you?"

Without looking up from his soup, Father Callahan huffed and said, "Nothing like that, traveler."

"Did you know this was going to happen?" Koneh asked.

This time, Father Callahan lifted his eyes to Koneh and smiled. "If I did, do you think I'd be caught here in the middle of *nowhere?*"

Father Callahan shook his head and then returned his attention to his soup. In between mouthfuls he said, "If the Pope or my superiors in my order knew anything about this they certainly didn't make the effort to contact any of their ministries in good 'ole Meh-hi-co."

"Your order?" Alexandra asked.

"I'm a Jesuit."

"Jesuit?"

Father Callahan nodded. "It's not as secretive as the History Channel would have you believe… we're actually the largest order of priests in the Catholic Church."

"Oh," Alexandra said, "I see."

Koneh leaned backwards and looked to the ceiling. Somehow, his ragged hood stayed in place. Alexandra wondered if it was stapled to his scalp.

Finished with his soup, Father Callahan rested his elbows on the back of Alexandra's pew and steeped his fingers. After studying Koneh for a moment, Father Callahan said, "Koneh. I've heard that name before."

Turning his icy gaze to the priest, Koneh said, "I guarantee you haven't."

Father Callahan curled his lips to the left side of his face. "Where did you say you were from again?"

"I didn't." Koneh's stare was terrifying enough to send a shiver down Alexandra's spine. She found comfort in her near-empty soup bowl.

After a few moments of silence, Alexandra finished her soup and said, "He doesn't like to talk about himself, Father."

"Forgive me, then. I mean no disrespect."

Koneh nodded.

"So," Father Callahan said with some levity in his voice, "where are you headed? Did you already answer that?" Father Callahan scratched his white and grey chin stubble.

"No," Alexandra said, "we didn't answer that one. To tell you the truth, I don't know either. My guide likes to keep his secrets. For now, we're just trying to find a safe place."

Alexandra smiled as she now had an ally, someone else who wanted the answers that Koneh kept safeguarded.

Koneh looked past her and said, "Tell me Father, what do you know of Eden?"

"As in 'The Garden of'?"

"If that's what you prefer…"

Father Callahan wrinkled his brow and said, "What's there to know? Eden is where God created Man. I have a bible if you're interested…"

Alexandra laughed.

After pausing for a moment to playfully scold her with his eyes, Koneh said, "Have you ever heard of an explorer named James Bruce?"

Father Callahan scratched his chin again and looked to one of the church's empty window frames. Then, he grinned and said, "Whew! I had to go way back there. Yes – James Bruce – he rediscovered the Book of Enoch in Ethiopia in the 1700s."

Koneh nodded and said, "1773 – and that's not all he discovered."

Alexandra's curiosity leapt to attention. "What else did he find?"

"Another book – the *full* version of the Book of Eden."

"That's non-canonical."

Koneh huffed. "Do you really want to debate the validity of church-approved and church-denounced material after all you have seen, Father?"

Father Callahan shrugged and said, "By all means, continue."

"You see, the Book of Eden went into great detail about the true nature of the Garden of Eden, Adam, Lilith, and Eve."

Alexandra put her hand up to stop Koneh. "Wait a minute," she said, "who's Lilith?"

"Adam's first wife," Koneh said.

"Non-canonical," Father Callahan said.

"May I continue?" Koneh asked.

"Please do," Father Callahan said.

"So," Koneh said, "the Book of Eden was long incomplete. The missing parts describe Eden's true nature, and how it is our heaven – the final resting place of mortal souls."

Alexandra raised her hand again like she was the slow kid in class who just didn't understand. "What do you mean, *our heaven?*"

"God's heaven is for God and His servants – angels. Mortal souls have no place there."

"Well," Father Callahan said, "Every shred of biblical and spiritual material contradicts that assertion."

Koneh raised a finger and smiled. "Except the full Book of Eden."

"Which may or may not have existed," Alexandra said. "Where is all of this leading, anyway?"

"Everything will be clear in a moment, please be patient for once," Koneh said, though Alexandra didn't detect malice in his voice. "Eden is described as the doorway between Heaven and Earth, a place where mortal and immortal souls coexist. The *gist* of Heaven is right in the bible, but the *place* is wrong. The place is on Earth – in Eden."

Father Callahan shook his head and frowned. "I'm with Alexandra. What does all of this nonsense mean?"

Koneh exhaled and said, "Yeshua failed to reclaim Eden for mankind. He was not supposed to die. His task was to reopen Eden to human souls so they could experience paradise for eternity."

"Yeshua?" Alexandra asked.

"Sorry," Koneh said. "Yeshua, the man you know as 'Jesus.'"

"Through his death, our sins were forgiven," Father Callahan said, his voice betraying annoyance with Koneh's outlandish assertions.

"Our sins can only be forgiven if Yeshua forgave them – but he did not," Koneh said.

"How do you know he didn't?" Alexandra asked. She thought Koneh only partially insane a day ago. Now she knew he was beyond all reason.

"I know because Eden has not been open to us for the past two thousand years, like it had been in the time of Genesis."

Father Callahan whistled. "Friend, I've heard some pretty crazy theories in my time, but that one takes the cake."

Koneh narrowed his eyes at the priest and said, "Tell me Father, who took your women?"

Clearly uncomfortable, Father Callahan leaned back in his pew and said, "Demons."

"Right. And who do you think these Demons are searching for?"

"I never thought I'd be saying this, but they are likely searching for the Messiah. It's all in Revelation."

"Makes sense that the New Messiah enters the world just like the last one – as a human child," Koneh said.

Alexandra curled her mouth in confusion. "Surely He would arrive more... protected."

Koneh turned his black-in-black eyes to her and her heart fluttered under his stare. Danger and mystery waited behind those eyes. "God works in mysterious ways," he said.

"Okay, okay." Father Callahan stood and paced in the aisle. "I'll admit that I don't understand what's going on. Though the quake, the blackened sky, and the demons lead me in only one direction. You said you had a point to all of this? Please, enlighten us."

"Very well," Koneh said. "You asked where we were headed."

Alexandra and Father Callahan leaned towards Koneh.

Koneh smiled and said, "I travel to Eden."

CHAPTER 7

"What? Eden?" Alexandra was exasperated. "First you tell me you talked to God, and now we're traveling to a mystical garden?"

"Surely this cannot be *that* difficult to accept. After all, you've seen an angel." Koneh said.

The image of Erzulie's unearthly beauty flashed into Alexandra's mind – the angel's ashen skin, the flowing dress, and those white-in-white eyes which provided a keen contrast to Koneh's bottomless black eyes.

"Wait a second," Father Callahan said as he stopped his pacing and turned towards Koneh. "You talked with God?" he asked in a tone of disbelief.

"That's what he *believes*, anyway," Alexandra said.

Ignoring the barb, Koneh turned to Father Callahan and said, "Yes, I was warned of the coming destruction and I was instructed that Eden would be our beacon."

"That's just…" Father Callahan's aggression faded as he appeared to lose himself in thought. Then, he turned to Alexandra and said, "And you've seen an *angel?*"

Alexandra nodded.

"What did it look like?" Father Callahan said and then abruptly changed his course. "Never mind that… something's familiar about…" After another pause, Father Callahan scurried out of the room, but Alexandra paid him little attention.

"Koneh, you failed to mention Eden when we talked about this before."

Shifting in his pew, Koneh said, "It remains… a delicate situation." He then stood and paced the aisle, much like Father Callahan had done a few moments earlier. Alexandra cringed when she noticed the frayed cloth covering his chest – the place he was shot less than twelve hours ago. What other secrets did Koneh possess? Now that Alexandra had an ally – Father Callahan – she was determined to discover those secrets.

"Well?" Alexandra asked.

Koneh halted and leveled his dark eyes upon her. "Is it really so hard to believe?" He asked the question with the usual rasp in his voice, like a senior citizen who smoked too many cigarettes in his day. "I am still getting a handle on all that has happened myself."

"Then tell me all *you* know!" Alexandra stood and met him in the aisle. Her voice softened. "Listen... I appreciate all you've done for me... but, you terrify me. Those men... you killed them, Koneh. I need to know why you think Eden exists and why you are headed there. Give me *something*."

This time, Koneh yielded under Alexandra's gaze.

He whispered, "I told you before – I am searching for answers and I hope to find them in Eden..."

"Why Eden?"

For the first time since she met Koneh, Alexandra felt pity for her companion. Though Koneh claimed to know where he was going, he seemed lost to her. Something in his voice cried-out for help. Alexandra could read that much. She found herself wondering about Koneh's true nature. Was he the killer on the bluff or the man who showed great caring as he cradled her wounded ankle? Further, why was she so drawn to him? She scolded her common sense for failing to keep her curiosity in check when it came to her new friend.

Koneh turned to face her again. The edge was gone from his scarred-smooth face and he said, "I believe Eden holds answers for us all. I cannot lie to you."

Alexandra touched his arm and smiled. "Then don't."

Koneh's eyes closed and Alexandra snapped her hand back to her side. However, the contact was less strange than the last time. There was nothing perverse about Koneh's reaction. He seemed genuinely relieved when she touched him.

Koneh's eyes opened and he whispered, "I also cannot tell you everything quite yet... I am sorry."

Alexandra sighed and grasped the pew banister with both hands behind her back. She leaned into the wood and said, "You're not making it easy for me to trust you, Koneh."

"I found it!" cried Father Callahan from the other room.

Before Alexandra could respond, the priest burst back into the main chamber of the church waving a bible.

"This is it. I knew I heard that before." Father Callahan almost tore the pages from the binding as he scanned through the back section of the holy book.

"Heard what, Father?" Alexandra asked.

Instead of responding, Father Callahan mumbled to himself and turned more pages. Alexandra looked to Koneh, who shrugged.

"Here it is." Father Callahan settled on a page and turned the book towards them.

Alexandra's lawyer eyes quickly scanned the page, but she was lost as the Bible was written in Latin. However, she noticed the text was full of scribbles, cross-outs, and hand-written notes in the margins – also in Latin.

"My Latin's not so good anymore," she said, scrunching her nose.

Father Callahan pointed to one of the notes and translated, "'And I beheld, Eden shall be the Beacon'."

"Whose book was this?" Koneh asked with piqued interest.

"It belonged to my mentor, Bishop Palusa from Rome."

Alexandra leaned towards the book and asked, "What else does it say?"

"Well," Father Callahan said, "on this page the word 'Lamb' is crossed out and replaced with the word 'Lion' several times."

Koneh looked from the book to Father Callahan and said, "Did Bishop Palusa have the gift of prophecy?"

Father Callahan shook his head and said, "No, no. He was… sick, in his older years."

"Sick?" Alexandra asked.

"Alzheimer's... and some paranoia. But he was a good man."

Alexandra noted the pain in Father Callahan's voice, so she decided to let the subject drop. However, her traveling companion was not so sensitive.

"Where did he live? Who did he study under?" Koneh said.

"Does it matter?" Father Callahan said as he snapped the book shut, "He's gone and this is just a coincidence."

"How many coincidences do you need Father?" Koneh said. "Tell me, when did he assign you to this church in Mexico?"

Father Callahan took a step backwards and dropped the Bible. The *thud* from the heavy book echoed in the ruined church. Dust billowed from the floor as the echo died.

"Strange that someone who was not in a position to make such an assignment sent you here," Koneh said. "But, you came anyway…"

"How… how could you know that?" Father Callahan left his mouth open after breathing the words.

"I don't," Koneh said. "Bishop Palusa and I shared the same vision or, at least, parts thereof. My vision led me to Mexico – to you, Father."

"Amen. Well, we should read the rest of the Revelation and see what else Bishop Palusa had to say," Father Callahan said as he knelt to retrieve the book.

"That's why I am here."

"Start from the beginning," Alexandra said as the small group huddled together over the book. Could this altered bible hold some answers?

Father Callahan wiped his hand across the dusty surface and opened the bible to the Revelation again. He pointed at the first scribble. "Here, the Messiah is described as having a sword in his hand *instead* of in his mouth."

"Well, that makes more sense," Alexandra said, suppressing the gruesome vision of Koneh's sword decapitating the shotgun man.

"The next one… okay, here," Father Callahan said. "The seven stars are instead the Seven Coursers – generals in the Messiah's army."

Koneh huffed. "Genghis Khan was said to have four hounds and four coursers serving him. They were his best warriors and generals. Interesting Bishop Palusa would choose the word Courser."

"Indeed," Father Callahan said as he scanned the next note. "This one's confusing. Bishop Palusa writes that he sees two swords, instead of a double-edged sword. 'Two swords to turn back the darkness.' It looks like he's just rambling here."

Koneh studied the hand-written notes and nodded.

Father Callahan continued, "Let's see, 'sword of my mouth' is crossed off here and replaced with 'sword of Eden's sin'…

whatever that means. Umm... the word 'thief' is replaced with 'vagabond' or 'wanderer'... my Latin's not perfect."

"Better than mine," Alexandra said.

Smiling, Father Callahan returned his attention to the pages. "Okay, now we're into the section where 'Lamb' is replaced with 'Lion'... interesting. 'The seven thunders told John to not write of God's mystery, which was revealed to him.' Here, in the margin, Bishop Palusa wrote 'God is not here for us'."

Alexandra shivered. Was all of this the senseless ramblings of an insane priest?

"Hmm... the first time the word 'testament' appears, Bishop Palusa circled it and wrote in the margin 'The Covenant will be upheld!' Further along, he crosses out the section on the saints and writes that the Church will fail to keep the commandments and will pursue the Lion. The rest of this page is smudged and unreadable."

"Lots of those notes look damaged," Alexandra said.

"Yeah, I'm having trouble with some of these," Father Callahan said. "Oh, okay. Here. He circled the section about the strange woman, the mother of harlots. Bishop Palusa simply wrote – 'she is not Babylon... she will be here, who is she?' Interesting. Wow. The line about Babylon being cast away and seen no more is crossed-out. Instead, Bishop Palusa writes that Babylon will be reborn in greater sin and evil. Wow."

"Why is Babylon so important?" Alexandra asked.

"The bible doesn't look too favorably on Babylon," Koneh said. "The city is credited to putting man's achievements before God's and for falling into unforgivable sin."

Father Callahan pointed to another Latin scribble. "Here is the passage I recognized from Koneh's words. 'And I saw a new heaven and a new earth. The sea will be as dust and Eden shall be our Beacon.' It's right there."

"Anything else?" Alexandra asked.

Father Callahan shook his head. "Lots of cross-outs, but nothing else legible."

Alexandra mulled the altered Revelation over in her mind, but it wasn't a cohesive whole. Perhaps only Bishop Palusa understood his notes. Perhaps not.

"Let's read the whole thing," Koneh said. "It's been a while for me."

Father Callahan flipped to the beginning of the section and said, "Good idea."

"You boys have fun," Alexandra said as she rubbed her burning eyes. "I'm going to get some rest."

Father Callahan nodded. "We'll go into the other room so you can sleep."

As the pair exited the main room of the church, Alexandra removed her leather jacket and laid in a pew. She used her coat as a pillow and curled her legs up to her stomach. After a few minutes her eyes settled on the altar and the crucifix.

"It's still so hard to believe," Alexandra whispered, though she wasn't sure if she was talking to herself or someone else.

Sleep eventually overtook her and she drifted away into her dreams. When she awoke, her hands were shaking. She opened her eyes and saw the church exactly as she left it. A few candles illuminated the walls and altar, and debris cluttered the floor. With a start, Alexandra sat up in her pew and brought her hand to her forehead – sweat.

One thing was different, however. Someone covered her with a blanket. Guessing it was Father Callahan, Alexandra pushed the blanket to the side, stood, and stretched her arms. In her sleep her hair became unraveled again. As she braided the waist-long strands, she entertained the notion of cutting her hair. The new style in San Antonio was knee-length, but she didn't find anything convenient about maintaining such long hair in her new environment.

Her ears adjusted to her surroundings. She heard low voices and the crackle of a fire in the other room. Outside, the wind whistled and Alexandra felt the chill it brought. She lifted her jacket and threaded her arms through the leather sleeves. If she ever met the man who lent her his jacket and duffel bag, Alexandra decided she would have to thank him.

Alexandra picked her way to the back of the church, where she last saw her new friends. As she approached, she heard Koneh's raspy voice.

"She is just a child… for something like this…"

The voice trailed away and Alexandra strained her ears at the other side of the wall. A moment later, without a sound, Koneh's hooded face appeared next to hers. Alexandra jumped.

"She is awake," Koneh said.

"Good!" Father Callahan said from the other room.

After composing herself, Alexandra said, "What were you two talking about in there?"

Father Callahan joined Koneh in the entryway and waved his hand. "Nothing, nothing. We were just getting to know each other a little bit."

Alexandra pointed to the altered Bible and asked, "Anything else of interest in there?" She wanted to ask if they were talking about her, but she felt petty for even thinking it. She reminded herself that she was not the center of the universe.

"Hard to say, but Bishop Palusa may have indeed received a vision from God – a corrected Revelation if you will." Father Callahan said. "Anyway, you must be hungry, my dear. You were asleep for almost six hours."

Alexandra's stomach answered with an audible growl.

Laughing, Father Callahan asked, "Is rice soup okay again for breakfast?"

Alexandra smiled. "Yes, that would be wonderful… and thank you for the blanket."

"Dear, that wasn't me," Father Callahan said.

"It was Father Callahan's idea," Koneh said with a nod. "I only performed the manual labor."

Father Callahan turned to Koneh and said, "That's not…"

Koneh interrupted him again. "Do you mind if I look over that Bible while you cook?"

"Please do," Father Callahan said.

Without further acknowledgement, Koneh grasped the book and stepped to a pew. Before he sat, he adjusted something under his rags. Alexandra guessed it was his sword. The one he used to kill several men. True, he acted in her defense, but how would she protect herself if that sword was ever turned upon her?

Father Callahan clapped his hands once and said, "Well then, I'll get started on that soup."

"I'll help," Alexandra said.

"Nonsense, dear. Sit, rest."

Alexandra looked over her shoulder at Koneh and whispered, "I need someone to talk to."

"Of course. You are free to watch me work, but mark my words," Father Callahan's face grew playfully stern, "nobody but

Father Callahan and the Almighty Himself are allowed to cook in my kitchen. Got it?"

"Yes, Father," Alexandra said as she bowed dramatically.

The pair shared a laugh.

"This way."

Alexandra followed Father Callahan into a study. Books clung to wooden racks along the far wall. Papers and debris littered the floor. The ceiling in this room appeared in worse shape than the main chamber of the church. Through the numerous holes, Alexandra spied the apocalyptic sky above. At the center of the room rested a makeshift fire pit, complete with spit and pot. The crackling she heard a few moments prior was from the small fire lapping the bottom of the steel pot.

"The water should be warm enough by now," Father Callahan said. "I've used all the chairs for firewood, so I hope the floor is okay."

Alexandra kneeled by the fire and said, "This is fine."

"Soon, it'll be the pews," Father Callahan whispered.

Father Callahan paused for a moment and then gathered some materials from a bookshelf – a spoon, some salt, and a small tin canister.

"What happened to your home?" Alexandra asked.

As Father Callahan scooped rice from the tin, he said, "Destroyed by the earthquake. I salvaged what I could."

"I'm sorry…"

"I'll make it fine, always have. God will provide."

Alexandra shifted off her knees and rested her bottom on the floor. She didn't know a tactful way to phrase the subject, so she just started talking.

"You know," she said, "Koneh believes Heaven and Hell have *fallen*. Does that mean anything to you?"

Father Callahan mixed the contents of the simple soup together and said, "Yes, yes… he told me his theories." Then, lowering his voice, he said, "To tell you the truth, I don't know quite what to think of your friend."

"Father," Alexandra said as she lowered her voice as well, "Koneh killed some men before we arrived. He has a sword."

Father Callahan halted in mid-stir and snapped his eyes to Alexandra. Lines and wrinkles gathered around his brown eyes and he appeared a bit older than when Alexandra first met him less than twelve hours ago.

"A sword you say? That's odd."

Alexandra nodded and said, "Yeah. In his defense, the men were about to rape and probably kill me. But, I... I don't know. Something felt *wrong* about the whole thing."

Father Callahan resumed his stirring and smiled gently. "Do not be ashamed to mourn the death of your enemy. All life is precious."

"I guess that's it," Alexandra said. "I haven't exactly been the best Christian... Catholic, whatever. If I do, in fact, have a newfound respect for life, I don't think our friend in the other room shares our feelings on the matter."

"Oh... after my talk with him, I think quite the opposite."

"Really? What did he tell you?"

"Oh, he made me promise to keep the priest-penitent privilege. I cannot say without breaking his trust, not to mention my own ethics."

Alexandra sighed.

"Almost ready," Father Callahan said.

Still on the previous topic, Alexandra looked into Father Callahan's eyes and asked, "Do you trust him?"

Father Callahan huffed and said, "I trust that he had a vision, one shared by my mentor in Rome. I also trust that he *thinks* he can find Eden. Of course, I don't usually place my trust in someone I've only known a few hours."

"I've known him a few days and I don't trust him," Alexandra said as her eyes wandered to the wall separating the study from the rest of the church. Trust him? Definitely not. Intrigued? Certainly.

"However," Father Callahan said, "I do trust Koneh."

Alexandra jerked her head back to her companion. "I thought you said you don't trust people you've just met?"

"I said I don't *usually* trust them. Your friend is an exception."

"He's an exception all right."

"Soup's done," Father Callahan said as he stood and produced two bowls from another bookshelf. "In fact," he said, "I trust him enough to follow him to Eden."

"You can't be serious Father," Alexandra said incredulously as she accepted a bowl of rice soup from the priest.

"Most serious," Father Callahan said with a smile on his weathered face. "As I said, I trust him."

"What did he say to convince you to go with him?"

Father Callahan sipped his soup, nodded, and then said, "There wasn't *one* thing, really."

Following suit, Alexandra brought the bowl to her lips and enjoyed the warmth of the broth. Though the soup was not very filling, it hit the spot.

"Don't the people here need you?" As soon as the words were finished, Alexandra regretted them. What right did she have to question a priest?

"Of course they need me," Father Callahan said. "However, I feel my presence here in Mexico is no accident. Bishop Palusa assigned me here for a reason. And now I know that reason."

"To follow a crazy man to a place that likely doesn't exist?"

Father Callahan pointed to Alexandra's chest and said, "You wear that cross. Have you no faith?"

After another sip, Alexandra rested the bowl on the floor and sighed. "I don't know where to place my faith anymore Father," she said.

"A soul without aim loses itself."

Alexandra frowned and said, "That sounds like a fortune cookie."

Laughing, Father Callahan said, "Yeah, I guess it does. I'm sure I read it somewhere. Appropriate, though."

Alexandra allowed some laughter to escape over the high walls of her self-control. She was never comfortable letting go of her composure. However, this priest wasn't stuffy and elitist like others she knew.

"I also believe," Father Callahan said, "that you are no accident, Alexandra. We were supposed to meet."

"Why do you think that?"

Scratching the gray stubble on his chin, Father Callahan said, "Hard to describe, really. It's just a feeling."

"Are you two all acquainted?"

Alexandra jumped and her knee smacked the empty soup bowl. It skipped across the floor and rolled to a halt near one of the bookcases.

Koneh leaned against the remains of the door frame. The light from the candles couldn't breach the shadow over his hooded face, but Alexandra knew what was there - scar upon scar.

Father Callahan looked from Alexandra to Koneh and said, "Well, not really. We didn't talk much about ourselves."

"You can play catch up on the road if you want. We need to leave," Koneh said.

Alexandra said, "Leave? What makes you think I'm going with you?"

Koneh and Father Callahan exchanged glances.

"I'm done with this," Koneh said as he dropped the Bible on the floor. "And you're not finished with her."

After the echo from the book faded, Koneh turned and walked into the main section of the church. Confused, Alexandra looked at Father Callahan and put her palms to the sky.

"What was that?" she asked.

Father Callahan smiled and said, "It was my job to convince you to come with us."

"Oh no," Alexandra said as she rose to her feet, "he's not going to get away with using you, Father."

"Alexandra…"

Father Callahan never finished his thought. Alexandra stalked after her secretive guide.

"No you don't, Koneh."

The target of her anger was perched on the back of a wooden pew. Loose wrappings from his tattered clothing draped over the arm and back supports. As Alexandra approached, Koneh watched her every move like a hawk watches a mouse in the field.

"If you want me to go with you on this foolish trip you'll have to ask me yourself."

"Consider yourself asked," Koneh said.

Alexandra stopped a few feet from Koneh and planted her fists on her hips. She decided she would have looked more menacing if she wasn't dressed in men's clothing.

"That's easy. My answer is *no*," she said.

"You'd rather stay here?"

"I'd rather get a straight answer from you Koneh!"

"You know some topics are off-limits."

"Fine," Alexandra said. "Give me one good reason why I should travel to Eden with you."

Koneh grinned and said, "I'll give you two. First: you need me."

"Are you sure about that?" She scowled, but she knew he was right. Though she was a Texan woman – she didn't need *any* man – these were extreme circumstances.

"Yes, you seem to need my protection. And I am happy to help." Before Alexandra could respond, Koneh said, "Reason two is equally simple: I need you."

Exhasperated, she said, "For what?"

"To finish what I start if I should fail."

"Why me?"

"Look around you, Alexandra. My choices are limited. You seem like you have a good heart."

"Why not the priest?"

"I saw you first," Koneh said.

"What about Erzulie?"

"She's not human."

"And?" Alexandra said.

"And," Koneh said, "Eden was made for *us* – for humans. Angels and demons have no place there."

Alexandra closed her eyes to keep the tears at bay.

Did she need him? The answer was there before Alexandra could analyze the question. Since waking up inside the overturned bus, Alexandra hadn't fared well. However, things could've been worse if Koneh wasn't around. In this new world, she *did* need him.

Did he really need her? Alexandra opened her eyes and examined Koneh. At times he'd shown compassion. For the most part, however, he was rude and coarse. His reasons for needing her didn't quite stack-up in Alexandra's mind. He was still holding back. If he needed her, he wasn't giving all the reasons.

Koneh stepped down from the pew and said gently, "The rules have changed." He moved closer and touched Alexandra's arm. "You cannot wait here for the next bus to Laredo or south Texas. There are no more busses."

"I don't believe that you need me," Alexandra said. "You can do this without me."

"If that's what you believe," Koneh said, "then tag along for *my* sake. I couldn't forgive myself if I knew you were wandering the Mexican wasteland alone."

Alexandra believed he would indeed feel guilt if he abandoned her. She also felt foolish for not placing her trust in him before. He saved her life without hesitation. He took a bullet for her! At least she could trust him to keep her safe. That was something. Though his exterior was frightening, Koneh's heart seemed to be in the right place. Further, and though she knew the thought was foolish, Alexandra wondered if she had a place in that heart.

"Okay, fine Koneh," Alexandra said. "I'll go with you for now. You convinced Father Callahan, so I guess I can't stay here with him. However, I'm still skeptical about this whole Eden thing. You'll have your chance to convince me on the road."

Koneh grinned and said, "Fair enough."

CHAPTER 8

"Do you even know *where* Eden is?" Alexandra said as she zipped her duffel bag and slung it over her shoulder.

Father Callahan waited for the pair at the crumbled entrance of his church, a backpack over his shoulders and walking stick in hand.

"Don't I still have time to convince you?" Koneh asked.

"I'm coming for now. However, I usually like to know where I'm going."

Koneh smiled. "Is the destination as important as the journey?"

Glaring at her companion, Alexandra said, "I'm confident whoever said that never dreamed of this situation."

"Perhaps not," Koneh said.

Alexandra sighed. "You didn't answer my question."

"Perhaps not." Koneh exited the church.

Grinding her teeth, Alexandra followed. How could someone frustrate and excite her at the same time? He wasn't playing fair.

Alexandra, Koneh, and Father Richard Callahan departed the small Mexican village with little fanfare. The men who populated the makeshift tents of the shanty-town appeared to resign themselves to a hollow existence. Their women and their lives were taken from them. One of those men, Renaldo, followed Alexandra to the edge of the town and gave her a flower – a cream-colored bougainvillea. He said it was his last blossom and Alexandra tucked the flower behind her ear.

Though Father Callahan wanted to stay and help the town rebuild, he told Alexandra that he believed he could serve a higher purpose by following Koneh to Eden. "First," Koneh said as they left the village, "we will head west, to Tampico. We can salvage supplies if anything's left of the port city. Plus, a boat would make this trip much faster."

Alexandra's reasons for following the raspy stranger were more selfish. She needed him. She both feared him and felt safe when she was with him. Though she wasn't sure she believed in the existence of Eden, she decided she'd rather find out for sure than be left wondering. What if it did exist? Even worse, what if she passed up her chance to live in paradise while the rest of the world crumbled and died? No, she wasn't going to miss *that* bus... if it existed.

They had only traveled for a few hours when Koneh stopped the group. The black and red velvet sky roiled above their heads and the wind cut through Alexandra's borrowed leather jacket. Alexandra thought she saw a hawk earlier that morning, but Koneh assured her she was mistaken. Beyond Alexandra's small group, no life stirred in the wasteland.

"What's the holdup?" Alexandra said.

Father Callahan stepped to her side and offered the canister of dry rice. Though not as tasty as the soup they shared in the church, the rice satisfied her hunger. Alexandra scooped a pile into her palm and pecked at the brown morsels.

"She's here," Koneh said.

The wind changed direction and gathered intensity. Alexandra heard the flapping of wings and saw a figure emerge from the murky sky. Erzulie.

Before Erzulie touched the dirt, she dropped a large sack to the ground. Dust plumed and then was scattered as Erzulie's dark wings scooped the air.

The fallen angel touched the earth with a slender gray foot and glided towards Alexandra. Erzulie's exotic beauty held Alexandra captivated for several moments and she couldn't muster the strength to glimse Father Callahan's reaction.

"I am elated to see you again, Lex," Erzulie said. Her voice was full of melodious undercurrents and her pure white eyes fixed upon Alexandra.

Tearing her eyes away from Erzulie's unearthly face, Alexandra said, "Father Callahan, meet Erzulie. She's a fallen angel... I guess."

Father Callahan's mouth hung open as he stared at the six and a half foot tall ashen-skinned woman. Erzulie folded her wings flat against her back and turned towards Father Callahan.

With a nod of her head, Erzulie said, "Pleased to meet you, Father."

Father Callahan fingered the golden cross at his neck, blinked, and then said, "Fallen Angel, you say. I always knew your kind to be called *Demons*, no?"

Koneh said, "Different species altogether, though I can see where the Church confused its facts."

"As far as priests go," Father Callahan said as he added some weight to his voice, "I am a tad more open to accepting the notion that not all of the Bible is meant to be taken literally. However, she looks much like the demons that carried off the women of my town a few days ago."

Erzulie opened her mouth to speak, but Koneh was faster. He said, "Subtle differences, Father. Think back to that day when the women were taken. Those demons had dark skin, yes?"

Father Callahan nodded but kept his eyes upon Erzulie.

"Now," Koneh said, "was their skin tinted gray like Erzulie's? Or, was their skin shaded red?"

Father Callahan scratched his chin and squinted. "Red, I guess," he said.

Koneh stepped towards Father Callahan and said, "Look to Erzulie's feet."

Both Alexandra and Father Callahan looked at Erzulie's bare ashen feet. Once again, the silver anklet captivated Alexandra.

Father Callahan huffed and said, "I guess she is a tad different. Those other demons had cloven feet – like a goat."

"Exactly," Koneh said. "Erzulie was once an angel. Those demons who took the women from your town are... something else."

"Beyond a few physical differences, what's the... well, difference?" Alexandra said.

Koneh said, "We could spend all day going over the two species history and physiology. However, I prefer the short version: angels were created in Heaven, and demons are created in Hell."

"Koneh speaks truth," Erzulie said. "We should get moving. This area isn't safe."

Without waiting for Erzulie to finish speaking, Koneh walked to the bag on the ground. "You did well," he said.

Erzulie turned to Alexandra and said, "I'm sorry, Lex. It would be more, but the army base was all but destroyed when I returned. Please forgive me for failing you."

"Forgive you?" Alexandra said. "It looks like you got a lot of stuff there."

"Open the top," Erzulie said to Koneh. "I grabbed a pair of boots for Lex."

Koneh untied the rope around the mouth of the bag and produced a pair of black army boots. He tossed them to Alexandra.

"You're a life-saver, Erzulie." Alexandra said as she pulled the boots over her feet. With some extra support for her ankle, perhaps she could finish healing.

"The remainder is food – army rations," Erzulie said. "The demons who hit the base before me seemed more interested in destroying vehicles, weapons, and ammunition. Some of the food survived."

"This is good," Koneh said as he tightened the rope. "We should have enough here for a few weeks."

"Great," Father Callahan said as he rolled his eyes, "I thought I'd seen the last of MRE's."

Koneh huffed. Alexandra guessed the noise was a laugh and asked, "MRE?"

"Meals, Ready-to-Eat. MRE's," Father Callahan said. "Though most of us called them 'Meals Rejected by Ethiopians.' American soldiers aren't known for their political correctness. Basically, they taste so terrible you'd almost rather starve than try to swallow them down, but they got everything a body needs."

"MRE's... can't wait," Alexandra said as she stood and tested her weight in her new boots. Then she stepped to Erzulie's side. "Thank you, Erzulie. The boots, the food. You did well."

Erzulie's white-in-white eyes softened and she said, "It is my pleasure to serve."

"Okay, okay. That's enough, Erzul." Koneh said. "I'll carry the rations – they're heavy."

"So," Father Callahan said, "this fallen angel is with you, Alexandra?"

Before Alexandra could answer, Erzulie said, "Yes, Lex and I are companions."

"We can move and talk," Koneh said as he shouldered the bag of rations and walked away from the group.

Erzulie frowned, "I should keep watch up high. We'll talk tonight Lex."

After spreading her dark wings, Erzulie shot into the sky. Alexandra closed her eyes from the dust and wind generated by the breathtaking departure.

"You keep some strange company, Alexandra Contreras."

Alexandra opened her eyes to Father Callahan's smile. "You're telling me," she said.

The pair kept pace behind their guide and munched on the dry rice. As they traveled, the smell of sulfur receded along with the wind.

"So, how do you know so much about army rations, Father?" Alexandra said.

"Well I wasn't always the well-spoken, finely dressed, widely studied priest you see before you."

"Oh, really?" Alexandra said as she nudged the priest, desperate to lighten the mood after the events of the past few days. "Okay, you have my attention," Alexandra said.

Father Callahan shifted his backpack and said, "Well, I grew up in New York City. Brooklyn to be precise. My neighborhood was pretty empty so my brothers and I had to kind of make our own fun."

"Sounds naughty."

"Nothing too bad. We played hide and seek in abandoned buildings, crawled around the underside of overpasses. Mostly a lot of trespassing and vandalism. Boy stuff."

"And this *boy stuff* got you into trouble?" Alexandra said.

Father Callahan grinned and looked towards the horizon, as if he was lost in memories. "Yeah, we vandalized the wrong place owned by the wrong person. Being the eldest, I took all the blame and my parents responded. They sent me to the army."

"No kidding. That's tough."

"I'm glad they did. I learned plenty about the world beyond Brooklyn. It's also where I rediscovered my faith through their Chaplain program. Once I was done with my four years, I completed seminary and was in line for a prestigious position in London."

"London – wow. Your parents must have been very proud."

"They certainly were. However I never made it to London."

"Why not?"

"Well," Father Callahan said, "I met Bishop Palusa in Rome and my life course altered. He opened my eyes to a world of faith larger than the Bible. Though he was not my superior, he assigned me to several research tasks in Rome. Then, I bounced around from church to church in Italy. Finally, Bishop Palusa sent me here, to Mexico. I've been here for the past twenty years."

Alexandra lowered her eyes as they walked. "Sounds like things didn't turn out as you hoped."

"Actually," Father Callahan said, "I'm happy things turned out the way they did. The people here are extraordinary. Though they may not have enough food for their family, they'll take a stranger in and feed that person their last slice of bread. They taught me more about living a good life than any rigid book or dogma ever could."

"I used to think highly of my brothers and sisters here in Mexico as well – until a mob of them chased me through the streets."

"Really? When was that?"

Alexandra's bruised ankle throbbed in response to the memory of the event. "A few days ago. Well, almost a week now. Koneh saved me."

"No kidding," Father Callahan said as he looked at their guide ten paces in front of them. Koneh seemed uninterested in their conversation.

"Yup. That's how we met. He salvaged a man's travel bag and that's how come I'm wearing these clothes." Alexandra waved her hand down her body like a metal-detection wand used at the airport. "Not exactly the latest fall fashion."

Father Callahan laughed. "I guess not. So you were born here in Mexico, Alexandra?"

"Yup, in a little town outside of Torreon."

"Oh, do you prefer Alexandra or Lex? That angel…"

"Yeah," Alexandra said with a chuckle, "you can call me Alexandra or Alex. Nobody calls me Lex anymore. Except Erzulie apparently. I'm still mystified by her. How could she know about that nickname from my childhood?"

Father Callahan shook his head and the two companions followed their guide for many hours. When they stopped to rest, the wind had quieted from painful surges to merely a constant annoyance. Amidst the squat cacti and low brush, the travelers set up their camp.

Father Callahan produced several blankets from his backpack and handed two of them to Alexandra. "Here, I noticed you don't have much."

"Thank you, Father," Alexandra said. "Koneh, how about we try some of those MRE's? Toss a couple this way."

Koneh looked to the reddish-black swirling sky and then to Alexandra and the priest. "We should ration what we have. One a day. You've already had rice, you'll be fine."

With a sigh, Alexandra pulled a water bottle from her bag. Before the group left the village, Father Callahan filled her empty bottles from the town's well. The water quenched her thirst.

Father Callahan followed suit with his own water bottle and said, "It'll take us a few more days to reach Tampico. What was the plan? Follow Route 70?"

Koneh circled around one of the cacti and said, "Yes, we'll see what's left of Route 70 and follow it into the port of Tampico."

"We probably won't have much traffic to fight," Alexandra said wryly.

Nobody laughed.

"I'd like to get us there as fast as possible," Koneh said. "So, few breaks, light sleep, and try to keep the complaints to a minimum."

Alexandra caught some movement out of the corner of her eye and looked to the air. Erzulie emerged from the darkness of the sky and landed a fair distance away from the cacti.

"You two - get some rest. We move again in four hours." Koneh left Alexandra and Father Callahan alone as he moved towards Erzulie.

Alexandra found a comfortable spot and laid one of the blankets on the packed dirt. Before settling down, Alexandra glanced to where she last saw Erzulie and Koneh. They appeared to be discussing something.

Exhausted from the day's walk, Alexandra slumped to the ground. She heard Father Callahan do the same. From her blanket, Alexandra said, "You have any more of that rice, Father?"

"We're rationing, remember?" he said. "Tighten up that belt!"

In response, Alexandra's stomach grumbled. She hated going to sleep with an empty belly. Memories of her early-twenties fad diets shouldered their way into the foreground of her mind. Celery was a poor substitute for the comfort food she rediscovered shortly before leaving for Mexico.

Alexandra pulled a second blanket over her body. The chill in the air forced her to wear her jacket. She longed for her real bed in San Antonio. Soft mattress, silk sheets, and fluffy pillows - she missed it all.

As she closed her eyes to sleep, she heard the flutter of clothing and the jingle of jewelry. Alexandra rolled to her other side and saw Erzulie perched on a rock two feet away.

The fallen angel smiled and locked her unearthly eyes upon Alexandra. "How are you feeling?" Erzulie asked.

"Tired... hungry... uncomfortable... hungry... smelly." Alexandra forced a smile to her lips.

"Do you want me to get you some food? I'm sure I can find more. All you need to do is ask."

Alexandra rested on her elbow and propped her head in her hand. "Don't be silly. I've dieted before. This won't be too difficult."

"What else can I get for you? Another blanket?"

"Really, Erzulie, I'm fine. Thank you, though."

If Koneh was right, and Erzulie could only imitate human emotion, then the angel was skilled in her imitation. She seemed sincere.

"You should get some sleep, Lex. I'll watch over you."

"I have so many questions."

"I know you do, dear. Save your strength. Our journey is just beginning."

Alexandra dropped her eyes to the ground. The angel didn't seem to understand. The questions Alexandra stirred in her head were ones of a divine nature. What was Heaven like? What was God like? How many passages in the Bible were legend and how many are fact? Her mind was a bee's nest alive with activity.

"I need to patrol the sky again. Get some sleep." Erzulie stood and stretched her gray-skinned arms. Her feathered wings followed suit and Alexandra marveled at the sight of exotic beauty beyond any she had ever seen.

"We'll talk tomorrow then," Alexandra said.

"Sure, dear. Tomorrow." Erzulie crouched. A moment later, she launched into the sky and disappeared into the roiling red and black.

Tomorrow. Alexandra closed her eyes and rolled the questions around in her mind. She wasn't sure she wanted to know the answers, but when would she have the chance to question an angel again?

Alexandra was drifting near sleep when she heard a coyote's dirge. Something wasn't quite right, however. The sound was deeper and less drawn-out than any coyote she had ever heard – and her hometown was inundated with the little yappers. No, this howl seemed unnatural to her. It was out of place in the desert she knew.

Her eyes shot open when she heard running. Koneh slid a sword from underneath his rags as he dashed past Alexandra's sleeping area.

"What's wrong?" Alexandra said.

Koneh halted and put his left hand against a tall cactus. With the usual rasp in his voice, he said, "Hounds."

CHAPTER 9

"Hounds?" Alexandra said as she bolted upright in her makeshift bed.

Koneh scanned the sky as another howl echoed through the wasteland.

"What's going on?" Father Callahan said from the other side of a rock.

Alexandra looked to Koneh to provide the answer. However, like usual, he ignored the question and moved from one side of the cactus to the other. He switched his sword from his right hand to his left and kneeled next to the tall plant. Only three feet away, Alexandra's eyes centered on Koneh's weapon.

When she was in law school, a younger Alexandra visited the Metropolitan Museum in New York City. She was fascinated by the Egyptian relics and artwork. History was not her favorite area of study, but after watching a few Discovery Channel specials on Egypt, she had become obsessed with all things Egyptian.

Her plan was to spend the whole day in the Egyptian wing of the museum. However, her friend Max dragged her off "just for a sec" to see the medieval display. As she was explaining the significance of hieroglyphs and their mistranslation through the years, the pair rounded a corner and Alexandra stopped mid-sentence. She held her mouth open in awe at the sight. Several mounted knights upon horseback dominated the center of the two-story room.

Alexandra's museum plan changed. She spent the rest of the day in the medieval wing with the armor, swords, and crossbows. Max explained the different types of medieval armors and the types of weapons invented to beat those defenses. "There's just something so romantic and elegant about the sword," he had said.

Koneh's sword was unlike any she had seen at the Museum that day. Only small pockets of silver shone through the layers of rust. The entire length of the three foot blade was pock marked with depressions and even a few holes. Instead of the fine edge Alexandra saw on the swords in the museum, this sword's edges were rough and uneven. As Alexandra studied the weapon and recalled how Koneh used it to end men's lives, she felt nothing romantic about the sword. Max was wrong.

"Stay down!" Koneh yelled as he leapt away from Alexandra.

Of course, Alexandra jumped out of her blankets. If someone said "don't look" to her, she would have looked. It was just the way she was built.

Several fast-moving forms emerged from the darkness. Koneh sprinted towards the center of the pack. Before the animals scattered, Koneh caught one in the swing of his sword and it tumbled to the ground. They were close enough for Alexandra to make them out – large dogs. Faster than Koneh, the dogs turned towards Alexandra and bounded in her direction.

"What is that?" Father Callahan said as he stepped to Alexandra's side.

Alexandra's words died of fright in her throat. Her heart beat against her chest like a convict against the walls of a burning prison.

She couldn't count them all, but she guessed there were at least five. The animals charged from several directions and Alexandra's legs shook with fear. As the animals closed, recognition snapped Alexandra from her stupor. These dogs were similar the one she encountered in the café.

"I've seen them before!"

Father Callahan nodded and stepped backwards.

"No, the one I saw didn't hurt me. Perhaps…"

Another form joined the fray. It was Erzulie. She swooped from the sky and impaled her sword into the side of one of the hounds. Both angel and beast tumbled to the ground.

"Run!" Father Callahan said as he turned.

However, one of the hounds was behind them. It pounced on Father Callahan as the remaining hounds cleared the small cacti and rocks and entered their camp. Alexandra swung herself to the other side of a cactus to avoid the lunge of one of the hounds. Another waited for her and leapt.

Alexandra raised her arms to protect her face as the animal slammed her to the ground and pinned her there. The shock from the impact left her woozy for a moment, but the hound's sulfurous breath and sticky drool sobered her almost instantly.

The beast closed its maw of yellow, jagged teeth and sniffed her chest. As it moved its nose across her shoulders she noticed the collar. Iron spikes protruded from the metal band. A broken chain dangled from a fixed ring and rested on her stomach.

Alexandra tried to move her arms, but the red-skinned beast kept her pinned to the earth. The hound rumbled a low growl and raised its head. Something pissed it off and Alexandra hoped it wasn't her own stench.

Then, Father Richard Callahan's voice filled the area. "Beasts of Hell! Be gone!"

Still growling, the animal backed off Alexandra's body. Father Callahan stepped to Alexandra and offered his hand. His other hand grasped his cross. The priest's eyes narrowed with intensity as he stared down the hound. Alexandra tried to stand, but found her legs lacked the courage. She scurried to a spot behind Father Callahan.

After glancing at Alexandra, the hound turned and bounded away. Father Callahan kneeled beside Alexandra.

"Are you all right?"

"Yes, Father. How did you do that?" Alexandra found she could stand and she scanned the area. The hounds were gone.

Father Callahan rubbed his chin and some of the edge was gone from his eyes. "I don't know, exactly," he said. "One moment I'm dog food, and the next moment... Strange really, I told the dog to leave me alone and it seemed really scared. Weird."

"They are cowed by those who have faith." Koneh appeared in the camp, sword in hand. "However, not all minions of Hell are so easily dispatched."

"Easy?" Alexandra said. "I almost got eaten!"

Koneh slid his sword under his rags and said, "Remember what Erzulie said? It appears the hounds are dragging women off to their masters. You were in no *immediate* danger."

Alexandra exhaled. "That's comforting."

"You survived unscathed."

"What if the Father wasn't here? I would have been dragged away for sure."

Koneh walked towards her and said, "Do you really think these hounds can out run Erzulie?" He waited for a moment before he continued. "Like I said. You were in no danger there."

"Erzulie…" Alexandra said as she searched the sky. "Where is she?"

"Hunting down the stragglers," Koneh said. "Get your things together. We must move."

"What? Why?" Alexandra's heart fell in her chest. She needed to sleep.

"Those hounds were in service of something much more terrible," Koneh said. "We would be wise to not be here when he comes looking for them."

"Who would come looking for them?" Alexandra was unsatisfied with Koneh's answers.

"More movement and less talk, Alexandra. Our time is short," Koneh said.

Though he was impatient, Alexandra caught him examining her body. Was he looking for wounds?

Father Callahan touched her arm and said, "Come, Alexandra. We can talk about this later."

With a sigh, Alexandra nodded. Father Callahan helped her pack her blankets and the group was on the move again. After a few minutes, Alexandra said, "Where's Erzulie?"

Koneh, a few steps ahead of them, said, "She won't be long."

"Shouldn't we go back and help her?" Alexandra said, though she didn't know how much help she could offer.

Alexandra felt Koneh's grin as she stared at the back of his hood. "She can more than handle a few hounds," he said.

"So, Koneh," Father Callahan said, "those hounds. Tell us about them."

Koneh stopped, kneeled, examined the ground, rose, and then resumed his pace. "Well," he said, "Not much to tell. They are used by demons as scouts and the ones we just met belong to a particularly nasty fellow."

"Really now?" Father Callahan said. "Who?"

"Derechi the Unclean… or, as Erzulie likes to call him, Derechi the Dirty."

"Can't say I ever came across that name in any of my studies," Father Callahan said.

"He replaced Moloch. I assume you've heard of him."

"Yes I have," Father Callahan said. "How do you know so much of Hell's dealings?"

"Wait a minute," Alexandra said. "Who was Moloch?"

Father Callahan turned to Alexandra and said, "Moloch was a cruel demon who…"

"Fallen Angel," Koneh said. "Most of the demons you know of are actually former angels. Remember the difference."

"Anyway," Father Callahan said, "Moloch encouraged the sacrifice of firstborn children by way of fire."

"That sounds… horrific." Alexandra tightened her jacket over her chest.

The group walked in silence for a few moments. Father Callahan stared at the back of Koneh's hood and fingered his cross. After what looked to Alexandra to be an internal struggle, Father Callahan said, "What happened to Moloch?"

Koneh halted the group and scanned the swirling red-black sky. He placed his fists on his hips and said, "You'll have to ask the angel who killed him."

Erzulie burst from the darkness and landed with less grace than Alexandra had seen her command on other occasions. She clutched a spiked collar in one hand and a slender sword in her other hand.

Father Callahan leaned towards Koneh and whispered, "Erzulie killed him?"

Koneh nodded and approached Erzulie. After straightening her legs and folding her wings against her back, Erzulie handed the collar to Koneh.

"The pack leader's collar," she said as she slid her sword into a sheath on her belt. "They won't be reporting to anyone now." As Erzulie spoke, she glanced at Alexandra several times.

"Good work, Erzul," Koneh said. "How much farther do you suggest?"

"A few hours should do it."

Erzulie stepped past Koneh and took Alexandra's hands in her own. Her pure white eyes bore into Alexandra. What was in those eyes? Was there real compassion or only the shadow of emotion? Alexandra couldn't tell.

"Just a little farther," Erzulie said as she struggled to catch her breath.

"You're… you're out of breath?" Alexandra said.

Erzulie smiled. It was a pure smile, a child's smile.

"Yes, Lex," Erzulie said. "I breathe air too."

The angel squeezed Alexandra's hands, released, and then extended her wings. Like before, she thrust her wings towards the ground and shot upwards. Alexandra remained fixated for a moment as she stared at the dark patch of sky where Erzulie disappeared.

"Let's get moving," Koneh said.

Alexandra's legs and ankle throbbed in protest as the group started walking again. She tried to push the pain and discomfort aside, but her efforts remained unsuccessful. Working out in the gym was far easier than trudging through a wasteland. Giant dogs never chased her through the rows of exercise machines. After an hour of walking, the group stumbled upon a deserted roadway.

"Route 70," Father Callahan said as he poked the pavement with his walking-stick, perhaps to ensure it was real.

"We'll take this for a few more hours and then try to get some rest," Koneh said.

Sections of the road lay overturned or sunken into the ground. After several hours, they found a ruined car. Alexandra decided to stay back while Koneh and Father Callahan searched the vehicle. She didn't want to see the faces of the deceased. She'd already had enough death for one lifetime.

Father Callahan took some items from the trunk. Koneh removed a gas can from the wreck and siphoned the gasoline from the vehicle. He then roped the can to the army pack full of rations and the pair returned to Alexandra.

"How did they die?" Alexandra said. She was surprised to find her emotions dulled by all that she had seen. Was she accustomed to death after this short time? No, how could she be?

"I didn't take the time to examine them medically," Koneh said. "But, the good Father offered a prayer for them. Let us continue."

They followed Route 70 for another half hour and then made camp off the side of the road. Erzulie landed and reported no activity as far as she could see. Koneh handed Alexandra and Father Callahan a ration pack from his bag. After Father Callahan showed her how to open the MRE and work the flameless ration heater, Alexandra devoured the bland contents. When she was finished, she made her bed and closed her eyes. She was asleep within moments.

What felt like only minutes later, Alexandra awoke to the sound of screeching tires. She shot forward and saw a tractor-trailer cab swerve to a halt on the road. Its headlights lanced through the darkness illuminating their small camp.

Koneh crept to Alexandra's side and said, "Stay here. The priest and I will check it out."

Alexandra rubbed her eyes and yawned as she nodded. Though the truck was a good distance away, Alexandra hid behind a rock. If things went sour, she was prepared to run.

As the two men approached the vehicle, Alexandra peered at the long dark shadows. If there were hounds out there...

The door to the cab opened and a man in a baseball cap jumped to the ground. Alexandra couldn't hear what they were saying, but Father Callahan shook the man's hand, so she assumed all was well.

After more discussion, the driver returned to his cab, killed the headlights, stopped the engine, and re-emerged with a backpack. He joined Alexandra's companions and walked towards the camp.

"Alexandra, meet Santino," Father Callahan said.

"Nice to meet you, Santino," Alexandra said as she looked him over. Mexican-American, maybe in his forties, dark hair protruding haphazardly from his Texas Rangers baseball cap, and clothed in jeans with a stained tee shirt.

With a thick Spanish accent, Santino said, "You too, Alejandra."

The last time Alexandra heard the Spanish pronunciation of her name was when her mother called, asking Alexandra to come to Mexico. Alexandra's mother said she had something important to say, but Alexandra couldn't abandon work on such short notice. One week later, Alexandra's mother died.

"We're the first people Santino has seen," Father Callahan said.

"Si, nuttin's left of San Luis," Santino said.

"He agreed to drive us to Tampico," Koneh said.

"Si, I have enough gasoline for the drive." Santino kept his distance and averted eye-contact from Koneh. Perhaps he was afraid of the scarred man.

"Give us a moment to pack our things," Koneh said.

"Wait a minute, I barely slept!" Alexandra complained.

Father Callahan touched her arm, smiled and whispered, "You were asleep for over six hours."

"Oh." Alexandra raised one of her eyebrows, a trait she inherited from her mother. "Six hours? Didn't feel like it…"

Father Callahan nudged her with his elbow as he stepped past her. "Come on sleepy-head. Pack up and move out."

The group broke camp and piled into Santino's roomy tractor-trailer cab. Alexandra cleaned debris and beer cans from her seat and noticed several pictures of topless women duct-taped to the walls. The pictures appeared to be from a Latino Hotties calendar.

As they drove, they saw many wrecked vehicles on the road. Santino was forced to plow through some of them at a low speed. At Koneh's direction, they didn't stop to look for survivors or salvage. The trip to Tampico took less than two hours.

Route 70 ended at a makeshift barricade of overturned cars, billboards, and sandbags. Santino slowed to a halt and said, "What now?"

Several men emerged on the barricade and shouted, in Spanish, for them to exit the rig and show themselves. The group complied and Alexandra glanced towards the sky. Still no sign of Erzulie.

"¿Hablan ingles ustedes?" Alexandra said. She felt more comfortable speaking in her stronger language.

"Yeah, we can talk English," one of the men on the barricade said as he shone a spotlight on Alexandra's group.

The light settled on Koneh and one of the men said, "Diablo!" Several of the men disappeared behind the barricade while the rest pointed rifles at Alexandra's group. Alexandra heard "Diablo!" repeated from behind the wall.

CHAPTER 10

"Wait!" Alexandra said as she threw her hands in the air. "He's not a demon – no un diablo!"

The men on the wall didn't respond. They kept their weapons trained on Koneh and the rest of Alexandra's group. Perhaps they waited for reinforcements from inside the barricade?

Alexandra stepped forward and said, "He was burned by radiation." She pointed at Koneh. "Radiacion."

"Don move, lady!"

Alexandra halted her advance and said, "Okay, but we're not here to pick a fight."

"I'll be the judge of that." A new figure appeared on the barricade. "Let's see what we have here."

The speaker was more American than Mexican, though his olive skin and dark hair revealed part of his heritage. Either he worked hard to remove the accent from his speech, or English was his first language.

"We're not taking in any more stragglers," the well-spoken man said. "Go back to the wasteland and find your own food."

Father Callahan stepped to Alexandra's side and said, "Now that's an awful attitude to have towards your fellow man in need."

"Padre! I-I didn't see you there."

Alexandra leaned towards Father Callahan and whispered, "You know him?"

"No," Father Callahan whispered in return.

"I'm Marco. Explain your friend, Padre. Was he burned by radiation like your beautiful spokeswoman claims?"

Father Callahan glanced at Koneh and said, "If Alexandra says it is true, then it is true. I only recently met these folks, but they have good hearts. We only wish a place to rest."

"Do you have something to offer Tampico?" Marco said. "Though you're a priest, that's not enough."

"Mi tractor trailer can haul or move anythin' you need," Santino said as he jacked his thumb over his shoulder towards his rig.

Marco looked past Alexandra's small group and rubbed his chin. "Let them in," he said as he disappeared behind the barricade.

Moments later, the men behind the wall pushed aside sheets of metal and wood. Alexandra, Koneh, Father Callahan, and Santino piled into the cab and drove through the entrance.

Tampico looked much like the village where Alexandra met Father Callahan, but on a larger scale. Some buildings were intact, but most were rubble. Empty oil drums and garbage cans housed fires and pockets of frightened people.

Koneh leaned close to Alexandra and said, "Women…"

Unlike Father Callahan's village, where all the women were taken by demons, Tampico seemed well-stocked with the better sex.

"Speaking of women," Alexandra said to nobody in particular, "Where's Erzulie?"

As Santino maneuvered the rig into a dark spot of the encampment, Koneh said, "Staying away for now. You saw how they reacted to me…"

The rig came to a stop and rattled its protest as the engine died. Everyone vacated the truck and Alexandra glanced around the ruined city center. Compared to everywhere else she'd been since her bus flipped, Tampico seemed like Mardi Gras. Well, Mardi Gras without the fireworks, neon necklaces, and joy.

People huddled in every nook. Fabric stretched over sleeping areas and across makeshift awnings for vehicles which now served as homes. Voices rose and fell from all corners of the area as if they were afraid to grow too long or too loud. The scent of burning meat wafted into the air around Alexandra's group and her stomach grumbled in response.

Koneh dropped the army duffel full of rations in the center of the group and said, "Why don't you have a look around, Father. Judging by their reaction at the barricade, I think it best I stay here, out of sight."

Father Callahan tapped his walking stick on the ground and said, "I agree. Perhaps they have some news of the rest of the world."

"I'll go with you," Alexandra said, as hungry for information as she was for food.

Koneh shook his head. "Too dangerous."

"Dammit Koneh, you don't make decisions for me," Alexandra said. "Just back off a bit."

"She'll be fine," Father Callahan said.

Alexandra stepped past Father Callahan and said, "I don't need you babying me either. I'm a grown woman for Christ's sake!"

With dramatic flair, Father Callahan said, "She's a grown woman!"

As she stalked away from the group, Alexandra suppressed a laugh. The Irish-American priest was goofy in an endearing way.

After a few moments, Father Callahan caught up to Alexandra and walked at her side. "Koneh's just looking out for you," he said.

"I know," Alexandra said. "I'm probably not much fun to be around, am I?"

Father Callahan smiled. "I miss *fun*."

The pair found Tampico to be pretty uniform in its disaster. What was worse, nobody seemed to know about anything beyond the barricade. After a few fruitless hours, Alexandra and Father Callahan returned to where they left Santino, Koneh, and the rig. However, only Koneh was there.

"Where's Santino? And the truck?" Alexandra asked.

Koneh stoked a campfire and then lounged with his back on the army duffel bag. "Marco came and said he needed the rig," Koneh said. "That was an hour ago."

Alexandra slumped to the ground in front of the fire and closed her eyes. She felt miserable. Her feet and back ached. Every inch of her body felt uncomfortable – like she was wearing someone else's skin.

"Koneh," Alexandra said, "toss me one of those MRE's."

Father Callahan sighed, "Yeah, might as well give me one too." Alexandra propped the ration on a rock and chuckled, as the directions clearly stated to "prop on a rock or something." After working the flameless heater, Alexandra waited for the meal to warm.

"They don't use a fire, just in case the soldier needs to eat in enemy territory," Father Callahan said. "No fire, no giving away your position. The army is smart."

"Indeed," Alexandra said.

After a few more minutes, her meal was ready. "Not that bad," Alexandra said as she devoured her chili and macaroni.

Nodding, Father Callahan said, "They've improved these since I was jarring around in camo."

"What'd you get?" Alexandra said, craning her neck in her companion's direction.

"Some spicy penne pasta!"

Alexandra tore the seal off her brownie dessert and mumbled, "Very nice."

After Alexandra and Father Callahan finished their meals, Alexandra decided to take another crack at Koneh's exterior.

"At least tell us where you're from," she said.

Father Callahan wiped his chin and said, "I've already been down that road… he won't budge. If you don't mind, I'm going to take a little nap."

Alexandra maneuvered closer to Koneh. "Go ahead, Father. We'll keep our voices low."

The priest mumbled something and was lightly snoring within seconds.

Koneh kept his eyes locked upon her as she sat next to him. "What are you doing?" he asked.

"Just getting a little closer," she said, afraid her interest was too overt. "I mean… I don't want to wake Father Callahan."

Koneh grinned. He saw right through her. "Of course not."

"So, you seem like this is all second nature to you," she said quickly. "I'd really like to know where you're from… more about you…"

"It's probably best you don't know much about me," he said. "I'm not someone you can be close to."

Alexandra wrinkled her nose. "Why not? That doesn't make any sense…"

He sighed. "You're just going to have to trust me…"

"Fine then," she said. "If you won't tell me where you are from, then tell me something about yourself."

Apprehensive, Koneh asked, "Like what?"

"Doesn't matter," she said. "I'll go first. I like bad movies."

"Bad movies?"

Alexandra smiled. "Yeah, real stinkers. I love curling up on the couch and just absorbing the mindless entertainment." She noticed her pack was a few paces away. "I think Father Callahan has the right idea," she said as she rested her head on his shoulder. "Do you mind?"

"No... I..."

"Your turn," she said as she closed her eyes. "Tell me something about you."

"Okay..."

After a minute of silence, Alexandra opened one of her eyes and looked at him.

"You meant *now*?" Koneh said playfully.

She closed her eyes again and waited. His shoulder was a comfortable one, and comfort was something she craved.

"Okay... well, I happen to like *good* movies," he said.

"Mmm hmm..."

"I also like plants," he said. "I can make pretty much anything grow in soil. Strange, I know."

"Strange... yeah." Though she wanted to enjoy her time alone with Koneh, her body demanded rest.

Alexandra drifted to that place between sleep and consciousness. She heard the sounds of the people around them, but she also wandered into and out of familiar dreams. Some time later, Father Callahan's voice came into focus.

"Alexandra... time to wake up."

"Why?" Alexandra reached to where she remembered Koneh's arm, but he wasn't there. Instead, she found her duffel bag under her head. When did that happen? She rose and noticed someone had put a blanket over her. Without asking, she knew it was Koneh. He eyed her from across the camp, watching her every move again.

"Marco's here," Father Callahan said.

Marco approached their camp. Alexandra's eyes were drawn to the holster and gun at his hip.

"Ah, glad to see the rest of you have settled in. Please," Marco said, "come to my villa on the hill so we can talk."

"Where's Santino?" Alexandra said.

Marco smiled at her and examined her from head to toe. "He's moving some heavier debris down near the docks. I almost offered to have one of my men relieve him, but your friend sure knows how to maneuver that rig. He's good."

"Why can't we talk here?" Koneh said as he eyed Marco from beneath his hood.

Without removing his eyes from Alexandra, Marco said, "Surely you want to escape the cold and perhaps enjoy some more food?"

"Hard to argue with that," Father Callahan said.

Koneh stood, but didn't join the group. "I'll stay here, with our supplies."

"Are you sure it's not too dangerous for me?" Alexandra said, though she regretted her words. Was she sending him mixed signals? She shook her head as she realized she didn't know why she enjoyed his shoulder as a pillow. Could she really be comfortable with someone so... alien?

Father Callahan nudged her and Alexandra said, "Thanks, Koneh. We won't be long."

When they were away from the camp, Marco said, "Interesting friend there."

Father Callahan laughed. "I think I said the same thing to Alexandra when I met Koneh for the first time."

"He's saved my life several times," Alexandra said. "And he's very resourceful, almost like he was prepared for all of this."

"Well," Marco said, "he better watch where he steps here. We've had problems with... well, *beasts from hell* is the only way I know how to put it."

"They took away all the women from my home village," Father Callahan said.

"¡Por el amor de Dios!"

"Indeed," Father Callahan said as he patted Marco on the back.

After about an hour, they reached the villa. The entire right side was gone. All that remained was a sheer cliff. However, the rest of the building looked to be in good shape.

"I used to watch the ships glide in and out of port from here as a child," Marco said as he stared off into the darkness. "Now, there are no ships... no water."

Alexandra and Father Callahan peered into the dark horizon but couldn't see much beyond the villa. Then, as if her mind remembered a dream shortly after waking, Alexandra said, "Wait, no water?"

Marco blinked and looked into her eyes. "Let's go inside."

The group settled into some comfortable couches inside the villa. Alexandra's eyes lobbied for closure, but she couldn't sleep yet. The nap on Koneh's shoulder wasn't enough. Why did her mind constantly return to him?

"We went out about three miles and still we couldn't find water," Marco said. "It's like the ocean disappeared from Tampico."

"That's a scary thought," Father Callahan said.

"I assume there was a quake here too?" Alexandra asked.

"Si-yes," Marco said, "many people died." His voice trailed into a whisper as he gazed towards a darkened window.

"So, you're in charge here?" Father Callahan asked.

Marco seemed lost in thought for a few moments. Then, he turned towards Father Callahan and said, "That is how things ended up, yes. My uncle was mayor, but he was out to sea when the quake hit us. We haven't found him."

"I'm sorry," Father Callahan said, "you're doing better here than where we came from."

"This is my home, no?" Marco stood. "And what a bad host I have been. Would either of you like some food or water?"

Throughout the conversation, Alexandra inched her way horizontal. Her eyes felt like they had cinder blocks attached to the lids. Surprised she had strength to speak, Alexandra said, "Water would be great."

"Same for me," Father Callahan said. From the next room, Marco continued the conversation. "Why don't you sleep here? It's certainly more comfortable than the ground."

Alexandra glanced at Father Callahan and said, "Sounds good to me."

Marco returned with two bottles of water.

"Have you heard any news?" Father Callahan said. "Any word from other cities? Anyone else?"

"No," Marco said. "Nothing on the TV or radio. No cell service. Nothing."

"That's been the story," Father Callahan said. "Seems like you have fared well here though."

"We tried to contact the American base, but nobody has made it that far yet. Too dangerous."

"There's a base?" Father Callahan said.

"Si, but it's pretty far."

As the two men spoke, Alexandra faded into sleep. Though she couldn't remember when she lost consciousness, Alexandra awoke refreshed on Marco's couch. A half-finished bottle of water was the only evidence of activity during the previous night. Pushing her hair aside, Alexandra snatched the bottle from the table next to the couch and finished the job.

"Hello?" Alexandra said.

Nobody answered.

Alexandra stretched and walked to a window. The red-black sky yielded little more of a view than the night before. After a quick look around the villa, Alexandra decided to head back to the rig and her friends. She traveled only a few steps when she saw movement on the roof of the villa behind her.

A melodious voice drifted down from the roof. "How does the morning find you, Lex?"

"Erzulie!"

Alexandra whirled and spotted the fallen angel perched on the edge of the roof. With a swoop of her dark, feathery wings Erzulie floated to the ground. She touched Alexandra's arm and bowed.

"I wish I could bring better news," Erzulie said.

Confused, Alexandra asked, "What's going on?"

Erzulie said, "Derechi's army marches on Tampico. They will reach the barricade in less than six hours"

Alexandra's heart quickened. "We should warn them."

"Koneh and Marco presently know."

"Where are they?" Alexandra asked.

"Koneh and the others are at Santino's rig. You know the way?"

"Yes. You're not coming?"

Erzulie smiled her perfect smile and squeezed Alexandra's arm. "These people do not understand who I am. I will watch you from the sky. I am always watching you."

With a *swoosh* of air and dust, Erzulie disappeared into the sky. Alexandra continued her jog to the rig. On the way, Alexandra watched people douse fires, gather their belongings, and barricade themselves into their broken buildings. They knew.

Alexandra also noticed a resignation in everyone's eyes. They believed they were doomed. Is this how the rest of the world fared? People existed as pockets of civilization grasping for life like a drowning man reaches for a piece of driftwood?

"How terrible," Alexandra whispered to herself. She reached the rig and was surprised to hear the engine running.

"Good, you're here," Father Callahan said. "I was just about to go get you."

Alexandra eyed Koneh as he secured an extra canister of gasoline to the flatbed. "What's going on?" she asked.

Father Callahan leaned towards Alexandra and whispered, "Didn't Erzulie tell you?"

"Yes… but, it looks like you guys are heading out."

"Well, we can't stay here," Father Callahan said.

Alexandra's eyes narrowed as she turned to Koneh. She said, "This was your idea, wasn't it?"

Koneh ignored her as he continued to pack the rig.

"Fine then," Alexandra said, "Have a nice trip. I'm staying."

"Get in the rig," Koneh said through clenched teeth.

"And what? Leave all these people?" Alexandra said incredulously as she swept her arm behind her.

Koneh stepped towards Alexandra and said, "You think you can alter their fate? What are you going to do, Alexandra? Litigate Derechi's demons to sleep? Get… in… the… rig."

Part of Alexandra wanted to follow Koheh's order, but that was part of herself she barely remembered. The lawyer and selfish daughter were fading into her *history*. She touched the flower in her hair and thought of Renaldo and his lost Maria. Though Alexandra didn't know these people, she felt a tugging at the back of her heart.

"I won't abandon them," she said, her heart breaking. Was she ready for this?

Without a word, Koneh scooped Alexandra off her feet and flung her over his shoulder like a sack of grass fertilizer.

"Let me go!" Alexandra said.

"Why don't you put the lady down, friend," Marco said as he joined the group with a pistol leveled at Koneh.

Koneh tilted his head to the side and peered at Marco from beneath his hood. Several moments passed as the two men glared at each other. Alexandra took the opportunity to try and wiggle free, but Koneh's grasp was ironclad.

"Fine," Koneh said, and he dropped Alexandra to the ground.

After Alexandra rose to her feet and dusted herself off, Koneh said to her, "Why do you want to die here?"

"You think this is suicide? That I'm giving up?" Alexandra said. "Maybe I don't feel like wandering the wasteland with you anymore, searching for someplace that doesn't even exist."

"You'd rather stay here? And fight against an army of thousands of demons?" Koneh said.

Alexandra nodded. "Yes. Tampico has food, water. This isn't such a bad place compared to everywhere else I've seen. Why not fight for it?"

"Because your fight is not here. Not yet," Koneh said.

Alexandra said, "That doesn't even make any sense!" She pointed at Koneh. "You know so much more than you've told me. I'm done. Yes, you've helped me, but I'm staying here."

Koneh took a step towards Alexandra but halted when Marco aimed his pistol towards Koneh's head.

"It's all right, Marco," Alexandra said.

"I need to talk with you." Koneh glanced at Marco. "Alone."

"Fine," Alexandra said.

Koneh led her out of sight of the group. Once they were behind a toppled building, he raised his hand to the air and traced several quick motions. Before Alexandra could ask what he was doing, Erzulie descended from the dark sky and landed next to the building.

"What's this all about?" Alexandra asked.

"I didn't want you to know until you were ready," Koneh said. "However, I don't know if that day will ever come… so, now is as good a time as any. Maybe you will come to your senses."

Alexandra crossed her arms and said, "You didn't want me to know *what?*"

Ignoring her question, Koneh said, "Normally, there's a protocol for this. However, under the circumstances, we'll do the best we can."

"You're not making sense again."

"Erzulie," Koneh said, "tell her who she is."

Erzulie stepped in front of Alexandra and grasped her hands. With a flick of her head, Erzulie's white-in-white eyes found Alexandra's plain human eyes.

"Alexandra Contreras," Erzulie said, "By the Word of Elah, I have come to…"

"We don't have time for the full speech," Koneh said. "Shorten it up."

Erzulie sighed and said. "My dear, you are the child of Elah, of

God."

"Child? What are you saying?" Alexandra asked. At once, she felt like she was swimming in a pool of old tires. She couldn't process Erzulie's words. A moment ago, Alexandra's attention was on the people of Tampico. This place appeared to be her best chance for salvaging her life. Now, her concerns about survival seemed out of focus. Alexandra struggled to remember where she stood.

Koneh's raspy voice sounded distant. He said, "Your blood, your destiny, is divine. It is *you* who will reopen Eden for us all."

Like she was attending a lecture on nuclear physics, Alexandra's brain couldn't connect all the information in a way that made sense. What were these two telling her? That she was the daughter of God? How was that even possible? They were mistaken.

Erzulie kneeled. While holding onto both of Alexandra's hands, the angel said, "Command me, my Lady."

CHAPTER 11

Child of Elah? Of God? Alexandra couldn't form a coherent thought, but she *knew* Koneh and Erzulie had to be mistaken.

Alexandra turned to Koneh and said, "What? You filled Erzulie's head with these... these lies?" Sweat rolled down from her temple as Alexandra strained to form the words.

"Think about it, Alexandra," Koneh said. "Everything has come easy to you – school, work, everything – because you were designed from superior material. In everything you ever put your mind to, you succeeded."

Alexandra curled her lip and said, "But that doesn't mean..."

"And what of your father?" Koneh said. "You never met him, did you?"

"He died before I was born."

"That's not what your mother told you. She told you your father was in Heaven," Koneh said. "She couldn't lie to you... she couldn't lie to anybody. She knew the score."

"What do you mean?" Alexandra asked.

Erzulie released Alexandra's hands and stepped to her side. The fallen angel looked different somehow. In a way, Erzulie seemed less alien to Alexandra than when they first met.

"I'm telling you that an angel informed her she was carrying Elah's daughter," Koneh said.

Alexandra shook her head. Her thoughts solidified as she parsed the information. Alexandra knew who she was and she wasn't the daughter of God.

"Your mother was also given instructions: how to prepare you for this day and for your duty," Koneh said.

"No… you're wrong about this," Alexandra said as tears gathered at the bottom of her eyes.

"What was your mother's favorite saying?" Koneh asked. "I know what it was, but I want to hear you say it."

Every morning, whether young Alexandra wanted to hear it or not, her mother came into her room and spoke the same words.

With tears rolling down her cheeks, Alexandra whispered, "Look upon the world with new eyes today, Alejandra."

"You see," Koneh said gently, "she was trying to prepare you for your task. However, she never finished. You didn't go to her when she was dying. She had so much more to teach you."

"If your goal was to reopen old wounds, you've succeeded," Alexandra said through sniffles and sobs. "I regret the daughter I became. I should've been there for her."

"The past is gone for us all. It's the future that we now mold," Koneh said.

Alexandra couldn't wipe the tears from her face. She was numb. Every time she allowed the weight of Koneh's words into her mind, she was crushed. How could this be true? The world spun and defocused. Up was down. Alexandra heard Erzulie's voice, but it was distant. The cream bougainvillea given to her by Renaldo fell to the ground, but Alexandra didn't reach to grab it. Then, Alexandra realized she was moving.

Alexandra opened her eyes and wondered why she couldn't remember closing them. She was in the back of Santino's rig. The quiet rumble of the engine flowed through her seat as she pushed aside a blanket, intent upon standing. A hand held her down.

"Quiet now," Father Richard Callahan said. "The last time you tried that, you banged your noggin'."

"What's… going on?" Alexandra asked with her hand on her throbbing head.

"Koneh walked you back to the rig," Father Callahan said. "You were barely able to stand."

"Leaving?"

Father Callahan nodded. "You kept saying you wanted to go home… over and over."

Alexandra didn't recall any of it. Again, she started to sit up. Father Callahan grasped her arm, but Alexandra said, "I'm fine."

Alexandra's determination must have carried through her voice, because Father Callahan complied. Alexandra rose enough to look out the side window. The people of Tampico watched as the rig made its way through the ruined city. Each miserable face imprinted itself into Alexandra's memory.

"Why do we get to leave?" Alexandra whispered.

Father Callahan leaned close and said, "Because you have more important things to do."

Without turning from the window, Alexandra asked, "You believe him?"

"I believe God works His mystery in strange ways sometimes," Father Callahan said.

Alexandra's eyes filled with tears again as she watched a woman load a shotgun while two children piled sandbags around their broken home. "The very thought is… impossible."

"In time, it may seem more possible…"

Now, Alexandra turned from the window and looked into Father Callahan's eyes. "You do believe him."

The front passenger door opened and Koneh joined Santino in the driver's section of the roomy cab. Koneh glanced at Alexandra and Father Callahan, but he didn't speak.

Alexandra returned her attention to the window and noticed the rig was moving past the barricade. Men with torches manned the walls and looked to the black sky from time to time. Though she wanted to stay and help them, part of her was relieved to be going. She wished she was strong enough to tell Santino to turn the rig around. However, the coward in her kept her tongue in check.

Nobody talked for hours. Alexandra's mind was as empty as a drum. She didn't want to think about Erzulie's proclamation of Alexandra's heritage.

"This looks good," Koneh said to Santino. The truck turned and Santino brought them to a stop.

The initial shock of this new twist demanded Alexandra's attention, but Alexandra pushed the ridiculous information to the back of her mind. She decided she would prove them wrong, though she didn't quite know *how*.

Alexandra raised her head and looked through the window at the dirt and black sky. The low scrub extended beyond the truck's headlights and the highway held no movement. After Koneh and Santino exited the cab, Alexandra shook Father Callahan's shoulder to wake him.

"Wha?" Father Callahan said as he struggled to open his eyes.

Alexandra smiled. "You were snoring."

"Was not. Priests don't snore."

The pair chuckled as they left the cab and stretched their limbs. Besides a few large boulders and an overturned dumpster the area was empty.

"Back to the wasteland," Alexandra said as she surveyed the horizon.

"We'll camp here for the night. Just stay close to the rig," Koneh said.

Alexandra turned back to the truck to get her duffel bag when she noticed four large barrels strapped to the bed of the vehicle.

"What are those?" Alexandra asked.

"Oh," Father Callahan said, "water and fuel... though Koneh never told me where he got them."

"Koneh..." Alexandra whispered. She reasoned he stole them from the doomed people of Tampico. Deciding to fight that fight another day, Alexandra tucked the information away for the time being.

Alexandra approached Koneh and said, "Where's Erzulie?"

Koneh opened his mouth to speak, but instead shrugged and pointed to the sky.

"Santino's going to have to meet her sooner or later," Alexandra said as she walked past Koneh and dropped her duffel next to Santino. "Mind if I sit?"

Santino smiled and adjusted his Texas Rangers cap, "'Course not."

As Santino scraped the bottom of a can of baked beans with a spoon Alexandra said, "So, where are you from Santino? Mexico?"

He nodded. "Si, but I live in Brazil."

"Brazil?"

"Si."

"Since he is on our way," Koneh said, "we have agreed to help each other."

"Wait a minute," Alexandra said, "we're going into South America?"

"Correct," Koneh said.

"I can't believe you're making me ask this," Alexandra said. "Eden is in South America?"

"Not exactly," Koneh said. "Our destination lies a bit more to the south."

Alexandra recalled the image of the multi-colored globe from her first schoolhouse. She remembered how she ran her fingers over the raised line of mountains down the west coast of South America. Rarely did she pay attention to the cap of white at the bottom of the globe. No mountains or cities were there. It was a boring spot on the model.

"Antarctica?" Alexandra said with one eyebrow raised.

"I know," Father Callahan said as he joined the group by the fire, "Sounds pretty ridiculous."

"No," Alexandra said, "ridiculous is what Erzulie and Koneh told me in Tampico."

Images of the people in the lost city pushed their way into Alexandra's mind. She wondered what happened to the women and children. Was Marco okay? Did anyone survive?

"You ask me questions," Koneh said, "and then you dispute the answers. Why do you ask?"

Alexandra shook her head. "I don't know why I ask you anything, Koneh…"

"Try to get some rest," Father Callahan said.

Scowling, Alexandra said, "I don't want rest… I want to know why we are going to Antarctica. How is it even possible?"

"Who are you going to ask?" Koneh said.

"Not you," Alexandra said dismissively to Koneh through narrowed eyes. She turned to Father Callahan and said, "You talk like you know something of our destination."

Father Callahan glanced at Koneh, "Yes, but most of my information is from Koneh."

"I don't care," Alexandra said. "Tell me what you believe."

"Okay," Father Callahan said as he pulled his blanket over his shoulders, "I don't understand much of the science, but I guess the North Pole shifts from time to time."

"Shifts?"

"Yeah, it's a major event. Climates re-align, ecosystems are wiped out… pretty serious stuff," Father Callahan said. "So, I guess Antarctica was once a paradise. It was there that God created Eden."

Alexandra held up her hand between herself and the priest. "Wait a sec. I wanted you to tell me what you believe. Are you saying you believe every word in Genesis?"

Father Callahan looked at Koneh and then back at Alexandra. "Yes," he said, "I certainly do these days."

"Okay," Alexandra said, "carry on then."

"Well," Father Callahan said, "I mean to say that *parts* of Genesis may have indeed happened. Other parts were supplemented by man's imagination. You see, Eden existed for quite some time – until the North Pole shifted and left Antarctica buried under hundreds of feet of ice and snow."

"And Koneh told you our job is to go and dig Eden out?" Alexandra said

"Not exactly," Father Callahan said. "You see, the North Pole shifted again. That's what caused the quakes, the darkness, and… well, I don't know why angels and demons are here."

Alexandra tried to wrap her mind around the pole-shifting concept. While she struggled with the logic of the idea, Father Callahan continued. "So, everything's kind of shifted north. Hopefully that means Antarctica is a more hospitable place than it has been for the past… well, many years."

"And you believe this?" Alexandra asked.

Father Callahan smiled. "Enough to hitch a ride with you and Koneh, yes."

"And we're going to… what?" Alexandra asked. "Reopen Eden like Koneh rambled about back when we met you, Father?"

"That is the plan," Koneh said.

Alexandra glared at Koneh and said, "I didn't ask you."

"Yes," Father Callahan said, "we will open Eden for all humankind. However I don't know how we are going to accomplish that."

"Shouldn't we at least have a clue?" Alexandra said. "Otherwise, it all sounds like a big waste of time and energy."

"Actually," Koneh said, "we were hoping *you* would have an idea."

Alexandra huffed. "Don't even mention that craziness about… me. I don't believe you."

"As you wish," Koneh said, "but search your memory. Your mother must have told you something relevant to our current situation."

"Relevant to our current situation?" Alexandra laughed through the words. "As pious as she was, I'm sure my mother never thought I'd be here... and talking to you, Koneh."

Koneh sighed and said, "I guess we will see what happens when we get there..."

"That's your plan?" Alexandra asked in disbelief and amazement.

Koneh shrugged. "I am just as lost as you are."

"Well, that's comforting," Alexandra said with a sneer.

"I think we're all a little lost," Father Callahan said, his gaze wandering.

Alexandra rested her head on her duffel bag and closed her eyes. She knew sleep wouldn't come easy. Her mind was teeming like a Texas ant hill. Where was Erzulie in all of this? Alexandra hadn't seen the fallen angel since Tampico and some questions needed to be answered.

"No fire tonight," Koneh said.

Alexandra pulled her blankets over her head to hide from her companions, and from the world.

After only a few hours of sleep, Koneh roused the group. "We are still too close to Tampico," he explained as everyone piled back into the rig.

As Alexandra faded in and out of sleep in the back of the truck, she overheard bits of conversation between Santino and Koneh.

"We stay on Route 180, si?"

"Yes, we shall see what is left of Poza Rica."

Alexandra's dreams swirled into an incoherent jumble. She was with her mother again, then she was in law school. Erzulie taught her Torts seminars. Like the reality around her, Alexandra's dreams carried her forward to a land of uncertainty. Why was she travelling to Antarctica? Alexandra's dreams didn't have the answer.

"Let's keep moving. It looks like someone already got to that wreck."

Then, Alexandra woke with a jolt. The rumble of the engine was gone, as were her companions.

Not much was left of Poza Rica. From Alexandra's vantage point, everything was rubble. Grateful to be free of the cab, Alexandra stretched her arms and legs. That's when she heard the distant whir of a motorcycle engine. Where was everyone?

A tug at the back of her mind told her she wasn't alone. Smiling, Alexandra raised her eyes to the top of the cab where Erzulie perched.

"Hi there, Erzulie," Alexandra said.

The angel kept her gaze on the horizon. "My Lady, perhaps the cab is a safer place for you right now. I do not know who approaches."

Alexandra cocked her ear to the sky. The motorcycle was closer.

"I'm sure it's all right, Erzulie," Alexandra said.

After a few more moments, Alexandra saw the silhouette of the figure on the motorcycle. The approach was erratic. Perhaps the vehicle was damaged?

Then, Alexandra recognized him. "Marco!"

The motorcycle's front wheel turned and flipped the vehicle, throwing the driver to the ground. Alexandra ran to Marco and helped him into a sitting position. Blood stained his shoulder and arm where his leather jacket was shredded.

Though he was out of breath, Marco said, "Good... found you..."

"Don't try to speak," Alexandra said.

Marco shook his head, "No... time... must..." The wounded leader of Tampico didn't finish. His eyes widened and focused on something behind Alexandra. Then, Marco drew his pistol from his hip holster.

Alexandra whirled to see Erzulie. "No!" Alexandra screamed as she pushed Marco's arm aside. The gun fired into the ground, spraying dirt and pebbles into the air.

"She's a friend!" Alexandra said.

"No," Marco said. "They are not your friends... Koneh... Koneh is going to kill you!"

CHAPTER 12

"I think," Alexandra said, "that Koneh could have killed me by now if he wanted to. You're delirious, Marco."

Marco wiped some blood from his mouth and shook his head. "You don't understand."

The ring of steel filled the air as Erzulie drew her slender blade and approached.

Alexandra turned to the fallen angel and said, "No, Erzulie. He's just… confused."

"Are you safe, my Lady?" Erzulie said as she turned her pure white eyes to Marco.

"Yes," Alexandra said. "This is just a misunderstanding. Marco didn't know."

The rest of the group came around the rig, Koneh, Father Callahan, and Santino. Koneh eyed Marco and asked, "What happened?"

"You know damn well what happened!" Marco said as he again lifted his pistol and aimed at Koneh.

"Please… put the gun away," Alexandra said.

Marco backed away from Koneh and scrambled to his feet. "Don't you see? He's a demon! Like the ones who slaughtered Tampico," Marco said.

"Koneh is no demon," Alexandra said. "He's our guide."

Father Callahan took a step towards Marco and said, "You've obviously been through much. Surely, you've seen enough violence today. Do you really wish to bring more upon us?"

Marco placed his other hand on the grip of his pistol to steady himself. "If I have to, I will. I know who Alexandra is and I'll protect her no matter the cost."

Alexandra noticed Erzulie and Koneh exchange a glance. Without waiting to see what her other companions were going to do, Alexandra stepped to Marco's side and placed her hands over his.

"Please," she said as she applied some pressure to lower Marco's weapon.

Marco conceded and dropped to his knees. "Forgive me," he said through tears, "I only wish to keep you safe. The demons told me about Koneh and what he plans to do with you."

"Slow down," Alexandra said, "and just start from the top. What happened to Tampico?"

"Destroyed... everyone butchered," Marco said through unsteady lips. "They were looking for you, Alexandra."

"Who told you that?" Koneh said as he took a step towards Marco.

Alexandra held her palm towards her friends and said, "We do this *my* way, Koneh. Stay back."

Marco leaned closer to Alexandra and whispered, "He's a demon... he's going to kill you."

"We'll get to that," Alexandra said. "Go on. Demons attacked Tampico?"

"Hordes of vile creatures. Our women... the children..." Marco shook as tears poured from his eyes.

"I know it's difficult," Alexandra said, "but try to put the pain aside for a moment. Tell us what happened to you. How did you escape?"

Marco sniffled. "I killed as many as I could, but we were overwhelmed. Then I was brought to the demon lord. He seemed to know who I was. He said he was looking for a woman and he described you perfectly. And there were dogs. I thought he was going to feed me to them."

Alexandra squeezed Marco's hand and said, "Did the demon lord tell you his name?"

Marco's eyes flicked back and forth and he said, "Si, Derechi."

"So, Derechi just set you free?" Koneh asked.

"Not at first," Marco said. "They asked me who you traveled with, Alexandra, and I told them. Then, they told me that all of Hell was looking for you, Alexandra. They were looking for you because you are..."

"Don't say it," Alexandra said. "It's not true."

Confusion spread over Marco's face as he looked into Alexandra's eyes.

"Please continue, Marco," Alexandra said.

Shaking his head, he said, "Well, the demon lord who finds you will be rewarded beyond measure. That's when they told me that Koneh was hunting you for the same reason, for his reward. They only let me go because I told them you headed north, on foot."

"No," Koneh said, "they let you go because they knew you'd find Alexandra for them. You fool!"

Koneh nodded to Erzulie, who sheathed her sword and shot into the sky.

"No!" Marco said. "I'm certain I wasn't followed!"

"Get the truck ready," Koneh said to Santino. Then, he turned to Marco. "You led them right to us." Koneh stalked towards the rig.

Alexandra's heart quickened as Koneh's analysis rung true in her mind. However, she didn't blame Marco. He followed his heart. He watched his neighbors and family get slaughtered at the hands of demons. She decided to give her new friend the benefit of the doubt.

"Can you ride that?" Alexandra asked as she pointed to Marco's motorcycle.

Marco's eyes brightened. "I think so."

She rose and said, "Good, follow us."

Father Callahan fell into step next to Alexandra as she walked back to the truck. "You think we can trust him?" he asked.

Alexandra looked over her shoulder at Marco and said, "I think he made a desperate mistake. I won't fault him for that after what he just witnessed."

Before Alexandra and Father Callahan reached the rig, Koneh appeared. "Leave him here," he said, "I don't trust him."

"I won't abandon him like we did the people of Tampico," Alexandra said. "I believe…"

Alexandra's words trailed off when she heard the flapping of wings overhead. An instant later, several forms descended from the inky blackness of the sky and landed on the ground around the vehicle. Though it was dark, Alexandra noticed their bat-like wings and goat legs. These were demons. Standing slightly shorter than Erzulie, their black-red skin almost matched the sky.

One of the demons charged forward, but Koneh was in front of Alexandra before she could raise her hands to her face. In one smooth motion, Koneh drew his sword from beneath his rags and sliced through the chest of the horned beast. The creature's unearthly cries died in its throat as it crumpled to the ground.

"Ziel-henel!" A female voice boomed from above the truck.

Two new figures emerged from the sky and landed on the top of the cab. One of them looked like Erzulie – ashen skin, black wings, and all-white eyes – but, this fallen angel was a male. The new angel's eyes focused upon Alexandra. The female was a demon, but her form was slighter than the other demons. Though dressed in a hooded robe, her remaining features were clearly demonic.

"I swear," the female demon said in a voice as grating as Erzulie's was melodious. "These demons grow duller and duller as the years roll on."

The remaining demons folded their wings to their backs and drew all manner of slashing weapons from their belts. The creatures didn't advance, however. The fallen angel atop the truck remained fixated on Alexandra. Her skin crawled as his eyes penetrated her.

"My, oh my… I had to see it with my own eyes," the female demon said. "Koneh, it *is* you."

Alexandra leaned closer to Koneh and whispered, "You know her?" Perhaps Marco was right. Was Koneh a demon?

Koneh ignored Alexandra's question and said to the newcomer, "Don't come any closer, Lilev."

The female demon, Lilev, smiled. "Fear not, I have no desire to lose more of my host on this little errand. That bitch Erzulie killed four of my minions before we had to put her down. I ordered the rest of them to keep their distance, but there's always some minor duke of Hell looking to challenge the legendary Koneh in battle. Pity."

Alexandra's heart plummeted in her chest. Was Erzulie dead?

"What do you want?" Koneh asked through narrowed eyes.

"Oh, just to understand what it is you think you are doing." Lilev said. "Why do you walk with the Mih'darl? Do you really think she is going to forgive you?"

Koneh said, "You couldn't possibly understand…"

As if she was continuing her thought, Lilev said, "The reward is substantial. The entirety of the Earth… all to the demon who delivers her safely to Iblis. Of course, I'm sure he would make an exception for *you*, my dear Koneh."

"Apparently," Koneh said, "age has not gifted you with wisdom. Do you really think he will share Earth with another?"

"Iblis is not interested in the wasteland that is the Earth," Lilev said. "His eyes are set upon another dominion to rule."

"Eden." As Koneh spoke, Alexandra formed the word in her mind.

Lilev stomped one of her cloven feet. "Tell me your intentions! Will you give the Mih'darl to me?"

"No," Koneh said.

Smiling, Lilev said, "Surely you wouldn't raise your sword against your own mother, would you?"

Father Callahan, Alexandra, and Santino turned their heads to Koneh.

Koneh gritted his teeth and tightened his hands on the grip of his weapon. "You are not my mother. You insult her memory with such pretensions."

"This is going nowhere," Lilev said as she spread her wings. "My master, Derechi, will know that the Mih'darl is protected by Koneh. That may stay his hand for a time, but not indefinitely. Reconsider your allegiance, my dear son. I would be most displeased to watch you suffer any further."

After her speech, Lilev lifted into the sky and disappeared. Moments later, the remaining demons followed. The fallen angel remained a few seconds longer. The corner of his mouth curled into a grin as he examined Alexandra. Then, he re-joined his companions in the canopy of darkness. Silence roared across the wasteland and between the people gathered at the truck.

"What just happened?" Alexandra said.

"Marco led them to us," Koneh said.

As if she was just pinched, Alexandra said, "Marco!"

The group ran to where they left Marco. The injured man from Tampico was curled in a ball next to his motorcycle.

"I'm sorry," he said with his head still buried under his arms. "I saw the demons… and I just froze."

Alexandra eyed the motorcycle. The vehicle looked like it was operable. Though glad Marco was unharmed, Alexandra's attention was elsewhere. Where was Erzulie? Was she injured? Questions needed answers. Alexandra lifted the motorcycle from the ground and straddled the seat.

"What do you think you are doing?" Koneh asked.

After a brief glance at the controls, Alexandra turned the ignition and sped into the wasteland.

When Alexandra was an intern for a local public defender, she worked on a case for a raped teen in a wooded park. Alexandra recalled the investigator's description of how he searched the entire area for evidence - alone. The investigator started from the scene of the crime and spiraled outwards until he covered a large enough area. Alexandra mocked his technique as she searched for Erzulie.

After a few minutes, she found her.

Erzulie rested in a pool of silvery liquid. Streaks of black marred her otherwise perfect ashen skin. One wing twisted under the angel's body. The other lay tattered at her side. As Alexandra approached the scene, Erzulie opened her luminous eyes and smiled.

"I am overjoyed to see you safe, my Lady."

Alexandra bit her lower lip and knelt next to Erzulie. "I'm so sorry."

"No need for apologies," Erzulie said. "They did not wish to destroy me, only incapacitate me for a time. I will be okay… with time."

Alexandra heard the rumble of Santino's truck and then the area was flooded with light. Koneh jumped from the vehicle before it came to a stop.

"Is she…" Koneh said. "Good, her eyes are open."

"I tried to escape them to warn you," Erzulie said, "but there were too many."

Koneh brushed Erzulie's hair from her face and said, "You did well, Erzulie. Alexandra is safe."

With tenderness Alexandra didn't realize possible from her scarred companion, Koneh lifted Erzulie from the ground and carried her to the truck. A part of Alexandra wished she was the wounded angel, carried off to safety by her protector. Her eyes lingered on Koneh until something else caught her attention. Alexandra dipped her fingers into the pool of silvery liquid and was intrigued to discover the liquid roll off like water, leaving no stains. Was this angel blood?

"How are you doing there?" Father Callahan asked.

Alexandra jumped. "Father, I didn't hear you. Me?" Alexandra exhaled. "I'll be fine. I'm more concerned with Erzulie at the moment."

"Koneh told me she'll be fine," Father Callahan said. "I guess angels are made from different stuff than us, eh?"

"Apparently," Alexandra said, only half-hearing the priest's words.

"Well, I think you need to stay out here for a few more minutes."

"Why?" Alexandra asked.

Father Callahan fidgeted with the straps on his backpack and said, "I think Santino figured out what is going on. He's cleaning his cab for you."

Alexandra looked beyond Father Callahan and watched Santino throw empty cans, debris, and calendar pages of nude women from his truck.

Returning her gaze to Father Callahan, Alexandra said, "There's nothing *going on*. You and Koneh are wrong about me... about my mother."

"And the female demon who called herself Lilev?" Father Callahan asked, "Is she wrong too?"

Something Lilev said popped back into Alexandra's mind. "Who is Iblis?" Alexandra asked.

Father Callahan nodded. "Yes, I heard that name too. I may be mistaken, but I believe Iblis was the Babylonian Satan or Devil." Scratching his new beard, Father Callahan continued, "However, I guess he could have been Sumerian... I forget."

"Yeshua... Elah... Iblis..." Alexandra said. "Good ole King James isn't helping us much now that we're face to face with all of this."

"Yeah, he would've done us a favor by keeping the original names from Hebrew, Babylonian, or wherever," Father Callahan said. "At least then we'd know who we're talking to, fighting, befriending, etcetera, etcetera."

Koneh approached and said, "We need to get moving. Everything's changed. Somehow they know."

"How's Erzulie?" Alexandra asked.

"She will recover," Koneh said. "Though, Marco made a quick exit from the truck when I put her in there. Santino is a bit nervous as well. Can you check on him, Father? Keep him from driving off?"

Father Callahan nodded. "Good idea."

As Father Callahan walked away, Alexandra worked through the questions in her mind. Was she really the daughter of Elah? Of God? No, she again returned to her conclusion that Koneh must be wrong. Though Alexandra was awestruck when Erzulie announced the news, Alexandra didn't accept or believe the outlandish assertion.

"There's just no way…" Alexandra whispered.

"What was that?"

Alexandra glanced at Koneh as more questions formed in her mind. Questions, questions. Always questions.

"Why did Lilev say she was your mother?" The question leapt from Alexandra's lips before her lawyer's brain could phrase it into proper direct examination form.

Koneh paused for a long time, even for him. The cold wind whipped like a train on tracks between Alexandra and Koneh. "I think it past time we start your lessons," he said. Koneh allowed the wind to subside. "After dinner tonight, we will discuss demons."

"That wasn't my question."

"We should get moving."

Alexandra rose and grasped Koneh's arm. "What about that other fallen angel?" She asked. "If that's what he was…"

Koneh nodded. "Yes. His name is Ael," Koneh said.

"You know him?" More doubts about Koneh's allegiance swirled through Alexandra's mind.

Though he was speaking to her, Koneh seemed to be in a different place. His eyes wandered to the dark horizon and he said, "An old enemy…"

Indication that the conversation had ended, Koneh wandered back towards the group. Alexandra mulled over the strange encounter and shivered. Ael's eyes, though similar to Erzulie's, frighteningly devoured her. Ael *wanted* her. And the unknown reasons *why* gnawed at her nerves. Shaking her head, Alexandra followed Koneh.

Alexandra sat in the back of the rig with Erzulie while Santino put some distance between them and the scene where they encountered the demons.

"Would you be more comfortable with your armor off?" Alexandra asked.

Erzulie opened her eyes and said, "That may help, yes."

Following Erzulie's instruction, Alexandra unbuckled the straps at the side of the breastplate and removed the glossy, black armor. The dress underneath clung to the fallen angel's breasts and Alexandra wondered how far the similarities between angels and humans went.

"Thank you, my Lady," Erzulie said. "You show me too much kindness."

Alexandra decided her questions for Erzulie could wait. "Save your energy," Alexandra said. "Get some rest… if that is what you need."

After a few hours, Santino pulled the rig to the side of the road and the group made a small camp.

True to his word, Koneh waited for everyone to finish their dinners. Then, he approached Alexandra and said, "Ready?"

In-between sips of her water bottle, Alexandra said, "Sure. Marco and Father Callahan were interested as well."

"If they wish," Koneh said.

As Santino slept on the other side of the camp, Koneh began his lesson. Alexandra sat cross-legged against her bedroll and pack. Next to Alexandra, Father Callahan lounged against a flat rock and scanned his Bible. Marco rested across from Alexandra, half inside his sleeping bag.

After taking in a long, wheezy breath, Koneh began. "Okay," he said, "as you all probably know by now, Erzulie is an angel and she's not built like we are."

Alexandra and Marco nodded.

"Angels were fashioned to serve the deity you know as 'God' in His heaven," Koneh said.

"Just curious," Father Callahan said, "how did you come by this knowledge you claim to be truth?"

Koneh cocked his head, as if listening to something in the distance. Then, he leveled his gaze at the priest and said, "Mostly from Erzulie, some of it from firsthand experience."

"Wait one second," Father Callahan said. "Do you mean to say you've been to Heaven?"

Koneh laughed, though the sound more resembled a throaty sneeze.

"No," Koneh said. "It is my understanding that humans cannot enter Heaven."

"Right," Father Callahan said, "Eden is our paradise – according to you."

Marco formed a "T" with his two hands, mimicking a basketball player's signal. "Time-out," he said. "What are you guys talking about?"

Alexandra said, "Koneh believes Eden is now accessible and that is where we're headed… for now."

"Eden?" Marco said with a look of utter incomprehension on his face.

"Details aside," Koneh said, "rest easy, priest, that I have my information on good authority."

Shrugging, Father Callahan said, "I just like to know my source, that's all."

Marco seemed to be stuck on Eden, as he repeated the word as a question to nobody in particular.

"Do not worry," Koneh said. "We will drop you off at the nearest city – if there is one. Only Alexandra and myself need to make the journey. We are getting off-track anyway. The purpose of this discussion is to teach Alexandra about demons. She may find the information useful someday soon."

"Hrmph," Father Callahan said through his nose. "I think we'll *all* find this information useful, provided it is based in truth."

Alexandra smiled. This priest was different than the unapproachable padres from her childhood. "Okay," Alexandra said, "objection noted. Please continue, Koneh."

Koneh peered at everyone's faces in turn from under his hood, as if he expected more chatter. After a moment of silence, he continued. "Very well," Koneh said, "Angels were constructed by Elah to serve him in Heaven. For several millennia, these angels performed whatever duties were appointed to them. Elah watched over the Earth through the eyes of his angels. However, Elah felt He could perfect the angelic design after observing the behavior of these crafty thinking creatures with souls – humans."

Koneh paused to look into everyone's eyes. "I cannot stress this enough," he said, "a soul is the fabric from which we are all spun. I do not know any more than this. The Earth provides the power necessary to maintain souls in all living creatures. This sort of power is incomprehensible to us and almost beyond a divine being such as Elah… almost."

Father Callahan shook his head and said, "Our souls come from Him. If you dispute this point, I don't think I can consider your assertions to be more than wild fantasy."

"I can only tell you what I have heard from a *divine being*," Koneh said as he jabbed his thumb in the direction of Santino's rig, where Erzulie rested. "I tend to believe her over two-thousand year old passages written by men who wished to selfishly twist a simple thought into a complex one."

Sighing, Father Callahan waved his hand and said, "Feel free to continue."

Koneh shook his head. "So, the reality of souls gets interesting when we start talking about demons."

Alexandra's heart quickened. At last, Koneh was delivering some of his secrets. Though everything he said could have been the ramblings of an insane man, Alexandra listened like a kindergartner at story time.

"So, Elah designed a more perfect angel. One that possessed a soul," Koneh said. "However after countless failed experiments, Elah found He would need to expend a tremendous amount of energy to create a soul. Resigning Himself to this fact, Elah nearly destroyed Himself and all of Heaven in His creation of an angel with a soul – Iblis."

"Satan?" Alexandra said.

"Or whatever your local culture calls him. Yes. I won't bore you with the story of the fall of Iblis, but while Elah slept after His divine miracle, Iblis was placed in control of Heaven. After several millennia, Elah awakened and Iblis did not want to relinquish control of Heaven. So a war ensued."

"Emotions…" Alexandra said.

"Right. Since Iblis had a soul, he was also prone to that most precious human weakness – emotion. During Elah's slumber, Iblis had swayed many of the angels to serve his command, rather than Elah's. So, after a long and bloody battle in Heaven, Iblis and his remaining angels were cast down from Heaven."

"It's amazing how much of the story was actually correct!" Alexandra said.

"Truth is usually the simplest answer," Koneh said.

"If you believe *that* to be truth," Father Callahan said. "You make some outlandish leaps there, friend."

Koneh shrugged. "Look where you are, priest. Tell me if the outlandish makes sense to you now."

Alexandra finished her water bottle and pulled a blanket over her legs and stomach. This was good stuff.

"So," Koneh said, "Iblis somehow formed his own realm."

"Hell?" Marco asked, joining the conversation.

"Not exactly," Koneh said. "Well, not as you were told. Remember, the men who wrote the Bible were also interested in power and control. Their Hell is much different from Iblis' Hell. Much like Heaven, Hell was merely a place where Iblis could rule his dominion. Sinners were never sent there and Dante certainly never travelled there. No human could... under normal circumstances."

As Koneh's voice trailed on the last word, Alexandra reasoned that Koneh knew a great deal about Hell. The truth of his words rang clear in her mind and a strange question popped onto her lips.

"Have you been to Hell?" Alexandra asked.

Koneh's black-in-black eyes peered into Alexandra's own eyes and he said, "That would be absurd, now wouldn't it?"

Alexandra felt a wave of victory, like when she cornered a witness on the stand. "That's not an answer," she said.

For several long moments, Koneh and Alexandra's eyes were locked. Koneh had never been this forthcoming, and Alexandra hoped for more information from her enigmatic guide. Was her question even founded? Yes, she decided, the question made sense in her new world. One that saw the fall of Heaven and Hell.

"No," Koneh said, after turning his gaze to the red-black horizon.

Before the word was finished, Alexandra knew it. "You're lying," she said.

Returning his gaze to Alexandra, Koneh and said, "Prove it."

Alexandra shrugged. "I'm not the one with secrets. I've got nothing to prove or hide, but those demons knew you and it's the best reason I've come up with so far."

"May I continue?"

Allowing the matter to drop, Alexandra said, "Please do." She tucked the information, and what it could mean, in the back of her mind.

"Your grace is immeasurable," Koneh said.

Knowing his meaning, Alexandra chuckled and said, "Immeasurably small?"

Father Callahan laughed and nudged Alexandra. "I guess he's not all doom and gloom."

A grin stretched across Koneh's scarred-smooth face. "So," he said, "Iblis continued the war against Heaven, but found his numbers dwindling. You see, Iblis could not construct angels of his own. He had his rebel angels and that was all. Each one lost was a soldier he could not replace. Elah, on the other hand, could construct new angels to replace the ones lost in battle. Iblis needed to get creative, and he did – with human souls."

After a short pause to gather his rags around his body, Koneh continued. "Just as Elah devised a way to allow souls to journey on to Eden after a human death, Iblis too found a way to capture souls. I don't know the details, but Iblis discovered how to trap the souls of wicked men and women into a vessel of flesh and bone. Those demons you saw tonight are the end result. A twisted mass of evil souls all crammed into a single being in servitude to their master."

"Wait," Alexandra said, "more than one soul?"

"Yes. Erzulie believes Iblis' method is imperfect and only the most depraved parts of the soul are salvaged by the process. So it requires more than one to sustain the creature we know as a demon. Eventually, the most dominantly evil soul comes to the foreground, with all the others simply powering the *life* of the demon." Koneh paused. "In truth, I don't understand the anatomy, science, and/or magic of it all."

"Magic?" Marco asked. "Like Voodoo?"

"Sure," Koneh said, "might as well throw that in as well. I'm just as human as you all are. It all sounds a bit like fantasy to me."

Alexandra allowed this new information into her working mind. Closing her eyes, she recalled the encounter with the demon, Lilev. Demons and angels. Servants of Iblis and Elah. Hell and Heaven. Earth caught in the middle. Questions and thoughts. Alexandra no longer believed that trial law was the most taxing of mental exercises. Sorting out her new world trumped even the most intense of courtroom situations.

After the storm of information passed, Alexandra formed a clear framework for her thoughts and assumptions on both angels and demons. One glaring difference leapt from her mind like a cinder block off a passing truck on the highway.

"So," Alexandra said, "are you telling me that demons have a soul and angels don't?"

"Somewhat ironic," Koneh said, "isn't it?"

CHAPTER 13

Alexandra awoke to the sound of fireworks in the distance. As her mind untangled from sleep, Alexandra realized fireworks seemed out of place in the wasteland. Opening her eyes, Alexandra noticed Koneh perched on a nearby rock.

Alexandra said, "Is that…"

Koneh fixed his fascinating eyes upon Alexandra and said, "Gunfire."

"Sounds like it's getting closer," Alexandra said.

"Yes, and a jeep too. Damn!"

"What?" Alexandra asked.

Koneh stood and adjusted something under his clothing – the sword. "There was an American military base in Veracruz during the war. I think they never left."

"You think they're Americans?"

"Definitely," Koneh said. "Army, by the length of their bursts and the weapons they are firing."

"What are you so nervous about?" Alexandra asked.

"Can you think of anything more dangerous right now than an army battalion without a commander-in-chief or laws to govern their behavior?" Koneh said. "We can't be sure what to expect. We need to avoid them."

"No problem," Alexandra said. "The wasteland is large. We'll just hunker down here in the darkness."

Koneh pointed to their large campfire and said, "They know where we are and we're not outrunning anybody in Santino's rig."

By now everyone in the small camp was awake.

"That sounds like gunfire," Father Callahan said.

"Si," Marco said, "auto fire."

Santino's face poked out of his sleeping bag, but he didn't speak.

"Stay in the truck with Erzulie," Koneh said to Alexandra. "Father Callahan, Santino, and I will investigate."

"Be careful," Alexandra said. "They're firing their guns at *someone*. Just make sure it doesn't become you!"

Father Callahan winked as he walked past Alexandra. "I know how to talk to army brats," he said. "I used to be one of them, remember?"

Santino grabbed a propane lantern and joined Father Callahan and Koneh as they walked towards the erratic jeep lights and muzzle flare.

Marco approached Alexandra, rubbing his eyes. "I'm sorry... about last night."

"Don't give it another thought," Alexandra said, "You've been through more than most of us..."

Though Alexandra believed Marco was tricked into helping Derechi and the demon Lilev, something tugged at the back of her mind. Was Marco telling the truth? Did he really avoid his own death by the grace of Derechi? Alexandra shook her head to clear her thoughts. Perhaps her internal compass was reeling from the activity of the past few days.

Alexandra jumped into the cab and closed the door. The new interior was more pleasant on the eyes and nose. The smell of beer still lingered, but it lost some of its pungency. Erzulie lay across the back seat, though she looked awkward in a vehicle made for humans.

"What's happening?" Erzulie asked.

"We may have trouble," Alexandra said. "There's an army jeep approaching... and they're shooting at something."

Erzulie raised her head and said, "I'll protect you, my Lady. Where is my sword?"

Alexandra looked around the cab and spotted the weapon resting on the dashboard. Curious about the archaic instrument of war, Alexandra grasped the handle and scabbard and then drew the blade halfway out. The metal was smooth, blac, and polished – nothing at all like Koneh's rusty sword.

"Forgive me," Erzulie said, "but I lack the energy to stand. I have failed you again."

"Don't be silly," Alexandra said. Then, after a long pause, she said, "Koneh told us you were constructed?"

"Yes."

"Elah created you? For what purpose?"

Erzulie smiled, "Every angel has a task. Mine was to champion Love, the most pure of the soul-guiding forces."

"How were you the *champion* for love?"

"I reminded humans of the importance of love in many ways. Always indirectly, of course. It was a very important station among the Seraphim."

Intrigued, Alexandra asked, "How did you remind us about love?"

"Oh, in small ways," Erzulie said. "A song on the radio at the right time… a chance encounter that would never have happened if not for my watchful eye… and many other things. Too many to discuss here and now."

"You can do stuff like that?" Alexandra asked.

"Yes, from Heaven," Erzulie said. "The way our two worlds interacted allowed for many possibilities."

Outside the truck, the rattle of gunfire ceased. Alexandra peered through the dingy windshield and noticed the headlights on the army jeep were stationary. Everything was calm in the distance.

Then, Alexandra turned back to Erzulie and said, "Koneh said something peculiar when I first met him. He said that Heaven had fallen. What does that mean?"

Erzulie frowned. "I do not know what happened, as I was in Jahannam."

"Where?"

"Hell."

"Oh… sorry," Alexandra felt like she had just asked a recently divorced friend how her husband was doing, only a thousand times worse.

"I was flawed," Erzulie said. "I failed to carry out my task."

"Koneh told me," Alexandra said. "You fell in love with a human?"

"That is not possible," Erzulie said. "I placed the life of a human above the duties of my position as Guardian of the White Sacrament. Such a thing should not be possible, but it happened… and I was exiled from Heaven because of my flaw."

"You made one mistake and you were discarded?" Alexandra asked with disgust in her voice.

"I do not make mistakes," Erzulie said. "I am flawed in some way. The result would be consistent were I presented with the same set of circumstances."

"Tell me what happened." Alexandra said, curious about the angel's first-hand experiences in Heaven.

"Perhaps another time," Erzulie said.

"Why?"

"They are returning."

Alexandra heard their voices in the distance.

"Get the first aid kit, Alexandra!" Father Callahan shouted. "Should be in the glove compartment!"

Alexandra proceeded as instructed and climbed out of the cab. The army jeep pulled to a stop in front of Santino's truck. Several men in fatigues deployed and pointed their guns into the air, scanning for enemies.

"Back here!" Father Callahan said as he waved Alexandra to the back of the jeep.

Inside, Koneh had his hands pressed against another soldier's neck. Blood trickled from between Koneh's wrapped fingers. The soldier didn't look like he was going to survive.

"We're going to switch bandages," Koneh said.

"Hold it!" one of the soldiers yelled.

Alexandra turned to see Marco on the other side of the rig with his pistol in one of his raised arms.

"He's with us!" Alexandra said. Then, she saw another soldier approach the rig. "Don't go in there!"

The soldier didn't listen. He opened the driver-side door.

"Koneh," Alexandra said. "Stop him."

Koneh nodded and left the wounded soldier in Alexandra's care.

Alexandra removed the old bandage around the soldier's neck and replaced it with one from Santino's first aid kit. However, the wound was large, so she also needed to apply pressure with her hands.

"They got a demon in here!" A soldier said from near the truck.

"Back away!" Koneh said. Though Alexandra couldn't see Koneh, she heard the ring of steel from Koneh's sword scabbard.

"Stand down!" Another soldier said. "Stow that weapon, friend!"

"Let's put the weapons down," Father Callahan said, his voice calm and even.

"Stay back, Padre!"

"I just don't want anyone to get hurt."

"Not another step!"

Alexandra's head spun. Perhaps she felt dizzy from the sight of all the blood. Maybe it was the steady decline in their situation. She knew she didn't want this man to die. However, she couldn't let the soldiers into Santino's rig. Erzulie was helpless.

Everyone was yelling now.

"I said stow that weapon!"

"Stop and think about what you are doing!"

"Another step soldier and you will wish you never came across us."

"That's it! You had your warning!"

Then, Alexandra yelled, "Stop!"

To her amazement, everyone turned and looked in her direction. Alexandra's breath was heavy and she felt her hands tighten on the soldier's neck. Faces open with shock, everyone was looking at the white light which radiated from the soldier.

Alexandra looked down and noticed that the light didn't come from the soldier. To her amazement, it was emanating from her hands.

CHAPTER 14

Alexandra was a child again. Her friend, Zana, followed her to the schoolhouse every day. Zana was a coyote who became a fixture when Alexandra gave him an apple – hence his namesake. Since that day, the animal had eaten many apples. Zana even tried to follow Alexandra into the schoolhouse on occasion.

When Zana went missing, so did Alexandra. She spent the day looking for the animal and found him at the bottom of a small ravine. Young Alexandra knew all about coyotes. She assumed Zana had tried to fly. Birds could fly, girls can go to school. So Zana naturally thought he could do both as well.

Zana was barely breathing when Alexandra found him. Tears rolled down her cheeks at the sight of her wounded friend. Her *only* friend. Then she touched Zana's hind leg and he jumped away from her. The animal licked his leg where Alexandra touched him and then yelped his way down the dried river bed. Zana was fine.

When Alexandra's mother heard of her daughter's trip to the ravine instead of school, Alexandra explained that she had to help Zana. Alexandra's mother didn't punish her. Instead, her mother smiled and said, "That's what I mean."

Now, almost thirty years after Zana and the ravine, Alexandra watched the soldier's wounds close.

The American soldier appeared a tad older than Alexandra. Grey and black stubble covered his jaw, cheeks, and neck. Ice blue eyes blinked open to greet Alexandra.

"Are you… am I in Heaven?"

Alexandra smiled. "Sorry, no."

"Then… I was…"

"Just relax," Alexandra said.

Alexandra turned over her palms and looked at her hands. The light was gone. What just happened?

One of the soldiers said, "Shit man, get on your knees." He slapped his forehead. "Oh shit, I said *shit*…shit!"

Two of the soldiers dropped to their knees. Another soldier asked, "Are you all right, General?"

The man at Alexandra's knees rose and removed the bandage from his neck. His wound was gone. The "General" looked at Alexandra and his eyes widened. "You… you're…"

Alexandra exhaled for the first time in at least a minute. "I don't know who I am."

I am a lawyer. I was born in Mexico. I am not married, but that isn't my fault. I am a fan of football, old books and awful movies. Alexandra tried to categorize herself in familiar ways. She knew if she looked into a mirror at that moment, she wouldn't recognize the woman in the reflection.

"I didn't choose this," Alexandra whispered.

"You cannot choose where you come from," Koneh said, "only where you are going once you discover the truth."

This time, Alexandra spoke louder. "I didn't choose this!" Though she tried to stop the tears, Alexandra's eyes disobeyed. She jumped from the jeep and stumbled into the darkness.

After a few steps she tripped on a bush and fell face-first into the ground. Alexandra's tears turned the dirt into mud around her face. She didn't bother to raise her head. She breathed the dirt and mud into her nose as she wept and pounded the earth with her fist.

Her thoughts cascaded like her tears. What does this mean? Am I destined for servitude and persecution? It's not fair! Someone else should have been chosen!

Alexandra rolled over onto her back and looked to the sky. "Why?" For several minutes she repeated the one-word question until her voice was hoarse and her body spent. After the mud dried back to dirt on her face, Alexandra realized she wasn't alone.

"I imagine Jesus had about the same reaction when he finally realized the truth," Father Callahan said from his seated position next to Alexandra.

Alexandra saw the truth of it all now. The daily teachings from her mother. Zana, Koneh, Erzulie, the soldier in the jeep – all of it fit neatly into her mental compartments to complete the undeniable fact. No longer able to hide from this truth, Alexandra felt exposed in a way she never thought possible. Her stomach threatened to empty its meager contents, but Alexandra maintained control.

"Why do I wish it isn't true?" Alexandra asked.

Father Callahan brushed the dirt away from Alexandra's face and said, "Oh, that's nothing to be ashamed of, my dear."

"I keep hoping," Alexandra said, "that I'm not who I think I am. Instead, I'm just some freak of nature."

"Above all, you are Alexandra Contreras. The very same woman I have grown to admire and respect," Father Callahan said with tears in his eyes. "Maybe we finish this small errand we're on and then be done with it all? Sound good? We can find a nice house... maybe even make Koneh tend the gardens."

Alexandra laughed and looked into Father Callahan's eyes. She saw love there. "I never had a father, but you are exactly how I imagined a father would be."

Father Callahan gathered Alexandra in his arms. They embraced in a hug Alexandra had never felt. The kind of hug fathers give to their daughters. Alexandra felt safe in that embrace.

After a few minutes, Father Callahan said, "We should probably rejoin the others."

Alexandra wiped some tears from her face and smiled. "Yeah, I guess we should talk with our new friends on better terms."

The group was more relaxed than before, when guns and swords were brandished and harsh words exchanged. When Alexandra and Father Callahan approached, the foul-mouthed soldier dropped to his knees again.

One of the other soldiers said, "What are you doing, Harris?"

The soldier on his knees said, "When in front of your Savior, you kneel!"

"There's no need for that," Alexandra said, "I'm nobody's savior."

The General stepped forward and said, "Thanks, but you probably saved *my* life."

Alexandra admired the General's strong physique and handsome features, even if a bit rough. "I... I don't even know what happened," Alexandra said.

"First, let's get some bookkeeping done," the General said. "I'm Todd Ryan. The two men by the jeep are Privates Greene and Jarvis. Next, the foul-mouthed black gentleman kneeling before you is Sergeant Harris. Lastly, care to explain to me why you have a wounded demon in your rig?"

Koneh stepped to Alexandra's side and whispered, "They want to take you back to the base."

Alexandra closed her eyes. Though she enjoyed the spotlight, this was almost too much.

"Slow down everyone," Alexandra said, "I'm going to go get some water and maybe some food. If anyone wants to talk to me about stuff after that, fine. While I'm eating, if anyone tries to talk to me about demons, army bases, or my divinity it'll have to wait."

Father Callahan chuckled and followed Alexandra to the rear of the rig. "You impress me at every turn, Alexandra Contreras," he said.

Alexandra downed some water and ripped open an MRE. In between mouthfuls of cold ziti, Alexandra said, "I think I scared them."

The rest of the group huddled around the jeep and talked. Every now and then someone would glance at Alexandra and then resume their discussion.

"Take your time," Father Callahan said. "You don't have to answer to them anymore. Instead, I think you'll find everyone will answer to you."

"Yeah, that's what I'm afraid of." Alexandra tossed the MRE container on the ground. No sense in saving the planet from pollution anymore.

"Litterbug," Father Callahan said as he dropped his own empty MRE.

"Okay," Alexandra said as she approached the jeep, "We'll start with the Sergeant."

The soldier pointed to his chest and asked, "Me?"

Alexandra nodded. "You. Don't kneel. It makes me uncomfortable."

Sergeant Harris looked away to avoid eye contact with Alexandra. Then, the soldier nodded and cleared his throat.

"General Ryan," Alexandra said, "before I answer your questions, you will answer mine."

General Ryan crossed his arms over his chest and said, "Ask away."

"What were you guys firing at back there?"

"Demons," General Ryan said. "We were returning from our airfield when we were attacked. The other three jeeps and the tank were destroyed. If we hadn't seen your campfire and your friend Koneh hadn't arrived, we would've died as well."

Alexandra glanced at Koneh who rested against the jeep and curled his fist. He appeared injured.

"Wait a sec," Alexandra said as she approached her guide. "Are you all right, Koneh?"

Koneh snapped his eyes up to Alexandra and said, "Yes, I am fine."

Koneh's right hand wraps were wet with a dark liquid, probably blood. He didn't look fine to Alexandra.

"You sure?"

Koneh waved his other hand. "Go... you have important things to do."

"Not until I'm sure you're all right," she said as she reached for his wounded hand.

Koneh pulled away and said, "Your concern is wasted on me. Finish what you started here and we can talk later."

After one more glance at her wounded friend, Alexandra said, "Okay, General Ryan. First, that is no demon in the truck. Her name is Erzulie, and she is a fallen angel. What's more, she's my friend. Attack her, and you attack me. Understood?"

General Ryan raised one of his eyebrows and said, "Very well."

"Secondly, what's this I hear about an army base? You wish to take me there?"

"Well," General Ryan said, "it's the least I can do to repay the people who saved my life and the lives of my men. Good food, maybe a warm bath, not to mention the safety my battalion can provide. I assumed you were headed to the base anyway, before Koneh told me you were just passing through."

Alexandra crossed her arms over her chest. "We *were* just passing though. However, I don't see the harm in accepting your offer."

Koneh stepped towards Alexandra and said, "No. Too dangerous."

For once, Alexandra understood Koneh's caution. Who knew what to expect?

"Okay," Alexandra said, "we'll follow you on one condition."

General Ryan said, "Name it."

"You and your men make no mention of Erzulie or what happened between you and me," Alexandra said. "We're just normal travelers passing through Veracruz. Nothing more."

"Done," he said. "May I ask where you are *passing through* to?"

"That's our business," Alexandra said. "I'm serious about this, General. Nobody says anything."

"You have my word," General Ryan said. "Okay men, pack it up. We're going home."

Everybody except Marco piled into Santino's rig and followed the jeep. Marco rode on his motorcycle. After an hour, they arrived at the base. Spotlights illuminated their arrival and the hum of generators filled the night air.

They passed through the steel gates and Alexandra noted the gun towers. They were ready for action. The interior of the base was dominated by squat bunkers and small, concrete buildings. Some light spilled through the windows of the buildings, but most were dark.

General Ryan gave Alexandra's group a small bunker to themselves. After Koneh carried Erzulie inside, everyone picked beds and settled in.

Alexandra addressed her group. "Okay, the same goes for all of you. Don't mention Erzulie, and definitely don't mention what happened between me and the General." Alexandra paused, not sure if she wanted to say what she was feeling. After a moment, she decided to speak her mind. "If anyone wants to stay here rather than continuing on with me, I understand. No hard feelings."

After Alexandra's speech, Marco left to explore the compound. Father Callahan and Santino were asleep before their heads hit their pillows. As Alexandra dragged a bed to be closer to Erzulie, Koneh stepped to her side.

"Listen," Koneh said, "I know what you are feeling right now."

"No, Koneh, you don't know how I feel right now," Alexandra said. "Why do I sometimes think I'd be better off if you never got between me and that mob the night we met?"

"You don't wish that. There is so much strength in you, Alexandra. You don't even realize it."

"So, now you're going to kiss my ass like everyone else?" Alexandra asked with a grin at the corner of her mouth.

Koneh huffed. "Maybe I should have left you to that mob."

"You know, Koneh, sometimes you're not a heartless jerk."

Koneh chuckled and said, "I should learn to space those moments closer together."

Alexandra laughed. "Quite the ride we're on. I never expected to be doing *this* during my thirties. This is supposed to be my best decade."

"It may be yet," Koneh said. "Get some rest. I will watch the exits."

"Sounds good, after I check on Erzulie."

Koneh studied Alexandra for a moment. Then, he said, "You really care for her, don't you?"

"Of course I do," she said.

"Even Yeshua treated His angels like servants," he said. "You are different, Alexandra Contreras."

Alexandra sighed. "Let's not start comparing me to... anyone. Okay?"

Koneh grasped Alexandra's hands and looked into her eyes. She tried desperately to read his emotions, but he was a complex subject. "The coming days and weeks will be difficult," he said. "Know that I am here... You can lean on my shoulder anytime you need, understood?"

She smiled and squeezed his hands. "Thank you, Koneh. That means a lot to me... really."

Koneh opened his mouth to speak, but he restrained himself. Averting his eyes, he dropped her hands and resumed his inspection of the bunker. What was he going to say? Alexandra's heart tore a little as she wondered if her feelings were genuine. Or, more realistically, was she just clinging to the man who had saved her life?

After parting with Koneh, Alexandra finished dragging the bed to Erzulie.

"He's quite the man, wouldn't you agree?" Erzulie said.

Alexandra looked over her shoulder. "Who? Koneh? He's something else, that's for sure. He's kind of secretive about his past, though. I don't suppose you could shed some light upon that subject?"

Erzulie said, "I cannot keep anything from you, my Lady. However, Koneh expressed his desire that I do not divulge anything about his past to you. He knows the rules, and now you do as well. He knows I would have no choice but to tell you if you so commanded. The choice is yours."

So, there was the cookie jar, opened and within reach.

"Never mind," Alexandra said, "he'll tell me when he's ready. Though, I don't understand all the secrecy. I trust him."

"Koneh is fearful of his past," Erzulie said. "Sometimes you humans do things and afterwards are vastly ashamed of them. This I'll never understand."

Alexandra curled into a ball on her bed and said, "You and me both, Erzulie."

"You must be tired, dear," Erzulie said. "Fear not, you are safe with Koneh as your protector."

Alexandra closed her eyes. "I don't doubt that. I have so many questions for you."

"I will be here when you awake," Erzulie said, "and every day after that for as long as you feel my service is worthy."

Alexandra smiled and said, "I'm glad you're here, Erzulie. Can you stay awake until I fall asleep?"

"Always."

The next morning was a fine morning for Alexandra. First, she took a two-hour bath. General Ryan left a present for the group of weary travelers – black army fatigues. Alexandra's set was made for a woman, and the clean fabric felt as refreshing as the bath. Koneh was the only one to refuse the new clothing. Erzulie remained in her original garb as well, as the U.S. Military didn't account for a seven foot wingspan.

Alexandra enjoyed a warm breakfast with Father Callahan, Santino, and the soldiers. Then, she spent the rest of the morning on a tour of the base with General Ryan.

"I'll tell you one thing," Alexandra said after the tour left them at the top of a tower, "the soldiers and their families are faring better than anyone else I've seen out in the wasteland."

"We were fortunate," General Ryan said. "The quake didn't hit us too hard. However, we have had our share of demon attacks." The General leaned against the railing and continued, "I used to come up here in the morning to watch the sun rise over the water. I'd give anything to see the sun again."

"I know what you mean," Alexandra said. After a day of avoiding the topic of what happened between her and the General, Alexandra felt anxious.

"So," General Ryan said, "we're alone now."

"Yes?"

He sighed. "You have to understand. Everyone here is desperate for hope. All we have seen is death and despair. Then, along comes a woman with the power to heal. And you ask me to keep this a secret? Why? What are you afraid of?"

"Everything," Alexandra said. "It's not like I've had a lifetime to prepare for this."

"So... are you... what? A saint?"

Alexandra sighed. "I don't know. Koneh seems to believe I am the... well, it's almost too ridiculous to say out loud."

"I think I know," he said. "Sergeant Harris believes you are the next Jesus Christ."

Alexandra threw her arms into the air and let them fall against her hips. "And there you have it! The most outlandish idea I've ever heard."

General Ryan rubbed his neck. "I dunno, how do you explain my speedy healing in the jeep?"

"I can't."

"Maybe we don't need it explained, maybe we do. I don't know what effect this kind of news would have on people," General Ryan said. "But, I imagine everyone would be overjoyed."

"I guess," Alexandra said. "I don't know. Koneh seems to think I'm Elah's daughter. At first, I thought he was crazy. Now? I'm not sure what to think."

"Elah?"

"Oh," Alexandra said. "Elah is God. Apparently, He or She has a name."

"I see."

"Did you feel or see anything when I healed you?" Alexandra asked, hoping for answers any way she could find them.

General Ryan rubbed his chin again and said, "Not really. After that demon wounded me, everything was pretty hazy until I saw you. I thought you were an angel."

Alexandra laughed. "I'm no angel, I can assure you."

"Nevertheless, your beautiful face brought me back from the darkness. I am forever in your debt."

Alexandra stared into the red-black horizon as she imagined the ocean in the distance. Why did she feel like she had more questions now that she had more answers? The paradox annoyed her.

"Well," General Ryan said as he slapped the railing, "I better get back to my duties."

Alexandra sighed. "Yeah, I should check on Erzulie."

"You know, you're welcome to stay as long as you like. Permanently even."

"Thanks. Some of us might."

"It's refreshing to have new faces around. Please consider it."

"I will," Alexandra said.

CHAPTER 15

Koneh swung his sword in a wide arc at Alexandra. Defending herself, Alexandra raised Erzulie's slim blade to block. However, the force of Koneh's attack was overpowering. Alexandra lost her grip on her weapon and tumbled backwards to the floor of the bunker.

"Damn!" Alexandra said.

Koneh planted the tip of his blade into the ground and said, "Do you know what you did wrong?"

Alexandra nodded and raised herself on her wobbly legs again. "I should have deflected the attack instead of meeting it head-on. I should have kept moving."

"Let us call it a day," Koneh said.

Alexandra didn't argue. She headed straight for the showers and enjoyed another warm bath. As she soaked in the suds, she replayed the day's training over and over in her head. Her mistakes were simple and correctable.

Alexandra spent the previous night convincing Koneh to train her. "I feel useless!" Alexandra said.

"Your soul must remain pure," Koneh said. "Let me bear the burden of sin upon my blade."

"And if I command you to help me?" Alexandra asked as her final resort.

"Then I will train you, but I urge you to remember, the more you sin the farther from Eden you will be."

Alexandra asked Koneh to explain what he meant by that remark, but he shook his head and told Alexandra to ask Erzulie how sinning worked. Unfortunately, the fallen angel had slipped into a twenty-four hour hibernation to finish healing her wounds.

Now, as Alexandra wiped herself dry from the bath, she planned to ask Erzulie about the workings of sin. On the way to the lockers, Alexandra stopped to examine her reflection in the mirror. Her bronze skin was drawn tight enough to show her ribs, yet her muscles bulged slightly around her arms and above her knees. Once her prize possession, Alexandra's hair spiked in every direction as it spilled down her back and over her bottom.

"I think I'm going to cut you," Alexandra said as she ran her hand through the dark strands.

"Now that would be a shame."

Alexandra jumped. "Marco?!"

"Si," Marco said as he emerged from behind a row of lockers and focused his eyes upon her.

Alexandra snapped her towel closed around her body and glared at the intruder. "Just what do you think you are doing?"

"Same as you – admiring."

"I wasn't…" Alexandra growled. "Get out of here!"

Marco held his hands up in defense. "Okay, okay. I'm leaving. Your boyfriend general stopped by. He wants to talk to you."

After a parting smile, Marco left the locker room.

Alexandra felt like she needed another bath after the way Marco's eyes devoured her naked body. Shaking her head, Alexandra walked to her locker and noticed a new set of black army fatigues on the bench. Two different sets of clean clothes in two days? Such an event was almost cause for celebration in Alexandra's mind. After looking around the room for more peeping Toms, Alexandra shed her towel and donned her new clothing.

Erzulie was still in hibernation sleep, so Alexandra left the bunker to find General Ryan. A group of soldiers pointed her in the direction of the chapel.

Father Callahan emerged from the chapel as Alexandra reached for the door.

"Oh," he said, "fancy meeting you here."

"I was looking for the General. Is he inside?"

Father Callahan nodded.

"Good," Alexandra said.

"How are you doing?"

"Me? I'm fine," Alexandra said, though she didn't convince even herself.

"Anything you want to talk about?" Father Callahan asked.

Even if Alexandra knew what she wanted to discuss with the priest, she wasn't sure she was ready. She felt like she was near the top of a roller coaster's lift hill, ready for the deep plunge. Maybe she'd have her feelings sorted after that first drop.

Alexandra shook her head. "Nah. Really, I'm fine."

"Okay," Father Callahan said. "I'm here if you need me. You know that, right?"

Alexandra hugged him and said, "Of course. Thank you."

Rows of candles lit the small chapel and threw long shadows into the corners. Like a church, the chapel had pews, an altar and a cross. However everything was miniaturized with only five rows of pews on each side and the altar reachable from the front seats. General Ryan looked up from one of the pews. He was the lone occupant.

"Hello there," he said.

"Hi."

After a long moment of silence, General Ryan asked, "Did you want to pray?"

"Me? No. I heard you were looking for me."

"Oh… yes. Please sit."

"What were you two talking about?" Alexandra asked as she sat in the pew behind General Ryan.

"Just confessing some sins," General Ryan said.

Alexandra smiled. "Someday I'll get around to that."

"I suppose you don't have to?"

"According to Koneh we're all bound by our sins, or something. I don't know."

"You keep some interesting company, Alexandra," General Ryan said. "One of my men said you were training with a sword this morning?"

Laughing, Alexandra said, "Training? More like gettin' my ass whooped."

"Well, whatever you were doing, it made today's headlines."

"Headlines?"

General Ryan waved his hand. "People were talking, that's all. We haven't seen a newspaper or heard anything on our radios from the U.S. since the quake. Any small amount of gossip is enough to send everyone buzzing."

"You've heard nothing?" Alexandra had assumed more people survived and that the army base was in contact with America. Was anyone left?

"Nothing," General Ryan said. "Our strongest radio was at our little airstrip. We were returning from there when we were attacked and stumbled upon your group."

"You couldn't get anything on that radio either?"

"It was destroyed."

"Oh."

After another moment of awkward silence, General Ryan said, "Well, enough about that. I just wanted to see how you were doing or if there was anything else I could get for you."

Alexandra leaned towards the General and whispered, "Chocolate."

"Chocolate?"

Alexandra nodded. "I would give my left arm for a chocolate bar... or cake... whatever!"

General Ryan laughed. "I think I can pull some strings. Come with me to the mess hall. We'll raid the kitchen together."

Alexandra spent the day again with General Ryan. She learned that he was born and raised in Raleigh, North Carolina. Stationed at the Veracruz base during the height of the South American oil rush, he was unmarried and had no children. Though Alexandra never cared for military men, she found she enjoyed her time with the General.

As the reddish-black sky turned to all black, Alexandra realized Erzulie must be awake. Alexandra thanked the General for the chocolate and returned to her bunker.

Alexandra found Erzulie and Koneh seated next to each other on one of the beds. The bunker was otherwise deserted. Alexandra guessed her friends were enjoying a late dinner in the mess hall.

"I don't mean to interrupt," Alexandra said as she approached Erzulie's bed.

Koneh stood and squeezed Erzulie's shoulder. "Not at all," he said. "I was just leaving. Our good General wanted to speak with me, but he's been indisposed all day. I wonder why that was."

Producing some candy bars from one of her many cargo pants pouches, Alexandra smiled and said, "He has chocolate!"

"Praise the Lord," Koneh said, "We are saved!"

Alexandra noticed Koneh still wore his tattered robe and hood. Apparently, the army clothes were too clean for his tastes.

"Good bye, sahil," Erzulie said.

After Koneh left the bunker, Alexandra sat next to the angel and asked, "Sahil?"

Erzulie paused and then said, "Sahil is angelic for... I guess the English equivalent would be *dearest one*."

"Oh," Alexandra said, "I'm sorry. I didn't know you and Koneh were..."

"No, you misunderstand. Koneh and I have known each other for... a very long time." Erzulie paused again. "He looks upon me as a friend... as close as a sister. That is our relationship."

"Mmm-hmm," Alexandra said, not sure what to think.

"My capacity to love is not the same as yours. I am designed to follow every divine command, nothing more."

Alexandra laughed. "That's not love, Erzulie."

"No, no. I'm not explaining myself correctly. Forgive me." Erzulie lowered her eyes and frowned.

"I'm just messing with you," Alexandra said. "Listen, forget it."

"As you wish."

Alexandra cleared her throat and wondered if Erzulie had taken her command literally. "Well, it's good to see you alert and moving again."

"You are too kind, my Lady. I failed you in the wasteland. When are you going to punish me?"

"Oh, I think you've been through enough," Alexandra said. "I have some questions for you."

"I am here to serve," Erzulie said.

Alexandra sighed. "On the other hand, let's start with an order. You can go back to calling me Lex and treating me like a friend rather than a queen. Things have changed since you told me who I am. Or, who I *may* be. I liked it better when we were just friends."

"Okay, Lex," Erzulie said as she tapped Alexandra on the shoulder with her fist.

"That's better," Alexandra said. "Now, I decided to ask Koneh to show me how to fight with your sword."

"Why?"

"I'm tired of feeling useless," Alexandra said, "Koneh didn't want to train me at first. He said I shouldn't sin. What did he mean by that?"

"Exactly what he said."

"He said you could explain to me the workings of sin."

Erzulie widened her eyes. "I'm not an expert on the subject. The truths of this universe are not for angels to know."

"Tell me what you know."

"Very well," Erzulie said. "The soul is at the center of every living being. As much as you need your bones, organs and blood, you require your soul to function. Just like your body, you can damage your soul if you do not take care. This is probably what Koneh meant when he talked to you about sin."

"So, what kinds of things damage a soul?"

"Elah revealed many of the basic sins through His teachings. Certainly, you know them well."

"So, the laws that govern life and the soul are God's laws?"

"Life is life," Erzulie said. "Everyone with a soul answers to those laws – even Elah. He has a soul like you and Koneh. Elah cares for His children on Earth, so He revealed to them the secret of life and how to preserve a soul."

"You mean The Commandments?"

Erzulie nodded, "In a way. Subtlety was no longer an option after Eden turned to sin."

"Eden turned to sin?"

"Surely you know the story," Erzulie said. "Though, it was far more than forbidden fruit. Sinning is just part of your nature, whether you evolve naturally or are created by Elah. To maintain the purity of Eden, Elah cast you from there."

Alexandra marveled at all of this new information. "Elah has a soul too?"

"Yes," Erzulie said. "All living creatures do."

"I guess I just never thought of Elah as *one of us*."

Erzulie smiled. "He is like you in so many ways. He cares for your souls and is saddened when you harm them."

"And sinning damages a soul?"

"Exactly," Erzulie said. "Koneh doesn't want you to needlessly take life. To do so would diminish your soul. Hence, he is hesitant to show you how to take life through battle."

"Why do certain things – sins – harm a soul? Who makes up the rules?"

"I do not know," Erzulie said, her ghostly eyes pinned to Alexandra. "However I calculate that the rules grew out of some form of natural law, the same as the rules that govern what is healthy and unhealthy for your body. Please note this is only my observation after thousands of years of studying life."

Thousands of years. Alexandra's mind struggled with the enormity of such a large number.

"How old are you, Erzulie?"

"By Earth's measurements," Erzulie said, "Eighty-four thousand, two hundred and fifty-three years, seventy-one days, six hours…"

Alexandra swatted at Erzulie's arm and said, "I don't need the seconds, thanks though. Wowee! That's a long time."

"By your standards, I see how it would appear so."

Quickly, Alexandra said, "Not that I'm saying you *look* old…"

"I'm not bound by human pride. There is no need to validate your accurate statement of my age in comparison to yours."

While Alexandra had Erzulie alone, she decided to ask some burning questions. "What's Heaven like?"

Erzulie blinked. "Heaven is difficult to describe in your language."

"Try your best."

"Heaven is a place of pure energy, but I feel that is not a strong enough description. Elah's presence is everywhere and we are connected to your world in many ways. Though *connected* is not an adequate word either. I'm sorry, Lex, I'm having trouble finding words to convey the description."

"What about Eden?" Alexandra said. "Have you ever been there?"

"Yes," Erzulie said, smiling. "Eden I can describe to you. Think of the most stunning painting you have seen. This can be a beach, mountain, river or meadow. Eden combines all the most beautiful aspects of Earth into one serene place. The sun warms your skin, but does not burn it. The breeze rustles your hair, but does not force you to blink. Animals and humans live in harmony with each other."

"Sounds wonderful."

Erzulie continued, "From what I know, *emotion* is strong throughout Eden. You will find you become more a creature of your heart than your mind. To a newcomer, like yourself, you may find it overwhelming at first. All your emotions are on the surface. However, Elah delights in a bared soul. So, that is how Eden is."

As Alexandra processed all the new information, the door to the bunker opened. Father Callahan, Santino, and Marco entered. The three men quieted their laughter when they saw Alexandra and Erzulie. Alexandra found she couldn't look at Marco, though she felt his eyes upon her.

Santino and Marco dropped onto their beds exhausted from a day full of lounging and eating. Father Callahan sat on the cot opposite Alexandra and Erzulie. A smile was stamped upon his wrinkled face.

"What are you so happy about?" Alexandra asked.

Father Callahan shook his head. "Nothing specific. This was just the first time things felt… normal. I led some of the soldiers in prayer. Good food, good company. Though we missed you."

"I got chocolate!" Alexandra said as she held a candy bar aloft like a trophy.

Father Callahan laughed. "Try not to indulge too much."

"Hey, I deserve it!" Alexandra said. "Especially after the beating Koneh gave me this morning. He didn't take it easy on me."

Growing serious, Father Callahan said, "Are you sure you want to learn about fighting? It's no easy task to bring yourself to harm another person. I found it very difficult when I was first in the army."

Alexandra shrugged. "I think our situation demands it. Besides, I can't rely on others to always rescue me."

"Okay," Father Callahan said, "I won't presume to know what's best for you."

Squeezing Alexandra's hand, Father Callahan smiled. Alexandra watched the tall priest walk to his bed and organize his possessions for the night.

"Perhaps you should get some sleep as well," Erzulie said. "Koneh will have you up early. He takes his instruction very seriously."

Alexandra yawned and stretched her arms to the ceiling. "Yeah, good idea. Night, Erzulie"

"Good night, dear."

Alexandra fell on the bed next to her angelic friend and sunk into the thin mattress. After a few moments, she felt weightless and free. Again, Alexandra found herself in the spring meadow of her dream-world. The same old woman from her previous dream sat atop a stump. The woman's eyes bore into Alexandra, but this time Alexandra was ready.

Alexandra approached, but the old woman spoke first. "So, you know more than last we parted. Your soul is ripe with self-knowledge."

"I'm not dreaming," Alexandra said.

"No, you are not dreaming," the old woman said. "I choose to bring you here to discover your allegiance."

"My allegiance?"

"Do you still hold the flame of loyalty to your departed God?"

"Departed?"

The crone frowned. "You didn't know that your God abandoned you? Abandoned your species? Where does your allegiance lay now, child?"

"Allegiance to whom? God?"

The old woman yelled. "Do you still serve your God?"

"I don't serve anyone!"

"I must know. On this, all things depend."

"Why do you care so much? Who are you, anyway?" Alexandra said.

"Answer my question, child!"

Alexandra frowned. She didn't know what to think about the old woman. "I will not answer your questions until you answer mine."

"Your consciousness is but a brief spark in an ocean of flames. Do not speak at me as you do your kind!"

"You seem to know who I am, what I am capable of. Until I know who you are, I don't need to answer to you."

The old crone nodded once. "That is why I must destroy you."

Words, shouts, and the scuffling of boots pulled Alexandra from the meadow. Like a stereo in-between stations, the buzz of the real world rung in Alexandra's ears. The inside of the bunker came into focus and Alexandra felt someone behind her. Outside the bunker, people shouted and trucks rumbled.

"Alexandra!"

It was General Ryan. Alexandra turned and blinked. "What's going on?" she asked.

"We need your help," General Ryan whispered.

Groaning, Alexandra rose and rubbed her eyes. "Okay, I'm coming."

General Ryan led Alexandra to the hospital bunker. Red and white assaulted her eyes as she processed the scene. Wounded soldiers laid on cots, medical staff rushed about, and the smell of blood and plastic clung to the air.

"They were attacked on their patrol by some large dogs, though I've never heard of a dog tearing a man's arm from the socket," General Ryan said as he led Alexandra to one of the beds. "This is Benjamin Howell."

Alexandra noticed that the nurses and doctors didn't approach Benjamin's bed.

"He's lost too much blood," General Ryan said as his voice wavered. "Look, he's just a kid. He doesn't deserve this."

"And you want me to do what?" Alexandra said as she locked eyes with the General and lowered her voice. "Save him?"

"I would if I had the power… but I don't. You do."

Benjamin groaned from under his bandages and blood drenched blankets. Alexandra didn't know where to begin, so she placed her hands on the young man's chest. Nothing happened.

"I don't know…" Alexandra said. "With you, it just happened!"

"He's dying, Alexandra!" General Ryan shouted. "Save him!"

Alexandra looked around the bunker at the nurses and doctors. All eyes were on her. Benjamin's chest moved less with each breath. He was dying.

A thought jumped into Alexandra's mind and she said, "Tell me about him."

General Ryan asked, "What?"

"Tell me about Benjamin!"

"Well… he's from Indiana. He joined the reserves to pay for college. Poor boy didn't expect to get called into active duty. The guys call him Strings, because he plays the guitar. He also loves zombie movies, girls and beer. The usual stuff."

Alexandra focused on the minor facts she learned about Benjamin. The kid sounded like someone she would like to meet because they shared something in common – they were both pressed into active duty against their will.

Eyes closed, Alexandra tightened her hands on Benjamin's chest and searched for the same surge she felt when she healed the General.

Then, her thoughts swirled around in her head and in her heart. This kid shouldn't die. He should live. I can save him. I can heal him. Alexandra chased all doubt from her mind. A whirlwind gathered inside the bunker. Papers fluttered and a few of the nurses exclaimed their surprise as a white light emanated from the spot where Alexandra's hands met Benjamin's chest.

The doors to the bunker burst open and the light from Alexandra's hand flooded through the opening. Soldiers gathered at the entryway and watched with open mouths as the light retreated and the wounded soldier stirred.

Benjamin opened his eyes.

Alexandra smiled and reached for Benjamin's forehead, but the motion caused her head to spin. She felt her knees buckle and she crumpled to the floor. The world went black.

"Easy now."

The voice was not the General's. Alexandra recognized Koneh's raspy whisper.

"Koneh?" Alexandra said. "When…"

"No more words," Koneh said.

Alexandra opened her eyes and the world was fuzzy. After a few moments, everything came into focus. A throng of soldiers and their families surrounded Alexandra as she floated across the ground. Wait, she wasn't floating. Koneh carried her across the courtyard towards their bunker.

"I said, stay back!" Koneh hissed as a soldier reached for Alexandra. The soldier recoiled and joined the faceless crowd.

Why was Koneh so mean to them?

People murmured and watched as Father Callahan held the bunker door ajar for Koneh and Alexandra. As they entered the bunker, Alexandra's head spun. She heard voices, but couldn't understand the words.

Alexandra knew some time had passed but she wasn't certain how much. As if revived with a bucket of cold water, Alexandra opened her eyes with a clear head. Her companions were packing their things and Koneh stood near the exit. Alexandra sat up in her bed and asked, "What's going on?"

"Apparently," Father Callahan said, "we're leaving."

"What?" Alexandra asked. "Who made that decision?"

Father Callahan pointed to Koneh.

Alexandra stalked to the door and asked, "Why are we leaving?"

Koneh didn't respond.

Alexandra huffed. "What's outside that door?"

"Everyone," Koneh said.

"Let me see."

"No."

Marco appeared behind Alexandra and said, "Why don't you let her do what she wants, man?"

"You cannot go out there alone," Koneh said. "It's too dangerous."

"Why is it dangerous?" Alexandra asked.

Koneh glanced over Alexandra's shoulder at Marco and said, "Because people don't know how to react. They're unpredictable."

Marco rested his hand on his holster. "Step aside," he said.

"It's all right, Koneh," Alexandra said. "Marco, you're not helping. Be someplace else."

After Marco walked away from them, Alexandra repeated gently, "It's all right, Koneh."

Koneh hesitated and then opened the door. Hundreds of soldiers, civilians, and children filled the area outside the bunker. When they saw Alexandra's face, some kneeled, some cried, and others shouted.

CHAPTER 16

The crowd erupted into a cacophony of weeping, shouting and wide-eyed gasps.

"There she is!"

"Help us!"

"My brother is sick…"

"It's her!"

"I don't believe it!"

"Can you heal me?"

"Please help my daughter!"

Koneh reached his arm in front of Alexandra and grasped the door. "You see what you have done? Foolish!"

Alexandra scanned the crowd. Soldiers and civilians alike pressed against each other to catch a glimpse of Alexandra. However, this wasn't the first desperate crowd Alexandra had faced.

Shortly after she made partner at her law firm, Alexandra was on the defense team for GreenTech - a biohazard waste corporation on trial for decades of environmental abuse. The people of Brackettville, Texas were poisoned for generations through the drinking water contaminated by the corporation.

The courthouse was mobbed the day GreenTech settled with the residents. Alexandra walked down the steps with her client and was spat on by a man in overalls with a sign that read "Their REAL punishment starts in HELL!" The crowd on that day would have torn her apart if the National Guard wasn't there.

Now, a very different crowd inched closer to Alexandra, but it was no less dangerous. Alexandra stepped backwards into the bunker and Koneh closed the door.

Why am I so terrified of them? She slumped against the door. *I shouldn't fear them!*

"We need to move," Koneh said as he glanced into her eyes and then walked to the rest of the group.

Father Callahan said, "Well, I think it's wonderful what you did for that soldier."

"She put herself in harm's way," Koneh said. "Again."

"It's her destiny to help those in need," Father Callahan said. "That much is obvious now."

"No…" Koneh said, "her path leads to Eden."

Marco joined the conversation. "Why don't you two ask Alexandra what *she* wants to do? No? Perhaps she doesn't want to go where you want her to go."

A fist pounded on the bunker door and Alexandra jumped.

"Alexandra!" said General Ryan from the other side of the door. "I need to talk to you!"

Alexandra grasped fistfuls of her hair with both her hands. "Everyone!" she said, "Back off!"

"I'm coming in!" General Ryan said.

Without answering, Alexandra locked the bunker door. The General rattled the door and said, "We just need to talk!"

"Go away!" Alexandra said between breaths.

"I can't do that. Not now."

"Why doesn't anyone understand?!" Alexandra said loud enough for the General to hear through the bunker door. "I'm not your Savior! I don't know how I healed you! Just… just leave me alone!"

Alexandra slid to the ground and buried her head in her hands. Tears poured from her eyes. Fear, confusion and frustration rushed through her thumping heart. Overwhelmed, she couldn't sort through the information and emotion. Everything tangled together in her mind. She was lost.

When Alexandra opened her eyes, Erzulie was at her side. The fallen angel's unearthly eyes stared through Alexandra.

"Quiet now, child," Erzulie said with the usual singsong in her voice. "Save your strength."

Though Erzulie's words carried little comfort, something in Erzulie's voice soothed Alexandra's nerves much like the sonic massage machines at the fitness center in San Antonio. As if her mind rebooted, Alexandra felt her emotions come back online and under control. Serenity returned and Alexandra wiped some tears from her cheeks.

"All right," Alexandra said. "Let me think a moment."

"It looks like you won't get the chance," Father Callahan said as everyone turned to watch the back of the bunker fill with a dozen armed soldiers.

"You left me no choice." General Ryan said as he followed his men into the main room of the bunker. "We had to ensure your safety."

Alexandra stood and said, "I assure you, I'm safe."

General Ryan nodded and said, "I'd feel a whole lot better if you just came with us and away from the demon."

Koneh stepped in front of Erzulie and Alexandra. Alexandra recalled the encounter with the thugs on the hill. She decided she didn't want to see a repeat performance.

"I'll handle this," Alexandra said as she touched Koneh's shoulder. "It's all right." After a moment, Koneh stepped aside and crossed his arms.

"You should come with us," General Ryan said.

Alexandra shook her head. "Not going to happen, General. We were just leaving."

"What? Why?" he said.

"Because we have other places to be."

"You're safe here. I won't let any harm come to you."

Alexandra sighed. "Then tell your men to leave."

After glancing at the soldiers, General Ryan said, "Green team. Dismissed! Standard perimeter."

With practiced precision, the soldiers fell back into the showers and out of the bunker.

"Well, how can I convince you to stay?" General Ryan said. "We need you here…"

Alexandra approached the General and said, "There's nothing you can do or say that will convince me to remain here. Listen, I'm not who you think I am. I don't understand it all yet, but don't put your faith in me. I know myself… and I'm not… well, I'm not anybody's savior."

"You healed me. And Benjamin," General Ryan said. "You saved my life."

Alexandra smiled. "You're welcome."

"You know, I can force you to stay."

Alexandra's smile retreated from her face. "You can try," she said. "But I think we both know you wouldn't follow through with that."

General Ryan's eyes fell to the ground and the lines around his eyes and mouth creased. "Where are you going?"

"You wouldn't believe me if I told you," Alexandra said. "Besides, the less people who know, the better."

"Very well," General Ryan said, "What can I do to help? I still feel I owe you... well, my life."

"I think I'll let you talk with the good Father here," Alexandra said as she motioned to Father Callahan. "He was once a military man and probably knows better than me what we need to survive our trip."

As the Father and the General discussed sundries, Alexandra packed her borrowed duffel bag. The bunker was comfortable and safe, but Alexandra felt uneasy when she considered making the base her new home. If Eden waited for them, then Alexandra was determined to find it. Perhaps Eden held answers. Maybe she could find peace, or a clue to what was happening to her.

When Alexandra finished packing her bag, Erzulie approached. "I want you to carry this," Erzulie said as she unbuckled her sword from her waist. "May it serve you better than it has served me."

"Won't you need it?" Alexandra asked.

Erzulie smiled. "Your safety is paramount. Besides, I have other tools at my disposal."

Alexandra nodded and kept the sword secured in its scabbard as she fastened it to her duffel bag. During her first lesson, Koneh told her to never draw the weapon unless she meant to use it. Something in his voice warned her that he was serious.

For the first time since the bus had flipped, Alexandra felt like she was in control – at least somewhat. She decided it was time to take charge.

"Okay everyone," Alexandra said. "This trip has been haphazard thus far. If we're going to do this, we're going to do it right."

Alexandra's gift for organization was one of the qualities that made her into her firm's top trial attorney. If only she had her digital data assistant, then she could have whipped together some charts and schedules. She missed her spreadsheets.

"Father Callahan is in charge of provisions," Alexandra said. "Father, get what you need from the General and let me know when we are two weeks away from running low."

Father Callahan disengaged from his conversation with General Ryan and smiled. "Yes, ma'am!"

"Santino," Alexandra said as she turned to the Spanish-American truck driver, "are you still interested in going home to Brazil? Or would you prefer to stay here?"

"I go with you, si?"

"Great. The rig is your responsibility. Get what you need for gasoline, oil and such. We leave in two hours."

Santino finished stuffing a blanket into his knapsack and nodded.

Alexandra faced Marco. Looking into his eyes, she wondered if he betrayed them to the demon, Lilev, or if he really was what he seemed – a miserable survivor from a ruined city. Whatever the case, Lilev didn't get what she wanted and Koneh kept everyone safe. Besides, Alexandra wanted to reconcile with her guilt over abandoning the people of Tampico. She couldn't abandon the sole survivor.

"Marco," Alexandra said, "everyone else is invested in this journey. You are not. However, you are welcome to join us."

The former leader of Tampico grinned and took a step towards Alexandra. "If it's all the same," he said, "I'd be muy glad to join you."

Alexandra nodded. "Very well. Work with Santino to get some maps or something. We need a good route into South America with stops at some major cities for supplies."

Marco winked and said, "As you command."

Ignoring the intimate gesture, Alexandra turned to Koneh, who watched her every move. "And you."

"Do you have a task for me as well, oh leader of men?" Koneh asked.

Alexandra nodded. "First of all, never call me that again. Second, you're in charge of our safety. Though I've protested in the past, you have done a good job of keeping me alive. Guns, ammo... if the General will part with it, get us what we need."

"I am ready for your command," Erzulie said as she stepped to Alexandra's side and smiled. "What can I do?"

"You can keep me sane," Alexandra said.

Though Alexandra knew the angel couldn't express emotion, a look of confusion spread over Erzulie's face.

"I do not understand," Erzulie said.

"Never mind," Alexandra said. "Your job remains the same. Watch the sky and alert us if anyone approaches. However I want you to be more careful. I don't want you hurt again. Stay safe."

"By your command."

The bunker buzzed with activity. After Alexandra gave the area one last glance, General Ryan approached her.

"That was impressive," he said.

"I'm a lawyer."

"Oh, well… yeah." General Ryan laughed. "I guess you're used to people listening to you. I mean, you know what they say about lawyers…"

"Save the lawyer jokes, please," Alexandra said, rolling her eyes. "And thanks for your help. We wouldn't make it too far without it."

"It's the least I could do," General Ryan said. "And remember, you're always welcome here."

"Thanks. That means a lot."

"Well," General Ryan said as he inhaled. "I'll clear out the courtyard so you can get moving."

"That would help," Alexandra said.

General Ryan opened his mouth to speak, but something held his words. Alexandra felt a connection to him, but she didn't know if she was attracted to the man or if the feeling was something else.

Without checking her words, Alexandra said gently, "I will return someday. I'd like to get to know you better."

General Ryan smiled. "I would very much like to get to know you better as well."

After the group secured their provisions to the back of Santino's rig, they drove towards the gate of the military base. People gathered on top of buildings and pleaded for Alexandra to stay. Many of the faces bore confusion and some appeared angry. Alexandra watched from the back of the cab. She wanted to explain to them why she left, but she knew they wouldn't listen. They were full of unrealistic hopes and expectations.

As the main gate to the base opened, someone repeated "Stop!" several times. It was Benjamin Howell, the soldier Alexandra healed.

"Wait! Stop!" Benjamin said as he ran to the side of the rig.

Santino looked over his shoulder and Alexandra nodded. "Stop the truck," she said as she opened the cab door and put a foot on the step bar. "What is it?" Alexandra asked.

The soldier looked to be in better health than when Alexandra last saw him. He wore green fatigue pants, a white tank top and a camouflage jacket. Benjamin's dog tags jingled to rest as he stopped and looked at Alexandra.

"I… um…" Benjamin fumbled with his words.

Smiling, Alexandra said, "You're welcome."

"No… I mean… yeah, thanks," Benjamin said. "I, uh… I want to go with you."

Marco pulled his motorcycle up next to the rig and said, "Everything all right, Alexandra?"

Alexandra nodded and then returned her attention to Benjamin. "Is General Ryan okay with your leaving?"

"Yeah, um… after I asked permission, he reassigned me. To you."

"Reassigned?" Marco asked.

"Yeah," Benjamin said, "Alexandra… Err, should I call you by your name?"

Alexandra nodded and said, "Please do."

"Okay, well, you, Alexandra, are now my CO – my commanding officer. I now take orders from you."

"Are you sure you want to do this?" Alexandra said. "We have a long, difficult journey ahead of us."

"I've never been more sure of anything in my life," Benjamin said. "Let me go get my stuff, I'll be right back. Don't leave without me!"

As the soldier ran to a nearby jeep, Koneh said, "If he climbs into the rig, he'll see Erzulie. Maybe it's better to wait to make that introduction?"

Alexandra glanced at Erzulie, turned to Marco, and said, "He'll ride with you for now."

Marco nodded and revved his engine.

After Benjamin secured his pack and guitar to the back of the rig, the group departed the military base. They traveled for the entire day on a lonely road through southern Mexico. The rig's headlights speared the red-black darkness as they followed Santino's route. If there was anything left of the towns they passed, no light betrayed their presence. Crumbled buildings, cracked roads and wrecked cars greeted them in an endless parade of ruin.

Santino and Marco agreed to stop the group outside of Villahermosa for the night. They setup camp and Father Callahan passed out some MRE rations to everyone.

As everyone ate, Alexandra approached Benjamin. "May I sit?" she asked.

Benjamin nodded and said, "Yes, yes! I'm sorry. Let me clean up my mess."

"No need," Alexandra said as she sat next to the soldier. "You already met Koneh. He's a bit strange, don't you agree?"

"Yeah," Benjamin said, "he kinda creeps me out. What's with his eyes?"

"I think he was burned by radiation or something," Alexandra said. "But Koneh is a good man. He saved my life and I trust him."

Benjamin nodded in-between mouthfuls of pot roast from his MRE.

"Well," Alexandra said, "there's someone else you haven't met. She's an angel. Well, a fallen angel. She's my friend."

"Fallen angel?" Benjamin said. "Like a demon?"

"No, not exactly." Alexandra turned her head to the sky and called, "Erzulie."

The campfire fluttered like a flag as the wind intensified. Moments later, Erzulie appeared from the darkness of the night sky and landed next to Alexandra. Erzulie eyed the soldier as she folded her black feathered wings against her back.

"Benjamin, meet Erzulie."

The soldier gaped as he stared at Erzulie. A chunk of pot roast fell from his open mouth.

Alexandra smiled, "Yes, she's quite beautiful, don't you agree, Benjamin?"

The young soldier nodded once.

"And she's my friend," Alexandra said. "Give her the same respect you would me, got it?"

Benjamin blinked and said, "Yeah... okay."

"Good. Now we're all friends," Alexandra said as she tore open her MRE. "Ohh... baked beans and ham. My favorite."

"I'll trade you," Father Callahan said. "I got ziti and meatballs again."

"Deal!"

After they exchanged rations, Father Callahan turned to Benjamin and said, "So, do you carry around that guitar for a reason?"

Benjamin nodded, "Yeah, I guess I'm okay with it."

Father Callahan motioned towards the instrument and said, "By all means... it's been a while since I've enjoyed some music."

Everyone gathered by the fire as Benjamin strummed a tune on his guitar. Though she couldn't explain it, Alexandra felt at home with the motley group. They were in the middle of a vast wasteland, with only the supplies on the rig to sustain them and Alexandra felt content. She looked at each of her companions as the music played.

Marco and Father Callahan clapped along with the rhythm, wide smiles on their faces. Santino leaned against his pack and tapped his foot as he enjoyed a cigarette. Even Koneh bobbed with the music. Then, there was Erzulie – the only nonhuman in the group. After a few songs, she joined the guitar with a melodious humming. No words, just notes. Erzulie breathed the most perfect melody Alexandra had ever heard. The music was intoxicating.

The next day of travel came too fast for Alexandra's liking, but they had to keep moving. Santino and Marco agreed that they should press on to Guatemala. However, once they arrived, it was clear that nothing was left of Guatemala City. The group spent the next day picking through the skeletal outskirts for supplies and gasoline.

After another several days of travel – and more sword lessons from Koneh - the group entered Costa Rica and Santino suggested they travel through the capital as well. Again, there was nothing left of the city. Ruined buildings, vehicles and too many bodies were all they found. When the group was about to make camp, they found a sign that read "Survivors," and an arrow pointing away from the ruined center of the city.

"Do we follow it?" Father Callahan asked as Alexandra inspected the sign.

She shook her head. "It's out of our way."

"Sometimes," Father Callahan said, "we aren't meant to travel in a straight line."

"And sometimes a straight line is all that is left for us," Koneh said as he approached. "We are ready to go. Not much here."

"There are survivors," Alexandra said as she pointed to the sign.

Koneh grunted, "Not for long. Demons can read too." He tore the sign down from its post and tossed it aside. "Now, these survivors might live a little longer."

As Alexandra weighed the cost of arguing with Koneh, Father Callahan said, "You don't know that. They might need our help."

"Or they could be dead already. Listen Father, we don't have time for this. Alexandra, we're ready to camp."

"Good," Alexandra said, "have Benjamin help you secure the area. I'll be there in a few minutes for my lesson."

Koneh nodded and walked back to Santino's rig.

Father Callahan sighed and turned to Alexandra. Before he could speak Alexandra said, "I know how you feel, Father."

"Good."

"But Koneh is right. It is dangerous to stop."

Father Callahan frowned and said, "You must do what you feel is right."

"Always," Alexandra said, "which is why we're going to find these survivors anyway."

CHAPTER 17

The sounds and smells of the camp greeted Alexandra as she walked past Santino's rig. Smoke from the fire stung her nose and throat. The rig's engine rumbled to a halt and Santino jumped down from the cab. In the distance, Koneh and Benjamin stood close together, engaged in conversation. Father Callahan squeezed Alexandra's shoulder and walked to the rig, probably to distribute everyone's rations for the night.

Alexandra felt a breeze and looked to the night sky. Moments later, Erzulie landed at Alexandra's side and said, "The area is clear, Lex."

"Thank you, Erzulie."

"Is there anything else I can get for you?"

Alexandra put her hands on her hips and said, "As a matter of fact there is."

Erzulie bowed and said, "All you need ever do is command."

"You confuse me, Erzulie," Alexandra said. "Koneh tells me you cannot feel emotions, that you are some sort of robot. I've been struggling with this for quite some time and I don't see it that way. You are always concerned with my well-being, and out of everyone I feel I can talk to you the easiest."

Erzulie brought her eyes to Alexandra's and said, "What you observe is merely imitation."

Alexandra frowned. "It seems strange that demons have a soul and angels don't…"

"Astute," Erzulie said. "However, most demons have a myriad of souls inside of them."

Alexandra narrowed her eyes and asked, "And what's inside an angel?"

"A host of materials you are no doubt unfamiliar with."

"But no soul?" Alexandra said, afraid to ask what those things could be.

Erzulie shook her head. "No soul."

"Yet more human than many humans I've met in my travels," Koneh said.

Enthralled by the conversation with her unearthly companion, Alexandra didn't notice Koneh's approach. He crossed his arms over his chest and eyed Alexandra.

"What's the one question you haven't asked yet?" Koneh said.

Alexandra mulled over the strange inquiry, but couldn't decide what Koneh wanted.

Koneh sighed and turned to Erzulie. "How do you kill a demon?"

Erzulie said, "Same as a human. Cause enough trauma to the body or organs and the entire unit will cease to function. However, their skin is much thicker than that of a normal human and their bones are fortified with eons of age. Only the truest of strikes can fell a demon."

"Which brings us to our lesson tonight," Koneh said as he drew his sword from beneath his tattered robes.

Alexandra took a step backwards and said, "One moment." She hesitated before asking her next question. "Erzulie, how do you kill an angel?"

Erzulie balled her fist and placed it upon her chest. "An angel's heart rests in the center of their chest. Any attack that penetrates the outer layers and skeleton has a chance of destroying the heart. Such a blow would kill any angel."

"Good question," Koneh said. "Are you ready now?"

"Heed his advice," Erzulie said as she spread her dark wings. "Koneh knows his trade."

Erzulie darted into the sky as Alexandra stepped to her pack and drew Erzulie's sleek blade from its scabbard. Before Alexandra could ready herself, Koneh was upon her. His motions were deliberate and obvious – to teach the basics.

"Mind your feet in each position," Koneh said. "Good. Just like I showed you. Remember, if you don't set your feet correctly, you will not have the balance you need. From your balance you will find your strength."

Sweat gathered around Alexandra's head and neck. Through labored breath, Alexandra asked, "So, how did you two meet?"

Koneh advanced and nodded as Alexandra sidestepped or parried each of his slow motion strikes. "Erzulie and I?" Koneh said. "That is a long story."

Parry, step, parry, parry, step. "I'm not going anywhere," Alexandra said.

Alexandra concentrated on the training while waiting for Koneh's response. After a minute or so, her teacher said, "When the rest of the world had given up on me, I was surprised to find an angel in my corner. She didn't appear to me as an angel. She looked human." Koneh paused after what appeared to be some internal reflection and lowered his sword. "Erzulie had faith in me. And for that, she was banished from Heaven."

"That doesn't make any sense," Alexandra said.

Koneh opened his mouth to speak and paused. After a sigh, he said, "Faster now."

This was the part of the lesson where Alexandra always faltered. Koneh was just too quick for her. After a few parries, Alexandra lost her sword and Koneh pointed the tip of his blade at her throat.

"Too slow," he said.

"No," Alexandra said as she retrieved her weapon, "You're too fast!"

Koneh rubbed his chin and smiled.

"What?" Alexandra asked.

"Switch," Koneh said.

"Huh?"

"Here," Koneh held the grip of his sword towards Alexandra, "switch."

Alexandra grasped the sword and strained at its weight. Erzulie's sword was much lighter. In return, Alexandra handed Erzulie's slender blade to Koneh.

"Now, slowly," Koneh said as he repeated the motions from earlier in the training session.

Alexandra's desire to talk about Erzulie was replaced with the arduous task of raising Koneh's heavy sword to the air. How could he fight with this thing?

"Good, faster," Koneh said as he increased the velocity of his attacks.

Through sheer force of will, Alexandra found strength enough to counter a few blows before her arms turned into noodles and she shook with exhaustion.

"No more," Alexandra said between breaths. "Too… heavy."

"Switch again," Koneh said.

When Alexandra gripped Erzulie's blade again, it felt light as a pencil.

"Go," Koneh said as he reengaged.

Koneh started as fast as Alexandra had ever seen. However, to her surprise, she was able to keep pace. Something clicked in her mind, and Alexandra understood the ebb and flow of what Koneh was teaching her. When she saw her opportunity, Alexandra turned the tide and went on the offensive. She felt the same exhilaration with her sword that she felt with her tennis racket during a rally. As she backed Koneh towards the fire, Alexandra let go and stopped thinking about her next moves. Instead, she *felt* them.

"You go girl!" Benjamin said.

"Woo!" Marco said, pumping his fist.

Alexandra swelled with pride. I get this, she thought.

Thud.

Alexandra had never been hit in the face – until that moment. The world spun a few times and Alexandra fell to the ground.

"Hey now!" Marco said.

Benjamin rose to his feet and said, "What was that for?"

Alexandra's head throbbed and the camp refused to come into focus.

"That was good," Koneh said as Alexandra felt her grip on reality returning. "However, the sword is not the only weapon your opponent has at their disposal. In this case, I used my fist. Against a demon, it could be claws, teeth or a tail. Always be ready." Koneh turned away and stopped after a step. "Lesson over."

"Dude, that was uncool," Benjamin said.

Through a pounding headache, Alexandra heard Benjamin and Marco voicing their displeasure in Koneh's direction.

Father Callahan helped Alexandra to a sitting position and placed a wet cloth to her mouth.

"You're bleeding, but not bad," he said.

Something inside Alexandra told her that Koneh was justified in his actions. "I *did* ask for this," Alexandra said to Father Callahan. "I wanted him to train me."

"Sometimes," Father Callahan said as he looked in Koneh's direction, "the lessons we remember most, are the ones that also hurt the most."

Alexandra winced. "I won't forget this one for a while."

Benjamin and Father Callahan helped Alexandra to her feet and brought her to the fire. The soldier glared at Koneh the entire time.

"It's okay, Benjamin," Alexandra said, "Koneh is training me."

"Still," Benjamin said, "he shouldn't be hittin' a lady — 'specially not *you*."

The two men lowered Alexandra to the ground.

Benjamin sat next to Alexandra and said, "Are ya okay? Really?"

Alexandra nodded and smiled. "Yeah, I'm fine."

"Why do you wanna fight with swords, anyway?" Benjamin asked. "Don't you guys carry guns? Guns kill demons good."

"And what happens when your ammo runs out, soldier?" Koneh asked.

Benjamin smiled. "I'll go get more."

"If only things were that simple..." Koneh said.

Benjamin leaned towards Alexandra and said, "Nice friend you have there."

"You get used to him."

Benjamin shook his head. "If you say so..."

After Benjamin wandered away, Alexandra closed her eyes. Just for a few minutes, she thought. The pain of the punch and the weariness from the travel overtook her.

Alexandra decided she must have fallen asleep at some point. She came to this conclusion because she now found herself at the edge of a large ocean. The breeze carried the familiar salt and brine to her nostrils. Waves crashed against the rocks below and Alexandra realized she wasn't alone. The white-haired crone was there.

"I'm dreaming again," Alexandra said.

"The world can once again be like this," the old woman said as she studied Alexandra. "But that depends on you."

"What do you want from me?" Alexandra asked, terrified of this woman in her visions.

"Only to see through your feelings. To know your intentions. You are not an open door, however. You must share with me your thoughts."

Refusing to yield to this stranger, Alexandra said, "You said before that God has abandoned us. What did you mean by that?"

"The taint of Elah has passed from this world and now I must heal it. You need to declare your allegiance so I can either show you the way or destroy you."

Alexandra studied the crone. "Who are you?"

Clouds filled the sky and thunder boomed overhead. The old crone rose to her feet and approached Alexandra. "Heed my words, child. You are both an ally and an enemy. Choose carefully the path you would take."

Like their previous conversations, this one ended almost as soon as it began. Even worse, Alexandra awoke with a foul taste in her mouth. A quick glance to her side revealed the source of the vileness – a mostly consumed hot dog MRE. When did she eat that?

Everyone else was asleep, except Koneh. Alexandra wrapped her blanket around her body and approached her guide.

"Mind if I sit?"

Koneh gestured to the ground with an open palm, but he didn't respond. Instead, he gazed upon the dark horizon.

Alexandra crossed her legs and dropped to the earth beside him. "Listen," she said, "we're going to go check on those survivors."

"That does not surprise me."

Alexandra rubbed her sore chin and attempted to read her companion.

"I hope you're not waiting for an apology," Koneh said.

"No," Alexandra smiled. "I asked for it."

"You did well last night. You are a good student."

Alexandra blushed like she did in the seventh grade when she talked with Antonio, the coolest boy in school. Young Alexandra always tried to find him at lunch time. They talked about kid stuff – the teachers they hated, TV shows, and how much they despised homework. If Alexandra had a first boyfriend, Antonio would qualify. Why she thought of Antonio as she talked with

Koneh, Alexandra wasn't certain. Maybe she was attracted to him, to the danger and freedom he represented.

"You are doing well," Koneh said as he leaned to catch Alexandra's eye. "And I don't just mean with the sword. Think of where you were a month ago when I found you. Quite a change, wouldn't you agree?"

Alexandra shook her head. "I still don't know why we're doing this, Koneh. You think I have some special power inside of me, but I don't."

"I think General Ryan and Benjamin Howell would disagree with you."

Alexandra glanced at the sleeping soldier. "I don't know what that was," she said. "It all seems like it happened to someone else."

"I know what you mean."

Sighing, Alexandra turned back to Koneh and gently placed her hand on his wrapped forearm. "Whatever secrets you have," she said, "I'm sorry I tried to pry them from you. You saved my life and I didn't even have the decency to respect your privacy. I know we're a bit different, but I want you to know that I'm truly grateful we found each other."

Koneh nodded and Alexandra saw the whole picture for the first time since she awoke inside the wrecked bus. She had been living moment to moment and never took the time to step outside of herself.

"We didn't meet by chance in that town," Alexandra said. "You were waiting for me. How could I have been so stupid?"

"Yes, Erzulie and I sought you out."

"To re-open Eden?"

"That is correct."

"Why?" Alexandra asked.

Koneh paused. "Because it is the only path left for me."

Though Koneh didn't answer her question, Alexandra refrained from pressing the matter. Koneh and Erzulie knew enough to seek her out. Lilev mentioned that Derechi, the demon lord, also had interest in Alexandra.

"We are on the run," Alexandra said.

Koneh nodded. "Everyone's looking for you."

"Why?"

"Because you are the only one who can re-open Eden for us all."

Alexandra huffed. "Yeah, no pressure or anything."

"Now that I know you," Koneh said. "I wish things were different."

"How do you mean?"

He exhaled. "You don't deserve this. It is too much to ask someone so young."

Frowning, Alexandra said, "I'm not exactly a *youth*. I've been around a couple of blocks."

"Not these blocks," Koneh said.

Again, Alexandra felt crushed by the weight of her task. Could she really re-open Eden? It was almost too massive to comprehend.

"Mind if I use that shoulder again?" Alexandra asked, her eyes pleading. She needed something stable in this world, and Koneh was her anchor.

He nodded and gently guided her head to his shoulder. She recalled the dormant flame she felt in her heart when Koneh carried her into the bunker. That flame grew stronger in response to his touch.

After a few minutes, Koneh stood and looked into her eyes. "I'm sorry," he said. "I should not permit myself... this is not allowed."

Alexandra held his eyes with her stare and said, "*What* is not allowed?"

"I cannot..."

Alexandra stood and wrapped her arms around his neck. Her feelings went beyond mere infatuation with her protector. She felt closer to him with the passing of each moment. Koneh excited her in a way no man had ever done. He was dangerous and caring, troubled and resolute in his path. Her heart needed answers.

"Nobody else is awake," she said, her face close to his. "What are you afraid of? I see the way you look at me..."

Koneh shook his head. "I am on a mission... I cannot indulge, even if I wanted to."

"You're saying you want to?" Alexandra inched closer. His scars didn't bother her and she wanted to know where each one was from.

"No," Koneh said as he disengaged from her embrace. "I'm saying... I wish this task fell to someone else... Someone who I could look upon as an instrument, nothing more. You are more than Elah and the Church expected from their Revelation, and I am sorry."

With Koneh clearly returning to business, Alexandra sighed. She said, "Why are *you* sorry? You didn't choose this fate for me. If this is indeed my fate."

Koneh held Alexandra's gaze a moment longer before he turned away. "I am sorry because you don't deserve to be moved like a chess piece by someone else's hand."

"I go to Eden because I wish to go," Alexandra said. "Nobody is forcing me. Why do you think that?"

Without answering, Koneh walked towards the camp. What was he holding back now? Was she really a chess piece in some sort of cosmic game?

The camp began to stir as the sky turned from black to reddish-black. Alexandra grabbed an MRE ration and walked to the rig where she found Santino and Marco.

"You look like hell," Marco said. "That monster gave you quite the bruise, no?"

"I'll live," Alexandra said. "Listen, we're going to head to where the sign pointed and hopefully find these survivors. Do either of you know the area?"

"That's what we were just talking about," Marco said.

Santino shifted his weight as he looked over his maps. He wasn't happy about something, but like usual, the soft-spoken truck driver kept to himself.

"What do you think, Santino?" Alexandra asked. "Do you know where we'd end up if we followed the sign?"

Santino adjusted his Texas Rangers cap and said, "I dunno... We go northeast to follow the sign. But, do we wanna go that way? Route 180 goes southeast to Panama and South America. Better to stay on 180, no?"

"We'll get back on Route 180, yes," Alexandra said, "but I need to know where you think this northeast road will take us."

"I think," Marco said as he glanced at the maps, "we'll come out near the coast... or, the old coast. Maybe where the big cruise ships from America used to make port?"

Santino nodded. "Si, I think that too."

Something still bothered Santino. Alexandra wanted to know what that was. "Okay, Marco," she said, "get everyone moving. We leave in thirty minutes."

Marco smiled and said, "Si, mi guapa flor."

Alexandra decided to let his flirtation slip and she turned to Santino. "Is everything okay, Santino?"

"Si," Santino said as he rolled his maps and tossed them into the cab of his truck.

Alexandra followed and said, "You know, Santino, you can talk to me. If something's bothering you, I want to know about it."

Santino paused and turned to Alexandra. "You travel on mission importante, no?"

Alexandra nodded.

"Then I am a sinner for wanting something for me."

"Nonsense," Alexandra said. "What do you want?"

"To see mi hija – my daughter."

"Oh," Alexandra said, "I didn't know…"

Santino said, "I don't wanna take you away from your mission."

Alexandra shook her head, "We were going in the same direction until now. I'm sorry. I shouldn't have taken your invaluable aid for granted."

Santino seemed ashamed. He wouldn't even meet Alexandra's

eyes.

"Listen," Alexandra said, "where's your daughter?

"Brasilia."

"The capitol city of Brazil?"

"Si."

Calling up the memory of the globe in her elementary school classroom again, Alexandra searched for Brasilia. Southern Brazil, past the Andes and Amazon Basin.

"Okay," Alexandra said, "that's still quite a distance away."

"Si."

"A deal then?" Alexandra said. "After we finish with this errand, we'll head straight for Brasilia. Sound good?"

Santino nodded and looked into Alexandra's eyes. For the first time, Alexandra noticed the lines under his eyes and at the corners of his mouth. He looked weary and defeated.

"But this is your truck," Alexandra said. "You can take it to Brasilia right now if you want. I wouldn't blame you one bit."

"No," Santino said, "you found gasoline and food... I stick with you."

Alexandra smiled. "Good. I'm not ready to say goodbye to you just yet. Thanks for all your help, Santino. I promise, you will see your daughter again."

The lines on Santino's face lightened when he smiled. "Si," he said as he hopped into his rig.

Alexandra sensed someone behind her and she whirled on her heel.

"A bit jumpy?" Koneh said.

"No, just... don't sneak up on me like that."

Koneh nodded and said, "Do you always go around making promises you aren't likely to keep?"

"Wha-?"

"What are the chances this man's daughter is alive?" Koneh said. "Or, for that matter, that he will survive the trip? Be careful, Alexandra, many things here are beyond your control."

Alexandra pushed past Koneh and spat her words. "Thanks for reminding me of that." How could Koneh seem so tantalizing to her and then turn cold a moment later? Was he trying to push her away?

Camp was almost broken when Alexandra reached her spot by the fire. Like a woman leaving a cheating husband, she gathered her belongings.

"Something wrong?" Father Callahan asked.

After Alexandra stuffed the last of her things into her pack, she flicked her braid to her back and said, "Nothing... It's just... Koneh pisses me off sometimes."

Father Callahan chuckled.

Glaring, Alexandra said, "I don't see why that is funny."

"Many apologies," Father Callahan said as he ran his hand over his bald scalp. "You two remind me of a brother and sister I knew back in Mexico. They fought all the time too."

"Did the sister eventually kill her brother?" Alexandra asked.

Father Callahan chuckled again and shook his head. "No, no. After many years they learned that they, in fact, were *not* related and then they got married."

Alexandra froze. "That's… strange."

"You cannot control some things," Father Callahan said. "Least of all, who you love."

This time, Alexandra laughed. "When I think of all the emotions I have towards Koneh, *love* isn't on the list."

"I'm not saying anything, my dear. Merely observations… observations."

"Well," Alexandra said with a smile, "If I ever do marry, you'll be the first to know."

"Oh?" Father Callahan said, "And why is that?"

"Because you are going to be the one reading from that Bible of yours."

With a bow, the priest said, "It would be my greatest honor."

Alexandra sighed. "Because you think I'm from Heaven?"

Father Callahan turned serious and said, "No, my dear, because I look upon you as I would a daughter."

Alexandra's heart swelled. She never knew the love of a father, and now she realized what she missed. With tears in her eyes, Alexandra hugged her friend, her adopted father.

CHAPTER 18

Route 180 was their course into South America before they made their detour. The highway was built and extended as part of the South American oil rush of the early 21st century. Middle Eastern crude oil supplies tapered off and the hard-to-reach oil became a hot commodity. Only after all the infrastructure was built, and people moved their families and fortunes did the truth strike – there was very little oil to be found in the lower Americas.

Leaving behind a wake of falsely promised labor and cleared rainforest, the wealthy oil-diggers abandoned the area. However, they also left behind a system of superhighways of which Alexandra and her group now took advantage.

"I guess this is the coast," Father Callahan said as he peered out the grimy windows of the cab.

Though she couldn't see too far, Alexandra marveled at the land's steep falloff into what was once the ocean. Like in Tampico, the ocean was gone.

"How are we going to survive this?" Alexandra said.

"It's like this to the north, too," Benjamin said.

Koneh said, "And I saw a new heaven and a new earth: for the first heaven and the first earth were passed away; and there was no more sea."

Father Callahan turned to Koneh and said, "Not that I doubt those words anymore... But, in the same breath we are promised no more death, suffering, or pain."

Koneh turned to Father Callahan and said, "Eden offers that promise."

Santino's rig stopped and the headlights painted the dark landscape. Alexandra marveled at the absence of the ocean. The new landscape seemed alien to her.

Moments later, Erzulie landed beside the rig and said, "The survivors are to the south. They take shelter in a ship."

"How many?" Koneh asked.

"A half-dozen or more," Erzulie said

"What do you want to do?" Koneh asked as he turned to Alexandra.

"The plan remains the same," Alexandra said, "We'll see if they need any help."

Koneh sighed. "Very well. Let's go, Santino."

Santino turned the rig south and they rumbled along a broken road for a while. They passed through the ruined buildings of a deserted coastal city. Upturned earth surrounded the road as they followed it to the shelf and saw the steep drop-off into the former ocean. Then, the truck stopped and Alexandra's eyes widened.

Illuminated by the rig's headlights, a beached cruise ship towered above the jagged landscape. Resting on its side against a long bank of sand, the cruise ship's white hull contrasted against the darkness of the earth below and behind.

Alexandra jumped from the cab and stepped to the edge of the small hill. Memories of her cruise from a few years ago popped into her head, but she never realized just how massive these vessels were. She gaped at the sight until Marco pulled his bike along side her.

Marco whistled. "Never seen anything like that before."

"Dear God," Father Callahan said as he gestured the sign of the cross from his head to his shoulders.

For a few moments, nobody spoke. The vision of the mammoth cruise ship was too shocking.

Tearing her eyes from the wreck, Alexandra looked to the sky and shouted, "Erzulie!"

A moment later, Erzulie appeared and dropped to the ground beside Alexandra.

"Your command?"

"Stay in the sky," Alexandra said, "but, remain close. We don't want to alarm these people."

Erzulie nodded and said, "As you wish."

"Okay folks," Alexandra said, "let's take it slow."

Everyone piled back into their vehicles and the group started down the steep embankment towards the beached cruise ship. A ruined pier extended to their left, but with no water underneath. The pier looked like a stretch of giant sized train tracks on the ground. As they neared the ship, Alexandra noticed a few torches and small camp fires. A man waved his arms like he was signaling an airplane. He appeared to be American or maybe European.

"Thank God!" the man said.

Alexandra stepped from the cab and said, "I'm Alexandra Contreras. We were on Route 180 where we saw your sign."

The man wore an unusual assortment of clothes. A life jacket rested over his chest, but someone had sewn canvas sleeves to the arm holes and a makeshift canvas hood to the back. His dress pants appeared quite worn and dirty.

"You're the first people we've seen," he said. "My name is Jason – Jason Nelson."

"Pleased to meet you, Jason, my name is Richard Callahan," Father Callahan said as he stepped forward and shook the man's hand. "How are you guys doing out here?"

Jason glanced over his shoulder at the ship and said, "Not bad, considering we've been stranded here for over a month. Luckily, the ship was stocked with supplies and food."

"How many of you are there?" Marco asked.

Jason looked at the ground and said, "Only eight of us are left. We were stuck on shore when the quake hit. Everyone was... everyone was dead when we found the ship here."

"Mind if we share your campfire for the night?" Alexandra said.

"God, no!" Jason said. "Everyone will be thrilled."

The cruise ship towered over the group. Every window was dark, and much of the structure looked damaged. Alexandra felt uneasy standing so close to the massive structure, as it appeared ready to topple at any moment.

"Here's the rest of our little group," Jason said as he led Alexandra to a gathering of tents and campfires. "There's Justin, Nicole, and Henry. Thomas is the teen at the grill cooking steaks. Francine is bundled up on that chaise over there. It's been especially hard on her because of her age. Working the fire is Carlos, a local we met on shore. My wife, Holly, is in that large tent over there... but she's sleeping. That's everyone."

The group was mainly comprised of Americans. Francine was the only one above the age of fifty. Most of them wore the life jackets with canvas sleeves. Alexandra introduced her group and everyone exchanged pleasantries.

"Please, you must let us cook you some food," Jason said. "We have plenty and it's going to spoil soon."

"I'm not going to argue with that," Alexandra said.

Jason led them to some white lounge chairs and said, "Enjoy! I'll be back in a few minutes."

Alexandra sank into the plush cushion. "I could sleep here."

Thomas and Justin, the two teen-age American boys, brought a plate of steak to Alexandra. "Here you go," Justin said with a smile.

"Thank you," Alexandra said as she took the plate, removed a slab of meat, and then handed the plate to Father Callahan.

Thomas sat down next to Alexandra with his own plate of food. Tall and lanky, Thomas reminded Alexandra of the Goth kids who plagued the malls in San Antonio. His nose and ears were pierced and his hair was dyed black. Thomas said, "So, we were wondering, how old are you?"

Surprised by the question, Alexandra blinked and said, "Excuse me?"

Justin, the other boy, sat down on the other side of Alexandra. His bleached hair spiked in every direction and he was a tad heavier than most teenagers. Justin stared at Alexandra's chest and said, "Well, Tommy thought you looked kinda old. But, then I said 'yeah, but she's also hot'. So, how old are you?"

"Old?" Alexandra said. "You think I look old?"

"Old to teenage eyes, maybe…" Marco said as he sat across from Alexandra. "Not so old to wiser eyes."

"Is this your boyfriend?" Justin asked, pointing his fork at Marco.

Alexandra felt like she was in high school again.

"Are these two scabs bothering you?" the teen girl said as she approached.

"Nicole, right?" Alexandra said.

"That's me," Nicole said. "Why don't you two bug off. Alexandra is way outta your league."

"We were just talkin'." Thomas said as the two boys rose and scurried back to their own campfire.

"May I join you?" Nicole asked. Freckle-faced and bright-eyed, the girl bounced from place to place with a spring in her step. Alexandra thought Nicole was plain featured, but then chided herself for reverting back to her old self. Petty observations and criticisms should have been a thing of her past and Alexandra smiled to hide her quick moment of shame.

"Of course you may join us," Marco said before Alexandra could respond. "And where are you from, my dear?"

"Connecticut," the girl said.

"America, then?"

"Born and raised," Nicole said.

"So, what happened to you guys?" Alexandra asked.

Nicole lowered her eyes. "It was awful. Thomas, Justin, me, and some friends from our school were on a cruise. We went ashore to shop when the earthquake hit. People were running and screaming. When it stopped, I found Justin and Thomas and then we met up with Jason, his wife Holly, and Henry the doctor. We recognized them from the ship and we all made our way back here. Oh, and Carlos from the town followed us too because he had nowhere else to go!"

Marco shook his head. "That must have been awful for you, so young." Marco placed his hand on the girl's shoulder.

Alexandra's skin crawled at the sight of Marco's advances. Nicole was far too young and vulnerable.

Tears gathered under Nicole's eyes. "Yeah, I don't even know if I'll ever make it home to see my parents."

"Shhh…" Marco said as he gathered the girl in his arms.

Nicole allowed Marco to soothe her. Then, she wiped the tears from her freckles and smiled. "You are all so nice. I hope you stay."

"We're here to help," Marco said.

After Nicole finished her food, she smiled and said, "Well, I need to go check on Francine. I'm kinda taking care of her."

"Sure, my dear," Marco said. "Remember, anything you need."

"Thanks," Nicole said as she jogged away.

Alexandra glared at Marco and allowed a few moments to pass. Then she said, "Were you hitting on her?"

Marco feigned a wound to his chest. "Me? You are mistaken, mi amor." Marco rose to his feet. "My heart belongs to another." With a wink, Marco walked back to the rig to talk with Santino.

Alexandra wasn't comfortable with this much attention from that man. Sure, Marco was handsome enough, perhaps intelligent enough, but something about him unsettled her nerves. At first, she believed his invasion of privacy at the military base was the cause for her discomfort but she wasn't sure of that anymore. Something troubled her mind each time she saw or spoke with Marco.

"I see you've met some of the younger ones?" Father Callahan said, snapping Alexandra from her thoughts.

Alexandra turned and smiled. "Grab a seat," she said. "I'm Ms. Popularity today."

Father Callahan chuckled. "You seem to attract attention wherever you go."

"No sh… no kidding."

Father Callahan waved his hand and said, "No need to sanitize your language around me. I've heard it all."

"Father?" Alexandra said as she reclined in her new favorite chair.

"Please, Alexandra, call me Richard."

Alexandra paused for a few moments and stared at the apocalyptic sky. Then, she turned her head to Father Callahan and said, "My mother used to call me Lex. It was the nickname she called me when I was young. I guess it took too much effort to spout my entire name whenever I was naughty – which was often." Alexandra smiled. "I would very much like it if you called me Lex as well."

"Very well," Father Callahan said. "What can I do for you, Lex?"

"I was wondering why don't you lead us in prayer at mealtimes, and other times?"

Father Callahan laughed. "With this bunch?"

"No, I'm serious. I think I'd very much like that."

"I would be more than happy to lead everyone in prayer at mealtimes," Father Callahan said. "However, I guess I come from a different school of thought when it comes to prayer."

Alexandra raised an eyebrow. "What school is that?"

"I believe that prayer is mostly *listening* and very little talking."

"Listening, huh?'"

"Listening," Father Callahan said. "Throughout my life, I have watched and listened as other people prayed. Usually, they prayed for things for themselves or people they knew, like God was some sort of cosmic Santa Claus out to bring us all presents of joy, healing, or prosperity."

Alexandra smiled, though she knew the priest was not cracking jokes. "Cosmic Santa Claus? That's kinda funny."

"So many people lean on their religion as the final answer, the place they can get what they need when all else fails." Father Callahan paused. "And sometimes, when their religious answers appear within their grasp, they abandon all sense of reason and selfishly expect gifts from their Gods."

"How do you mean?"

"Have you ever seen *Jesus Christ Superstar* on LightDisc?"

Alexandra shook her head. "Never heard of it."

"It was a mid-20th century musical. My father took me to see it when I was a boy. The man who wrote the dialogue wrote an amazing line for Jesus Christ in the play. You see, while Jesus was healing the sick and crippled in Galilee, the crowd grew massive and demanding. Everyone wanted to be healed. Everyone *expected* to be healed. In the play, Jesus bursts from the throng of people and screams 'Heal yourselves!'"

Alexandra wrinkled her nose and said, "That doesn't sound like something Jesus would say."

Father Callahan shrugged and said, "Who knows what kind of toll all of that took on Jesus or what it will take on you." He touched Alexandra's arm. "If things become too overwhelming, I'm here."

Alexandra's lower lip trembled. "I'm afraid," she said. "I'm afraid of the future. I don't know how to handle all of this."

"You don't need to handle it all alone," Father Callahan said, "We're all here to help."

Alexandra nodded. "I know… I know."

Koneh approached from the beached cruise ship and stopped in front of Alexandra and Father Callahan. "Ready?" he asked.

"For?" Father Callahan said.

"She knows," Koneh said.

"Time for my training," Alexandra said as she rose to her feet.

Father Callahan reclined in his chaise and smiled. "Take it easy on him, Lex."

Alexandra laughed. "I'll try."

After another exhausting training session with Koneh, Alexandra approached the cruise ship and washed her face from a communal bucket of soapy water. She longed for the indoor plumbing of her apartment.

"Alexandra?"

Wiping her face, Alexandra saw Jason approach.

"Alexandra," he said, "I want you to meet my wife. She's awake now."

"Sure."

Alexandra followed Jason into a large tent. Along the walls, clothes filled drawers laid piled on top of each other. Several plastic bins were stacked near the far wall, filled with rope, tools, diapers, and canned food. Holly rested on the air mattress bed in the far corner. She was pregnant.

"You must be Alexandra," Holly said as she clutched her stomach and rolled into a sitting position. The woman's thin blonde hair stuck to the sides of her face and neck. She wore a large patterned sun dress and sandals. Her belly appeared ready to burst.

"Likewise," Alexandra said, "Wow, you're very pregnant."

Holly smiled and said, "Yeah... any day now."

"We were lucky," Jason said, "Well, lucky considering the circumstances, I guess. Henry, the man you met earlier, is a doctor. So Holly's been pretty well taken care of."

Alexandra recalled the doctor. Mid forties, short and squinty-eyed. "A doctor. That's fortunate," Alexandra said.

"Please," Holly said, "grab a folding chair. Where are you guys from? What have you seen? Is the rest of the world like this?"

Alexandra unfolded a chair and said, "Well, most of us were in Mexico when the quake hit and we've seen some pretty strange things on our trip."

"Trip?" Jason asked, "Where y'all headed?"

"Brasilia," Alexandra said. "We're trying to get Santino back to his home to see his daughter."

Jason whistled. "Brasilia? That's pretty far."

"You know," Alexandra said, "there's a United States Army base to the north, near Veracruz. We could take you there, if you want."

"There's people there?" Holly asked.

Alexandra nodded. "A whole base full of U.S. Army boys and their families."

"That sounds perfect!" Jason said. "And you would take us there?"

"Of course," Alexandra said, dreading the conversation with Koneh she now brought upon herself.

"Well," Jason said, "I'll tell everyone. Of course, we can't leave until Holly gives birth. But that should be any day now. Man, we got a lot of work to do. I gotta... I gotta get everyone together!"

Holly leaned towards Alexandra and said, "Don't mind my husband, he gets a bit scatterbrained sometimes."

Alexandra smiled. "Jason," she said, "go find the priest, Father Callahan. He can help you get everything ready to go."

"Okay," Jason said as he looked at his wife. "You all right for a bit?"

"Yup!" Holly watched her husband exit the tent. "So, where are you from?"

"San Antonio," Alexandra said. "Well, I was born in Mexico but I live in Texas."

"We're from Woodland, just outside of Boston."

Alexandra nodded. "I know the area."

"We booked this cruise a year in advance. I didn't plan on being pregnant."

"Sometimes, things don't turn out the way we plan," Alexandra said.

After exchanging more pleasantries, Alexandra yawned. The long days in the wasteland were taking their toll.

"You look beat," Holly said. "Why don't you go get some rest?"

Alexandra stretched her arms. "Yeah, that's a good idea. Nice to meet you, Holly."

"You too."

Alexandra stumbled from the tent and dropped to the ground near the fire. Her bones and muscles ached from her training session.

"We need to talk."

"I'm sleeping," Alexandra said without opening her eyes.

"You promised these people we'd take them back to the base?" Koneh said. "On foot, that'd be a week or more in the opposite direction."

"Tomorrow," Alexandra said, though she wasn't sure her words were coherent. "I'll argue with you tomorrow."

The aroma of cooked bacon awoke Alexandra from her slumber. Every muscle cried in protest as Alexandra rose and walked to a makeshift table where Father Callahan served breakfast.

"She lives!" Marco said as he extended his arms and mimicked a zombie.

"Pretty much everyone else has eaten," Father Callahan said, "but, I saved some for you."

"Thanks," Alexandra said as she sat on a folding chair and tasted the bacon. "You're Henry, right?"

The other man at the table nodded.

Henry appeared to be in his early forties. His hairline was receding, but he seemed to be in good shape.

"A doctor?" Alexandra asked, still not fully awake.

"General surgeon," Henry said. "Your crew seems to be in good health. Do you want me to take a look at that bruise?" The doctor pointed at Alexandra's chin.

"Nah. Doesn't even hurt anymore."

"Suit yourself," Henry said as he rose and left the table.

"Not much of a talker," Alexandra said as she forked some scrambled eggs into her mouth.

Father Callahan smiled. "Not everyone is. Are you all set?"

Alexandra nodded.

"Okay, I gotta go check on some supplies. I think you're making the right decision, by the way."

"Huh?"

"Bringing the people back to the base," Father Callahan said.

"Yeah, well, we can't just leave them here."

Father Callahan nodded and walked to Santino's truck.

After she devoured her breakfast, Alexandra noticed Father Callahan and Marco talking near the rig. They seemed animated. Alexandra approached the two men and Marco turned in her direction.

"We're going back to the base?" Marco asked.

"What did you expect me to say? They'll be safe there," Alexandra said.

"You know," Father Callahan said, "If we turn our back on our fellow man, how much better are we than the demons we have met?"

"Then tell them where the base is and we keep moving, no?" Marco said. "We don't need to babysit them."

Alexandra sighed. "Do you really think they'd survive the trip without us?"

"They done just fine so far…" Marco said.

Alexandra frowned and couldn't understand why anyone would question her on this, though she knew Koneh was next. Wasn't this the right thing to do?

To clear her head, Alexandra stalked off, away from the encampment. Not watching where she was going, Alexandra almost bumped into Carlos.

"Sorry," Alexandra said.

"No problemo," Carlos said as he shifted the weight of the branches and brush in his arms.

"Gathering some firewood?" Alexandra asked. Before the words were gone from her mouth, Alexandra chided herself for asking the obvious.

"Si…"

Carlos never finished his sentence. A large creature burst from the underbrush and attached itself to the man's jugular. Blood sprayed into the air. Alexandra recognized the attacker. A hound!

Alexandra froze as she watched the animal tear Carlos's neck apart. Her knees lost their strength and she almost toppled to the ground. That's when she noticed two more hounds crouched and ready to pounce.

The first hound leapt but was plucked out of the air. With a surprised *yelp*, it landed ten feet away and crashed into a rock. Not wasting any time, the second hound snarled and advanced on Alexandra.

Erzulie landed in front of Alexandra and said, "Get back to the ship and tell Koneh we have trouble."

"Will you be…"

"Go!" Erzulie yelled as she charged the hound.

This time, Alexandra's legs responded and she sprinted towards the beached cruise ship. However, she knew she wasn't alone. The hound that killed Carlos was close behind her.

"Help!" Alexandra screamed.

Alexandra thought she could feel the beast's sulfurous breath on her back. She cried for help again.

Bang!

A single gunshot rang out across the scrub and Alexandra dove to the ground. The first shot was followed by a short series of gunshots and then the area was silent. Risking a glance, Alexandra removed her arms from her head. Marco was the closest to her, his gun raised. Off to the side, Benjamin kneeled and prepared another shot with his assault rifle.

"I think we got it," Marco said as he lowered his pistol and approached Alexandra.

Koneh and Father Callahan ran to the scene. Alexandra glanced over her shoulder and saw the motionless form of a large canine. The creature's dark fur glistened from numerous wounds.

"Erzulie!" Alexandra said as she jumped to her feet.

"Where is she?" Koneh asked.

Alexandra pointed. "Over there! Another hound!"

"Stay put," Koneh said. "Marco, Benjamin – watch Alexandra!" Koneh dashed towards Erzulie's last known location.

"Are you okay?" Father Callahan asked.

"Yeah," Alexandra said. "Let's go."

"Didn't Koneh say to…"

"I don't care!"

"Then we're going with you," Benjamin said as he removed a pistol from a hip holster and held it out for Alexandra. "Here."

Alexandra reached for her own belt, but Erzulie's sword was back in the camp. "Dammit," she muttered. Alexandra logged a mental note to never again be caught without a weapon at her side. She grasped the pistol and strained to recall her one trip to the indoor range.

Alexandra, Father Callahan, Benjamin, and Marco reached the bloody scene. Koneh and Erzulie stood over the bodies of two hounds and a very dead Carlos.

"Damn," Alexandra said. "How did they sneak up on us like that?"

"Many apologies," Erzulie said. "I wasn't fast enough to save this human."

"No," Alexandra said, "I don't blame you." For the first time, Alexandra noticed Erzulie's fingernails. They were an inch longer than the press-on nails Alexandra sometimes wore and blood dripped from their ends. Alexandra guessed they were also a bit sharper than her press-ons.

"We don't have much time to waste," Koneh said.

Alexandra crouched to catch her breath and said, "Why?"

Erzulie stepped forward and said, "A demon army approaches from the northwest."

"How many?" Benjamin asked.

"Standard host, ninety-nine strong," Erzulie said.

"Derechi?" Marco asked.

Erzulie narrowed her eyes and said, "I don't think so. However, I didn't risk a closer inspection."

"How certain are you that they are not from Derechi?" Marco said.

Erzulie said, "I'm not certain. But I didn't see any Reavers. Derechi's war-hosts usually travel with one or more."

Before Alexandra could ask what a Reaver was, Father Callahan said, "How far?"

"No more than a day," Erzulie said.

Quickly thinking the situation over, Alexandra said, "Can we outrun them?"

Koneh said, "Only if we leave now and abandon these people. They have no transportation and the last operable vehicle we saw was a few days back towards Route 180."

Alexandra turned to Koneh and said, "That's not acceptable."

"How do you intend to fight ninety-nine demons and…"

Erzulie interrupted. "Ninety-six, now."

Koneh drew a labored breath and said, "…ninety-six demons. Do you intend to talk them to death?"

Alexandra reevaluated the situation in her mind. They could leave in Santino's rig and maybe bring along a few others with them. Who stays behind? How could she make that kind of decision? Alexandra never thought she'd be in this kind of situation, one where she could be deciding her own fate and the fate of others. To her surprise, Alexandra found she cared more about these strangers than herself. They deserved a chance. Holly's unborn baby deserved a chance.

"I'm staying," Alexandra said. "I'm not going to force anyone to stay with me. Go if you want, but I'm not leaving these people to die."

Alexandra turned around and took a step towards the cruise ship.

"Wait," Koneh said as he grasped her arm. His voice was soft, barely a whisper. "Wait."

"What?"

Koneh held her arm and said, "You realize what you are doing? If we leave, everyone behind will likely perish. If we stay, then you are putting the entire group in danger. I cannot protect everyone."

"Everyone is free to make their own decisions," Alexandra said. "I'm not ordering anyone to stay."

"We're not going to just leave you behind," Father Callahan said.

"Then, that is your decision, Richard," Alexandra said.

Koneh looked into Alexandra's eyes and said, "People are going to die."

Alexandra had her flawed response ready. "But not through any action or inaction of mine."

CHAPTER 19

"That looks good!" Alexandra yelled. "Stop there."

The hydraulics on Santino's rig hissed and the vehicle rumbled once more before falling silent. Father Callahan, Marco, Koneh, Benjamin, and a few of the survivors constructed a makeshift barricade with sheets of metal and wood. Santino's rig formed the remainder of the "wall" that extended from the base of the beached cruise ship and around Jason and Holly's tent.

The cruise ship survivors didn't take the news of Carlos's death very well. Most of them now huddled inside Jason's tent with Holly. Alexandra, however, reasoned they were more afraid of the demon army that now approached.

"It's time," Alexandra said as she turned to her guide in all of this, Koneh.

Koneh let loose a low whistle. Moments later, Erzulie dropped from the sky and scanned the panicked faces of the cruise ship survivors as they peered out from the tent.

Addressing the group, Alexandra said, "Erzulie is an angel and friend. If it comes down to it, don't mistake her for the enemy."

"An angel?" Nicole asked.

"Yes, and as I said before, my friend."

Alexandra expected some jeers from Thomas and Justin, but the two teenagers instead resumed their work on the barricade. Perhaps they sobered to their new reality, like Alexandra was forced to do after the toothless man and his gang chased her down the street.

Turning away from the group, Alexandra leaned close to Erzulie. "How close now?"

Erzulie's melodious voice responded, "Not long now, Lex. The hounds and belchers will reach us within the hour."

"Belchers?"

"You need some help?" Koneh said as he broke away from Alexandra and approached Father Callahan. The priest, Thomas and Justin attempted to lash pieces of metal and wood together to reinforce the wall.

"Are you prepared for what will happen next?" Erzulie said.

Alexandra shook her head. "I haven't been ready for any of this."

Erzulie smiled and said, "You sound just like him."

"Who?"

"Yeshua."

"You mean, Jesus?" Alexandra said. "You met him?"

Erzulie nodded. "Yes, before I was cast down, Elah sent me to his only son to help Yeshua in his time of need."

"So, Elah does stuff like that? Sends his angels to aid those in need?"

"Well," Erzulie said, "not very often, no. Only when something is very important to Elah."

"I see…"

A violent banging interrupted Alexandra's conversation.

Bang… Bang… Bang…

Curious, Alexandra approached the barricade. Everyone watched as Koneh drove nails into the steel with one stroke each.

Bang… Bang… Bang…

"There," Koneh said as he handed the hammer to Benjamin. "You should be able to handle the rest of the wall, it is wood."

"Where'd you learn to do that?" Alexandra said.

Koneh shrugged, "I knew a great blacksmith who was way ahead of his time." Koneh turned to the angel. "Erzulie?"

"Yes, sahil?"

"Get up there and find those flyers. They have to be out there somewhere."

Without a word, Erzulie shot into the black-red sky. That simple act still amazed Alexandra.

"Flyers?" Alexandra said.

Koneh nodded. "We know they're out there, we just don't know *where*."

"I have a theory," Alexandra said, not sure why she decided to talk to Koneh about the subject at this moment.

"About?"

"Erzulie," Alexandra said, "Well, all angels for that matter."

"Talk and walk," Koneh said as he moved away from the barricade and into the wasteland.

"You see, I think angels do have emotions. I mean, the human brain is essentially a biological computer, right?"

Koneh huffed. "I see where you are going with this and you are wrong."

"Just hear me out," Alexandra said.

Koneh shrugged and pulled a long knife from beneath his robes. He planted the weapon tip down into the ground and kept walking.

Alexandra said, "You see, we're programmed as well. Perhaps Erzulie's programming is more limited than ours, but it's all the same. I mean, you've talked with her, you see how well she imitates emotions. Perhaps she is beyond imitation now?"

After about fifteen feet, Koneh drew another bladed weapon and repeated the planting process. He turned to Alexandra and said, "The difference is simple. As humans, we rely on our emotions to override our programming. Look to yourself for evidence. You stay to protect these people because of your guilt over Tampico."

"It's more than that," Alexandra said.

"I know, but you realize yourself that this is an illogical decision. Our chance of victory is slim, but your compassion for these people has overridden any sense you might have to flee and save the biological computer inside your skull."

Koneh paused for a moment and then continued. "You see," he said, "Erzulie is incapable of that. Though she seems loyal and friendly to you now, if she was ordered to kill you, she would do so without hesitation. She is programmed to obey Elah's command. She has no emotional strength to resist such a command. Her emotions are merely imitation."

Alexandra processed the information. "So," she said, "one day Erzulie could be my enemy?"

"Possibly," Koneh said as he continued his semicircle around the barricade. "Time will tell whose command she finds strongest – her master's in Jahannam, man's divine law on Earth, or yours."

Koneh drew yet another blade and stuck it in the ground.

"Okay," Alexandra said, "what the hell are you doing?"

"Your responsibility is to kill any demons that make it past me. Make sure Marco and Benjamin keep their lines of fire away from me."

Alexandra noticed Koneh's semicircle of knives and other bladed weapons was about twenty feet away from the barricade.

"You're going to be out here?" Alexandra asked, confused.

Koneh nodded.

"Who are you?" Alexandra said as she searched her companion's black-in-black eyes for any clue to his thoughts. "I mean, we're probably going to die here, so you may as well spill all the secrets you've been hiding from me."

Koenh looked into her eyes and said, "If I had my way of things, I would keep no secrets from you. Not ever you."

Once again, she felt a connection with this mysterious man. When they were alone, the world faded into the background, and Alexandra was acutely aware of the beating of her heart.

She stepped next to him, paused, and then embraced him. His hands reached around her back and she closed her eyes. She felt *right* in his arms.

"I… I have things I want to say to you," she said, "but, I'm not sure how to do it."

Koneh tightened his grip and said, "Forgive me this one moment of peace… I do not have the strength to let you go."

Alexandra whispered, "Then don't."

The wind passed over them for the next few moments. Alexandra's heart sighed in relief. She was finally close to Koneh. His mysteries were unraveling and she felt drawn to the man underneath the secrets.

Then he pushed her away and said, "You should return to the group." He averted her gaze.

"We're not going to make it, are we?" she said.

"I don't intend to die here. I will keep you safe."

Alexandra raised one of her eyebrows and said, "How can you know that?"

"I suppose I don't," Koneh said. "However, confidence is half of victory. I forget who told me that, but it seems fitting."

Though it went against her better judgment, Alexandra saw hope in Koneh's words. As she walked back to Santino's rig and behind the barricade, she allowed the hope to grow a little. Maybe they'd make it out of this after all, she thought.

Everyone else was inside the barricade. Thomas and Justin smiled when they saw Alexandra.

"Whoa!" Justin said as he pointed at Alexandra's midsection, "Where'd you get a sword?"

Relieved the boy wasn't pointing at her crotch, Alexandra said, "An angel gave it to me."

"You mean that hot chick with wings?" Thomas said as he leaned against the barricade in his best GQ pose. The boy turned a pistol over in his hand. "I got one of my own."

"Who gave you that?" Alexandra asked.

"Soldier boy," Thomas said, "since I'm the only one who knows how to use it."

"I know how to shoot a gun," Justin said, defending his manhood in front of Alexandra.

Thomas chuckled. "Yeah, but you won't hit anything with it."

"Fuck you, loser."

"Are these two bothering you again?" Nicole emerged from the tent and stood beside Alexandra. "Because I can have Marco beat them up for you."

"You've been talking with Marco, have you?" Alexandra said. "And where is our Latin loverboy?"

Nicole blushed and pointed to the tent. "He's inside with Father Callahan, Benjamin, and the others. They're talking about the barricade and stuff."

"Good," Alexandra said as she took a step towards the tent. "Keep an eye on these two, okay?"

"That would mean I'd have to look at them, blech!"

Alexandra smiled and paused before she entered. Francine, the older woman, rested on a chaise next to the tent. As if still on vacation, Francine took a sip from her sports bottle and reclined. Intrigued, Alexandra changed direction and knelt next to Francine.

"Hello my dear," Francine said as she lifted her sunglasses. Her flowered dress contrasted against their surroundings like a neon sign on the face of a burned down building. Deep lines pooled around Francine's mouth, eyes, forehead, and neck. From her wrinkled mouth, her southern accent weighed thick in her speech. "We haven't had a chance to speak too much. I am Francine Burns-Holyst, from Georgia."

"Sorry, I've been... busy."

Francine waved her hand and said, "Nonsense, my dear. You seem like an important young lady."

Unsure what Francine knew, Alexandra said, "How do you mean?"

"Well, your friends inside the tent talk like you ah the one giving orders 'round here," Francine said. "That, and you have an air about you. I can sense when someone is important."

"I'm nobody important," Alexandra said. "I'm just a girl in the world."

Francine chuckled and almost spit her drink as she burst into full laughter. After a few moments, Alexandra said, "Did I say something funny?"

Francine shook her head and said, "Please forgive my lack of manners. You just reminded me of a song from my youth. Of course, you've probably never heard that song… you kids and your fractal rhythms."

"I hate that fractal stuff," Alexandra said. "It gives me a headache."

Still chuckling, Francine said, "Me too, my dear, me too."

Alexandra dove into chaos as she entered the tent. Marco and Father Callahan were arguing over something. Jason kneeled next to his wife, Holly, who was struggling through her breathing as she looked ready to give birth.

Alexandra rushed to the pregnant woman's side and asked, "Is the baby coming?"

Henry, who was on the other side of the cot, removed his hand from Holly's belly and said, "She's still a ways off, several hours at least."

Holly closed her eyes and cried.

"It's okay, dear. You're doing great," Jason said as he patted his wife's hand.

Through tears, Holly said, "No, it's not okay. Our baby doesn't even have a chance. Look at the world we are bringing her into! Look at it, Jason!"

Alexandra knelt next to Holly and put her hand on the pregnant woman's forehead. "There is hope," Alexandra said. "You have an angel protecting you."

Holly opened her eyes. "An angel?"

Nodding, Alexandra said, "And an American soldier, a priest, myself, and many others. I swear to you, your baby will make it into this world."

Holly's sobs subsided and she closed her eyes.

"Let her rest in-between contractions," Henry, said. "She'll need her strength."

"Won't we all," Alexandra said under her breath as she rose.

"Thanks," Jason said as he walked with Alexandra towards Father Callahan. "You're the only one who has been able to calm her down."

"I can't even imagine what she is going through," Alexandra said. As she approached her friends, Alexandra caught the tail end of the argument between Father Callahan and Marco.

"You're not going out there and that's final," Father Callahan said.

Marco smiled and said, "Well Padre, you're not in charge." Marco turned to Alexandra. "I think I should hop on my bike and check things out. I don't mind the risk."

Alexandra dismissed Marco with a wave of her hand and said, "Erzulie's already scouting the area. She's much faster than you on your bike. Go check on Benjamin outside. He might need some help."

Marco mumbled something inaudible under his breath and stalked away.

"I hope it's okay," Father Callahan said. "Everyone is looking to me for direction when you're not around."

"Believe me," Alexandra said, "I never wanted to be in charge. You're probably the biggest expert on Hell we have, so…"

"Well," Father Callahan said, "I can only imagine Erzulie would be our resident expert now. Or Koneh."

"Oh yeah. That makes sense."

"How are you holding up?" Father Callahan said.

Alexandra shrugged. She felt queasy and weak from holding back her tears. However, her lip trembled as she said, "Pretty scared."

"Shall we talk outside?" Father Callahan said as he gestured to the tent entrance.

"Excuse us, please?" Alexandra said to Jason.

"Sure, I should get back to Holly anyway."

Alexandra pulled her leather jacket tight around her body as she emerged into the cold, black world. The sky yielded little light or warmth. At the edge of her range of vision, Alexandra spotted Koneh. He sat twenty feet away from the barricade, with his back to her. Alexandra's heart shriveled when she thought about the danger he faced. Could he survive? Would she get the chance to express her uncertain feelings?

"Listen," Father Callahan said once they were alone, "I have faith that you are who Koneh believes you to be."

Alexandra raised her hands to stop him, but Father Callahan said, "Let me finish."

"Okay, Richard."

Father Callahan cleared his throat, wiped his hand across his bald scalp, and said, "With that faith comes a truckload of guilt. I don't know what I'm supposed to be doing. It was no accident that we met. God had a plan for it all. I feel I was supposed to lead you in a certain direction and now we are on the verge of destruction. I guess I'm asking for forgiveness. I feel I have failed you."

"I… I don't know what to say. I mean, you know where I stand on the whole *Child of Elah* thing."

Father Callahan nodded.

"However," Alexandra continued, "the more I open my eyes, the more I believe *something* is going on. Koneh, crazy or not, found me right away, which tells me he was waiting for this. We then met you, and you have that altered Bible, which I'm sure tells us something we need to know. I dunno. Maybe some of this was set in motion by the powers that be or, rather, the powers that *were*."

Henry, the doctor, brushed past Alexandra as he left the tent and mumbled something about a cigarette.

After the doctor was out of sight, Father Callahan said, "So you see, I was meant to guide you in a certain direction, and I have failed. I'm sorry, my dear."

"Bah," Alexandra said, "Maybe you were just put in my path to keep me sane. Lord knows how I'd be if I only had Koneh and Marco to talk to."

As if on cue, Marco's bike rumbled to life outside the wall.

"What?" Father Callahan said, "Marco's leaving!"

Alexandra and Father Callahan climbed through Santino's rig and watched as the bike and its rider disappeared into the darkness.

"That bastard! He's running," Alexandra said as Koneh joined them.

"I don't think that was Marco," Koneh said.

"What do you…" Alexandra's question died in her throat as Marco appeared from the barricade. He fumed.

"Who the hell stole my bike?" Marco said.

"The doctor, Henry," Alexandra said as she recalled the look in Henry's eyes when he passed Alexandra moments ago. The man was terrified.

"Dammit!" Marco said as he threw a balled rag to the ground.

"What do you want to do?" Koneh said, "We could send Erzulie after him."

"No," Alexandra said, "we need everyone here."

"I'll go after him," Marco said as he removed his pistol from his holster and checked the magazine. "There wasn't too much left in the tank. He won't get too far."

"We need you here," Alexandra said. "Revenge will have to wait."

After looking in the direction of his stolen bike, Marco returned the pistol to his holster and said, "Si, I will, of course, stay at your side."

"Where's the doctor?" Benjamin said as he joined the group outside the barricade. "Holly's having another contraction."

Marco said, "The good doctor abandoned us."

"No…" Benjamin said.

Alexandra opened her mouth to reassure everyone, but she never got the chance. She heard the flapping of wings. An instant later, Erzulie dropped to the ground and to her knee. Silvery liquid ran down her left shoulder.

"They're here," Erzulie said. "I took out their flyers, but the hounds and belchers are upon us."

"Everyone, back to the barricade!" Alexandra yelled.

"How large is the advance force?" Koneh said as he grasped Erzulie's arm and inspected the wounds.

No pain registered on Erzulie's face or in her all white eyes. "A full thirty-three," Erzulie said.

"Thank you, sahil," Koneh said, "Stay above the tents and help them out."

Erzulie nodded.

"And stay safe, "Alexandra said

As Erzulie lifted herself into the sky, Alexandra turned to Koneh and said, "That goes for you as well…"

Koneh settled his gaze upon Alexandra, but he didn't speak. He looked into her eyes for a few moments and Alexandra thought she saw tenderness there. He then strode out into the wasteland towards his ring of planted knives.

CHAPTER 20

Alexandra wondered no more what a "belcher" was. As the first wave of demons crashed against the makeshift barricade, she knew. A demon, as tall as a large dog, hopped over the wall and snarled at her. Just in time, she turned away as the creature launched a ball of flame from its mouth like a grill lit after too much gas escaped from the tank.

Flames roared over Alexandra's back, scorching her hair. However, her leather jacket absorbed the brunt of the attack and left her mostly unharmed. Surprised, the creature paused long enough for Justin to crush it with a metal pipe. The demon cracked like a dozen eggs hitting the floor.

Risking a glance to the outside of the barricade, Alexandra spotted Koneh. The mysterious warrior moved in his semicircle, cutting down hounds and belchers as they approached. Bursts of flame lit the landscape, but Koneh seemed impervious to their attacks.

Rat-tat-tat-a-tat-tat!

Benjamin's assault rifle turned a nearby hound into giblets. Thomas and Justin hooted at the sight. Was this just a video game to the teenage boys from America? Did they not realize the danger they were in?

Alexandra didn't have much time for thought, as she turned to face a snarling hound. The sword she held now felt heavy, as did her knees. Alexandra never wanted to hurt anyone or any*thing*. What if this creature was just tortured into its current existence? What if it had no choice? Yet, here she was, ready to strike it down.

"Move!"

The command came from behind her. It was Marco. Stepping to the side, Alexandra flinched as the hound leapt.

Pop-pop-pop!

Marco's pistol rung in her ears as the creature recoiled from each shot. However, it still advanced.

Pop-Pop!

Two more shots from Marco's pistol sent the creature to the ground for an instant. Then, it growled and charged him.

Click.

"I'm out!" Marco said as he stepped backwards.

Recalling her training, Alexandra slashed with Erzulie's sword. The stroke cut through muscle and bone on the hound's flank and it yelped as it tumbled into the barricade. Panting, the creature lay at the base of the wall and closed its eyes.

Alexandra's hands shook and her legs trembled. The stink of her burned hair filled the area, but she found it bearable. She never thought she could bring herself to kill another living creature. Where was the feeling of revulsion she expected? Why did a part of her feel so comfortable with Erzulie's sword in her hand?

"They're pulling back!" Thomas said as he waved his pistol in the air.

Indeed, the remaining belchers and hounds leapt over the barricade and gave Koneh a wide berth as they retreated into the darkness.

"Look out!" Thomas said as he turned and pointed his gun to the sky.

"Wait!" Alexandra said, but too late.

The boy fired a single shot at Erzulie, but missed.

"Stop!" Alexandra said. "She's on our side, remember?"

Erzulie descended to the ground and gathered her dark wings against her back. The angel's metallic breastplate was covered in new scratches and dents. Small cuts crisscrossed her skin and silvery angel blood congealed around the wounds.

"The main force approaches," Erzulie said with her usual melodious tones. "Have your men with guns focus on the larger demons as they won't go down easy."

Alexandra nodded and said, "Are you okay?"

"Don't be concerned for me," Erzulie said. "I've been in many battles."

"Oh no!"

The cry came from Nicole.

"No, no no…"

The girl kneeled next to the still form of Francine. Lying on her chaise, the older woman looked peaceful. Her sunglasses on, the only evidence of her passing was a dark spot in the middle of her flowered dress. Somehow, Alexandra missed what happened.

"Is she dead?" Alexandra asked, surprised at her coarseness.

Nicole nodded and turned a tearful face to Alexandra. The girl seemed incapable of speech.

"I see them!" Benjamin said from his position atop Santino's rig.

"Get inside," Alexandra said, pointing to Nicole. "Benjamin, Marco – focus your fire on the larger ones!"

The soldier nodded and peered down the barrel of his weapon. Marco rammed another clip into his pistol and looked over the wall.

"More?" Father Callahan said from the entrance to Holly's tent.

Alexandra nodded and said, "How are things going in there? Everyone okay?"

Father Callahan lowered his eyes and said, "A hound got into the tent. Jason's badly wounded and Holly's not doing so well."

"Keep them together," Alexandra said, "We're not out of this yet."

"By your leave," Erzulie said, "I will continue to protect the flanks from being overrun. I will also keep an eye on the tents."

"Thanks, Erzulie," Alexandra said as she joined Marco at the wall.

Like a full marching band running for cover under the rain, a mob of figures careened towards the barricade. Unfazed, Koneh stood at the apex of his semicircle. How was he going to survive? Would she get the chance to tell him that her feelings were stronger than she first thought? That she maybe loved him?

Now was not the time for such thoughts as more pressing matters knocked on her door. She performed some quick math in her head. If they started with ninety-nine, and maybe fifteen were killed, that left over eighty demons. All eighty at once, they would crash against the makeshift barricade like a wave against a sandcastle.

Rat-tat-tat-a-tat-tat!

Benjamin's assault rifle sung its tune. As the army closed, Koneh lifted a knife from the ground and hurled it at the nearest belcher. The creature breathed a final puff of fire before being trampled by the larger demons.

Alexandra lost sight of Koneh as the demons rushed past him and rammed the barricade. Marco and Thomas joined Benjamin. The roar of gunfire was almost louder than the thunder cloven feet.

Most of the demons were the size of a human male with exaggerated spines, claws, and two ram-like horns on their heads. Alexandra's heart sank when she noticed that some of the newcomers were much larger. These demons stood about ten feet tall and wielded large swords, axes, or spiked chains. These giant demons destroyed sections of the barricade with each stroke of their weapons. However, Benjamin and Marco kept them harassed with constant gunfire.

"One down!" Benjamin said as one of the larger demons toppled through a hole in the barricade, its bones exposed from numerous wounds.

As the smaller demons and belchers used the fallen demon as a doormat, one of the larger ones pointed his sword at Benjamin and said, "Flan-nese!"

A small group of belchers hopped onto Santino's rig and Benajmin's gunfire stopped as the area was covered in flames.

Alexandra was forced to return her attention to the barricade. Erzulie swooped in and engaged the large demon. Marco and Alexandra backpedaled as the horned demons approached.

"Any ideas?" Marco said as he reloaded his pistol.

Too frightened to speak, Alexandra readied her sword. Demons rushed them.

Pop-pop-pop!

Marco fired a series of expertly placed shots and several of the demons tumbled to the ground. As the others advanced, Alexandra recalled Koneh's training session about *reach*. Since her sword covered a better distance than the horned demons claws, Alexandra kept them at bay for as long as she could. She scored some superficial wounds, but she knew she would have to leave herself open to engage.

Several of the horned demons turned away from Marco and Alexandra, as Thomas and Justin got their attention. Through the corner of her eye, Alexandra saw the section of wall behind the two

American boys shatter, and a large demon with a chain roared. She lost sight of the boys as the horned demons pressed forward.

Rat-tat-tat-a-tat-tat!

The rest of the approaching horned demons scattered as bullets rained down from above. Alexandra peeked at the rig and saw Erzulie jump from the top of the vehicle. Benjamin resumed his attack.

"That'll help," Marco said as he overturned a table and took cover.

Alexandra turned to see one of the boys – she wasn't sure which one – flung over the wall by the large demon with a spiked chain. The other boy was nowhere to be seen. Mustering all her strength, Alexandra subdued the urge to vomit.

As Koneh predicted, people were dying. For the first time in her life, Alexandra believed she was going to die. Even worse, the death would probably be unpleasant.

The demon that breached the wall smiled and pointed a clawed finger in Alexandra's direction. More horned demons poured through the openings in the barricade and rushed in her direction.

Pop-pop-pop!

Marco fired from his new position and Benjamin downed the large demon with concentrated fire. Some of the horned demons ripped at the tents and entered.

"Dammit!" Alexandra said, "They're in the tents!"

Moving along the base of the beached cruise ship, Alexandra approached the tents. One of the smaller horned demons charged her and seemed unphased by several gunshot wounds. Alexandra readied her sword and watched the creature's claws. After several moments of positioning and feints, the demon lashed out with its tail and opened a stinging cut on Alexandra's cheek.

With a squeal, the creature lunged at Alexandra and she raised the tip of her sword enough to impale her attacker. Blood spattered Alexandra's face and arms. Gurgling, the demon fell to the ground.

Stepping over the corpse, Alexandra dashed through the ripped side of Holly's tent and this time, she vomited.

Fire from a burning corpse illuminated the interior of both tents. Blood and someone's body parts were everywhere. Father Callahan stood in front of Holly's bed, his cross outstretched and his arms bloodied. Crimson stains on the canvas walls gave the interior the look of old floral wallpaper.

"Stay back, creatures of Hell!" Father Callahan said.

A pair of horned demons advanced on Father Callahan and Holly. Then, one of the demons turned and approached Alexandra.

At that moment, Alexandra found a new resolve within herself. She couldn't let her friends die. She had to be strong for them. Armed with a new strength of will, she closed the distance with the demon. However, as she stared into the grisly face of her enemy, her resolve faded away just as quickly as it had arrived. All of Koneh's training drained from her mind like water through a strainer. Fear gripped Alexandra as she wondered how she got to this place. Two months ago she owned an upscale apartment, played racquetball, and dined at expensive restaurants. Now, she was bloodied and carrying an angel's sword. She witnessed the slaughter of her new friends. Blood dripped from the canvas of the tent and from her gashed cheek. What was she doing?

A howl pierced the tent and the two horned demons scurried from the area.

"Are you all right?" Father Callahan said, his hands trembling.

"How long can you keep them at bay?" Alexandra asked.

Father Callahan shook his head. "Unfortunately, not very long. Not long enough."

"Well," Alexandra said, "it's something. Get outside and help Marco and Benjamin. You may be able to give them the few moments they need to keep the tent clear."

Father Callahan nodded, wrapped his rosary around his forearm and rushed from the tent. More gunfire, shouts, and roars echoed off the hull of the beached cruise ship and into the tent. Exhausted, Alexandra turned to the cot.

Though pregnant, Holly pulled her knees to her stomach and buried her face in her arms. She appeared in shock, as she drew one sharp breath after another. The cot sagged from the combined weight of its occupant, blood, and water. The stink of sweat, vomit, and burnt flesh greeted Alexandra's nostrils as she stepped around the carnage on the floor of the tent.

"Holly?" Alexandra said, wondering why she felt the need to whisper.

There was no response. Holly's body shuddered with each intake of breath. Then, Alexandra saw what may have thrown the woman into shock – Jason's crumpled form. The American's mangled life jacket still clung to his body, like the chewed wrapper on a candy bar. His limbs were no longer attached. Something tore the man to pieces.

Outside the tent, Benjamin and Marco's guns popped at random intervals. Someone shouted incomprehensibly, but Alexandra didn't care. She rested her sword against a crate and joined Holly on the cot.

"Shhh…" Alexandra said, "Don't think about anything but your baby."

Turning Holly away from the sight of her husband, Alexandra hugged the sobbing woman and scanned the rest of the interior. She counted three main entrances - the original opening, the tattered side where Alexandra entered, and the cutaway to the other tent. Jason's limbs and blood covered almost everything. Where was Santino? He was in this tent when the battle started. Were his body parts amongst the grisly mess?

"What did I do?" Alexandra said.

Before Holly or anyone else could answer her question, Alexandra heard a loud sniffing at the ripped side of the tent. A large snout pushed its way into the opening, followed by two smoldering eyes – a hound. This wasn't any normal hound. Alexandra recognized this hound as the one from the café where she sought refuge from the toothless man.

Sustaining a low, guttural growl, the creature advanced into the tent. Smoke leaked from its nostrils as the canine locked gazes again with Alexandra. Cursing her own carelessness, Alexandra glanced at her sword which rested just out of reach. The hound followed her eyes to the weapon and grinned. Unlike a normal dog, this canine seemed intelligent and aware.

Alexandra wanted to call for help, but she knew that nobody could arrive in time. The men from Father Callahan's town now spoke the truth of Alexandra's fate. The demons were killing all women and babies.

"I'm so sorry," Alexandra said into Holly's ear, "I'm sorry I might not be strong enough to save you."

If this was her fate, Alexandra decided that Holly shouldn't share it. Alexandra pushed the pregnant woman aside and leapt for her sword. However, the hound pounced on her leg and Alexandra crashed to the ground. She turned to face her attacker and was greeted by a vicious headbutt. Stars exploded across her vision and she felt herself spinning and falling.

Through waxing and waning consciousness Alexandra felt she was at her dentist's office again, going under anesthesia for her wisdom teeth extraction. She fought the encroaching darkness as Holly's life hung in the balance.

Then, Alexandra fell to the ground. Wait? Wasn't she already on the ground? Her vision cleared and she was surprised to find herself outside, a good thirty feet from the barricade. How did she get here? The hound growled and turned to the sky. A dark, winged form lunged at the canine and the two bodies tumbled across the ground. With a yelp, the hound separated and retreated into the darkness.

Alexandra recognized her friend and said, "Erzulie!"

Erzulie glided into the air and dropped at Alexandra's side an instant later. Silvery liquid oozed from under Erzulie's breastplate and matted many of her black feathers together on her wings.

"Are you harmed?" Erzulie said as her eyes scanned Alexandra's body.

"No," Alexandra said as her brain flipped over like a pancake in her skull. "I'm just… a little woozy."

Erzulie extended her wings and said, "I'll go finish that hound."

"Wait," Alexandra said, though she struggled to form the word. After centering her eyes, Alexandra said, "Help them… help Holly."

"As you comm…" Erzulie stopped and swayed on her feet. Her eyes fluttered.

"Erzulie?"

The angel blinked and then focused on Alexandra. "Many apologies. I am a little… woozy, as well."

"Don't apologize – just go!" Alexandra said.

Nodding once, Erzulie shot into the air and flew over the remains of the barricade. At the edge of her vision, Alexandra saw some hunched forms moving away from the beached cruise ship. The backdrop of gunfire was replaced with silence. Was it over?

Through monumental effort, Alexandra rose to her feet. She moved as fast as she thought she could, without losing consciousness, to Holly's tent.

"We're over here!" Marco said.

Alexandra picked her way through the rubble and bodies of demons. A few people were gathered at the center of their encampment. Holly rested on a chaise, her hands over her face. Nicole kneeled on the ground beside the pregnant woman. Marco waved his pistol to catch Alexandra's attention and Erzulie perched behind Holly. Benjamin stood on the roof of Santino's rig, his gun scanning the horizon.

"This isn't everyone," Alexandra said.

Marco stepped towards her and said, "Alexandra, listen…"

"Where's Koneh? Richard? Santino?"

Without waiting for an answer, Alexandra climbed over the rubble of the ruined barricade and looked to the last spot she saw Koneh. A carpet of demonic bodies covered the area. Was Koneh's body amongst them? To the far side, Alexandra caught some movement with her eyes.

"Santino's fine," Marco said, "He got knocked out when some crates fell on him. But you need to know something."

Ignoring her companion, Alexandra ran to the spot where she saw the movement in the wasteland. When she reached the area, Alexandra didn't see anything. Then, one of the large demons twitched from his position facedown in the dirt.

Alexandra stepped backwards and grasped for the sword at her belt, but the weapon wasn't there. Still dazed, Alexandra struggled to remember where she left her sword.

The demon twitched again and rolled onto its back.

"Look out!" Benjamin said from his elevated position.

Marco rushed forward and yelled, "Alexandra!"

Prepared to wring her vengeance with her own two hands, Alexandra stood her ground. But the demon didn't open his eyes. Instead, a very bloody Koneh pulled himself to his feet from under the massive form of the demon.

All of Alexandra's emotions crashed at that moment – elation at seeing her friend alive, terror over watching so many people die, and guilt about putting her friends in so much danger. Alexandra hugged Koneh as tears streamed down her face and stung her wounded cheek.

Managing a few words, Alexandra said, "You're alive!"

Koneh stumbled in Alexandra's grasp.

"Easy," Alexandra said. "Are you hurt?"

Covered in blood, Koneh's rags appeared more shredded than before. His left arm hung limp at his side and his breathing came in long wheezes.

"Priest..." Koneh said. "Gone..."

"What?" Alexandra said.

"That's what we were trying to tell you," Marco said. "The Padre is dead."

"Padre?" Alexandra said, her head clearing. "You mean, Richard? Father Callahan?"

Marco nodded. "Si."

"No," Alexandra said, her thoughts swirling. Father Callahan couldn't be dead. He was just in the tent with Holly and me. He was just sitting by their campfire. He was just telling me how he looked upon me as his own daughter. He was just...

CHAPTER 21

Alexandra ran.

Father Callahan couldn't be dead. He was Alexandra's voice of reason in this new, chaotic world. How could this happen?

"Over here!" Benjamin said, the flashlight on the barrel of his gun pointed at a motionless form on the ground near Santino's truck.

"No, no, no…" Alexandra said as she knelt beside her friend. "You don't deserve this."

Father Callahan was face down, his clothing wet with blood. Alexandra plucked his battered rosary from the dirt and held it to her chest. Her tears had stopped and she felt like there were none left. Then, the pain turned to guilt as Alexandra realized she was responsible. She was the one who ordered him from Holly's tent and into danger.

"It's my fault," Alexandra said

With a hand around Alexandra's shoulders, Erzulie said, "The Father's death was not of your making."

"Maybe we should be blaming you then, demon?" Marco said, his eyes locked upon Erzulie.

Koneh slumped to the ground near the group. His voice little more than a whisper, he said, "The mere fact you called her a demon speaks to how little you know about the situation."

"And what the hell are you?" Marco said. "No human could have survived that. You are a demon too, aren't you?"

Benjamin descended from the top of the rig and joined the group. His hair and eyebrows were gone and his face was blackened from the belchers. "Why are y'all arguing?" He said, "Koneh just killed a bunch of those things. You really think he'd do that if he was one of them?"

"I dunno," Marco said as he pointed at Erzulie, "She's one of them too and she was fighting them."

"Stop laying blame," Alexandra said. "I made the decision to stay. I'm responsible. Let's just leave it at that."

Supported by Santino and breathing through contractions, Holly approached the scene. The pregnant woman's eyes scanned the group until they found Alexandra.

"The priest told me everything," Holly said, an edge in her words. "He said you are the Christ, here to save us all. Is it true?"

There was no wonderment in Holly's voice, no warmth. She sounded like a woman who felt betrayed.

Shaking her head, Alexandra said, "It's not true, I'm sorry."

"She healed me," Benjamin said. "I was a goner and she healed my wounds with light from her hands." He paused, looked at Father Callahan's body, and said, "Wait, you can heal the Father!"

"I cannot bring back the dead," Alexandra said, amused at the words coming out of her own mouth. "That's impossible."

"Jesus resurrected the dead," Holly said.

"You healed General Ryan too," Benjamin said. "You can heal everyone here, right? Bring them back?"

"Erzulie," Koneh said, "don't say a word."

"See!" Benjamin said, "Koneh knows. He knows and he doesn't want the angel to tell us."

"I know that you are all fools," Koneh said.

"He was your friend, si?" Marco said. "Can you not heal him, Alexandra? Like you did for the General and Benjamin?"

Her face twisted into a frown, Holly said, "What are you waiting for? Heal him!"

Cornered, Alexandra placed her hands upon Father Callahan's back. She strained to recall how she felt when she helped the other two men, but her mind couldn't focus. Alexandra wanted her friend back. She poured all her guilt, sadness, and anger into her hands and squeezed her eyes shut.

Nothing happened.

After a few minutes, Alexandra opened her eyes and removed her hands from Father Callahan. He was gone.

"What's this?" Holly said. "I thought you said she could heal?"

Benjamin shrugged and said, "She healed me."

"Why don't you all just leave her alone for a few minutes," Koneh said.

"But she can save my Jason!" Holly said.

"No, she cannot," Koneh said. "Let her grieve over her friend."

Marco slapped Benjamin on the back as they turned away and said, "Maybe she's not who you think she is?"

Holly burst into tears and said, "My poor Jason…"

Santino led her away from Father Callahan's body.

"You too, Erzulie," Koneh said.

Erzulie removed her arm from Alexandra's shoulders and joined the rest of the group near the tents. A cold wind blew through the area. For several long moments, Alexandra and Koneh sat in silence. Alexandra's body ached from the strain of the battle and the loss of her friends. Part of her envied Father Callahan. At least he didn't have to worry anymore.

"Was this over guilt?" Koneh said.

"What?"

Koneh wheezed. "Your decision to stay and fight. Were you still guilty from leaving Tampico? Or were you pursuing some higher purpose?"

"I didn't know," Alexandra said, "I didn't know something like this could happen."

"What did you expect?" Koneh said, coughing through the words. "Five of us had the capacity to fight. Five against ninety-nine. I told you people were going to die."

"I just didn't think…"

"Why did you stay?"

Alexandra said, "I couldn't just leave them…"

"Why?"

"I don't know! Because I still feel guilty about Tampico. Because I care what happens to them. Because I didn't want more guilt? Pick one!"

Instead of responding, Koneh looked into Alexandra's eyes.

"What do you want from me?" she asked, her voice hoarse.

"How do you feel?" Koneh said, "now that you made the decision and people are gone…"

"What kind of a question is that?" Was Koneh trying to make her feel worse?

"I just want you to remember how you feel at this moment," Koneh said. "This world is one where you will lose friends and loved ones. Death and despair will become commonplace, and you must decide how to handle it."

"Why?"

"Because if you let it consume you… if you allow your heart to succumb to the grief, you won't survive."

Alexandra closed her eyes. "I hate this world."

"Do you think that's how Richard would feel?" Koneh said. "If your places were switched, would he hate the world?"

"I don't know…"

"Don't choose the easy answer," Koneh said. "That's not you."

Alexandra opened her eyes. "I don't know what you want me to say."

"I don't want you to say anything," Koneh said. "Just don't forget why you chose to make a stand. And don't forget the friends you've lost along the way."

"I won't forget Richard. He was like a father to me," Alexandra said, her voice unsteady. "I just wish we had more time together."

"Time is one of those tricky things. It's fast to slip through our fingers and we regret each lost moment the instant it's gone," Koneh said. "If we constantly turn around to examine our footprints, we'll miss the road ahead."

"That's easy for us to say, we're still alive and we have regrets," Alexandra said as she looked at the still form of her friend. How could he be gone?

"Do you think Richard would want you to live your life in the past? Haunted by your regrets?"

"Why do you keep asking me what Richard would want?"

Koneh sighed. "Because this is the way we honor our friends who have fallen," he said. "It is the only way."

What would Father Callahan want? Would he want her to continue to Eden? To reopen paradise for mankind? Of course he would. Father Callahan had faith in her from the moment they met. Was that faith misguided? Could he have predicted that following her into the wasteland would have led to his own death?

"I think he'd want me to carry on," Alexandra said. "He'd probably tell me to *cry tough* or something like that. He liked to talk with funny old sayings."

"He was an impressive man," Koneh said. "I don't know if I would have followed us if I were him."

Alexandra chuckled wryly. "Yeah, what made him think following a lawyer, fallen angel, and *you* was a good idea?"

"I told him who you are," Koneh said. "And he believed me. Probably because of that Bible."

"How did you convince him?"

Koneh shrugged. "I really didn't have to, he was desperate for hope."

Tears again filled Alexandra's eyes. "He doesn't deserve this."

"No… he doesn't."

Koneh grasped his left arm and turned it over in his hand. He was severely wounded, though his face betrayed no pain.

"You know," Koneh said, "I might not make it with you to the end."

Alexandra forced a laugh. "I saw you stand up after that man unloaded his shotgun into you. You'll be just fine."

Koneh dropped his left arm to the ground and closed his eyes. Perhaps he was in some pain, after all. Alexandra felt like a fool.

"I'm sorry," she said.

"As long as I have fight left in me," Koneh said, "I will remain at your side. However, once I'm gone you must remain strong. Stay true to yourself. You know right from wrong better than I ever could."

"I don't know," Alexandra said, "seems like every decision I make is the wrong one."

Koneh shook his head. "You did well, and you didn't let this old fool change your mind. The demons didn't get what they came for."

"No," Alexandra said, "but, they took away more than I wanted them to."

After a few long minutes of silence, Marco approached and said, "We talked and we decided to bury everyone at the base of the ship. Benjamin and Santino are gettin' some shovels. Erzulie is watching over Holly."

Alexandra snapped from her daze and said, "Yeah, that sounds okay."

Pointing over his shoulder, Marco said, "We got you a shovel too. Figured you'd want to help."

Alexandra nodded. "Are you okay?" She said to Koneh. "Can you move?"

Koneh nodded and rose to his feet. "I'll dig too," he said.

Nobody spoke as they dug shallow graves for their friends. Alexandra was numb. Was *this* her new life? Chased through the streets by mobs, accosted by rapists, expected to perform miracles, attacked by demons, and forced to bury her friends. Alexandra loathed every part of it.

She was certain of one thing: God existed. So, if God was here, why was the world doomed to so much suffering? Or was the old woman in her dreams correct? Did God abandon them? If Alexandra was to figure it out, she decided she needed to open up her mind even further. She accepted that she had some important role to play. Koneh believed her fate was to open Eden. The woman in her dreams hinted at something Alexandra could accomplish as well, to bring the world back to life again. What did the old woman mean by that? Could Alexandra fulfill everyone's expectations?

"Maybe… maybe you should say something?"

Benjamin's words brought Alexandra back to the present. So automatic were her motions, Alexandra didn't notice the passage of time. The bodies rested under mounds of new dirt. Six mounds. Their names burned themselves into Alexandra's memory: Thomas, Justin, Francine, Carlos, Jason, and Richard.

"Me?" Alexandra said. What could she say? The man she looked to as a father was gone. Two teenagers from America were cut down before they had a chance to enjoy their lives. An expecting husband was torn to pieces by demons while his wife watched. A local man and an elderly passenger were also dead. The doctor watching over the pregnant woman abandoned his patient. What words could she offer to make any of it seem right?

As if Erzulie sensed Alexandra's distress, the angel sang. The words of the ancient funeral song flowed like ribbons from Erzulie's perfect mouth.

"Amazing Grace
How sweet the sound

That saved a wretch like me!"

All the sweetness from Alexandra's life drained away. All the things she found comfort in were now gone as well. Her world was empty.

"I once was lost,
But now am found;
Was blind but now I see!"

Alexandra closed her eyes. Erzulie's dirge, though beautiful, offered no comfort. Darkness stretched out before Alexandra and she felt lost.

"'Twas Grace
That taught my heart to fear,
And grace my fears relieved;
How precious did that grace appear
The hour I first believed!"

How could she believe in a God who would allow such things to happen? The world was full of suffering even before Alexandra's bus flipped. War. Poverty. Disease. Hatred. Was this new world simply an extension of the old one?

"Through many dangers, toils and snares,
I have already come;
'Tis grace hath brought me safe thus far,
And grace will lead me home."

Home. Erzulie sang the word like it was the sweetest word Alexandra ever heard. She longed for her refrigerator and takeout menus. Central air, silk bathrobes, satin sheets and bubble baths. All gone. Alexandra would give anything to return home.

"The Lord has promised good to me,
His Word my hope secures;
He will my Shield and Portion be,
As long as life endures."

Life. Alexandra thought she was protecting life. Instead, death visited them six fold. Was a sad mound of dirt waiting for her next? A week from now, would Erzulie be singing over Alexandra's grave?

"Yea, when this flesh and heart shall fail,
And mortal life shall cease,
I shall possess, within the veil,
A life of joy and peace."

Eden. Koneh believed Eden awaited them. A paradise. Was her companion correct? Or was he delusional to a dangerous extreme? Alexandra wondered if peace waited for her in Eden.

"The earth shall soon dissolve like snow,
The sun forbear to shine,
But God, Who called me here below,
Will be forever mine."

Alexandra opened her eyes and looked to the black-red sky. For over a month the sun had refused to shine. Was the yellow star still out there, waiting to give life back to the earth?

"When we've been here ten thousand years,
Bright shining as the sun,
We've no less days to sing God's praise,
Than when we'd first begun."

The last word of the funeral song drifted across the still wasteland. Everyone stood by the graves for a few minutes. Then, one by one, they departed.

Alexandra knelt at Father Richard Callahan's grave and said, "Koneh's not here to scold me so I'm going to make a promise." Alexandra chuckled, wiped a tear from her face, and continued. "I will reach Eden. If, by chance, you and Koneh are right in all of this then maybe I'll see you again. I would very much like that… I miss you already, my friend, my adopted father."

Smiling, Alexandra touched the dirt and rose to her feet. She tightened her sword around her waist, tucked Richard's rosary into her pocket and zipped her leather jacket. Glancing once more upon the six graves, Alexandra turned and walked towards Santino's rig.

The group salvaged what they could from the camp turned battlefield. Amongst the debris, Alexandra found Father Callahan's altered bible. She turned the leather book over in her hands. Was all of this predetermined by the words at the end of that book?

"Alexandra!" Marco's voice carried through the air. "It's Holly!"

"She's ready to go," Koneh said as he intercepted Alexandra. "Any minute now."

Holly squirmed and screamed on the chaise next to Santino's rig. The woman appeared possessed.

"Tell me someone knows how to deliver a baby," Alexandra said.

Benjamin and Marco shrugged. Nicole bit her lower lip and shook her head. Santino stared at the scene from the driver's seat and Alexandra noticed that Erzulie was missing.

Koneh sighed and said, "Someone get the propane burner going and boil some water. Find some clean cloth as well."

As bodies spun into motion, Alexandra turned to Koneh and said, "You can... deliver a baby?"

Koneh's eyes narrowed. "I'd have prefered the doctor stuck around for this duty," he said.

"Is that a yes?"

"That is a yes," Koneh said.

Without another word, Koneh walked to the pot of water. "Get her whatever she needs," Koneh said to Nicole. As the water came to a boil, Koneh drew a small knife from under his rags and dropped it in the pot. He then unwrapped the bandages from his hands, revealing scarred fingers.

Alexandra stepped forward and said, "What are you doing?"

Koneh pushed his hands into the boiling water and groaned.

"You are loco, my friend," Marco said.

Alexandra jumped as Erzulie appeared from the sky and landed at her side.

"I found him," she said.

"Who?" Alexandra asked, though she knew the answer as soon as she opened her mouth.

"The doctor."

"We may still have time," Koneh said. "Go get him."

"Where is he?" Alexandra asked.

"On the freeway," Erzulie said, "About twelve miles away. The bike appears to be out of gas."

Alexandra exhaled and said, "Benjamin, stay here with everyone. Erzulie, fly back there and keep an eye on him. Marco, Santino and I will go get him with the rig."

"Just hurry," Koneh said.

Santino maneuvered the truck through the brush and onto the freeway. The vehicle's headlights cut through the darkness as Marco and Alexandra rode in the back of the roomy cab.

Wrestling with the thought of asking Marco about Tampico, Alexandra fidgeted with her ragged hair. Lost for the best way to approach the subject, Alexandra decided to just speak her mind.

"What happened in Tampico?" she asked.

Marco blinked and looked her in the eyes. "What?"

"I'm sorry if I seem uncaring, but I need to know. What happened after we left?"

"Well," Marco said as he shifted in his seat to face her, "the same thing that we just lived through, basically. The belchers set fire to our barricade and most of our men died there. Then, the man-sized demons ran through the streets and tore open anyone they came across. I've never seen so much blood. Not even after the quake."

"I'm so sorry," Alexandra said. "I was… I wasn't exactly thinking straight and I let Koneh make a decision for me."

Marco frowned and said, "Koneh is a monster, no? Why do you stay with him?"

"Well," Alexandra said, "if he meant to harm me, I think he could have done so easily by now."

"Not all pain is of the physical sort," Marco said as he leaned towards Alexandra. "Maybe he's planning something special for you."

Not ready to concede that point yet, Alexandra let the topic drop. Something deep inside told her she could trust Koneh. However, she wasn't prepared to have a debate over the issue.

"This is it," Santino said over his shoulder.

Alexandra and Marco hopped from the rig after Santino brought the vehicle to a halt. Henry, the doctor, cowered against a wrecked car.

"I guess he's frightened," Erzulie said.

"I thought I told you to just watch him," Alexandra said.

Erzulie shrugged. A human shrug. "He was going to run away, that wouldn't have been good."

Alexandra approached the doctor and said, "Henry, listen. Holly is giving birth. We need you."

Henry mumbled to himself and appeared incapable of speech.

"Dammit," Alexandra said, "We don't have time for this."

Marco returned from inspecting his bike and said, "I got the doctor's bag. There's maybe some useful stuff in here?"

"Maybe," Alexandra said, her eyes still on the cowardly doctor.

"If we get the bag back in time," Marco said, "Maybe Koneh can use what's in here?"

"Good idea. Erzulie, fly it back to them," Alexandra said.

"As you command."

Erzulie lifted into the sky and disappeared.

"You're coming with us, Henry," Alexandra said as she turned to Marco. "Can you lift…"

The question died in her throat as she found herself staring into the barrel of Marco's pistol. Where did he get a silencer?

"Not a word," Marco said as he shifted his aim to the doctor and squeezed the trigger.

"No!" Alexandra said as she lunged for the weapon. She was too slow. With a thud, Henry slumped to the ground. Marco stepped backwards and yelled in Santino's direction. "Stay put, or she dies."

"What the hell are you doing?" Alexandra said as her hand strayed to the sword at her side.

"You're not *that* fast," Marco said. "Drop the sword to the ground."

As Alexandra complied, the truth of Tampico resonated in her mind. "You didn't escape," she said. "They let you go."

Marco nodded as he stepped towards the rig. Six shots later, a majority of Santino's tires hissed in protest as they flattened.

"Why?" Alexandra asked, though she thought she knew the answer.

"I made my bargain," Marco said. He pointed his pistol at Alexandra. "Now, let's take a little walk."

CHAPTER 22

"This should be good," Marco said. "You can stop now."

The lights of Santino's rig were a distant speck. Alexandra wondered if Santino was smart enough to fill Marco's bike with gas and go for help. Or would it be too late?

Marco drew a different kind of gun from under his jacket and fired a green flare into the dark sky.

"What was that for?" Alexandra asked.

"I told you," Marco said, "I made my bargain."

A plan formed in Alexandra's mind. Maybe she could rush him. "So, they want me alive?" Alexandra said, not sure who *they* were.

Marco looked to the sky. "Si."

Alexandra calmed her nerves and readied her attack. She reasoned she would get one chance and she decided to take it.

"It would be a pity to blow off one of those beautiful knee caps," Marco said as he lowered his pistol to Alexandra's knees.

Alexandra froze. Was he bluffing?

"You know," Marco said as a grin spread across his lips, "they might take a while to get here. Plenty of time for me to get more out of my bargain."

With one smooth motion, Marco advanced on Alexandra and cracked her on the side of her head with the butt of his pistol. She fell to the ground and Marco pinned her. He growled as he reached for the waistband of her fatigues.

Perhaps Marco thought Alexandra was more subdued from the pistol-whip? Perhaps he lost control of his common sense in the heat of the moment? Whatever the reason, Alexandra was aware enough to deliver a sharp knee to his groin. She followed her attack with a twist of her attacker's wrist. Though she didn't mean to break his bones, she heard his wrist snap and the gun fall to the dirt.

Pushing Marco from her, Alexandra rolled to her side and scooped the pistol as she came to her feet. Her attacker groaned and held his broken wrist.

Shoot him or let him go? In the split second she gave herself to decide, Alexandra couldn't pull the trigger. She turned and ran towards Santino's headlights.

Still woozy from the blow to the head, Alexandra tumbled to the ground several times before reaching the truck. To her delight, Alexandra found Santino fiddling with Marco's bike. An empty gasoline container rested nearby.

"No time," Alexandra said as she lifted her sword from the ground and handed Santino the pistol. "We probably have company."

Santino nodded and said, "Si, we can go."

Alexandra hopped on the back of the bike and put her arms around Santino as he kicked the starter. Moments later, they raced down the freeway towards Koneh and the others.

Alexandra caught movement in the corner of her eye in time to see a winged form crash into them. Both passengers were flung from the vehicle and Alexandra rolled on the pavement several times before resting on her back. In addition to being flame retardant, the fatigues from General Ryan also resisted shock. However, Alexandra's bones still screamed their pain from every joint.

"Kono day rah," one winged creature said to another as it landed and advanced upon Santino's motionless body.

There were two. Alexandra forced herself to her feet and drew her sword. The weapon wavered as Alexandra scanned the area. One demon was almost upon Santino, though Alexandra didn't know if he had survived the crash. The other demon stood about fifteen feet from Alexandra, its teeth bared as it snarled at her.

The cut on Alexandra's cheek burned as if a warning to be wary of their tails. Alexandra's knees wobbled and she wasn't sure she could fight, but she took refuge in the possibility these demons were here to capture her, not kill her. However, Santino might not get the same offer.

"Back away from him," Alexandra said, projecting the strongest voice she could muster.

"Jemo rah," the closer demon said.

"I'll take that as a no," Alexandra said as she closed the distance and swung her weapon at her enemy.

The demon caught her arm with its own clawed hand and shredded her jacket, scraping her forearm. Alexandra tumbled to the ground and lost hold of her sword. Pushing against the pavement, Alexandra forced herself to her feet again. She couldn't give up on Santino.

"Jemo rah," the demon said as it flicked its tail in her direction.

Surprised by her own speed, Alexandra grasped the tail and yanked. The creature toppled to the ground and squealed. By now, the other demon broke away from Santino and bounded towards Alexandra. Alexandra wasn't fast enough this time. The monster slammed into her like a charging bull and flung her backwards. Again, Alexandra fell to the pavement and rolled to a stop.

This time, her muscles wouldn't obey. Alexandra lifted her head to watch, but felt too weak to stand. Moments later, the demon convulsed and gurgled. Before the body dropped to the ground, a winged figure slashed open the other demon's chest and all was quiet.

"Erzulie!" Alexandra said.

The angel rushed to Alexandra's side. "Are you hurt?" Erzulie asked.

"I'll be fine," Alexandra said. "Please, check on Santino."

Erzulie lifted into the air and dropped next to Santino.

"He's just unconscious," Erzulie said. "Maybe a concussion."

Alexandra planted the tip of her sword into the freeway and pulled herself to her feet. The bike's engine still rumbled. Alexandra found the vehicle and righted it.

"Stay with him," Alexandra said. "I'm going for help."

"You will be vulnerable."

"I know."

Alexandra twisted the throttle and raced along the ruined highway. Every few moments, she risked a glance at the red-black sky, but it didn't stir. After several miles, she came to the lights and piles of equipment that represented their camp.

Benjamin ran to her side and steadied the bike as it came to a halt.

"You okay?" he asked.

"Santino's hurt and Marco betrayed us," Alexandra said as she dismounted and stalked towards the camp.

"What?"

Alexandra didn't answer him. She needed to get everyone moving. More demons were probably on the way. Marco's betrayal stung like the cuts on her cheek and forearm. Why would he do such a thing? What did they promise him?

The camp was too quiet.

"What's wrong?" Alexandra said as she stopped and turned to Benjamin.

Benjamin smiled and said, "It was the most amazing thing. A little gross, but pretty freakin' cool."

Alexandra didn't need to ask. The baby was born. She rushed into camp and spotted Holly on the cot, holding a small bundle of cloth. Nicole pressed a wet towel to the new mother's forehead and smiled.

"Can you believe it?" Holly said as she turned a tear-streaked face in Alexandra's direction. "So much beauty in such an awful place."

Alexandra dropped to her knees at the side of the cot. Holly was correct, the baby was the most precious thing she'd seen in over a month. Alexandra's heart expanded as she looked upon the child.

"I decided to name her 'Delia.' Jason always liked that name best," Holly said as she pushed aside a small fold of cloth to better display her baby's face.

"How?" Alexandra asked.

Nicole pointed to Koneh, who stood near the same bowl of water where Alexandra last saw him. "He was mean and ordered us around," Nicole said, "but he delivered the baby."

Numb, Alexandra walked to her friend. "You did this?" she asked.

Koneh didn't respond. Instead, he stared at her from beneath his hood. What was he thinking?

"I'm amazed," Alexandra said. "You are... unbelievable."

Koneh huffed and leaned towards Alexandra. "She's not out of the woods yet," he said.

"What do you mean?" Alexandra said, lowering her voice to a whisper.

"She has an infection," Koneh said. "I can only do so much. Maybe her body will fight it off, but that's unlikely."

"An infection? Well, how bad could it be?" Alexandra glanced over her shoulder.

"Without antibiotics," Koneh said, "It will probably kill her eventually."

"I'm not losing anyone else," Alexandra said. "Did Erzulie bring the doctor's bag? Are there antibiotics in there?"

Koneh shook his head. "I looked. Nothing. Though, the doctor may be able to keep her going a while longer. Did you find him?"

Alexandra lowered her eyes. "Marco betrayed us," she said. "He killed the doctor and shot the tires out on the truck. Santino's unconscious, but Erzulie is watching over him. And I feel like I just got run over."

"You look it," Koneh said. "I knew something was up with Marco… damn. What's the danger right now?"

"I don't know," Alexandra said. "He fired a flare into the sky and two winged demons came. I can only assume more are on the way."

"That's a good assumption," Koneh said. "We need to get everyone moving."

"My thoughts exactly. Do you think Holly can move?"

Koneh rubbed his chin and said, "She shouldn't, no. However we have no choice. I'll go look for a vehicle. You stay here with everyone else. Tell Benjamin what's going on, but no one else."

After Koneh disappeared into the darkness, Alexandra brought Benjamin up to speed and the soldier fortified himself in a good position to watch over the camp. Alexandra joined Holly and Nicole and doted over the baby. After an hour, Holly and the baby needed their sleep. Nicole made them comfortable.

"You look pretty beat-up," Nicole said. "Are you in pain?"

"Honey, everything hurts." Alexandra chuckled.

"Ouch! Your hair," Nicole said as she winced at the sight.

"Yeah," Alexandra said as she ran her hand through the singed mess, "that belcher got me good. You know, I was thinking about cutting it anyway."

Nicole primped her bob of auburn hair and said, "Short is fab."

"Can you help me?" Alexandra said, desperate to focus on something other than the battle at the cruise ship. "Do you know where we could find a pair of scissors?"

Nicole smiled and disappeared behind some corrugated crates. A moment later she appeared with a large pair of sewing scissors.

"These will work!" Nicole said. "Are you sure?"

"What the hell," Alexandra said. "I'll do anything to take my mind off everything that has happened over the past twenty-four hours."

A few hours later, Koneh rumbled into camp with a silver station wagon. The windows and hood were gone, but the vehicle otherwise seemed fit for travel.

"Okay," Koneh said, "we must leave some things here for now, at least until we see if the rig can move again. Load up only the essentials."

Koneh paused as he passed Alexandra on his way to the cot. He looked at Alexandra's new hair style and grinned. "You looked better with long hair," he said and continued his preparations.

With only a few things to pack, the camp broke down faster than Alexandra expected. Holly rested in the back seat with Delia. Crates were emptied and refilled with rations, water, blankets, tools and gasoline. Most of the crates were tied to the roof of the station wagon. After everything was packed, Benjamin broke from his position and joined Alexandra and Koneh.

"Looks pretty clear," the soldier said, "though I can't see much in this sky."

"That's okay," Alexandra said. "Let's get moving."

After everyone piled into the station wagon, Alexandra paused and gazed at the mammoth cruise ship. Before the tears could gather over losing Father Callahan, Alexandra swung into the vehicle and closed the door.

They arrived at another bloody scene. Two demon corpses occupied the middle of the highway, the doctor lay on the ground in a pool of blood and Santino rested unconscious in Erzulie's arms.

"Is everything okay?" Alexandra asked.

Erzulie nodded, "His condition hasn't changed."

Koneh and Benjamin inspected the rig.

"Damn," Benjamin said, "he shot out six tires. That mother-"

"Let us salvage the important stuff," Koneh said.

As the two men consolidated equipment onto the station wagon, Holly, Nicole and Alexandra fed the baby.

"This isn't as easy as I thought it was going to be," Holly said as she fought to keep Delia attached to her breast.

"She'll get it," Nicole said. "My younger sister was the same way at first. She'd just cry and cry and cry... my mom cried a lot too."

After much coaxing, crying, and frustration Delia filled her small belly and went back to sleep. Alexandra longed for the innocence in the baby's eyes. Delia knew no fear, loss or despair. Not until she realized her father was gone, at least.

Alexandra remembered Koneh's diagnosis. Holly had an infection and without help she would probably die. The baby might know more loss, after all. The earth had become a terrible place to be born into.

"We are ready," Koneh said. "We had to ditch some supplies to put Santino in the back, but it's all stuff we can probably find along the freeway."

"Great," Alexandra said.

Koneh grasped Alexandra's arm and asked, "Can I talk to you for a minute?"

"Sure."

Once they were away from the others, Koneh said, "We still have a way to go and at this rate of loss we're not going to make it far."

Alexandra nodded.

"We just have to drive," Koneh said. "There are places we can stop to get supplies, but if we stop every few miles to check on a sign or to help some people, we won't make it."

Alexandra lowered her eyes and said, "I know." If she could somehow help improve the long-term, she knew she had to stop thinking so short-term. Though that logic made the most sense, Alexandra felt uneasy about leaving everyone she saw to their fate in this new world. She reached back to flip her hair, but she only grasped air. To fill her need to fidget, Alexandra untied and retied her short ponytail.

"Sometimes," Koneh said, "the most important battles are the ones we choose to avoid."

"I know. I just... I couldn't turn my back on them."

His voice no more than a whisper, Koneh said, "Sometimes you must."

After a few moments of silence, Alexandra asked, "Do you really believe we can make a difference by reaching Eden?"

"With all my heart, I do."

"How can you be certain it's real?"

Koneh shifted on his feet. "Whether you believe me or not, Elah did come to me. He told me something that most people long for – knowledge of *why* we are here. Not collectively, but individually."

Though skeptical, Alexandra nodded and allowed Koneh to continue.

"He told me my purpose was to see you safely to Eden," Koneh said. "If He believes you can make a difference, then who am I to argue?"

"I didn't ask for this," Alexandra said. "God decides the paths we must follow? What about free will?"

Koneh shook his head. "I don't have answers for you. All I know is I was tasked with a mission from my Creator."

Alexandra met Koneh's eyes and asked, "And you'll complete that mission no matter the cost to me?"

Koneh blinked. "I have weighed the price you may yet pay..."

"And if it came down to it," Alexandra said, "would you let me walk away?"

Koneh narrowed his and asked, "Are you saying it's down to that now?"

"No, I'm still willing to see this through, but I really need to know whose side you're on. Marco taught me a valuable lesson today."

Koneh grasped Alexandra's shoulders with both of his hands and said, "My promise to you is all that I have left. You will reach Eden alive. I will not betray you. If nothing else, you must believe this."

"Do you say that because you have to obey my commands, like Erzulie?"

Koneh shook his head and opened his mouth to speak, but he was interrupted by Benjamin.

"Sorry guys," the soldier said, "but we're ready to go."

Alexandra attempted to read Koneh's all black eyes. However, his emotions hid in the darkness. Sighing, she said, "We can continue this conversation later?"

"Of course."

CHAPTER 23

They stopped after a few hours of hard driving. Alexandra scooted from the hatchback and found the rest of the group at the front of the station wagon. Erzulie perched nearby on an overturned school bus.

Santino approached and said, "Gracias, Alejandra. I can maybe make it to see mi hija now."

Alexandra smiled and hugged her friend. "I surely hope you get to see your daughter again, Santino. If nothing else, it means we got all the way through Brazil - alive."

"We made good time," Benjamin said. "This part of the freeway seems pretty intact. Hopefully, our luck holds into South America."

"If not, Santino has some tricks up his sleeve to keep us moving in the right direction," Koneh said.

Alexandra nodded and said, "Excuse me for a moment."

Like a gargoyle overlooking the street, Erzulie perched atop the burned-out shell of a bus. Her eyes scanned the sky for danger. All that remained of her armor was an arm piece, evidence of the battles Erzulie had fought in service to Alexandra and her journey to Eden. Her tattered white dress fluttered in the wind. If Erzulie suffered wounds from their previous encounter, none remained on her perfect skin.

"Hello Lex, are you well?" Erzulie said.

"Funny," Alexandra said, "I was going to ask you the same thing."

"You need not worry for me."

Alexandra climbed to where Erzulie perched and sat next to her companion. "That's the thing about friendship," Alexandra said, "I will always worry."

"Friendship?"

Chuckling, Alexandra said, "Yeah sistah, you're my friend."

"I am your servant," Erzulie said. "I don't understand why you think-"

"Thank you," Alexandra said as she touched Erzulie's arm, "you continue to put yourself in harm's way and though I worry for you, I am grateful."

"It is my duty."

"Just be careful, okay?"

Erzulie smiled and said, "You always say the same thing. You don't need to repeat your orders. I understood them the first time."

"Okay," Alexandra said, returning the smile. "I just don't want you to forget, that's all."

"I cannot forget. My memory is more than adequate to store more orders than you are capable of giving over your brief lifetime."

Alexandra laughed. "Well, that's comforting."

"I'm glad you think so."

"Do you think…" Alexandra's question was cut short by Benjamin, who waved to Alexandra.

"Looks like we're moving out," Erzulie said as she stood and stretched her black, feathery wings.

"Yeah," Alexandra said, "just be…"

"Careful," Erzulie said. "I know."

After several days of uneventful travel with Santino at the wheel again, the car stopped at a large rise in the freeway. The asphalt lifted into the air forming a high bridge above the burnt treetops.

"What's this?" Alexandra asked.

Nicole shielded her eyes from a sun that wasn't in the sky and said, "Wow. How high do you think it goes?"

"They call it the Gran Cielo here in Brazil," Koneh said as he joined the group outside the station wagon. "The American company who built it during the failed oil rush dubbed it the Great Flyover. It serves as a bridge over four hundred miles of forest and jungle. Lucky for us, it leads right to Brasilia."

"Do you think it's all intact?" Alexandra asked.

"It would save us a ton of time if it is," Koneh said.

Benjamin rubbed his chin and said, "Yeah, that's a lot of jungle to cover if we can't drive over or through it."

"What do you think Santino?" Koneh asked. "You've probably driven on this thing more than anyone else."

Santino shrugged and said, "The Gran Cielo is muy grande, muy strong."

"Well," Koneh said, "this part looks okay. All we can hope is the rest survived the quake just as well."

"Maybe we should make camp," Alexandra said. "I know it's not time yet, but Santino looks exhausted and maybe we should sleep on this one."

Koneh nodded. "Very well."

After unpacking some supplies, the group settled into camp.

"It's just so empty," Nicole said as Alexandra joined her and Holly for an MRE ration.

"What's empty?" Alexandra asked.

"Everything," Nicole said, "the freeway, all those towns we passed. You'd think we'd come across some people."

With Delia tucked under one arm, Holly ate a rare meal. The infant never left Holly's side and Alexandra wondered if the behavior was normal. Now that Alexandra thought about it, nobody else had held the child.

"How does it feel?" Alexandra asked. "To be a mother for almost a week now?"

Holly smiled but didn't meet Alexandra's eyes. "Oh, great," Holly said.

"Mind if I hold her?" Alexandra asked.

Holly glanced in Alexandra's direction and said, "She's sleeping now. Maybe later."

Alexandra nodded and studied Holly. Without proper postnatal medical care, Holly looked awful. Her skin was red in some areas and gray in others. Though she didn't complain, Holly made frequent trips out of sight. Alexandra could only guess from the bloody rags that Holly was in much pain and discomfort.

"Okay girls, I'm going to go talk shop with Koneh. Get some rest," Alexandra said.

After a few minutes, Alexandra found Koneh and Erzulie talking near some rubble on the side of the freeway. Like so many times in the past, Alexandra felt she was barging into a private conversation.

"What's going on?" Koneh asked as he peered at Alexandra from beneath his hood. If there wasn'y anything romantic between Erzulie and Koneh, why did Alexandra's heart skip every time she saw them together? Why did she care if they *were* together? Did she really feel something for him?

"Nothing... I just... Have you seen Holly?" Alexandra said.

"Yes," Koneh said, "she's not doing too well."

"Can't you help her?" Alexandra asked.

Koneh shook his head. "I'm not a doctor. Plus, she won't let me near her or her baby."

"Do you find her behavior odd?" Alexandra asked.

Koneh shrugged and said, "Could be the onset of the infection, the loss of her husband, the rough trip. Pick a catastrophe."

"She won't let anyone hold Delia."

"I'm not around babies much," Koneh said. "You think there's something wrong with her mentally?"

Alexandra reached for her hair again, but found only the small ponytail. She decided she needed a new nervous habit. "I wish I knew. Something's not right, though," Alexandra said.

"Maybe it is too much for her," Erzulie said.

Alexandra sighed. "I think it's too much for me..."

"I'll let you two talk," Erzulie said.

"You don't need to..." Alexandra started, but the angel was gone before she could finish.

Alexandra held Koneh's gaze for a moment before he looked away. What was he thinking? What did he feel? She didn't know how to ask these questions.

"How's your arm?" she asked, choosing the easy road for the moment.

"Fine," he said, returning his piercing eyes to her. "How's yours?"

"Wrapped and healing well," she said.

Koneh traced his finger along his cheek. "And the cheek? That one looks nasty."

Alexandra reflexively touched her own cheek. "I disinfected it with an alcohol wipe. It still stings."

Koneh smiled. "You're starting a collection."

"Of wounds?" Alexandra nodded. "Yeah, I guess so."

Though she enjoyed comparing scars with Koneh, Alexandra returned to business. "What do you think about the Flyover?" she asked.

"Erzulie scouted ahead and she said it's intact."

"Good," Alexandra said as she attempted to read his face. He remained an unreadable wall.

"You want to ask me something," he stated.

"Yes," she said, hesitating. Was she so transparent? "I… what did you mean before when you said you might not make it to the end with me? Do you..?"

Koneh waved his hand. "I'm just feeling… old. Tired. I thought I was ready for this ordeal, but maybe I was wrong. I should've been able to protect you at the cruise ship. I'm sorry."

"Why is everyone apologizing to me?" she said. "What you did out there… well, I'm still trying to figure it out. I can only imagine things would have been worse if you weren't here, protecting us all."

"Are you sure about that?" he said. "What if Marco was right? What if I plan to betray you? Have you considered that possibility yet?"

"I think you could've done anything you wanted with me by now," she said, unsure why he would open this topic.

"What if I'm waiting until we reach Eden?" he said. "Certainly a willing hostage is easier to transport than a reluctant one."

Alexandra hesitated. What if that *was* his plan? Then she smiled and said, "Then why would you tell me now and put me on my guard?"

Koneh grinned. "Maybe I'm an evil genius. I figured I could put you off balance, throw you off until I can spring my trap."

She studied his face for a moment, attempting to unravel his mystery. "No," she said, "I don't think that is your plan. You're not that clever."

Koneh huffed and looked away. "Don't underestimate me. I'm capable of awful things."

"Really?" Alexandra said, scooting closer to him. She was hopelessly drawn to his mystery, no matter how dangerous that became for her. "What sort of awful things?"

He returned his eyes to her and said, "The way you look at me… You mustn't. I'm not… This isn't allowed."

Alexandra reached towards his face and traced his jaw with the back of her hand. "You said that before," she whispered. "I just want to be closer to you, get to know you better. Is that so terrible?"

Koneh intercepted her hand and gently pushed it aside. He closed his eyes and appeared to be embattled with some internal struggle. After a few moments, he opened his eyes and said, "I must not falter... when you say these things... when you touch me..."

He stood and turned his back to her. "You should focus on your task," he said. "And I on mine."

Without another word, he returned to the camp.

Alexandra was now certain of her feelings. Sure, Koneh protected her like he was her own personal knight, but her heart had moved beyond infatuation. She cared for him in a way she hadn't known before the quake. She sensed that he harbored feelings as well, but he restrained himself. Perhaps he had more self-control than she did?

"That's no surprise, Lex," she said to herself.

She put her hands in her fatigue pockets and meandered back to the camp. Benjamin's voice carried across the freeway.

"Oh yeah!"

"Bueno!"

"You lost it!" Benjamin said.

Santino crouched in the front section of a ruined pickup. Benjamin leaned on the frame and turned to Alexandra as she approached.

"We think we got it working," Benjamin said.

"Got what working?"

Santino pointed to the dashboard. "El radio."

"We tried the radio in the rig and the station wagon," Alexandra said. "Nothing's coming through."

Benjamin smiled and said, "This is a satellite radio."

"Oh!"

"There it is!" Benjamin said as Santino scanned the stations and stopped.

A crackling voice played through the one working speaker on the dash.

"...pal city forty-one... fift... orth. Twelve, twenty-seven east. Medit... way for African survivo... Zagreb pen... points east. Avoid Berlin and north... of... der... radiation... repeat in... minutes... may God... you."

The speaker went silent.

"That was better than before," Benjamin said. "Keep trying the other stations."

Alexandra looked to the sky and said, "Satellite, huh?"

"Makes sense," Benjamin said. "But we had one at the base and all we ever heard was a dead line."

"Something new then?" Alexandra said.

The soldier nodded, "And they're tapping into several stations. Seems to be the same message though."

Alexandra rejoined the group while Benjamin and Santino fiddled with the radio.

"The world may not be so empty after all," Alexandra said as she sat next to Nicole.

"What do you mean?" Nicole asked.

"Santino and Benjamin found a message on that satellite radio over there."

Everyone except Holly congregated at the ruined truck and its working satellite radio. The message came through several more times, but not as clear as the time Alexandra heard it.

"Hard to tell what the intent of that message is, but the latitude and longitude coordinates for Rome were in there," Koneh said, pointing at the dashboard.

"And they mentioned Berlin," Benjamin said.

"And God," Nicole said.

"Who do you think they are?" Alexandra asked, though she didn't expect an answer.

After a few hours of silence on the satellite radio, the group settled down for the night. The pavement offered no relief to Alexandra's throbbing bones, but sleep was a welcome companion.

Alexandra found herself in a dense jungle, the sound of life teemed all around her. Sunlight streamed through the treetops and onto the jungle floor in vibrant streaks. The white-haired woman knelt next to a small brook. Another dream.

"I know where you are going," the old woman said as she rose and turned towards Alexandra. "You must tell me your intentions once you reach that accursed place."

As the crone approached, Alexandra struggled to remain focused on her thoughts and surroundings. What should she tell the old woman? What should she hold back?

"I will tell you," Alexandra said, "but I need to know something first."

The old woman stopped and glared into Alexandra's eyes. "You are an interesting one," she said, "not at all like I expected. However, do not assume I must answer to the likes of you. The taint of Eden must be purged from the land. Only then can the Earth begin to heal. Only then will the filth of Elah be forever gone from this world."

Taken aback by the crone's words, Alexandra said, "You want Eden destroyed?"

The white-haired woman pointed a bony finger at Alexandra and said, "You, Child, have the power to either destroy or revive Eden. Tell me your intentions!"

CHAPTER 24

Alexandra awoke and noticed the camp was still quiet. Benjamin, Holly, Santino and Nicole all slept either on the ground or in a nearby vehicle. The full darkness in the sky told Alexandra that nighttime was still in control. After her eyes adjusted, Alexandra spotted Koneh crouched beside an overturned oil rig. Alexandra stretched her weary limbs and rose to her feet.

"Couldn't sleep?" Koneh asked.

"I've been having some strange dreams."

"Is that so?"

Alexandra sensed something in Koneh's tone and said, "You know something of my dreams, don't you."

"From what I understand, you are glimpsing the future."

"I dunno," Alexandra said. "Sometimes, maybe… But, I think there's more…"

Koneh raised his hand and said, "I don't want to know."

Confused, Alexandra said, "Why not? Maybe we can figure some stuff out together."

Koneh shook his head. "I spent much of my life seeking the future and it has brought me pain and disappointment. Please, if you have seen anything, I don't want to know about it."

"If you really think I'm seeing the future…"

"No, I don't want to know."

Alexandra studied him for a few moments before allowing the subject to drop. "Fair enough," she said, "we can talk about something else."

Koneh nodded and returned his gaze to the dark horizon. When Alexandra first met the scarred man she thought him insane and callous. Now, after almost two months in the wasteland, Alexandra felt connected to Koneh in many ways. He was her protector. He was full of knowledge and experience. He cared for

Erzulie in a way that made Alexandra's heart yearn. Did he feel the same about her?

The love of a companion was something Alexandra thought she'd *get around to* someday in her busy lawyer's life. Excuses to avoid commitments came easy when she worked seventy hours a week. Now, she realized she missed something important. Would she ever feel the comfort and completeness of someone else's love?

Alexandra thought she found something else in Father Richard Callahan. He filled yet another hole in her life. The void that had been left by never knowing her father. Then, as soon as Alexandra realized how wonderful a father could be, Richard was taken away from her.

"I miss him," Alexandra said.

Without turning, Koneh said, "He was a good man. In some ways, I envy him."

"How do you mean?"

"Well, he doesn't have to worry about whether we will run out of food, water, gas or companions. He's feeling no pain right now."

Alexandra wiped a tear from her eye and smiled. "I can almost hear him arguing with you over the best way to deliver the baby. That would have been fun to watch."

Koneh chuckled. "Father Callahan always had an opinion and he wasn't afraid to voice it."

"He had faith right to the end," Alexandra said as she struggled with the memory of the battle. "I found him in Holly's tent warding off those demons. He stood his ground. Then I asked him to help Benjamin and Santino. I sent him…"

Koneh turned to Alexandra and said, "Listen. That wasn't your fault."

Now, the tears came. "It *was* my fault…"

Alexandra closed her eyes and pulled her knees under her chin. Nothing Koneh said could change what happened. Alexandra caused the death of her friend. Father Callahan deserved better than a shallow grave at the base of a beached cruise ship.

Sobbing, Alexandra buried her head in her arms and succumbed to the wave of grief and guilt. She couldn't remember when it happened, but Koneh held her as she cried. She found comfort again in Koneh's arms, relaxing long enough to find a sliver of peace.

"You will see him again," Koneh said.

Alexandra lifted her tear-streaked face. The weight of her task again threatened to crush her. How could she open Eden? She didn't even know where she was going. Fear, uncertainty, anger and hopelessness threatened to overtake Alexandra. However, she commanded her mind to focus so she could work everything out. Though she knew she lied to herself, Alexandra wiped the tears from her face like they were the last tears she would shed.

"How do you think we're doing, really?" Alexandra said.

"This is no small errand we are on," Koneh said. "I won't lie to you. This is an impossible journey but I'm not planning on failing you."

Impossible journey. The words carried more weight coming from a seemingly invincible man. Alexandra heard the word *impossible* before, but never had it ringed so true.

"If it's impossible why are we even trying?" Alexandra said.

"Because it is all we can do. Because it is what we *must* do," Koneh said. "There comes a point in our lives when we must make our stand. Why not for Eden?"

"Are you doing this because God commanded you?" Alexandra asked.

Koneh shook his head. "No. The choice to seek Eden is my own. Though I knew my chances for success were low when I started."

Alexandra turned away from him and battled her tears. Was the reward of Eden worth the risk to her life? Was she seeking Eden for the right reasons? What were her reasons? Alexandra closed her eyes and flushed her questions. Now wasn't the time to doubt. Her friends were relying on her to lead them to Brasilia.

Opening her eyes, Alexandra said, "Well, we have more immediate things to deal with. Like the Flyover, Holly's condition, the new baby and our own survival." Alexandra said.

Koneh nodded. "Holly isn't doing well."

"Are we close to Brasilia?"

"Not really," Koneh said. "And there's no guarantee anyone there is alive."

"You know," Alexandra said, "the worries of my life before the quake seem so trivial now. I mean, my world would end if I missed an episode of *Orion Prime*. Now, I can't even remember the plot of that senseless show."

"I remember the exact moment I first felt as you do now," Koneh said. "It was the moment I realized that my life would never be the same."

"What happened?" Alexandra asked, desperate for more clues to Koneh's personality.

Koneh shook his head and said, "I was a foolish youth, absorbed in my own pride. You wouldn't want to hear about it…"

"No," Alexandra said as she touched Koneh's arm, "I want to… I want to know more about you. I think we've been together long enough. At least tell me where you're from. I've had a hard time placing your accent."

"I've moved around quite a bit," Koneh said. "I doubt I have an accent that can be tied to any single location."

"Good morning!"

Alexandra jumped.

"Sorry," Benjamin said, "I didn't mean to scare you."

Lost in conversation, Alexandra didn't notice the activity in the camp.

"Nicole is cooking up the last of the bacon from the ship," Benjamin said. "Might as well enjoy it before we're back to MRE's."

After a parting glance which only strengthened the longing in her heart, Alexandra left Koneh at the overturned oil rig and joined the group next to the station wagon.

"What were you guys talking about over there?" Nicole asked as she handed Alexandra a plate.

Alexandra dropped to the ground and used the rear tire for support. "Travel stuff," she said as she devoured a piece of sizzling bacon.

"Oh."

Santino leaned into the station wagon and offered a plate to Holly.

"I'm not hungry," Holly said.

Santino turned to Alexandra and said, "She needs to eat. You can say to her?"

Sighing, Alexandra rose to join Santino in the window. "Holly, please eat something. Delia needs you to be strong."

Apart from the bulge at her midsection, Holly appeared almost skeletal. Deep red lines cradled the woman's bloodshot eyes. A yellow crust formed at the corners of Holly's mouth and pimples raged across her face.

"I said I'm not hungry!"

Alexandra took the plate from Santino and rested it on the seat. "We'll just leave it here in case you change your mind."

"No good," Santino said as they walked away from the car. "That baby should cry but she don't anymore."

"Do you think Delia will be okay?" Alexandra asked.

He looked over his shoulder and said, "If she were my baby…" Tears formed in Santino's eyes and his mouth wavered. "If she were my little girl…"

Alexandra touched Santino's arm and said, "We'll get there. You'll see your daughter again."

Nicole joined Alexandra and Santino. "Well, I don't think they look right," she said.

"No, they don't," Alexandra said as she followed Nicole's gaze to the station wagon.

The group sped along the Flyover for two days. The claw-like remains of the forest below the highway hid the ground, but no animal or human movement was seen. Holly's condition worsened and everyone only spoke when necessary. The weight of losing so many friends at the cruise ship had finally settled on the survivors and the mood turned dour.

Alexandra's thoughts wandered to the white-haired woman. Were the dreams *real*? Did she really exist somewhere, content to speak to Alexandra through dreams? Why would anyone want Eden destroyed? Every attempt to piece together the information met with failure. Alexandra wished Father Callahan was still around to help her sort everything out.

At the end of the second day, in the middle of Alexandra's soul-searching, the highway began to rumble.

"What was that?" Nicole said, clutching the back of the seat.

"Sounds like a quake," Benjamin said.

"Stop the car!" Koneh said.

As soon as it began, the quake subsided. Santino punched the brakes, which jostled the occupants of the dented station wagon. Then, Santino adjusted his Texas Rangers ball cap and pointed out the windshield. "Extremo," he said.

Alexandra, Benjamin and Koneh exited the car and stood at the edge of the Flyover. Roughly fifty feet of highway was missing!

"I dunno how high we are," Benjamin said as he peered over the torn edge of road, "but, maybe we can climb down?"

"That's one option," Koneh said as he rubbed his chin.

Erzulie landed on the pavement next to Alexandra. "The road looks intact beyond this break," the angel said.

"What about the forest beneath us?" Koneh said.

Erzulie shook her head and said, "Very rough terrain down there. Your path would be a difficult one through fallen trees, sinkholes and upturned earth."

"How high are we?" Benjamin asked.

"We stand one hundred and sixty meters above the ground," Erzulie said. "The fall would undoubtedly kill you."

Alexandra examined the impressive angel and said, "How much can you carry while flying?"

"That's the other option," Koneh said.

Erzulie carried Koneh over the chasm while Santino, Benjamin and Alexandra unpacked the station wagon.

"Did you guys make it over there all right?" Alexandra asked after Erzulie returned, empty-handed, on Alexandra's side of the broken highway

Erzulie nodded. "Koneh is securing the area as we speak."

"Good," Alexandra said, "bring Santino over next. Find a car and make sure Holly will be comfortable in the back seat."

"By your command," Erzulie said.

Alexandra inventoried their supplies while Erzulie and Santino made the trip over the chasm. Five jugs of water, thirty-four MRE rations, twenty gallons of gasoline, six sets of fatigues, several packs of diapers, two containers of powdered baby formula, one portable grill, two small propane tanks and various utility tools and snacks.

"We're definitely running low," Alexandra said to herself.

"Hi," Nicole said as she rounded the corner of the station wagon.

"Hi there," Alexandra said. "Has Erzulie returned yet?"

"Yeah, she took Benjamin over. I helped Holly out of the car…"

Nicole's voice trailed away when both Nicole and Alexandra noticed Holly teetering near the edge of the broken highway. Alexandra raced to the mother and baby.

"You're not taking her!" Holly said.

Erzulie stood several feet from Holly, but the angel didn't advance.

"What's going on?" Alexandra asked.

"She won't let me carry the baby over," Erzulie said.

Alexandra turned to Holly.

"Stay back," Holly said, a wild look in her eyes. "I'm not letting that demon take Delia."

"Calm down," Alexandra said. "We need to get you and Delia to the other side. Do you understand?"

Spittle sprayed from Holly's mouth as she spoke. "That demon isn't going to touch my baby!"

Alexandra took a step towards the deranged woman and said, "Okay. We can talk about this."

The wind intensified, and Holly stumbled near the edge. Alexandra gasped as Holly and Delia fell from the broken highway and into the darkness below.

CHAPTER 25

Alexandra was stunned as she watched Holly and Delia disappear from the edge of the broken road. However, Erzulie's angelic reflexes sprung into action. She spread her wings and followed Holly into the darkness below.

A small scream escaped Nicole's lips. Everyone else was on the other side of the chasm, at least fifty feet away and out of sight.

Alexandra waited for several strained minutes. The image of Holly's fall was fresh in her mind. Dropping to her knees, she remained a good distance from the lip of the chasm. She was numb from all the death around her.

More time passed.

Neither Alexandra nor Nicole moved. The wind howled around them and the rustling of clothes was the only motion. Was this really happening? Alexandra stared at the broken edge of the road. How could she continue?

"Too much," Alexandra said, though her voice was weaker than the wind. Friends and enemies have been killed in her presence. She bloodied her own hands during the battle at the beached cruise ship. What was it all for? A place? Heaven on Earth?

What if they were wrong?

Eden may well be a fantasy. Everyone's death would become hollow, a waste of precious vitality in a world devoid of any comfort or remorse. How would she deal with that final truth, if it came to that?

Alexandra turned her tear-streaked face to the dark sky and screamed.

"What do you want from me?"

The weary woman from San Antonio turned wasteland leader repeated the words until her throat stung and her voice turned hoarse. Nicole, hesitant at first, encompassed Alexandra in a hug. They both sobbed.

Alexandra didn't see or hear Erzulie return to the surface of the flyover highway, but when Alexandra opened her eyes, the angel came into focus at the edge of the chasm.

"Erzulie?" Alexandra said.

"I am sorry, Lex. I couldn't save them both," Erzulie said as she strode towards Alexandra.

So, that was it. Another death. Though Alexandra knew this would be the likely outcome, the truth of the angel's words stung like a fresh wound.

Erzulie continued. "Delia is safe on the other side with the others."

"Delia…" Alexandra said. Was she wrong to feel relief over Erzulie saving the child over the mother? Who should make those decisions?

Nicole smiled and hugged Erzulie.

Though Holly was gone, Delia now had a chance in this doomed world. A small victory for Alexandra was still a victory. She decided she would take it.

Wiping the tears from her face, Alexandra said, "Thank you, Erzulie. You were truly heroic."

Alexandra and Nicole joined the rest of the group on the other side of the flyover highway. Few words were exchanged over dinner. By the time the reddish dawn came, Erzulie had flown all the supplies over the chasm and Santino waited in their new transportation – a rusty black pickup truck.

Since Santino knew the most about babies, Alexandra offered to drive. Santino and Nicole made themselves comfortable in the back of the pickup truck along with Benjamin who watched the skies with his assault rifle. Koneh navigated as they followed the flyover. Koneh also continued with the sword lessons, though Alexandra felt like she wasn't really progressing. After two days, they reached the ground again and followed route 180 for another three sunless days into the capital of Brazil – Brasilia.

Alexandra reined the pickup to a stop before a ruined bridge. The remaining sections of bridge stretched out like a broken stone path at the base of a massive dried out lake. The reddish sky gave the group a glimpse of the other side and the many lights from what Alexandra hoped were survivors.

With Delia in one arm, Santino hugged Alexandra and said, "Gracias."

Erzulie appeared in the sky and dropped to the ground beside Alexandra.

"There are many humans in Brasilia," Erzulie said.

Alexandra's heart leapt.

"How do they look?" Koneh asked.

Erzulie said, "They seem to have managed quite well. Many of the buildings are functional and some vehicles drive on the roads. The cathedral seems to be the place with the most people."

"Did you see any weapons? Troops?" Benjamin asked.

"Oh yes," Erzulie said. "In fact, a small group of jeeps and soldiers are gathering on the other side of this empty lake as we speak. No doubt, they are curious about us."

"Did they see you?" Alexandra asked.

Erzulie smiled. "Of course not."

"That's a large city," Alexandra said. "Erzulie, I don't think you need to fly around the whole time we're inside. We may rest up for a while."

Erzulie turned to Alexandra and said, "I'm quite strained from the battles and constant flying. I'm sorry, but if we were to go into battle again, I may fall."

Koneh said, "I was already thinking about that. Why don't you stow the wings and join us on this one."

"Stow the wings?" Alexandra asked.

Koneh grinned. "Angels are remarkable creatures."

"How?" Alexandra asked.

"She can fold them under her skin," Koneh said.

"Is that acceptable?" Erzulie asked.

Alexandra blinked. "Of course!"

The angel removed what was left of her armor, which fell to the pavement with a metallic *thud*. Then, with a child's innocence, Erzulie removed her dress to expose her naked ashen body. Santino and Nicole turned away. Benjamin and Alexandra stared as Erzulie flattened her black, feathery wings against her back.

"Okay, soldier. Show's over." Koneh grasped Benjamin's bicep and turned him around. "Give the lady some privacy. This will take some time."

Over the next hour, Erzulie contorted her wings until they disappeared under her skin. While the group enjoyed a brief meal,

Alexandra found her eyes drawn to the naked angel time and again. The procedure appeared both majestic and gruesome to Alexandra's human eyes.

"I know what you're thinking," Koneh said as he leaned towards Alexandra.

Alexandra shifted her attention to her companion and said, "What?"

"You're thinking, why hasn't she done this before?"

Alexandra shook her head. "That wasn't on my mind, no."

"Well," Koneh said, "the process will take another three days, as the wings further compress themselves under her skin. She may not walk or move quite right until the process is finished and she cannot bring them out again either."

"No wings for at least three days?"

"Correct," Koneh said as he watched Erzulie retrieve some fatigues from the back of the pickup. "But I think she needs the rest."

"Do you love her?" Alexandra said, not sure why she asked the question. She was both curious and jealous. However, her jealousy was the foolish kind she felt when she saw a gorgeous woman with a man her age. Sure, the people were strangers, but that didn't matter.

Koneh huffed. "Love is one of those tricky words."

"You told me before that you are human," Alexandra said. "Don't you have feelings? Emotions?"

As the rest of the group carried on their own conversations, Alexandra studied Koneh. The sharp lines of his face contrasted the uneven scars which painted every patch of his grey skin. Those black-in-black eyes betrayed no emotion. Whether he was killing an enemy or chatting about demonic physiology, his eyes held their secrets. This both frustrated and excited her.

Then, Koneh closed his unreadable eyes. "Sometimes I envy Erzulie and her limitations," he said. "Sometimes I feel too much."

Alexandra lowered her eyes and thought of Father Richard Callahan again. Guilt and sorrow swirled together in the pit of Alexandra's stomach. Was his body still under that shallow mound at the base of the beached cruise ship? Did his soul patiently await her arrival in Eden? Did everyone's soul wait for her?

The magnitude of her responsibility threatened to overwhelm her again until she heard Koneh's raspy voice. "She's finished."

Erzulie approached the camp dressed in black army fatigues. Her long dark hair was tied into a ponytail, with each strand in perfect alignment. A pair of sunglasses hid Erzulie's all-white eyes, but nothing could hide the ashen pallor of her skin.

"Do you think it'll work?" Alexandra asked.

Koneh said, "We'll use the radiation story. It has worked for me so far."

"Well," Alexandra said, "look at her. She's more beautiful than any supermodel, and you're... well..."

Koneh huffed. "Just stay in the back of the truck, Erzul. And find a hat."

Alexandra rose and took Erzulie's hands, reversing their positions from when they first met.

"Wow," Alexandra said as she inspected the transformed angel. "It doesn't matter what you're wearing, does it? You make those fatigues look like runway material."

Erzulie's face shifted into a look of confusion. "Like an airport?"

Alexandra laughed. "No, like you could walk down a runway at a fashion show and dazzle the photographers."

"Ahhh, that makes more sense."

"Indeed," Alexandra said.

"Okay," Koneh said, "enough clothes talk. Let's go see how friendly those soldiers are."

Maneuvering the dried out riverbed proved more difficult and time-consuming than Alexandra first thought. However, the sight of civilization kept everyone awake long past their usual hour. When the truck reached the other bank, one of the awaiting jeeps flashed its lights and a man called to them.

"¿Quem sao voce?"

Alexandra stopped the truck, killed the engine and turned to Santino. "Are they speaking Portuguese?"

Santino nodded. "Si, I know it."

"By all means. Make a good impression."

Santino passed Delia to Nicole and waved at the soldiers. He exchanged a few words in Portuguese and then a short man in a plain green jumpsuit descended the slope.

Smiling, the Brazilian soldier said, "Welcome to Brasilia. Please, please come!"

"What's your name?" Alexandra asked.

While Santino maneuvered the truck up the embankments, everyone else climbed up with the Brazilian soldier.

"Cedro."

"I'm Alexandra. This is Benjamin and Nicole," Alexandra said as she waved her hand in the direction of the pair. "Nicole has Delia in her arms. Behind them are..." Alexandra paused. Did she fabricate names for her two unusual companions? What if the Brazilian military detained them? Deciding that the simplest solution was always best Alexandra said, "Koneh and Erzulie." Pointing to the pickup Alexandra said, "And Santino's in the truck."

"Yes," Cedro said, "good to meet you." The Brazilian soldier's eyes lingered on Koneh and Erzulie for a few moments, but he didn't appear shocked.

"How have you fared?" Alexandra asked.

Cedro paused his climb to remove his helmet and wipe his brow. "Very much death. But we go on. Padre Hernon is good to keep us together. He talks to visitors, so I tell him where you are."

"Do you get many visitors?" Alexandra asked.

Cedro resumed his climb. "No. Very little visitors."

Switching from small talk, Alexandra asked, "Is there a place we can stay?"

"Yes! I take you to Tryp Hotel, yes?"

Nicole gasped and said, "A hotel?"

"Yes," Cedro said, "many rooms to use. You pick."

"What about supplies?" Alexandra said. "Can we buy or trade for gasoline and food?"

Several more Brazilian soldiers waited in and around their jeeps. Some of the soldiers smoked cigarettes, others chatted in Portuguese.

Cedro nodded to one of the soldiers leaning next to an empty jeep. Then Cedro said, "Yes, very many gasoline and food. You see. You ride with me, Alejandra? Truck can follow."

"Sure," Alexandra said.

After a few more minutes, Santino popped over the ridge in the pickup. The vehicle rumbled and protested, but Santino prevailed. Benjamin helped Nicole and Delia into the truck and then joined Koneh and Erzulie in the flatbed.

Alexandra approached the driver's window on the pickup and smiled at Santino. "I know you are anxious to see your daughter. All I ask is you drop us off at the hotel and then take the truck wherever you want."

Santino smiled. "Si, many thanks to you, Alejandra."

Alexandra kissed Santino on the cheek. Then she patted his forearm and said, "Your rig brought us most of the way. It's *you* we should be thanking."

As they drove through the dark city, Cedro acted as Alexandra's tour guide.

"Very many buildings crumbled, but very many okay." Cedro said.

As they passed buildings and campfires, Alexandra marveled at how intact Brasilia was compared to Tampico and the other places she had visited. The people appeared less downtrodden as well. They almost seemed cheerful. Perhaps the shock of the earthquake and loss of loved ones had passed. Maybe they were moving on with their lives.

The jeep turned onto a wide road and the central city plaza stretched out like an endless field in front of the headlights.

"What's that?" Alexandra asked, pointing to a tall structure at the center of the field.

"Television tower," Cedro said.

Cedro turned the jeep into a large, mostly empty parking lot. The tall Tryp Hotel looked like it had been blanketed by a layer of ash, but otherwise appeared to be in good health.

At Koneh's suggestion, they claimed some rooms on the second floor. Nicole settled into her room with Delia while everyone else unpacked the supplies.

"Good luck," Alexandra said to Santino. "You know where we are."

Santino nodded. Then, with tears in his eyes, he hugged Alexandra.

"Gracias," Santino said. "I was not born here, but this is my home. You brought me home."

"We'll see you tomorrow?" Alexandra said as they parted.

"Si."

Koneh shook Santino's hand and said, "You did well."

Though Santino was weary of Koneh at first, those feelings had long since been replaced by the bond of friendship.

Erzulie embraced Santino and said, "You are very brave, Señor Santino. I hope you find your daughter. The love between a father and daughter is a special gift."

Alexandra winced at the angel's words and thought of Father Callahan. Her guilt refused to be ignored.

After Santino departed, Koneh turned to Alexandra and Erzulie. "So," he said, "ready for your lesson tonight?"

Alexandra glared at him and said, "Seriously? Tonight?"

"Sometimes," Koneh said, "the battle comes to you when you are least ready. I thought you knew that lesson already."

After training with Koneh, Alexandra found her room and dropped into her bed. Sleep came easy on the comfortable mattress.

Alexandra awoke refreshed but sore. Sword training proved more taxing than a game of racquetball. And more frustrating. At the gym in San Antonio, she feared nobody on the racquetball court. In the wasteland, however, she found plenty to fear.

"Are you well?"

Alexandra jumped out of bed.

"When did you get here, Erzulie?" Alexandra examined her naked body. "And where did my clothes go?"

Erzulie cocked her head to the side. "I arrived in your room two hours ago and noticed you were still in your clothes. So I removed them and washed them for you. I also brought you a bucket of soapy water to clean yourself with, as the running water and electricity are both nonfunctional. Is all of this acceptable?"

Both annoyed and grateful, Alexandra sat on the edge of her bed and said, "You don't need to do all of these things for me, Erzulie. You are not my servant."

"But of course I am your servant," Erzulie said. "All angels were built to serve. This is not something to revile or pity. Rather, this is a fact of our existence."

Alexandra ripped open a granola bar. In-between mouthfuls she said, "Well, I'd rather you treat me like a friend, like we talked about before. You're nobody's slave. Okay?"

"I'm sorry that I cannot explain myself to you. It is my own failing."

Alexandra shook her head. "You're not a failure! If God discarded you because he thought you were flawed, well, then He was wrong!"

Erzulie lowered her eyes and said, "Your words are kind, but I am self-aware of my own flaws."

Alexandra sighed and walked to the bucket of soapy water. "I'm not going to win this argument, am I?"

Erzulie smiled, rose to her feet with the grace of a trained dancer, and left the room. Alexandra took advantage of the time alone to bathe and open Father Callahan's altered Bible. Though Alexandra couldn't read Latin since her early days in law school, she flipped to "Revelations" and studied the cross-outs and notes in the margin. Did this book hold some clue to her future or was it just the ramblings of a man driven insane?

After relaxing for the better part of the morning, Alexandra slipped into some clean fatigues and ventured from her room. A lone propane lantern flickered at the end of the hallway, throwing long shadows.

"Good afternoon," Koneh said.

"Why are you lurking about?" Alexandra asked.

"Our friend Cedro came to visit this morning," Koneh said.

"Yeah?"

"Looks like the man in charge here is Padre Lucio Hernon, a priest," Koneh said. "And he wants to talk to you."

Alexandra narrowed her eyes. "What did you tell them?"

"Nothing," Koneh said. "I'm not the one who's been advertising."

The scene at the army tent crept into Alexandra's mind. She healed Benjamin and she still didn't know how. Why couldn't she heal Father Callahan? Jason? The others who died at the cruise ship?

"I got the impression they're just looking for news or information we may have," Koneh said. "It will probably be quick and harmless."

"Sounds good. When do I go?"

"As soon as Benjamin wakes up. He stayed in Nicole's room last night."

"Why Benjamin?"

"Because he's going with you," Koneh said.

Alexandra sighed. "I don't *always* need protection."

"I'm not sure how well organized or informed the Catholic Church has remained over the past few months," Koneh said. "So, like anyone, we'll treat them with caution for now."

"Why aren't you coming with me?" Alexandra asked, though she already guessed the answer.

Koneh flashed a look of frustration at Alexandra and said, "I'd rather not raise any more eyebrows than we have to."

"Fair enough," Alexandra said as she turned her attention to Nicole's door. "Have you knocked?"

"The baby stopped crying an hour ago. So, I was letting them get some sleep."

"Oh," Alexandra said, "how much has she been crying?"

"Off and on, all night," Koneh said.

"A bomb could have detonated in the hotel last night. I wouldn't have heard it."

Koneh huffed. "You looked quite ragged."

The cry from the other side of the door started low, but then it grew into an all-out cacophony of infant screams.

"Wow, she's really unhappy," Alexandra said as she knocked on the door. "Nicole! Benjamin!"

Moments later, Benjamin opened the door and rubbed his bleary eyes. "What's going on?"

"We're going to meet someone," Alexandra said. "Grab your clothes and bring the pistol."

"Okay."

Alexandra fidgeted with her short ponytail as she waited for Benjamin in the hotel lobby. Some people, mostly locals, milled about the lobby and restaurant.

Then, Santino entered the hotel and Alexandra's heart sank. The look on his face told a familiar story Alexandra had come to know in this new world. Santino had lost his daughter.

CHAPTER 26

"I'm so sorry," Alexandra said as she held Santino.

Though Santino wasn't crying, Alexandra noticed the red circles under his eyes and the lines across his face. The man had been upset for many hours.

"They say the building fell," Santino said. "They say people inside screamed for days. Then, no more screams."

Alexandra searched her heart but couldn't find any words of comfort. Even when her friends in San Antonio called her in despair, Alexandra never really listened to them. She wasn't good at this.

"Where's her mother?" As a lawyer, Alexandra never asked a question like this, where she wasn't sure of the answer. Some of the possible answers could bring Santino to tears again and she scolded herself for taking the risk.

"She's gone," Santino said. "Very long ago."

Alexandra quickly decided that asking Santino questions about his family would bring the man more pain. Then an idea popped into her head.

"Do you want to see Delia?" Alexandra said.

Santino nodded. "Si, I like that very much."

Alexandra led Santino to Nicole's room and knocked on the door.

Benjamin, now dressed, opened the door and smiled. "Good to see you, Santino."

Nodding, Santino entered the room and scooped Delia into his arms. Though the pain on Santino's face remained, love was also there. Santino had grown close to the infant over the past week since Holly had plummeted off the Flyover. In the old United States, adoption under these circumstances would take months or years. However, in the wasteland, Alexandra learned to follow her heart.

"Santino," Alexandra said, "I can't imagine the pain you are feeling. Delia shares your pain, but from the opposite end. If you'll have her, I can think of nobody more qualified or deserving for this special baby girl."

Confusion and then joy spread over Santino's face.

"If you're not ready for this, I understand," Alexandra said. "I'm meeting with the leader of Brasilia in a few moments. I can ask him if anyone wants a child. However, I think this is the best place for Delia. She's safer here than in the wasteland with me. I think you are the best one to make that decision for her, Santino. Should I mention something to the Brazilians or will you take care of Delia?"

Santino looked into the infant's eyes. Then, he raised his tear-streaked face and said, "Si, I take Delia."

"Good, it's settled," Alexandra said. A part of her recoiled at her own arrogance. Was she making new law as she went along? Who was she to decide the fate of an infant who had lost both parents to this new Earth? Was she just trying to hide her own guilt over the battle at the cruise ship?

Despite the questions in her mind, Alexandra felt her decision was a wise one.

Nicole clapped her hands together and hugged both Santino and Delia. "I haven't fed her yet. She's probably hungry."

"Si," Santino said, though his eyes remained on Delia.

"I'll get the bottle ready," Nicole said as she sprang into action.

Alexandra and Benjamin departed the hotel and followed Cedro's directions to the Catedral Metropolitana Nossa Senhora Aparecida – The Cathedral of Brasilia. Though the streets were occupied by a few more people and vehicles than the night before, Brasilia was still quiet and dark for a city of its size.

The Cathedral of Brasilia looked like a massive teepee, rising from a bed of white stone. Crumbled statues lined the main entrance courtyard. Pillars of concrete stretched inward from a circular base to a point near the top, and then angled outwards and towards the sky. Gigantic sections of brown and tan cloth waved in the breeze between the skyward reaching concrete columns. Locals of Brasilia huddled around trash can fires and picnic tables scattered about the wide courtyard area. The scene reminded Alexandra of nighttime tailgating outside of Cowboys' Stadium after a football game.

Equally as impressive as the exterior, the inside of the Cathedral drew a low whistle from Benjamin. The interior appeared to be one large teepee room, with fiberglass angels hanging from the slanted spines of the concrete pillars. Propane lanterns lined the room along its circular base, but couldn't pierce the darkness of the roof high overhead. The many pews were filled with people, though mass wasn't in session.

Benjamin and Alexandra waited only a few minutes before they were lead into an inner office by a woman with a nametag. Seated behind a large steel desk was a slight middle-aged Brazilian man with thick grey hair and glasses. The Padre wore black robes and several silver rings.

"Hello! I am Padre Lucio Hernon."

"Hello," Alexandra said. "I'm Alexandra, and this is my friend, Benjamin."

"Please, Alejandra, sit." Padre Hernon motioned to the two chairs in front of his desk. "Benjamin, sit."

"Thank you for seeing us," Alexandra said. "My friends and I have travelled far and we are grateful for your hospitality."

Padre Hernon waved his hand and said, "Brasilia is friend to all. You come from Mexico, yes?"

"Yes," Alexandra said as she wondered what Koneh was so worried about. The Padre seemed quite pleasant.

"You have news?"

Alexandra told the Padre about the quake, Tampico, the Army base at Veracruz, the beached cruise ship, the garbled message on the satellite radio and the Flyover. However, Alexandra left out the battles, Erzulie, Alexandra's healing hands, the altered Bible, Holly's fall and most everything Koneh said. She wasn't ready to show her aces just yet.

After listening without interrupting, Padre Hernon leaned back in his chair and studied Alexandra and Benjamin. Though the Padre appeared simple and humble at first, Alexandra reevaluated the man. As Padre Hernon digested the information, she reviewed her story in her mind to confirm she didn't divulge any dangerous facts.

"We heard that same message on our radios," Padre Hernon said. "We think we sent a reply message to Rome, but we have not heard back yet. From what we know, Pope Victor the Fourth survived the quakes and is gathering information from Rome."

"Oh, that's good news!"

"Yes, it is. So, why did you leave Veracruz base?" the Padre asked.

"Santino wanted to get home to his daughter," Alexandra said. "We promised to help him. We were saddened to find out she had passed away."

"And Santino was in Mexico with his baby?" Padre Hernon asked.

"Yes," Alexandra said. "He has brought his other daughter back to Brasilia. Her name is Delia, and she is a newborn."

"The mamã?"

Alexandra shifted in her seat and said, "The mother... died."

Padre Hernon studied Alexandra for a few moments. She usually avoided lying as it always got witnesses in trouble on the stand. One misstep and the whole lie came crashing down.

"And you're a soldier?" This time, the Padre addressed Benjamin.

Benjamin nodded. "Yes, Father. U.S. Army."

"Why did you leave Veracruz base?"

Benjamin looked to Alexandra, who had the answer ready. "General Ryan had no news of the outside world," she said. "Since we were travelling so far, he thought it a good idea to send someone with us, both for protection and to gather some information."

"I understand. We have law in Brasilia. God's law. I see the cross on your neck, so I think you know the laws?" Padre Hernon said as he gestured to Alexandra's Confirmation necklace. "Follow God's law and you stay for as long as you want."

"Thank you," Alexandra said. "We don't want to cause any trouble. Some of us are staying and some of us are moving on."

Alexandra wished she could retrieve her words. She said too much and now the lie could dissolve under the judging stare of the Padre.

"Moving on?" Padre Hernon said. "Where do you go?"

From the other side of the witness stand, Alexandra enjoyed the rush she felt when she caught someone in a lie. It made her job so much easier. Now, she was the witness. Committed to this course, she spun a scarf of lies to wrap around her blunder.

"Yes," Alexandra said as she strained to keep her voice even and her face calm. "I'm going home to San Antonio, to see what's left."

Padre Hernon raised an eyebrow and said, "Why did you not do that first? San Antonio is close to Mexico. Not so close to Brasilia."

"We came here for Santino," Alexandra said, clinging to her lie like a life raft. "I have no family in San Antonio. I can wait."

Padre Hernon studied Alexandra for a few moments and said, "That is very generous to help a friend so far."

"We're only doing what we can," Alexandra said.

"You have more friends with you, yes?" Padre Hernon said.

Alexandra realized the Padre was setting her up, a lawyer's tactic.

"Yes," Alexandra said. "An American girl and two more friends of mine."

"I hear," Padre Hernon said, "that some of your friends are sick? They look sick?"

"They aren't sick," Alexandra said. She realized she had to be careful with her words. "Just weary from a long trip."

"I see." After a few more uncomfortable moments, Padre Hernon said, "Well Alejandra, I have more meetings today. Stay in the hotel as long as you want. Be safe, follow God's law, and may God be with you."

"And also with you," Alexandra said, recalling the rote from her church days.

Once outside the cathedral, Alexandra exhaled and put her hands on her knees.

"Yeah," Benjamin said, "he was a tough little nut."

Though Alexandra didn't think Padre Hernon bought her whole story, she hoped she misled him enough to leave her group alone.

"Just don't tell Koneh what happened," Alexandra said. "I don't want to have to defend myself twice today."

"No problem."

After Alexandra survived another training session with Koneh, everyone ate dinner in her room. Santino cradled Delia while the baby slept, Benjamin and Nicole shared an oversized chair, Erzulie sat next to Alexandra on the floor, and Koneh paid equal attention to the conversation in the room and the darkness outside the window.

"This is great," Nicole said as she devoured her hamburger. "Where did you get these again?"

"Right on the street," Benjamin said. "The guy will cook you anything. I think he said these are soy burgers."

Alexandra took comfort in the warm food. "Thank you, Benjamin. Did you have to pay?"

The soldier nodded. "Yeah, I gave him one of my guitar picks. No need for those now, since we had to abandon the non essentials."

Delia stirred in Santino's arms but she didn't awaken.

"How's she doing?" Nicole asked.

"Good, good," Santino said. "Brave lil' girl."

"I can't believe we made it," Nicole said. "I mean, so many people died."

Alexandra recalled the grave mounds at the base of the beached cruise ship. "Too many."

"Well," Benjamin said, "we still got a ways to go."

Nicole bit her lip and nodded.

"Don't worry," Alexandra said, "you can stay here if you want to."

"Really?" Nicole said.

Alexandra smiled at Nicole, but Erzulie responded. "Of course," Erzulie said. "Alexandra doesn't wish to put you in any more danger."

"That goes for you too, Santino," Alexandra said. "You have more important responsibilities now anyway."

Santino smiled at the sleeping infant in his arms. "Si, gracias, Alejandra."

"Hell," Alexandra said, "I might stay here myself! What's not to like?"

"Not much, *Alejandra*," Benjamin said.

Nicole turned to face her chair-mate and said, "Alejandra?"

Benjamin laughed and said, "Yeah, everyone's calling her that here. It's kinda funny."

"That's her name," Koneh said, joining the conversation.

"Huh?" Benjamin said.

"Before she Americanized it," Koneh said. "The name her mother chose for her was Alejandra."

Like water over a fire, Koneh doused Alexandra's mood.

Koneh continued his assault. "One letter. How much did it cost to change that one letter, Alejandra?"

At times, especially now, Alexandra felt like the cost was too high. She changed her name to further distance herself from her home and her mother. In Alexandra's desire to gain acceptance in her beloved America, she lost a part of who she was, the person her mother raised her to be. Now, in the wasteland of the Earth, Alexandra felt the pain of her past vanities.

Without responding to Koneh, Alexandra left the hotel room. Koneh looked into her soul and exposed her shame. Yes, she was a selfish girl in the past. Did Koneh need to show that to everyone?

Alexandra departed the hotel and found a comfortable patch of burnt grass overlooking the central city plaza with the massive TV tower. After a few long minutes alone with her thoughts, Alexandra whispered, "Who am I?"

The red-black sky held no answers for her. Then, she heard Koneh's familiar footsteps. Like a predator, Koneh approached from behind and made almost no sound.

"May I join you?" Koneh asked.

Alexandra motioned to the ground, but didn't speak. She wanted to hear what he had to say.

"Nicole said I was being a... well... I don't quite remember the slang she used. Anyway, I wasn't really sympathetic to your feelings. So, I guess I'm here to apologize."

"You guess?"

Koneh sat facing Alexandra and said, "I'm sorry you were hurt by my words."

"Do you even know how to apologize?" Alexandra stared down her companion. Then, her voice softened and she said, "Listen, I didn't walk out because I am mad at you. I left because you're right. I've been a selfish, self-absorbed brat for most of my life."

Koneh shook his head. "That's not how I see it."

"Yeah," Alexandra said, "what do you see? Because, to tell you the truth, I don't know who I am anymore."

"I'm not going to tell you who you are," Koneh said. "Your own actions at the cruise ship speak louder than any words."

Tears rolled from Alexandra's eyes at the memory of the battle. "You mean, when I condemned half of us to death?"

"Where would Nicole and Delia be right now if you hadn't stayed to help them?"

Like a computer programmed to respond to a certain command, Alexandra's response was automatic. "Where would Richard be if we didn't stop?"

As if Koneh prepared a counterpoint he said, "Do you really think Richard would count his life above that of a newborn's? Of anyone? You tarnish his memory by even suggesting he would leave those people to die."

"You would have left them," Alexandra said.

Koneh opened his mouth to speak, but he paused. Then, after a few moments, he locked his eyes upon Alexandra and said, "My duty is to bring you to Eden, no matter the cost."

"Is that all that is important to you? Your duty?"

Koneh turned away from Alexandra. "It's all I have left," he said. The edge was gone from his voice. What was he feeling? Alexandra still found her guide difficult to read.

"You have Erzulie and the friends we've made along the way," Alexandra said.

"Friends have a way of coming and going."

"Not Erzulie."

Koneh sighed. "Erzulie is not my friend."

"You never answered my question before," Alexandra said. "Do you love her? Does she love you?"

Koneh stood, his back still to Alexandra. "I think I felt love for Erzulie once, a long time ago. However, like all love, the trip is short when it's on a one-way street."

"What happened?"

Koneh looked over his shoulder and said, "Nothing. How could anything come from nothing? Without the capacity to return my love, Erzulie and I… well, that's a long story. Let's just say we went our separate ways."

"Until all of this?"

"Something like that," Koneh said.

"I want to hear what happened."

"I'm not sure I can recall the events as they happened, anyway," Koneh said. "We humans have a way of reinventing our past to fit how we think things happened. Nostalgia and the barrier of years distort our view of what was. I fear I may be guilty of this when it comes to Erzulie. I had hopes..." Koneh's voice trailed away.

Alexandra stood and faced him. Her voice soft, she said, "And do you have hopes now? Besides Eden?" She stepped closer, within arms reach. "Is there nothing else in this world for you?"

He looked into her eyes. "I... I am no longer here for myself," he said. "At the end of this road..."

Alexandra encircled his neck with her arms. She wasn't going to allow this conversation be interrupted. Not this time. She brought her face close to his and said, "Don't think about the *end* of the road. I'm talking about here and now."

"You must not..."

"Must not what?" Alexandra inched closer with her lips.

Koneh closed his eyes and said, "This is not me... Don't look at me as I am now. I didn't choose to look like this."

She ran her hand across his cheek and said, "I don't see the scars... the eyes... all I see is a man I want to be closer to. Don't you feel the same?"

"No," he said.

Still gentle, Alexandra said, "I don't believe you. Why do I feel like you constantly try to push me away?"

After a long pause, he opened his eyes and said, "Because I am."

"Why? What are you afraid of?"

"I cannot... let go," he said. "Eden must come first."

"And there's no room for *your* feelings? For the things you want?"

Koneh's eyes narrowed and he whispered, "You tempt me too much. My self-control is only so strong."

"Let go," she said. "I'm not afraid..."

Without warning, Koneh pulled her close and pressed his lips to hers. Alexandra's heart and world exploded like a long restrained force was unleashed within her. She pressed against his body. The pain, guilt and sorrow from the past months drained from her soul as she enjoyed that moment of joy.

Then, as soon as it came, the moment ended when Koneh pushed her away.

"We cannot," he said, unable to meet her questioning eyes.

Alexandra collected her thoughts after the rush of passion and exhaled. She wanted him more now that she experienced her first touch. She stepped towards him, but he held his hand towards her to ward her away.

"No," he said. "That was a mistake and I'm sorry."

"A mistake? I thought you felt…"

He shook his head with a pained look on his face. "I'm not allowed to feel such things. Not for you."

Frustrated, she said, "Why not? Who's making the rules?"

His face grave, he said, "I am. I must. To reach Eden, I must not feel, only *act*. This is too important."

"To let your feelings show?" she said. "I don't agree."

"You don't have to agree."

"But I have to live with it? Is that what you're saying?"

Koneh appeared lost. "I… I shouldn't have kissed you."

"Because it's not allowed?" Alexandra asked, her voice mocking.

"No," he said, "Because now I may be unable to control my feelings. Because now I know how you feel and my pain is only deepened. Because now… now I am conflicted."

Softening her tone, she said, "Conflicted? This isn't complicated…"

"It is, Alejandra," he said sadly. "There's so much you don't know. I should be more careful when we are together. You must distance yourself from me. You cannot touch or watch me like you do. I must not be reminded of…"

"Our kiss?" she asked. "Was it so terrible?"

Koneh held her gaze for a moment. Then, looking away, he said, "No, quite the opposite. If circumstances were different…" He shook his head as he disappeared into the darkness. "I cannot…"

Alexandra watched him as he walked away and out of sight. She touched her lips and still felt fire there. She knew she loved him, but she didn't know how or *if* she should tell him. His motives seemed noble, but Alexandra couldn't abide by his rules. She *needed* to be close to him. She decided she would convince him that their feelings could only strengthen them. Somehow…

Then, after a few long minutes alone in the darkness, Alexandra returned to the hotel. Sleep came quickly again and so did Alexandra's dreams. She couldn't recall every detail, but she remembered confronting the boy child on the throne again. This time the throne was in a palace at the center of a large city. A barren, rocky landscape surrounded the city. Alexandra couldn't remember what she or the boy said, but she felt the dream was important.

Santino brought Delia to his home the next morning. After saying a few good-byes, Santino departed the hotel parking lot in a friend's jeep. Though Alexandra knew she would see Santino and Delia again, their relationship had changed. Instead of a travelling companion, Santino was now a friend who lived in Brasilia. He no longer shared Alexandra's burden. A burden she never accepted nor wanted to share.

"What now?" Nicole asked. "Are you still going to Eden?"

"I don't know," Alexandra said. "For now, I'm glad to have a roof over my head and a mattress to sleep on."

"Amen, sistah," Nicole said. "I'm looking forward to some R&R."

Benjamin smiled at Nicole and said, "Me too."

"Okay," Alexandra said, "what's going on with you two?"

Nicole and Benjamin blushed. "We're kinda dating," Nicole said.

Koneh huffed and said, "Whenever you're ready for your lesson, Alexandra, I'll be in the back lot."

"Isn't it a little early for a lesson?" Alexandra asked, her eyes searching for some lingering effect on his face from their kiss. However, he was unreadable and detached.

"You're not progressing," Koneh said. "So, two a day until I see some improvement."

After he disappeared into the hotel, Alexandra turned to Nicole and said, "Aren't you a little young?"

"I'm fifteen."

"And you?" Alexandra asked, pointing at Benjamin.

"Twenty."

"New love is one of the most amazing moments you humans can feel," Erzulie said. "Enjoy your time together."

Alexandra prepared a speech to warn Benjamin and Nicole about the dangers of their new world and the uncertainty of their temporary home. However, after Erzulie's words, Alexandra's speech fizzled. Erzulie was right. Why should they be afraid? Joy in this new world was fleeting. Of course they should enjoy their time together.

"Well," Alexandra said, "Just don't do anything stupid."

Nicole raised her eyebrow and said, "Like?"

"I don't know! Use your heads."

"I brought condoms with me," Benjamin said. Nicole's blush deepened. "Just in case."

Alexandra smiled. "All right, I'm not your mother. Listen to Erzulie and enjoy yourselves."

Leaving the new couple alone, Alexandra and Erzulie found Koneh in the hotel's rear parking lot. The other residents in the hotel didn't visit the lot too often, so Koneh chose the spot as their sparring ground.

Koneh watched Alexandra as she stretched. "I think you made a wise decision," Koneh said.

Alexandra reached for her toes and said, "About what?"

"Santino and Delia."

"Thanks. It made sense to me."

Koneh fidgeted and averted Alexandra's gaze. Then he said, "You were right about the cruise ship as well. If we left them there, then I would have never had the chance to deliver that baby."

"I didn't realize it meant that much to you." Alexandra recalled Koneh's trepidation before delivering the baby. Most of the time, Koneh appeared confident and under control. Koneh's vulnerability hid far beneath the surface, but it was a side of him Alexandra found she liked. She exposed that part of him when they kissed and Alexandra wanted to indulge farther. However, he was clear that they needed to remain distant from each other. Was that possible? Could she bury her feelings like she buried her friends?

"We've discussed his experience at length," Erzulie said. Though Koneh glared at her, Erzulie continued. "Sometimes, change is good for the heart."

"Indeed," Alexandra said as she studied Koneh. "How very interesting. Do you think you have changed?"

Koneh shrugged. "I remember that feeling – the joy of new life in the world. It's just been a long time."

"Okay," Alexandra said. "I think the three of us have been together long enough. I'm not trying to be a bitch, but what's the deal Koneh? Sometimes, you say things and I just don't understand.

Where are you from? Why won't you tell me more about your past?"

Koneh drew his rusty, jagged sword and pointed it at Alexandra. "Get through my defenses and I'll answer any question you pose."

"And what we talked about last night?" she said, desperate to taste him again. "If I break your defenses, can we revisit our new arrangement?"

"We can revisit that too," he said hesitantly.

She breathed deeply and for two seconds closed her eyes while her heartbeat quickened. Then, drawing her own sword, Alexandra said, "Well, that's better than your usual stonewalling. You're on!"

CHAPTER 27

Alexandra didn't succeed in breaking Koneh's defenses during any of their twice-a-day training sessions over the ensuing week. However, she felt like she made some progress with her footwork and positioning.

"Power and speed," Koneh said on many occasions. "Don't think about it while we're sparring, but figure out a way to ignore your own physical limitations. The human soul can push the body to pretty extreme limits. Once you accept that as truth, there's no attack you cannot execute and no defense you cannot muster."

Though Koneh's words made sense, Alexandra didn't know how to rise above her physical limitations and the doubts in her mind. How could she swing her blade fast enough to deflect the brunt of Koneh's strikes? Strength was one thing. Alexandra's muscles had toned and firmed over the past few months. But how could she move like Koneh moved? Koneh seemed to anticipate her attacks. He was just too fast.

Though Koneh expressed disapproval over staying in Brasilia so long, he didn't force the matter. Everyone seemed to be enjoying the downtime. Alexandra respected Koneh's desire to remain distant, though it took a considerable amount of self-control on her part. If he needed some space, she decided she'd honor his wishes. Yet, the memory of their kiss haunted and excited her each night.

Padre Hernon sent a messenger to Alexandra asking for another meeting, but for two days Alexandra ignored the request. She didn't want to face the Padre's intense stare again. What if he suspected something?

Alexandra spent most nights on the small hill that overlooked the Brazilian city's central plaza and TV tower. Alone on her hill, Alexandra found time to think.

As Alexandra meditated on the past week in Brasilia, she succumbed to the weight of her eyelids and fell asleep. When she awoke, the redness had retreated from the sky and Alexandra gathered her things to head back to the hotel. With a *woosh* of air, Erzulie landed on the backside of the hill. Then, Alexandra remembered that Erzulie had folded her wings before the group entered the city. Whoever landed wasn't her friend.

Alexandra reached for her sword. "Shit," she said as she remembered leaving the weapon in her hotel room. She assumed Brasilia was safe.

A grating female voice answered Alexandra. "Indeed."

Then, Lilev appeared from the darkness. Alexandra whirled to face the demon. "What do you want?" Alexandra asked, though she had a guess.

Lilev folded her bat-like wings against her back and pointed a clawed finger at Alexandra. "You are unwise to think yourself safe. I could tear the flesh from your bones if I wanted."

Though Alexandra received death threats while she worked for the State's Attorney's office, none of those people were as frightening as the demon named Lilev. Alexandra's throat dried and she couldn't speak.

"However," Lilev said as she stepped towards Alexandra, "that will have to wait. I have an offer for you."

The demon was an arm's length away when Alexandra found her strength. She took a step backwards and said, "Stop right there."

Lilev smiled to reveal two rows of jagged yellow teeth.

"Of course." Despite her words, the demon mirrored Alexandra's movement and continued to advance.

Alexandra noticed the demon's eyes were much like Koneh's. Pure black.

"He cannot save you now," Lilev said. "Yes, your assumption is correct. I can skim your thoughts laden with fear when we are this close, Lamb."

How was this possible? Like a frantic beekeeper trying to put a lid on a dozen angry nests, Alexandra attempted to blank her thoughts and focus on the demon. Her efforts were futile. She may as well have tried to stop the rain from falling.

Lilev snapped forward with her clawed hand, but Alexandra stepped to the side to place more distance between them.

"Aha," the demon said, "I see Koneh's training in your movements and in your mind. How very interesting."

"You said you had an offer," Alexandra said, commanding her voice to remain even.

"Indeed," Lilev said. "Listen to my words as I will not repeat them."

Alexandra nodded. This demon had little of the grace that Erzulie commanded and Lilev's movements appeared jerky, like some other consciousness fought for control under the surface. Lilev's voice grated like metal scraping against metal.

"I will tell you where your enemies are and how much time you have left," Lilev said. "I will also help you in your journey by delaying my master's main force."

Alexandra raised her eyebrow and said, "Even if I believed your words, what would you want in return?"

Lilev snorted. "You will know the truth of my words as soon as I speak them. You are the Mih'darl. Truth is like a light in the dark for you, is it not so?"

"What if I'm not the…" Alexandra struggled with the word, "…Mih'darl?"

"Koneh wouldn't be with you if you weren't, Lamb."

Alexandra weighed the importance of this information and said, "Okay, what do you want in return?"

"I don't care about Eden," the demon said. "I want to look into your dreams, dear child, that is all."

"My dreams?"

Lilev nodded. "Do you agree?"

"How?"

"I need to touch you," the demon said. "And you need to cooperate by opening your mind to me."

"How do I know you won't just kill me after you get what you want?"

"You sense truth in my words, yes?" Lilev said.

Though Alexandra wanted to run to Koneh and Erzulie for protection, she sensed only a hint of deception in Lilev's offer. However, Alexandra believed the demon would honor a bargain.

"Tell me," Alexandra said as she found the strength to make some demands of her own, "why do you want my dreams?"

"The future concerns me," Lilev said, "nothing more."

Alexandra recognized the demon's tactic. The creature was giving as little information as possible to avoid being caught in a lie. Well-coached witnesses often employed this trick. However, Alexandra knew how to peel the layers of a simple answer and get to the juicy core.

"I cannot see the future," Alexandra said.

"Your thoughts tell me you believe otherwise. Don't try to lie to me, Lamb."

"What about the future concerns you?" Alexandra asked.

"No more questions!" Lilev said. "If you accept my offer, we will have a bargain and I will not harm you this night. Decide!"

"Very well," Alexandra said. "You tell me your information and if I find it useful I will allow you to see my dreams."

"You will find it useful, child."

"Good," Alexandra said, "then agree to my terms and we will have a deal."

Lilev leaned back on her cloven feet and studied Alexandra for a few moments. Then, through her wicked teeth, the demon said, "Agreed."

"Okay. Tell me what you know," Alexandra said.

Lilev nodded. "My master, Derechi, heads for Eden now. Iblis has promised the Earth to the demon who delivers the Mih'darl and Derechi's hounds have already sniffed you out. Derechi may be the only one besides Iblis, Koneh and myself who know the location of Eden, so the Unclean One has an advantage. If you delay any longer, you risk facing Derechi's entire army. I will keep them at bay for as long as I can, but even mighty Koneh cannot win a battle against such large numbers. You would be wise to leave this city now and head for Eden before the main force arrives."

"So," Alexandra said, "Eden is empty right now? Nobody else knows where it is?"

"Koneh knows, so you should make haste. If you leave now, you will still have to deal with Derechi's advance force."

"I see. And how large is this force?"

Lilev waived her hand and said, "Oh, small enough for Koneh to handle. Maybe thirty greater demons. The best flyers are already scouring locations told to them by Derechi. It won't be long now."

"And we can make it there before the main force?"

"If you leave now, yes."

Alexandra sensed truth in the demon's words, but could the creature be trusted? Would Lilev kill Alexandra anyway once the creature got what it came for?

"You reek of fear," Lilev said. "And you should, for you and I are enemies."

This time, the demon snatched Alexandra's wrist.

"Now," Lilev said, "open your mind to me and allow me to see what you have seen when you sleep."

The presence of the demon in Alexandra's mind was overwhelming. Lilev filled every corner of Alexandra's thoughts. Alexandra fought against the violation.

Through clenched teeth Alexandra said, "You... will honor... the bargain."

"If you don't let me in, human, I will be forced to kill you," Lilev said. "Pity that would be as I may have use for you again."

Alexandra mounted one last stand with her dissolving willpower, but the demon remained. Then, Alexandra let go and allowed Lilev free reign. Darkness overwhelmed Alexandra and she fell to the ground. When Alexandra tried to open her eyes, the world spun around her little hill. Forcing the nausea away, Alexandra struggled to remain conscious. Where was Lilev?

The world settled to a halt. Alexandra scanned the hill. Though Lilev was gone, the demon's words rang clear in Alexandra's head, "...you would be wise to leave this city now and head for Eden before the main force arrives."

Was Eden mankind's last chance for happiness on this scorched Earth? Alexandra didn't know the answer, but she believed the demon spoke truth about Derechi's army. Before this moment, Alexandra wasn't sure of her path. Now, however, Alexandra realized that Eden was her destiny. Alexandra felt a new determination to find the mythical birthplace of humanity. Demons and humans would fight for Eden and Alexandra knew she had some part to play. If Alexandra's group had a chance, now was the time!

CHAPTER 28

"I'll miss you, Alex," Nicole said.

Hugging her friend, Alexandra said, "I'll miss you too."

After saying farewell to Santino and Delia, packing the truck, bartering for some cold weather clothing and resupplying the pickup, Alexandra, Koneh, and Erzulie were ready to leave Brasilia.

"Are you sure?" Benjamin asked as he handed a full gas can to Alexandra.

Earlier that day, Alexandra told Benjamin to stay in Brasilia. Perhaps he could find peace with Nicole and the couple might build a life together. In the end, Alexandra resorted to *ordering* the soldier to stay and protect Nicole, Santino, and Delia.

Alexandra smiled and hugged Benjamin. "We've been over this."

Benjamin blinked back tears and kissed Alexandra on the cheek. "Thanks," he said, "for saving my life."

"Just remember our deal," Alexandra said.

Benjamin nodded and pulled Nicole close. "I'll look after them."

"I'm counting on you."

"Oh! I almost forgot." Benjamin pulled a pistol from his belt and held the grip towards Alexandra. "I know you've been training with swords, but you might need this."

Alexandra grasped the weapon. "Thank you. I wish I could say I won't have to use it."

"We're ready," Koneh said.

After Alexandra reported her encounter with Lilev to Koneh and Erzulie, Koneh grew quiet. Erzulie confirmed that Lilev was bound by her bargain with Alexandra, so the demon would honor any pact made. While they secured their supplies, Koneh kept silent. Alexandra assumed Koneh was thinking things over and preparing his scolding for her. Or maybe he was reconsidering his wish to not express his feelings? Alexandra's heart hoped for that.

Alexandra winced as the memory of Lilev's mental invasion resurfaced. Why did the demon want to know about her dreams? Was the future really in there somewhere? To Alexandra, her dreams were a tangled mess with the white-haired crone at the center of everything. Did this old woman hold some key to the future? Alexandra shook her head. She didn't know anything for certain.

"Be safe," Erzulie said as she hugged Benjamin and Nicole.

"I won't forget you," Nicole said.

At the edge of the city, Alexandra stopped the truck. A row of jeeps and Brazilian soldiers blocked their way. "This might be trouble," Koneh said as he opened his door and stepped from the cab.

Erzulie stayed in the flatbed while Alexandra and Koneh approached the jeeps. The Brazilian soldier, Cedro, met them in the road.

"You must go back," he said. "Padre Hernon wants to ask you questions."

"I'm sorry, Cedro," Alexandra said, "but, we're not going back into the city."

Cedro frowned and averted Alexandra's gaze. "I have orders," he said, "You must go back or we take you back by force."

Koneh huffed, but before he could speak, Alexandra said, "Fine, we'll go back. We're not looking for a fight."

"I'm sorry to do this," Cedro said. "You must be cuffed."

Koneh leaned towards Alexandra and whispered, "Last chance. This might not go well, especially for Erzulie."

"Are her wings out yet?"

Koneh glanced towards the truck and said, "Should be."

"I don't want to get in a fight here," Alexandra said. "We'll cooperate, but they're not taking Erzulie."

"I'll follow your lead," Koneh said.

Raising her voice, Alexandra said, "Erzulie, we'll be back. Fly now!"

Without hesitation, Erzulie burst from the flatbed and disappeared into the dark sky. The soldiers seized Alexandra and Koneh.

"I suspected you were dangerous," Padre Hernon said to Alexandra from the other side of the bars. "You bring demons to Brasilia? Not wise."

"That wasn't a demon," Alexandra said. "She's a fallen angel and I ordered her to escape because I didn't think you'd understand."

The Padre laughed, but there was no joy there. "You think I don't understand? I tell you what I understand. You bring demons to Brasilia, your friend with the scars is a demon and you lied about who you are."

"And who do you think I am?" Alexandra asked, raising herself to look down on the priest.

Padre Hernon stepped forward and said, "Do not try to intimidate me. You are a servant of Lucifer and you will be punished for your crimes. We spoke with Rome. They warned us about imposters of the Christ. Stories of you have come to us now as well. We have a man who will identify you as false."

"Identify me?" Alexandra glared at Padre Hernon. "What are you talking about? What does Rome have to do with anything?"

Padre Hernon shouted over his shoulder. "Bring him down."

A few moments later, Marco appeared beside Padre Hernon. Alexandra's blood roiled.

Marco winked and said, "Si, that is her."

Alexandra glanced at his bandaged hand and asked, "How's your wrist?"

He fumed, but he didn't respond.

"And what did she do? So we have a record," Padre Hernon asked.

"She claimed to have healing powers," Marco said. "And she led a demon army into Tampico. Everyone was butchered."

Alexandra grasped the bars and said, "Marco! you bastard! What are you getting out of this?"

"Oh," Marco said, grinning, "she also killed a priest named Father Callahan."

Alone in her windowless cell, Alexandra wondered what happened to her friends. Was Erzulie waiting for them in the sky? Did Padre Hernon arrest Santino, Nicole and Benjamin too? What would happen to Delia? Was Koneh in another cell? Worse?

Alexandra didn't want to fight the soldiers of Brasilia. Was that the correct decision? Of course it was. How long would the remains of humanity last if they fought amongst themselves? Was it even a matter of *us* versus *them* anymore? Were the lines blurred beyond all recognition?

One thing was certain, Alexandra felt she could pull that trigger on Marco now. His betrayal had gone beyond his servitude to Derechi. He seemed to want Alexandra out of the equation. But why? According to Lilev, there was a reward on Alexandra's soul. If they had the right girl. She still wasn't convinced she was the new Messiah. Sure, she healed General Ryan and Benjamin, but maybe she was just a freak of nature? What if Bishop Palusa's altered Bible was simply the ramblings of a crazy man? What if Koneh was mistaken? What if Erzulie was as flawed as she insisted? Alexandra might die at the hands of the Catholic Church for merely denying Marco a roll in the sack. Alexandra shivered. What a way to go.

Alexandra recalled the overturned bus, the zombie-like mob, those evil hounds, meeting Koneh, Erzulie's grace, Father Callahan, abandoning Tampico, vivid dreams, healing General Ryan and Benjamin, the battle at the beached cruise ship, Marco's first betrayal, the demon Lilev, the birth of Delia and Holly's plummet. Did she really experience all of these things?

Like a swinging door, Alexandra's thoughts returned to Koneh. Time and again, the man had put himself between Alexandra and mortal danger. Though Koneh claimed to be on a mission from God, Alexandra didn't always believe him. Koneh cared for her, but he was afraid to express his feelings. Their kiss seemed like a lifetime ago, but she attempted to remember every detail of that sweet moment.

Alexandra curled into a ball on the cold slab and closed her eyes. She remembered another emotion she enjoyed near Koneh. Security. Alone in her cell, Alexandra desired his company and protection.

"Where are you now, Koneh?"

When no answer came, Alexandra drifted into sleep. A field of razor-sharp rocks extended out from where Alexandra awoke. The red-black sky above threw shadows across the narrow paths between them. In the distance, Alexandra saw something shine and then disappear.

A dream.

"Yes," said the white-haired crone.

Alexandra spun. The old woman was perched atop one of the jagged rocks. Alexandra felt insignificant under the stare of the crone.

"Where are we?" Alexandra asked.

The old woman shrugged and said, "This is your vision. I come to peer upon my enemy."

"Enemy?"

"You travel to this place," the white-haired woman said. "You must tell me your intentions."

Alexandra climbed. Since she knew she was dreaming, the cuts from the stone didn't hinder her. The razor edged rocks extended as far as Alexandra could see. Then, in the distance, something sparkled and was gone again.

"Eden is that way," Alexandra said.

The white-haired woman appeared next to Alexandra. Her eyes were like an endless ocean and Alexandra almost lost herself within their shifting depths.

"You must tell me your intentions!" the white-haired woman said.

Alexandra returned her gaze to the intermittent sparkle on the horizon and said, "I don't know."

"Your soul is in conflict."

"I don't understand everything that's going on around me."

"Nor are you meant to. You are an instrument. His instrument. You either succeed in His task or you fail, nothing more."

Alexandra turned to the crone and said, "I'm more than that!"

As if Alexandra hadn't spoken the crone said, "But He doesn't know what I hid. Deep within you I buried the knowledge to remove the taint of Eden forever. You are my instrument as well."

"I am nobody's instrument!"

After studying Alexandra for a few moments, the white-haired woman said, "My time is short. You will be here soon and I must prepare for what is to come."

"And what is that?"

The white-haired woman looked into Alexandra's eyes and said, "Whatever you make."

"I don't understand."

As the field of razor rocks faded away, she struggled to follow the white-haired woman.

"Tell me more!"

Before the dream ended, the old woman stopped and tears appeared in her eyes. "I must rest and think on my transgressions. Am I as much at fault as He for what I have done to a soul? I fear we will not speak again until after you have made the future. If I was wrong, then I extend my regret to you for what I have done…"

Alexandra awoke. Before she had time to analyze the dream, Alexandra heard footsteps. Torchlight breached the darkness as several faces appeared outside Alexandra's cell.

A group of priests and soldiers led Alexandra to the square in front of the Cathedral of Brasilia where Koneh waited next to a wall. Blood stains and bullet holes marred the surface and Alexandra wondered why she hadn't noticed this grisly landmark before. A firing squad waited for them. Marco was there too, and he edged closer to Alexandra as they lead her towards the wall.

"One thing I thought you should know before you die," Marco said. "Your friend, Koneh, won't die here, but you probably knew that."

Her words laced with venom, Alexandra said, "I'll make sure he hunts you down."

"I plan to be far away from here in just a few moments," Marco said. "But do you want to know *why* he won't die here?"

Alexandra attempted to ignore Marco. She hated him. However, Marco's next three words rang clear and true.

"Koneh is Cain."

CHAPTER 29

The truth and absurdity of Marco's words settled in Alexandra's mind. Koneh was Cain, the first murderer.

The events of the past few months locked together like the final pieces of a puzzle. Koneh was telling the truth about everything. He was human, he wasn't burned by radiation and he spoke to God.

Numb, Alexandra found herself next to her scarred companion. Only one word escaped her lips, "How?"

"No talking!" One of the soldiers slapped Alexandra across the face.

Padre Hernon's voice carried from somewhere to Alexandra's left. The Padre was listing her crimes. Alexandra didn't care. She looked into Koneh's deep black eyes and said, "You are Cain."

Koneh exhaled. "What?"

"Tell me it's not true and I'll believe you," Alexandra said, ignoring her inner voice which validated Marco's words.

"I'm sorry," Koneh said, "to have dragged you out here. I would have retrieved you from that cell yesterday, but I wanted to draw out our accuser." Koneh scanned the crowd. "And I think I see him now."

Koneh snapped the chains binding his wrists and traced a pattern in the air with his hand. A moment later, Erzulie appeared and attacked the firing squad. People screamed and shots were fired. During the confusion, Koneh led Alexandra away from the wall and down an alley where their truck idled.

"Wait here," Koneh said. "I'm going after Marco."

Alexandra leaned against a dumpster for balance. "All right," she said, "just answer one question."

"We don't have time…"

"How?" Alexandra said. "Tell me how this is possible. Were you thrown back to Earth when Hell collapsed, like Erzulie?"

"No," Koneh said, "my fate was handed to me by Elah. For my sin, I was cursed to walk the Earth until final judgment."

Koneh's unexpected response sobered Alexandra's thoughts. "Wait," she said, "you're telling me that you've been wandering the planet for…"

Finishing Alexandra's thought, Koneh said, "Thousands of years."

Koneh disappeared into the chaos. So, it was true. Koneh was Cain. He didn't deny it. Alexandra's thoughts defocused for several minutes as the weight of his words collapsed around her.

Then, automatic gunfire erupted from the streets. Alexandra crawled to the edge of her alleyway and spotted Koneh running towards her.

Bullets ripped through the area bombarding the walls and denting the dumpster. Alexandra threw herself to the ground and put her arms over her head. Then she heard a scream from the street and saw a little girl fall.

Peering at the bloody body from under her arms, Alexandra's heart thumped. More bullets pelted the area like deadly hail. Koneh stumbled but maintained his course. He noticed the girl too.

Koneh halted his dash and locked eyes with Alexandra. No words were exchanged, but Koneh glanced at the motionless girl. Then, Koneh dropped a figure to the ground. Marco.

"Save her!" Koneh shouted, and he turned towards the pursuing soldiers.

Marco scurried to the side of the road and out of Alexandra's field of vision. As Koneh charged the soldiers, Alexandra wondered if she was about to lose him before she was able to ask her many questions.

Alexandra rallied the courage to stand and sprint into the dangerous street. The girl's stomach was covered with blood and her breathing came in irregular gasps. She was dying. Tears filled Alexandra's eyes. This is exactly what Alexandra wanted to avoid when she surrendered to the soldiers – needless violence.

Alexandra placed her hands on the girl's stomach and closed her eyes. Koneh might die and Alexandra wouldn't be far behind. But, that was the line. Alexandra decided at that moment the violence would go no further. The girl would live.

Light flooded the area and the gunfire ceased. Onlookers gasped as a gentle wind swept through the street-turned-battlefield.

The girl opened her eyes and Alexandra's heart floated. Though the situation was her fault, Alexandra took comfort in the fact that she made things right. That feeling gave her strength and she marveled at her own power. Perhaps she would reach Eden after all.

Alexandra smiled and said, "What's your name?"

"Medina," the girl said. "Are you..."

"Just a friend," Alexandra said. "A friend who is sorry for what just happened to you."

The soldiers dropped to their knees and prayed in Portuguese. Bloodied and battered, Koneh staggered to Alexandra and said, "The Padre may not be so awed. We should go."

A woman ran from a nearby building and scooped Medina from Alexandra's arms.

With tears in her eyes, the woman said, "Obrigado... obrigado."

"We need to move," Koneh said.

"Right," Alexandra said, risking one more glance towards Medina.

They climbed into the idling truck. Koneh took advantage of their opening and sped through the deserted city streets. In moments, the city disappeared into the darkness behind them.

"Who got the truck ready for us?" Alexandra asked.

"Benjamin," Koneh said, checking the rear view mirror.

"Are they going to be all right?"

Koneh nodded and gritted his teeth. He was in pain. "Santino's getting everyone out in his jeep. They're headed back to the Veracruz base."

"Do you really think Padre Hernon will follow them? Or us?" Alexandra asked.

"He might," Koneh said. "He was spouting scripture to me and he even doused me with holy water. I think he's the real deal."

"What about Erzulie? Is she going to meet-up with us?"

Koneh nodded. "That's the plan."

"I hope she's okay, Alexandra said.

"She... will..." Koneh's head hit the steering wheel. Alexandra grasped the wheel and brought the truck to a stop before they crashed. Koneh had succumbed to his many wounds, which Alexandra now noticed. How many bullets did he take?

Alexandra laid Koneh on the ground and looked to the sky. Where was Erzulie?

"Wha-?" Koneh struggled to speak.

Alexandra knelt beside him. "Don't talk. You passed out, which is understandable."

"I'm... fine," Koneh said as he rose to a sitting position. "Just a little off balance."

"Well, you took quite a beating back there. Lots of bullets."

"True..."

"We saved the girl," Alexandra said.

"I remember..."

Alexandra examined Koneh. Cain. How could it be true? She was certain she loved him. Though how could she love someone so evil? Was he the murderer from the Bible or was he the daring man who just risked both their lives to save Medina?

Koneh drew an uneven breath. Then he said, "It's no excuse, but I'm not who I once was. I think something's happening to me."

Surprised by this change of direction, Alexandra said, "What do you mean?"

Koneh leveled his eyes at Alexandra and said, "I think I'm dying."

"I've seen you take a bullet before..."

"Not from the wounds," Koneh said. "This is... something else."

"This is the second time you've talked like this," Alexandra said.

"Before, I wasn't sure. Now, however, I know something's wrong."

"What are your symptoms? What's making you feel this way?"

Alexandra needed evidence. Too many of her friends had died. She wasn't going to lose Koneh to some mystery illness. Not him.

"I'm not sure." Koneh looked away and said, "It's just this feeling..."

"You were going to say something else," she said. "More secrets?"

He shook his head. "I just want you to know I don't want to fail in my task, but I fear I might. Protecting you... Everything has led to this."

Alexandra didn't know how to respond to his words. Did she tell him to leave so she didn't have to *watch* him die? Could she handle such a loss?

Alexandra examined him. Though she wanted to know *everything*, she wasn't sure she was ready. Koneh didn't deny Marco's accusation, so the truth wasn't in dispute. However, she didn't know where to go from that truth.

"Okay," Alexandra said, "I don't know how to deal with that right now."

"Just wanted you to know..."

"Let's talk about something else," Alexandra said, desperate to push aside her terror over losing him. "What name should I call you?"

"Koneh is the name my mother gave to me. I'd prefer you use that."

"Your mother..." Alexandra attempted to wrap her mind around the importance of her protector. Everything had changed. Or had it? Alexandra felt like she always knew the truth. Her heart stayed the course, but her mind warned her this love could never work.

"Sometimes," he said, "I still miss her..."

Alexandra looked into his eyes and allowed the pain to gather in her heart. It throbbed like an old, deep wound. Could she *make* her love work? Or was she doomed to watch it wither and die before it even had the chance to blossom?

Ignoring her pain, she said, "I don't even know what questions to ask."

Koneh huffed. "That's amusing. Aren't you going to question my motives? Ask me when I'm going to kill you?"

Alexandra shook her head. "No. All I have to go on now is my own heart. You must know how I feel for you... And your actions have been nothing short of *heroic* for as long as we've been together."

"Heroic? I've never been accused of that before..."

Her eyes full of standby tears she said, "What happened to you?"

"I told you," Koneh said. "I was cursed by Elah to roam the earth, forever an outcast."

"Why?"

"If you remember *Genesis*," Koneh said, "the gist is there."

"I want to hear it from you."

"It's not something I'm proud of."

Alexandra said, "I want to hear it in your words."

Koneh sighed. "My parents were a direct act of creation, as was Lilev. You might know her as Lilith."

Alexandra shook her head. She didn't recognize the name.

"Lilev was credited by some theologians as the first wife of Adam. Indeed, this is true. However, Lilev was cast from Eden by my father before she bore him any children. There are many legends about Lilev and I find it difficult to follow them all."

"She called you her son. What is that about?"

Koneh frowned. "After I was exiled from my home, Lilev took me under her protection and treated me like a son. But we're getting ahead of ourselves."

"Sorry," Alexandra said, "please continue."

"So I wasn't born in Eden. My parents were exiled before I was born, but not as the Bible tells it. Instead, I was born in the wilds, along with my brother, Aboh. Ironically enough, both creation stories are true. We soon found we weren't the only humans on earth."

"How can both be true?"

Koneh shrugged. "Some scholars and theologians sniffed at the truth through the years. Someone was bound to get it right, considering humanity's obsession with sitting around and *thinking*."

"Okay, so you met other humans?"

"I don't have all the answers, but from what I understand, humans evolved on this planet quite on their own as science and nature took their course. Elah planted Eden and created Man. Well, His version of mankind. We met these *other* humans in the wilds and the most basic of human instincts took over."

"You fought?"

"No, my brother and I both fell in love with the same woman."

"Oh."

"To be fair, we were teenagers, so I think it was more *lust* than love. You get the picture."

Alexandra nodded.

"Well, she fell in love with Aboh and I was left alone with my jealousy."

"I see."

"Mind you," Koneh said, "things were a little different then."

"I cannot even imagine. I still can't believe we're having this conversation."

Suddenly, a question popped into Alexandra's head.

"How old are you?" Alexandra asked.

Koneh stood and smiled. "That's the first question I usually get. Let's get moving again. I can drive."

"You better let me," Alexandra said.

After Alexandra put more distance between their truck and Brasilia, she said, "So, how old?"

"Ask Erzulie. She might have a more accurate estimate than I do."

"Estimate?"

Koneh turned to Alexandra and said, "Elah created Eden roughly seventy-five thousand years ago. I haven't exactly celebrated my birthday from year to year. Especially since the calendar has changed several times in that span."

Alexandra couldn't come to terms with that large a number. Now, the questions flowed.

"How have you survived?"

Koneh returned his attention to the dark highway and said, "We're getting *way* ahead of ourselves now."

"Okay, okay. Aboh, your brother, and this woman were in love. What was her name?"

"Her name was Ebba," Koneh said. "She was as beautiful as a fresh snow. I… I'm not proud of what I did. Just know that I'm not that man anymore."

Alexandra said, "You killed your brother because of your jealousy…"

"Not exactly," Koneh said. "As I've said, the world was a different place then. We were but children in the grand path of evolution and children do whatever they want, no matter who they hurt. This will be difficult for you to hear, but you must know. I was jealous of my brother. I took Ebba for myself."

"You raped her?"

Koneh paused. "Yes."

Alexandra gritted her teeth. "Maybe you were right to keep some things from me."

"No," Koneh said, "I want you to know these things. Elah commanded me to keep nothing from you once the time was right. Somehow, my past is vital to your future."

"I don't see how this is important…"

Alexandra slammed the brakes and stumbled from the truck. She fell to her knees and closed her eyes. What was she doing with him? Did she actually feel something for a man who is capable of rape? Murder? Would anything stop him from raping her? Marco was right, Koneh was a monster.

Erzulie's voice floated through the air. "Are you all right, Lex?"

Alexandra sat on the ground and wiped the tears from her face. The wave of relief over seeing Erzulie alive was overshadowed by Alexandra's newfound revulsion towards Koneh. "I don't want to be near him right now."

"So, you know," Erzulie said. "I've watched Koneh since he was a boy. Through the long years of his sentence on Earth, I've seen him change."

"People don't change *that* much. Evil is evil."

"I know it must be difficult for someone so young to understand, but don't fault him before you hear his whole story."

"He raped a woman," Alexandra said. "That is unforgivable."

"Elah believed in forgiveness. So much that He manipulated the principles of a human soul to allow it to heal through forgiveness."

"How could anyone forgive Koneh? How many women has he raped? How many people has he killed?"

"Ebba was the first and only woman Koneh raped. He was so disgusted with himself afterwards, he went to a cliff to end his own life."

"Really?"

"Yes, and do you want to know what happened?"

Alexandra nodded.

"Koneh's father, you know him as Adam, came to him and told him that what he did wasn't a sin. Elah didn't hold these native humans in the same regard as His children of Eden. And Koneh was a fool for feeling guilt over his crimes against what Elah considered to be an animal."

"That's horrible!"

"Koneh rose up against Adam and said that these humans were *not* animals, that they were just like him. Aboh came to his father's defense and Koneh slew his brother. When Elah came to speak with Koneh to question him about Aboh, Koneh rose against Elah Himself."

"Koneh took a swing at God?"

Erzulie smiled. "He was quite the undisciplined youth."

Alexandra furrowed her brow in an attempt to focus on what she was hearing. "No kidding," she said.

"Elah was taken aback. He cursed Koneh to walk the Earth, with these *animal* humans, until the time of judgment."

"None of that is in Genesis," Alexandra said.

Erzulie shook her head. "I view Koneh much as I do the human race as a whole. Through the millennia, humans have grown more self-aware. Some things that were once commonplace, like slavery, are now crimes abhorred as much as murder. Since Koneh uniquely lived through the entirety of civilized humanity, I see the changes reflected in his soul. Ever since his father came to him on that cliff, Koneh has been searching for something."

"What is he looking for?"

"Peace. All he wanted was a chance for a life of happiness. His guilt over his own transgressions weighs heavy upon his shoulders. He knows he suffers in a prison of his own making."

"Yeah, maybe he deserves to suffer for his crimes."

"For thousands of years? I have watched Koneh bear unimaginable physical and emotional pain throughout the millennia. A lesser man would have cried for mercy after the first hundred or several hundred years. Koneh only once asked for release from his sentence. Besides that one moment of weakness, he has carried the guilt of his original crimes with him through the ages."

"What moment of weakness?"

"When Elah sent His first son to forgive the sins of men, Koneh tracked Him down."

"Jesus?"

"Yes, that is the name you know. You see, Koneh's curse can only be broken by *divine* forgiveness. Koneh cornered and threatened Jesus in an effort to obtain forgiveness."

"What would happen if Koneh was forgiven?"

"He would finally be allowed to die."

Alexandra wiped some tears from her face. "Oh."

"However, Jesus saw through Koneh's bluff. He didn't intend to follow through with his threat. In the end, Koneh walked with Jesus for a time and the two became friends."

"That's a lot of information to process," Alexandra said.

"What does your law call the leniency it gives to criminals who also act on behalf of others?"

Alexandra smiled. "Mitigating circumstances."

"That's it! I'm often amazed at how human law oftentimes unravels the very secrets that science cannot define. A soul is dampened by a murder, but if that murder is in defense of a loved one, the soul isn't diminished quite as much as if that murder was over a sum of money."

"We're not talking about an affirmative defense murder," Alexandra said. "We're talking about a calculated rape."

"Your judicial system is cumbersome but enlightened. You also have provisions in place to release dangerous criminals from your prisons if they demonstrate good behavior and a genuine feeling of remorse."

"True. But if Koneh is capable of such an awful crime…"

"I'm not here to convince you of anything," Erzulie said. "You just needed to know the truth. Koneh didn't kill his brother over an offering to Elah, like in your Bible. Nor is Koneh the same man who raped the object of his obsession. Think on these things."

Alexandra closed her eyes to digest the new information. Could she forgive him? Probably not. Was Koneh just angling for forgiveness? Was that all he wanted from her? Maybe, but Alexandra thought she felt *something* from him during their kiss. Did he feel the same towards her? Was there something left of him to love? Or was he just another monster in the night?

"Is he really dying?" Alexandra asked.

"We're not sure what's happening, but Elah's curse seems to be weakening ever since the earthquake."

So, it was true then. Koneh would be taken from her too. Now that Alexandra knew the truth about him, did it matter?

"I don't know what to think or how to feel," Alexandra said.

"You look exhausted," Erzulie said, cupping Alexandra's cheek with her slender hand.

Alexandra smiled. "Well, we did fight our way out of a city today."

Erzulie kissed Alexandra's forehead and said, "You were very brave."

The pair embraced and Alexandra said, "This is almost too much. I'm wondering who I am more and more each day."

"Shhh, quiet now."

"Listen, I just want to sleep out here tonight. Can you bring me my bedroll and something to eat? And can you watch over me?"

Erzulie smiled. "Of course."

As Alexandra slept under the vigilant eye of her angelic protector, her thoughts returned to Koneh time and again. The same questions revolved in her head like a carousel. After much tossing and twisting, Alexandra finally fell asleep.

A cold, barren plain stretched out in front of Alexandra. Koneh walked ahead of her. Where were they going?

Another dream.

They came to some ruined buildings and Koneh entered. Alexandra followed. People huddled inside, frightened. Koneh raised his sword and Alexandra discovered she couldn't cry out to tell him to stop. He butchered every last person and then turned to face Alexandra, sword in hand.

Was this the end? Was Koneh's betrayal finally at hand? Was this a glimpse into the future?

Then, Koneh pulled back his hood. Instead of the scarred-smooth skin and black eyes, Alexandra saw her own face. She killed those people...

CHAPTER 30

Unsettled by Koneh's confessions and her dreams from the night before, Alexandra rode in the bed of the pickup. Koneh gave Alexandra the space she needed for the next few days. They only spoke to discuss their supplies, the growing cold and their route.

Then, the highway ended.

Erzulie landed, folded her dark wings against her back and approached. "We are not far from where the road divides. The part that heads west is intact several miles in that direction. However, the section we need is unusable."

"Seems like a good place to camp then," Koneh said. "In the morning, we'll see if the truck can make it across the broken ground. Erzulie, take a look farther to the southeast and let me know what you think."

Erzulie nodded and shot into the dark sky.

After Koneh started the fire, Alexandra decided it was time to talk to him again.

"May I sit?"

Koneh nodded.

"Listen, I've been thinking."

Koneh touched Alexandra's arm and said, "May I go first? I've been thinking as well."

"Of course," Alexandra said.

"You are right to hate me."

"I don't…"

"Please, let me finish."

Alexandra's heart ached as she looked into Koneh's eyes. Though she knew the truth about him now, she felt safe and *right* when she was with him.

"I have done terrible things," Koneh said. "I do not ask for forgiveness, nor your understanding. The fact that you remained with me, on this journey, even after you learned the truth… Well, it means everything to me. However, I'm also torn with the desire to turn around and leave you safe in the city of your choosing and never see you again."

"What?"

"When I started this journey, I didn't know you. Elah set me on my course and I viewed my quest as a chance for final redemption. A chance to show everyone that my time was finally here. I was going to show them that Koneh stood the test of time and still had the strength to lead the Mih'darl to Eden, thus saving humanity. My reasons were selfish."

"I… I didn't know," Alexandra said.

"Please… don't speak. I might not be able to finish if I hear your voice again. You don't know what your voice means to me."

Alexandra bit her lower lip and nodded.

"After speaking with Elah, I set out to find you. It wasn't easy. Other forces were looking for you. Well, they were looking for your mother. You see, all of Hell believed you would be born on the day Heaven fell. That is why the demons are searching for an infant. However, Elah gave me a headstart. He told me you were born on the millennium and that you were not a man.

"The demons I raced against had a headstart as well. Somehow, they gleaned the location of the Mother – *your* mother! With Erzulie's help, I arrived in time to save your mother from a fate of torture and suffering, but regrettably, I couldn't save her life."

Alexandra covered her mouth with her hands and gasped. Could this be real?

"Of course, it was easy to find you after that. I watched you from the shadows for a few weeks. In that time, I plotted this journey and how I would manipulate you to be a willing partner in restoring my soul. I mislead you into thinking I saved you from that mob when we first met. The truth is, I could have pulled you from the bus long before the mob arrived. We could have been safe and with Father Callahan before you were chased down that street. However, I needed to save you so you would stay with me long enough to trust me.

"Then, it happened. The beauty of who you really are shone through the dust of the old world. Your true sense of what's *right* in this world hasn't faltered since we first met. You were right to want to leave me in the beginning. I was manipulating you from the start.

"This journey is my final battle, the last great act of the mighty Koneh. The Church, the remnants of Hell, the humans of the Earth and the remains of Heaven would look upon my accomplishment and recognize my sacrifice. In my dreams of how the end would transpire, you would forgive me and my name would live on in the timeless pages of the new holy books. At last, I would have the perfect peace, one in which I was remembered quite differently than in the Old Testament."

Koneh lowered his eyes.

"Alejandra, my lie ends here and now. You deserve better than to be a pawn in this cosmic game of chess between Elah, Iblis, the Church and myself. Elah set your DNA in motion eons ago to accomplish this task, in case you were needed. Iblis chases you down so he can have Eden for himself. The Church would use you for their own agenda if they knew who you were. And I, I betrayed your trust so I could have my last moment of glory and a chance at redemption.

"I have killed many men, including my own brother. I abandoned an angel when she showed me compassion. However no sin weighs as heavy on my soul as my betrayal to you. You, Richard, and the others could have been quite happy in Brasilia or wherever. I should have let you live in ignorance of your divine heritage. Instead, I led you down a path you would never have chosen.

"I don't ask for your forgiveness. All I ask is you follow your heart and tell me how I can best serve you. My quest is now to bring you wherever you want to go. I will protect you until my bones crumble to dust. Or you can leave me in the wasteland. My life is in your hands. Do with me what you will."

Koneh bowed his head and fell silent. For several minutes, the wind was the only sound between them. Alexandra couldn't remember what she planned to say to Koneh. His speech left her searching her heart for answers.

Then, she decided to bare a part of herself as well.

"I never had any dreams," Alexandra said quietly. "There were things I *wanted* – my apartment overlooking the Riverwalk, my large investment portfolio, a judgeship... However, those weren't dreams, not like other people have dreams of raising a family, finding love, helping others. Am I wrong to not dream of these things?"

"I do not know."

"I think I'm wrong to *not* have those dreams. In a way, we have both been selfish. Perhaps we can learn from our mistakes?"

"What do you mean?"

"Well, if Eden really can be the place you say it is, how can we turn our backs on it? You have the strength and knowledge to lead me there. Somewhere in my soul, I have the key to open the gates for all of humanity. Eden sounds like a proper enough dream for me. We can open it. Not for your reasons, and not for mine. Instead, we can open it for everyone else in this world, everyone who had dreams of living their lives before Elah selfishly left us in ruin."

Confused, Koneh said, "Elah? He has left us? How could you know this?"

"You didn't want to hear about my dreams before. Do you want to now?"

"No," Koneh said. "I trust that you know the truth."

"Very well," Alexandra said. "Let's stop worrying about who was wrong and who was right. Instead, let's just act with what strength we have left and get to Eden."

Koneh looked into Alexandra's eyes. "You are an amazing woman, Alexandra Contreras."

"Then you'll help me?"

"Until my last breath."

CHAPTER 31

Koneh maneuvered the pickup through the scarred land. Progress towards their destination crawled in comparison to the distance they covered on the superhighways of South America. However, Alexandra was content to be moving *forward*.

After her talk with Koneh, she felt more comfortable around him. His age seemed impossible. However, like the red-black sky and absence of the ocean, Koneh stood before Alexandra every day as a constant reminder that the impossible was not beyond her reach.

The bitter cold stung Alexandra's lungs and penetrated her skin. Alexandra covered her head with a wool hat and wore a parka over her leather bomber jacket. At camp the next night, Alexandra put all her strength into her training session with Koneh, but she still couldn't break his defenses. She learned that Erzulie had retrieved Koneh's sword in Brasilia and Alexandra felt safer knowing his favorite weapon was at his side.

As she enjoyed the last MRE ration, Alexandra pointed to Koneh's sword. "How do you swing that heavy thing so fast?"

Before Koneh returned the blade to its resting place under his rags, Koneh turned the weapon over. Firelight reflected off patches of silver under the sections of rust, dents and notches. "A good friend made this for me when I was on the island nation you know as Sri Lanka. Back then, we didn't call it that and the forges used to produce this type of steel are gone forever."

"Back when?" Alexandra asked.

"By the calendar you know," Koneh said, "probably about four hundred B.C., give or take a few decades."

"Okay, you have my full attention."

Koneh grinned. "Have you ever heard of Damascus Steel?"

Alexandra searched her memory, but couldn't find any reference. "No."

Erzulie perched on the pickup truck and joined the conversation. "All is quiet as far as I can see."

"Good," Alexandra said. "Stick around. Koneh is going to tell me about Sri Lanka and Damascus steel."

Erzulie nodded.

"So," Koneh said, "Damascus steel was first encountered by Westerners around the time of the Crusades. European knights returned home with remarkable, almost legendary, swords. These weapons could cut through rock and still retain their edge. Many a knight fell because his sword shattered under the assault of a Damascus blade."

"Wow. I must have missed that History Channel special," Alexandra said.

"Indeed. Even today's scientists cannot duplicate Damascus steel."

"How's that possible?"

Koneh shook his head. "I don't know all the secrets, but it's probable the material used to forge Damascus weapons was used up by these early smiths. I do remember the forges though. Hundreds of them lined a mountainside. When the monsoon winds came, the forges would flare hotter than anything possible elsewhere in the world. It was in one of these forges that my friend crafted me this sword as thanks for protecting his son during a war in India."

"It survived all these years?" Alexandra ran her hand along the rough surface and wondered how many men, women and demons died at the end of Koneh's weapon.

Koneh huffed. "Erzulie believes a part of Elah's curse upon me has kept the sword intact for the past two and a half millennia, but I'm skeptical."

"The steel would have long since lost its strength," Erzulie said. "Much like the human body, the molecular structure of these crude metals breaks down over time. It's simple science, as you call it."

"Why do you call what was done to you a *curse*?" Alexandra said. "I think you've used that word several times."

"Seems fitting," Koneh said.

"What was it like?" Alexandra said. "In those first years, I mean. What was the world like? What were the people like? I can't even wrap my mind around the large amount of time you've... Well, it's just a lot of time."

"To tell you the truth," Koneh said, "I cannot recall too many specific details as the years accumulate. I do remember my parents hating their new world. It was a place where they were forced to work for their food and comfort. After my act of defiance, I roamed the wilds. Everyone was just trying to survive."

"Erzulie told me that there were people on earth? Before Adam and Eve?"

"Yes," Koneh said. "We have mixed to the point where there is no bloodline that extends solely back to Eden or one that is purely evolutional. I think it's safe to say we're all one race now, despite Elah's efforts."

"Despite His efforts?" Alexandra said. "What do you mean by that?"

This time, Erzulie answered. "Elah created His new vision of the human race to be superior in form and function. However, once He realized that the humans He created carried the same flaws as the indigent humans of the Earth, He closed Eden to everyone."

"And He tried to kill all the *native* humans by shifting the poles," Koneh said, finishing Erzulie's account.

"Elah tried to kill everyone?"

"Not exactly," Koneh said. "Even after Eden was lost, He still felt His creations to be superior, so He attempted to rid the world of the other line of humans, the naturally evolved ones. However, that attempt failed and the rest is... well... history."

"Elah failed?"

"Through the bravery of one man," Erzulie said. "Koneh."

"I must apologize for my cheering section," he said. "It didn't quite happen that way."

Alexandra raised her eyebrows. "What *did* happen?"

"Elah warned His chosen messenger about the coming destruction. You know him as Noah," Koneh said. "More than one boat was indeed built and a handful of survivors did indeed set sail from the former shores of Eden. Some of them landed in Mesopotamia and founded the earliest permanent human settlements. Others were scattered across the globe. However, all of them were direct descendants of Adam and Eve. Save one."

"One?"

"Koneh managed to defy Elah, again," Erzulie said. "He rescued a young native girl and stowed her on one of the ships. She was in love with a man from Noah's tribe and would later be responsible for keeping the human race mixed."

"How many boats? What was the flood like? I have so many questions!"

"Unfortunately," Erzulie said, "Koneh was seen as the enemy and Noah's tribe was able to keep him from the boats when they set sail."

"So how did you survive?"

"I think it was at the time of the Great Flood that I finally believed Elah's words when He told me I would wander the Earth forever an outcast," Koneh said. "Though I managed to stow the girl on a boat, I was stranded on the shore when the Earth trembled and the waves came. I don't remember much of those years beneath the water, but I awoke when the land of Eden was at the bottom of the world. I made my way to what is now South America, a reverse of almost the same route we are taking today."

"This is unbelievable."

"If only..." Koneh said.

"I can understand why you'd want a little peace," Alexandra said. "Seventy five thousand years..."

"Well," Koneh said, "this isn't about me. It should never have been."

"Do you think we'll make it?" Alexandra said. "I know we've come quite a ways, but Lilev said Derechi is marching towards Eden as well. Can we beat him there?"

"My dear," Erzulie said, "when Koneh acts, even Elah pauses."

Koneh sighed. "Erzul..."

"Elah has passed to many worlds throughout the eons," Erzulie said. "Though I didn't have access to His archives, other angels have noted that Koneh is the only mortal to ever stand against Elah. This is why Elah chose Koneh for this important task. We will reach Eden."

"But Elah has abandoned us!" Alexandra said.

"Do you know that for a fact?" Koneh said.

"Well, no."

"We don't really know what happened," Koneh said.

Alexandra's mind and body ached. "I think I'm just a little overwhelmed," Alexandra said.

"Of course you are," Erzulie said. "This is quite a burden for one so young."

Alexandra forced a smile. "Compared to you two, I'm not even on the calendar."

After a few days of fighting the unforgiving terrain, the truck bent an axel and could travel no further. Koneh, Alexandra and Erzulie packed the most necessary supplies and continued their journey on foot.

"Just like we started," Alexandra said.

"In many ways," Koneh said as he struggled with the weight of the water containers.

Alexandra glanced over her shoulder at the lifeless pickup and said, "Do we have enough to make it back?"

"Once Eden is restored," Erzulie said, "we won't have to."

The white-haired crone's words echoed in Alexandra's memory. "Eden must be destroyed."

Why would Alexandra destroy Eden? No, her goal was now clear. She would restore Eden and the people of the Earth would have a place to go. A place of peace.

At camp that night, Alexandra noticed something.

"Koneh," she said as a shiver penetrated her two coats, fatigues and tank top. "You haven't eaten in days." Though Koneh didn't eat as much as the others when they were all together, he shared the occasional MRE ration.

Satisfied with his fire, Koneh stood. "Don't worry about me. I've gone longer than this without food. Wait here. I'm going to see if I can find more scrub for the fire."

Koneh disappeared into the darkness.

"He's lying," Erzulie said. "But, you probably sensed that."

Alexandra nodded. "Why would he starve himself?"

"To ensure you have enough food for the return trip, if needed," Erzulie said. "Koneh always has a backup plan."

"But won't he…"

"Die?" Erzulie smiled and touched Alexandra on the cheek. "He won't die from starvation, but he's already suffering. He just doesn't want you to see his pain."

"That's just stupid. He should eat!"

Erzulie shook her head. "You won't convince him. Your life is far more precious to him than anything else right now. He will endure anything for you, if necessary. Even die, if that's possible."

"Nobody should be dying for anybody else," Alexandra said as she settled into her thermal sleeping bag.

"Martyrs are looked upon with the highest regard," Erzulie said. "To die for love, that's something even more special."

Alexandra propped her head on her arm and said, "Love?"

Erzulie looked into Alexandra's eyes. "You don't see it?" the angel said.

"See what?"

Erzulie shook her head. "If your own heart doesn't recognize love, then I cannot help you."

"You mean… Koneh?"

"I thought it was obvious," Erzulie said. "However, I have known him for quite some time."

Alexandra frowned. "I don't think Koneh feels…"

"Ask him," Erzulie said. "Or tell him how you feel. Hiding from a feeling does a great disservice to your soul. You'll be so much happier if you just talk to him."

Alexandra allowed her thoughts to wander through the forest of her feelings towards Koneh. Could she forgive him? Love him after all she knew? She wasn't sure.

"What was it like?" Alexandra asked. "To be the angel of love?"

"How do you mean?"

"Well, you mentioned your duties before, but… I dunno," Alexandra said. "Why are angels tasked with keeping watch on mankind?"

"I cannot speak for my counterparts in Heaven," Erzulie said, "but, *love* is the most powerful and wonderful force on this planet. Even Elah marveled at how you humans rally around this one concept time and again. He wanted to study and promote this all-powerful force, so he sent his angels to Earth to discover its secrets."

"Love's secrets?" Alexandra said. "If you know them, please don't hesitate to share."

"I know this," Erzulie said. "The purest love is amongst the most precious and unyielding forces in the known universe. To open your heart in this way takes no effort, yet you humans spend your time building barriers to prevent this kind of pure feeling. As you grow from a child to an adult, you lose the ability and willingness to share unconditionally. This is why Eden is so vital. Elah believed humans can learn how to love like children again."

Love.

Was it really that simple? Did the human race complicate life beyond all previous recognition? The love of a child. Alexandra remembered that love. When her mother was her world and nothing of importance existed outside her home. Then, slowly, *life* began. School, friends, her career – Alexandra drifted away from that love and away from her bare innocence.

"Unconditional, all-forgiving, everlasting," Erzulie said. "These are just a few of the amazing traits which accompany this pure love. Even Elah couldn't match this kind of love. You humans are special."

Drifting into sleep, Alexandra explored her feelings but couldn't capture her own heart. Why was it so elusive?

Every night seemed to hold dreams for Alexandra as she neared Eden. This time, she was in a ruined building with Erzulie. Someone else was there as well – an American man in a nice suit.

"Did you not think I would be prepared for this moment, Lamb?" the man said.

Alexandra drew her sword from her belt and advanced upon the speaker. "I don't want to kill you, but I will," Alexandra said. There was something dangerous about the man, but Alexandra couldn't place it.

The well-dressed man smiled and said, "Erzulie, I command you to seize the Mih'darl!"

Erzulie turned her sword on Alexandra and then Alexandra awoke from her dream.

Reluctant to unzip her sleeping bag and face the harsh wind, Alexandra enjoyed a few more minutes in her warm cocoon. Then, she joined Koneh as he salvaged some wood from the dead fire.

"It's getting colder," Koneh said. "Are you all right?"

Alexandra probed her cracked lips and said, "Yeah, I'm fine." Her words were accompanied by visible clouds of breath. She missed the San Antonio warmth. Though she wanted to talk to

Koneh about her feelings, she allowed the urgency of their trip to be her excuse. She kept silent.

After a painful and cold training session, the group broke camp. Alexandra had done some hiking in the Rockies and the Appalachians, but the dried ocean floor was far more unforgiving. The terrain was comprised of steep cliffs full of soft handholds, vertical drops and collapsing shelves. They ascended one incline only to be greeted with a dangerous drop and another upward slope. Ground gave way in some areas and tortured her feet in other spots.

The days and nights blended together for Alexandra. Talking was painful as the air invaded her lungs and froze her throat. Training with Koneh was excruciating, but Alexandra persevered. Koneh insisted that she needed to keep her joints loose as in the end they may have to fight their way to Eden.

Some number of nights after her dream about the businessman and Erzulie's betrayal, Alexandra awoke to Koneh dousing the fire with dirt.

"What's going on?"

"Erzulie spotted flyers," Koneh said.

The area fell into total darkness and Alexandra waited for her eyes to adjust before finding her sword and Benjamin's pistol. She squinted to keep the surrounding terrain in focus as very little light escaped the clouds above. As always, the wind cut through her layers of clothing and chilled her bones. Various items in the camp teetered against the wind and made noise. Alexandra hoped it wasn't enough to surrender their position.

Then Alexandra heard a distant sound. The flapping of wings. For several long minutes, Alexandra strained to spot the source of the sound in the sky. However, the sound disappeared and only the wind remained.

Koneh moved close to Alexandra and said, "Let's get moving. Quietly."

They packed the camp and moved away from the area, all the while keeping a nervous eye overhead. After that, Alexandra relied on her thermal sleeping bag for warmth at night. There were no more fires.

More days passed and Alexandra's body wore down. Each laborious step brought pain to her bones. She required more time to rest than before and her fingers and toes felt frozen together.

"Tell me a story," Alexandra said after a brutal day of trudging across the wasteland.

"A story?" Koneh asked.

"Yeah."

"What about?"

Alexandra shook her head. "I don't care."

"All right," Koneh said, eyeing Alexandra with a look of concern on his face. "I'll tell you of the fall of Moloch."

"The fallen angel Erzulie killed?" Alexandra's teeth chattered as she spoke.

Koneh smiled. "Yes, that one. Fallen angels aren't normally able to leave Hell and travel to Earth, however Moloch found a way. Every year, Moloch would steal away and spread disease amongst mankind. At first, Elah believed the disease was just from natural causes. However, after the pattern continued, Elah decided to send one of his angels to Earth to investigate."

Alexandra scanned the camp for her friend, but didn't see her. "Erzulie?"

"Yes," Koneh said. "Erzulie tracked Moloch to his lair on Earth and confronted the plague-bearer. However, she was surprised to find Moloch was not alone. A saint was there with the fallen angel."

"A saint?"

"From what I understand," Koneh said, "true saints are granted immortality in Heaven. Somehow, this saint made his way back to Earth to assist Moloch."

"What was his name?"

"I forget," Koneh said. "However, this is important because angels are not allowed to harm saints nor fail their missions. In my mind, this was the turning point for Erzulie. Like a human, she weighed her mission against the standing rules of sainthood and she acted."

"What did she do?"

Koneh smiled. "She killed them both."

Alexandra gasped. "Really?"

"Through their conversation, Erzulie discovered the saint was working with Moloch to devise and spread disease. Moloch had promised the saint reincarnation and permanent life on Earth. Apparently, Heaven wasn't good enough for the saint. Erzulie made a very human decision."

"I see," Alexandra said. "Was she punished?"

"No, that wasn't the act that caused her fall," Koneh said. "Elah praised Erzulie for her actions and promoted her to the ranks of the Seraphim, the highest choir of angels."

Alexandra absorbed the story and wondered how many like it Erzulie and Koneh had to tell. The amount of accumulated knowledge and experience between her two companions was staggering. Alexandra allowed some hope to wander into her survival equation. She might make it after all.

"What did cause her fall?" Alexandra said. "You guys have hinted at it a few times now."

"That's a long story."

Alexandra shivered and pulled the lip of her sleeping bag against her chest. "I want to hear it."

"She tells it better than I do," Koneh said.

"Just... don't argue with me," Alexandra said. "Tell the story."

"Very well. Let's see," Koneh said. "Are you familiar with the Boxer Rebellion?"

Like her muscles, Alexandra's mind was slow to react to stimulus in the freezing cold. "No, only the date. I rarely forget dates. 1899, right?"

"Roundabouts," Koneh said. "Though the financial crisis and natural disasters leading to the conflict began a few years prior."

"I'm sorry, where did this happen again?"

"In China."

"Oh."

"So," Koneh said, "the Boxers organized as an anti-Christian and anti-foreign movement with support from the Chinese government. They began by disrupting trade and communications. Then, they started slaughtering missionaries and Chinese Christians. Though I've fought many wars in my long years on Earth, something about religious genocide got to me. I became involved by helping Chinese Christians reach safety. Naturally, that brought me in direct conflict with the Boxers and I killed my share of them before the rebellion was over."

"Somehow that doesn't surprise me," Alexandra said. "But I'm surprised by the date. Erzulie hasn't been a fallen angel for long, has she?"

"Not compared to most, no," Koneh said. "So, then the foreign countries took interest in their destroyed embassies and murdered missionaries. An Allied force landed on Chinese shores and quelled the rebellion. Of course, I'm leaving out some details, but this next part is important."

"Okay."

"The allied forces – including Germany, England, and the United States – were terribly brutal in their suppression of the Boxers. I was forced to get involved again. The Germans called me the *Grey Devil*, as I harassed them for months after they pillaged and raped their way across the Chinese countryside. They would declare a village to be aligned with the Boxers and then the troops would slaughter everyone. Inexcusable, even in wartime."

Koneh paused and Alexandra realized she had closed her eyes. "Bored yet?" Koneh asked.

Alexandra opened her eyes and said, "No, no. This is interesting. I guess I'm just tired, that's all."

"We can finish this story tomorrow."

"Please, continue."

"As you wish," Koneh said. "Well, I fought against the Allied forces and tried to get word to the Chinese government about what was really going on. From what Erzulie tells me, my actions were noticed in Heaven and Elah dispatched one of his warrior angels to go and put an end to my interference."

"Why did Elah want to stop you?"

Koneh huffed. "I don't know, but I was supporting the people who killed Christians so perhaps that drew His ire and He sent an angel to stop me."

"I thought you couldn't be killed?"

"The angel's task was to incapacitate me until the conflict was resolved. Apparently, Elah approved of the retribution delivered upon the Boxers, uneven as it was in my eyes."

"The angel was Erzulie?"

"No," Koneh said, "the angel was an archangel named Hojn. I didn't want to kill him, but warrior angels aren't interested in talking things through. They have their mission and they carry it out. Killing Hojn only angered Elah further and he decided to send Erzulie. In the past, she had stayed my hand and talked me out of certain courses of action. Elah reasoned she could do the same this time."

"I'd love to hear those stories too," Alexandra said.

"Not tonight, Alejandra," he said tenderly.

"Please continue," Alexandra said as she closed her eyes. "I'm listening."

"Well, Erzulie wasn't talking me out of anything, not that time. When she realized why I was doing what I was doing, her new order from Elah came in direct conflict with her station as the Seraphim of Love. She returned to Heaven to inform Elah of her failure and Elah discarded her like a broken appliance."

"You said before that Erzulie fell because she thought she was in love with a human. Where's that part of your story?"

"She told Elah that she loved me."

Alexandra opened her eyes. "What?"

"Apparently, she came up with her own answer as to why she put my life above her mission from Elah," Koneh said. "Needless to say, Elah wasn't pleased with that answer. I don't know why Erzulie came to that conclusion."

"Maybe," Alexandra said, "she has risen above her limitations and can actually *feel* now."

Koneh shook his head. "Not possible."

"After all you've lived through, after all you've seen," Alexandra said, "how can you be sure?"

Koneh shrugged. "I guess I'm not."

Alexandra took her small verbal victory to sleep with her that night. No dreams came and the next morning felt harsher than the last. Alexandra and Koneh trudged through the unforgiving terrain for several more days until they reached the former ice shelf of Antarctica.

Like in Alexandra's dream, razor-sharp rocks extended in every direction.

"This is it," Alexandra said. "I've seen this place."

CHAPTER 32

The razor rocks protruded from the earth as if thrust to the surface by some powerful underground force. Their tips pointed in extreme and contrasting angles towards the red-black sky. Alexandra's group camped under the cover of one of the large rocks which provided relief from the brutal wind and protection from spotters in the sky. With frostbitten fingers, Alexandra built a fire. The risk of cold exposure had finally outweighed the risk of being detected.

"We passed some dry plant debris a few minutes ago," Koneh said. "If we want this fire going all night, we'll need some more fuel. I shouldn't be long."

Alexandra nodded and warmed her hands. "How are you doing, Erzulie?"

Erzulie sat next to Alexandra and smiled. "The cold doesn't hinder me."

Alexandra examined her companion. "I don't suppose you radiate body heat, do you?"

"Unfortunately, I don't," Erzulie said. "In fact, quite the opposite."

Alexandra returned her attention to the fire and said, "We haven't had a chance to talk lately. You and me, at least."

"My apologies."

Alexandra nudged Erzulie. "Don't apologize. You kept us safe over the past… week? Two weeks?"

"Actually, it has been…"

"Don't tell me," Alexandra said. "I'm not sure I want to know."

"As you command."

"Speaking of commands," Alexandra said as she remembered her last dream. "Are you taking orders from someone? Do you have a... master?"

"My master is Iblis, of course," Erzulie said, "but, with no standing orders or reserve commander on record I am bound to obey the orders of my last master, Elah."

"So what happens now that neither of those two are around?"

Erzulie smiled. "You are next in the chain of command, so I must follow your orders, my Lady."

"I see," Alexandra said. "Not sure I understand the hierarchy though."

"You need not worry about such things," Erzulie said. "I have a low probability of failing you. If Derechi was here, we'd see more evidence of his army. We are ahead of him."

Alexandra was more concerned with her dream than Derechi's army, but she didn't know how to broach the subject of her dreams with her angelic friend.

"I've seen this place in my dreams," Alexandra said. "I've seen other things too."

"You have the gift of foresight," Erzulie said. "In time, you will learn to master it."

"In my dream, I was here with a white-haired woman," Alexandra said. "Does that mean anything to you?"

Erzulie turned to Alexandra and said, "Perhaps. Tell me more."

"Well, she said I would make the future. And I am her enemy."

"That's all?" Erzulie asked.

"No," Alexandra said. "I think the first time I dreamt of her, we were in a volcano and then near the ocean. The white-haired woman said the Earth can again be a place of beauty and life... or something like that."

"Did she reveal her name?"

Alexandra shook her head. "No. But she did say she wanted Eden destroyed."

Erzulie gasped. "So it has happened. The One has contacted you."

"The One?"

"This being doesn't have a name," Erzulie said, "yet, Elah feared and respected The One."

Alexandra's heart shriveled in fright. Was she really having nighttime conversations with a being feared by God? A being that wanted her destroyed? This was chilling. "Who is she?" Alexandra said, desperate for information. "Why did Elah fear her?"

"Well," Erzulie said, "the One appears in your mythology as Mother Earth, Gaia or merely *nature*. However, The One is far more enigmatic than can be presented in a story or parable. Elah believed The One an ancient soul trapped on Earth since its creation. Keep in mind, The One has appeared to Elah in many forms through the millennia, with the white-haired crone being the most common."

"What else do you know?"

Erzulie said. "Elah feared The One because she held some sway over the souls of the Earth. How much control and to what extent, I don't know. Only Elah came face to face with The One and our archives made little mention of her."

"Do you know what she might want from me?" Alexandra asked. "Why would she even contact me?"

"You said she wants Eden destroyed?"

"Yeah," Alexandra said, "though I don't know why she would tell me that."

Erzulie studied Alexandra and said, "Because if Elah is truly gone from this planet, you are the only one with the power to destroy Eden."

"Why the hell would I do that?"

"Perhaps The One is making her play for dominance on Earth," Erzulie said. "We can only speculate. However, Elah and The One were enemies. No battles were fought, but Elah issued a standing order to prevent The One from entering Heaven or Eden."

Alexandra closed her eyes. "This cosmic-level stuff is confusing," she said.

"I'm sorry," Erzulie said, "but my station kept me from studying such things in the archives."

"It's not your fault," Alexandra said, "I'm just terrified that this being has taken such an interest in me. If Elah feared The One, then I'm pretty mortified to fall asleep again. Especially if the white-haired crone is my enemy."

CHAPTER 33

Koneh nodded. "This feels right. Erzulie?"

The angel nodded and said, "Not far now. I will stay close."

"Be careful," Alexandra said. "We don't know what's out there."

Erzulie extended her wings and launched into the air. Moments later, she was gone.

The wind howled through the canyons of rock and Alexandra pulled her scarf over her mouth. Over the last week, the air had grown even thinner and colder. At least Alexandra thought it was a week. Time lost all meaning in the wasteland.

Though the wind couldn't gather momentum and slice through her layers of clothing anymore, gusts and squalls made their way into the rocky paths. Alexandra fought to keep her footing and resorted to a trick which kept her moving. She thought of home.

Hour long showers.

Silk sheets.

Alexandra felt some moisture on her scarf, but it wasn't from her breath. Her lip was bleeding again.

Tofu salad.

Orion Prime.

Clean drinking water.

Koneh supported Alexandra with his arm. "Tough wind today," he said.

Alexandra nodded. Talking irritated her cracked lips, dry throat and raw tongue.

"Do you need to rest?"

Though his eyes were impossible to read, Alexandra thought she saw compassion on Koneh's face. Did he really care if she lived or died? Yes, Alexandra believed he cared. If he really loved her, like Erzulie said, then he cared. However, she didn't have the time or energy to explore such thoughts.

"Let's rest," Koneh said as he helped Alexandra to the ground. "How are you feeling? Should we stop for the day?"

Beyond exhaustion, Alexandra strained to form her words. "No. Keep going."

Koneh eyed her and said, "Okay."

"Running low anyway," Alexandra said as she pulled the last can of ravioli from her backpack. After this, it was crackers and trail mix.

"We have enough," Koneh said.

"You eat," Alexandra said. "Must eat…"

Koneh opened the Ravioli and handed it to Alexandra. She intended to push the can back towards her friend, but Koneh dropped the food and drew his sword. Realizing he was about to attack her, Alexandra rolled to the side and drew Erzulie's sword from her belt. Was this betrayal?

They sparred for a few seconds before parting. "What are you doing?" Alexandra asked, sobered by the sudden attack.

Without responding, Koneh advanced. Alexandra parried his swings and back-pedaled. Remembering one of Koneh's lessons, Alexandra didn't allow herself to be cornered against the rock wall, so she maneuvered into a better position.

"Well done," Koneh said.

This was a lesson.

Alexandra's bones creaked and her muscles strained against the cold. A few months ago, she would have been annoyed at Koneh's inconvenient timing for a lesson. However, the realities of the journey had sunk into Alexandra's psyche. She expected the unexpected.

After the lesson, Alexandra slumped to the ground.

"I thought… Nevermind," Alexandra said.

Koneh leaned against the jagged rock wall and said, "You thought I betrayed you?"

"It went through my head," Alexandra said.

Koneh sighed. "What must I do?"

"I'm just tired," Alexandra said. "You… you've done so much for me. I didn't mean to…"

"It doesn't matter," Koneh said. "Save your apology and eat that ravioli. You need your strength."

Alexandra reached for the can and Koneh drew his sword again. This time, his weapon nicked Alexandra's parka. She wasn't fast enough.

"The lesson," Koneh said, "is one I learned at an early age."

With just enough energy to stand and swing her sword, Alexandra felt her muscles weakening and her knees wavering. How could she fight if the need arose?

"Your enemy will never let you rest," Koneh said. "Especially when they think they have you. Let them see you tire, let them see you bleed."

Alexandra parried and pushed her advantage. Was he building her confidence or was she actually winning?

"Then," Koneh said, wheezing. "You strike and make them regret their transgressions against you."

Koneh was cornered against the jagged rocks and Alexandra intensified her assault.

"Make them wish they never heard your name..." Koneh said as he stumbled and dropped his weapon.

Alexandra sliced into Koneh's shoulder and shrieked.

"I'm sorry!" she said as she dropped her sword.

Koneh glared at her and drew a dagger from beneath his robes. He lunged, but Alexandra was faster. She kicked the weapon away and pushed Koneh to the ground.

Unsure if she should continue to bludgeon her teacher, Alexandra said, "Are you okay?"

Koneh rolled to retrieve his sword, but Alexandra reached the weapon first and held the point to his chest.

"Very good," Koneh said before he fell to the ground unconscious.

CHAPTER 34

"It's not bad," Erzulie said. "Of course he'll live."

Erzulie returned from her scouting mission to find Koneh unconscious with a viscous sword wound in his shoulder.

"He told me never to hold back during training," Alexandra said. "And I didn't know if he was just teaching me another lesson by letting me win. I didn't know."

"My Lady, Lex," Erzulie said, "Koneh would never let you beat him. He doesn't believe a student learns anything when it is handed to them."

"How was I able to beat him?"

Erzulie examined the wound a final time and said, "The curse upon his body is weak. I don't think he can hold on for much longer."

Alexandra lowered her head and closed her eyes. How could she travel the wasteland without Koneh at her side? After seventy-five thousand years, why did he have to die so soon after she met him? Through the bitter cold, a few tears ran down Alexandra's cheeks.

"He will fight for you," Erzulie said, "to his dying breath he will see you into Eden."

Alexandra gazed at Koneh's closed eyes and peaceful face. She had never seen him like this. "I just wish I had more time with him... I feel like he just told me that Heaven and Hell have fallen and I need to face the realities of my new world."

Erzulie touched Alexandra on the arm and said, "Your time is so brief, yet look at all that you have accomplished. Would you have ever, even in your most fantastic dreams, imagined yourself here in Antarctica?"

"No," Alexandra said, "definitely not *this*."

Koneh stirred and opened his eyes. When he realized he was on the ground, he whirled and scanned the area.

"What's going on?" he asked.

Alexandra offered Koneh his sword and said, "You passed out on us there for an hour or so. Sorry about your shoulder."

"Your student defeated you," Erzulie said.

Accepting the weapon, Koneh eyed Alexandra and said, "It's about time."

"Are you okay?" Alexandra asked.

Koneh rotated his arm and said, "Yes, I'm fine. Nice work."

Alexandra wanted to turn back. If it meant she could have Koneh in her life for a little longer, Alexandra told herself she would abandon Eden. Who travels to Antarctica anyway? Sure, the poles have shifted and the ice is gone, but she didn't know how much more she could take. Her entire body screamed for a reprieve and Alexandra regretted her decision to leave the Veracruz base.

"Now that you are both conscious," Erzulie said, "I have some news. Climb that rock and see for yourself."

Alexandra followed Koneh up the slope of a nearby rock outcropping. On the dark horizon, just like in her dream, Alexandra saw a flickering light in the distance.

"Is that Eden?" After all she had survived, Alexandra found words difficult in the face of her goal.

Koneh nodded. "The gates of Eden."

"Eden." Alexandra breathed the word and her heart leapt.

With her goal in sight, Alexandra's doubts from moments ago retreated into the long shadows of the rocks. New life invigorated her cold and weary bones. Alexandra narrowed her eyes but couldn't discern anything more about the intermittent and brilliant light in the distance.

"That light is visible for miles, especially from the sky," Alexandra said. "We might not be alone out here."

Koneh grinned. "Good thing everyone else is looking in the Middle East."

"What?"

"The truth of Eden has been hidden," Erzulie said. "Hidden even from the angels of Heaven. Only those who have been to Eden can find their way back."

"Koneh and Lilev," Alexandra said.

"Exactly," Erzulie said.

"Even so," Alexandra said, "how could it remain hidden? Seventy five thousand years is a long time."

"Buried," Koneh said, "beneath hundreds of feet of ice and snow."

Alexandra shook her head. "It's just so unbelievable."

"I know how you feel," Koneh said. "I've seen the entrance. When I was still in my youth, I ventured to the forbidden place and gazed in wonder at the silver gates. Beyond those gates, I knew a paradise of trees and water waited. Until now."

Paradise. Could it be real?

"How much farther, do you estimate?" Koneh asked.

Erzulie cocked her head. "Maybe a day or two. Do you want me to get a closer look?"

"No, stay close for now. Alexandra is right. We don't know who else is out there, but I have a good idea."

"Derechi," Alexandra said. "Do you think they're already here?"

Koneh pointed to one of Erzulie's wings and said, "They have the advantage. Well, their advance force does, at least. We move faster than an army, but slower than a group of fliers. They are most definitely here already."

"Can we make it?" Alexandra asked.

"I told you before," Koneh said. "I have one last fight left in me and this is it. You will reach the gates of Eden."

CHAPTER 35

For two days, Erzulie led them in the direction of the flickering light in the distance. Koneh and Alexandra walked the winding paths between the jagged shards of upthrust rocks. The place looked almost alien to Alexandra. Alone with her thoughts, Alexandra felt like she was driving without her GPS. Each step she took felt like another turn on a road farther away from the places she knew. Her heart quickened as she realized she was committed to such an unsure path.

Like a distant voice waking her from a dream, Alexandra heard Erzulie's words carry from the sky.

"Above you!"

Koneh whirled and drew his sword in time to slice open a flying demon. Blood sprayed from the creature as its body slammed into a rock.

Erzulie landed on the ground. Silvery blood oozed from a gash in her forearm.

"Flyers. Lots of them," Erzulie said.

Koneh looked to the sky. "Derechi's advance force."

Alexandra drew her slender, black sword from its scabbard.

"We'll stick to the paths," Koneh said. "Stay above us and don't wander too far."

Erzulie nodded and then shot into the sky.

"Will she be all right?" Alexandra asked.

Koneh pulled one of his daggers from under his tattered clothes and said, "I'll keep an eye on her."

A shriek pierced the air and Alexandra glimpsed Erzulie spin in the air to meet a winged attacker. Then, more shrieks reverberated through the canyons and a dozen more winged enemies appeared in the sky.

"Here they come," Koneh said.

Alexandra stood next to her companion and studied her enemies' approach. A moment later, the flying demons scattered and landed.

"Stay close!" Koneh said as he released his dagger into the air, catching a demon in the head.

Claws scraped against rock and the beasts were upon them. Koneh's sword flashed in Alexandra's peripheral vision as he decapitated one demon and impaled another.

Alexandra parried a clawed attack by a red-skinned demon and then she slashed with her sword, missing the creature's head. Moments later, Erzulie landed and ripped the red-skinned demon's wing from its socket. Two more demons landed behind Erzulie, and the angel floated backwards while fending off her pursuers.

Alexandra whirled in time to block a barbed whip wielded by a squat, horned demon. The demon snarled as it lashed out with its tail, but Alexandra was ready. Spinning from the tail, Alexandra wrenched the whip from the demon's hand and impaled the monster on her blade. It crumpled to the ground. Two more horned demons appeared and Alexandra back-pedaled. The newcomers hopped over their fallen comrade and advanced upon Alexandra.

"Koneh?!"

One of the demons toppled face first into the hard ground, a dagger imbedded in its back. Then, Koneh appeared behind the other one and ran it through before the beast could swing its weapon.

Koneh dashed to Alexandra's side and said, "Are you all right?"

"I think so. Where's Erzulie?"

Koneh's eyes widened and he pushed Alexandra to the ground. With a *whoosh*, a demon flew between them and Koneh ducked to avoid the creature's sword. Then, Alexandra realized it wasn't a demon. It was a fallen angel!

The fallen angel, a male, landed and turned to face them. His face was chiseled and strong. Muscles bulged along his arms and legs. Like Erzulie, he wore charred armor. This was the same fallen angel who was with Lilev after Tampico. And, like that time, Ael locked his white-in-white eyes upon Alexandra. Grinning, Ael turned to Alexandra's protector.

"Koneh," the fallen angel said.

"Ael, I didn't know you served the Unclean One," Koneh said as he circled in front of Alexandra. "I thought you were merely Lilev's dog."

"Jono Mih'darl," Ael said as he lifted himself into the air and raised his sword.

Koneh stepped backwards and then propelled himself towards his descending attacker. Koneh caught Ael in the breastplate with his foot and dented the armor. With a flap of his wings, Ael retreated into the air and gripped his sword like a lance.

"Jaharl ono de lorien, Koneh," Ael said as he again darted towards Koneh.

This time, Ael landed and attacked Koneh with a series of swift sword strikes. Koneh back-pedaled and parried each one.

Koneh huffed and said, "You're not the first angel to try."

As they fought, more of the squat, horned demons landed. Alexandra glanced at her friend during the second before she was forced to run from the swarm of new enemies. Looking back, Koneh caught her eye and nodded before he was forced to focus on Ael. For a moment, her heart worried for Koneh, but the immediacy of the battle pressed her forward.

Allowing her intuition to guide her, Alexandra raced along the winding paths and attempted to lose her pursuers. There were just too many! A horned demon squealed and appeared from behind an outcropping. Alexandra stepped into the creature's advance and swung her sword through its midsection. As the demon crumpled to the ground, Alexandra saw something in the corner of her eye.

Ael landed in her path and raised his sword. Alexandra stumbled to the ground, but Koneh was there. Panting, he darted in front of Ael and parried the attack.

"You cannot protect her," Ael said, his voice strong and clear.

Koneh gritted his teeth and turned to Alexandra. "Go!" he said.

Alexandra circled around the two combatants while Koneh kept Ael at bay. When she cleared the area, she glanced backwards to see Ael soar into the sky and again land in front of her. There was no escaping an angel!

"Your fight ends here, Lamb," Ael said. "Accept your destiny and throw down your weapon."

Alexandra's sword wavered and Ael smiled. He stepped towards Alexandra and then reeled when a knife buried itself in his breastplate with a loud *clink*.

Koneh rushed towards Ael and said, "Go now! Run!"

As Alexandra stepped to the side, Ael mirrored her movement and disarmed her with a swift flick of his sword.

"I cannot kill you," Ael said, "but I will disable you until my master arrives."

Ael swung his sword towards her leg, but he never finished his stroke. Koneh leapt in the air and sliced one of Ael's wings clean off his back. The fallen angel tumbled to the ground and Alexandra retrieved her weapon.

Koneh pushed Alexandra in the direction of the flickering light and said, "Now!"

Alexandra ran.

This time, Ael was forced to deal with Koneh and couldn't take to the air.

The air!

Alexandra scanned the sky for some sign of Erzulie. Was her angelic friend still alive? Some loose stones fell on the path and Alexandra spotted Erzulie struggling with a large, winged demon on the rock above.

Alexandra ran to the base of the outcropping as the demon slammed Erzulie into the surface of the jagged rock. The demon raised his weapon and Alexandra threw her sword to her friend.

"Erzulie!"

In one smooth motion, Erzulie caught the sword and plunged the tip into the demon's chest.

More demons landed between Alexandra and her friend. Erzulie shot into the sky, but she didn't fly far as she was forced to fight her way through the enemies still in the air. Alexandra backed away and decided she couldn't get any closer to Erzulie. The only clear path was to the massive silver gates. Now without her sword or her companions, Alexandra ran through the narrow canyons.

The demons closed the gap, but Alexandra pulled Benjamin's pistol from her belt and fired at the nearest enemy. The demon tumbled to the ground from several gunshot wounds. Alexandra emptied the clip into the closest demons and then threw the weapon aside.

After widening the gap with her pursuers, Alexandra found herself running on a flat expanse towards the glimmer she saw in her dreams. The jagged rocks behind her, Alexandra found new strength in her muscles when she realized where she was. Demons hopped, flew, and raced towards her from all directions.

Alexandra reached the gates. She looked over her shoulder, but couldn't see her friends. Were they still alive? Should she run to them? Could she still help?

A horned demon crashed into Alexandra and sent her tumbling across the rocky ground. She rolled to her feet and grasped at her empty scabbard. Erzulie had the sword.

"Damn!"

Alexandra calculated the distance between herself, the horned demon and the gate. The math wasn't in her favor.

At the edge of her vision, Alexandra saw a large pack of demons embroiled in a melee. Her friends were still alive. Alexandra crouched, ready to sprint for the gate when the horned demon moved.

The creature leapt into the air and Alexandra dashed below its claws. She reached out to touch the gate.

A moment later, she fell to the ground. The *grassy* ground. Alexandra blinked as sunlight filled her eyes. The bitter cold of the rocky plain was replaced by a comforting, warm breeze. Through squinted eyes, Alexandra saw a green meadow stretch before her. A stream ran through the grass and into a lightly wooded forest. In the distance, snowcapped mountains reached into the blue sky. Blue Sky!

At last. Eden!

CHAPTER 36

Alexandra's wounds and weary bones no longer cried for attention. Instead, Alexandra felt like she was swimming in a warm bath. Her pain melted away with every breath she took. A deer drank from the stream and lifted its head when Alexandra rose from the grass. Overhead, clouds drifted in an ocean of blue. The breeze reminded Alexandra of those perfect endless days she knew as a child.

"So, this is Eden."

Alexandra turned and noticed that the gate was gone. Rolling green hills extended into the horizon where the gate should have been. Serenity reigned here. Alexandra struggled to remember how she arrived and why she came. She knew she was someone important, but why was she here? The question was replaced by a sense of peace and wholeness.

With a child's innocence, Alexandra shed her winter gear and grimy clothing. Naked, she dipped herself into the stream. The water was cool, but not cold. Her cuts, bruises and wounds became a distant voice. Alexandra lost track of time as she lay in the grass and allowed the sun to dry her body. An eagle flew overhead. The warm breeze washed over the grass and lightly touched her bare skin.

Then, Alexandra noticed a strange looking animal hide resting at the water's edge. Wait, that wasn't an animal's hide. It was a tattered jacket. Her jacket! Alexandra remembered.

Koneh!

Alexandra grasped the jacket and held it close. Her friends, Koneh and Erzulie, still fought on the other side of the gate. They fought so she could reach Eden. Her heart thumping, Alexandra struggled to maintain the memory of her friends. She didn't want to forget again. Alexandra pulled her black fatigues over her legs and strapped her bra into place. She grabbed her jacket, but left the rest of her ruined clothes on the grass.

Where was she going?

Alexandra scanned the horizon in all directions, but didn't see the silver gates. Then, a light flickered in the distance on the slope of the closest snowcapped mountain.

Well, it's something, she thought to herself.

Alexandra followed the stream to the base of the mountain. The sun remained fixed in the sky, so Alexandra wasn't sure how much time had passed.

The climb was gratifying, but not strenuous. Within a few hours, Alexandra reached a plateau and her destination – a silver tree. Alexandra's stomach growled when she noticed the translucent fruit hanging from the branches. Then, another feeling welled in her stomach when she noticed the lone person standing near the tree. It was her mother! Recognition didn't register at first in Alexandra's mind. She appeared exactly as Alexandra remembered and her smile caused Alexandra's knees to buckle.

CHAPTER 37

"Mama..?" Alexandra didn't weep, but her eyes welled. Could this be real?

"Alejandra, my dear," her mother said. "I've missed you so much."

"I've missed you too..."

"Shh," her mother said as she gathered Alexandra into her arms and stroked her daughter's shortened hair. "I can sense your regret, but that isn't necessary, not now. You are here and all will be made right."

Alexandra looked at her mother through swollen eyes. Yes, this was real. "How?" was the only word she could manage.

"I have been waiting," her mother said. "God brought me here and He told me you would come. You once said to me that my faith was a one-sided contract. Do you still believe this?"

Alexandra shook her head. "I'm not sure of anything anymore."

"Did you at least follow my advice?" her mother asked. "Did you look upon the world with new eyes each day?"

"I don't know," Alexandra said. "I don't know what you meant by that."

Her mother smiled. "You were chosen to be the caretaker of Eden," she said. "God sent you to redeem the world, and here you are. All you need do is touch the tree and Eden will be open for the pure of heart. I was preparing you for your task, nothing more. The choice is a simple one, but only you can make it," she said gently.

Her mother motioned towards the brilliant tree.

"Is it that easy?" Alexandra asked.

Nodding, her mother said, "God loves us all, and this is His gift. Do you have doubts?"

"No," Alexandra said, "this is why I'm here. It's just all so unbelievable..."

"I have watched you over these past few months," her mother said. "You have endured pain, hardship and loss. Yet, you also found love. In Eden, *love* is all you'll ever know."

Love? Did she find love? Were they meant for a life together?

"Wait," Alexandra said, her face growing cold. "You've *watched* me? How?"

Her mother pointed to a silvery pool beyond the tree. "From there. It shows me whatever is in my heart at the moment I gaze upon its surface."

Alexandra stumbled to the pool of still water. Almost immediately, Koneh's image danced on the surface. He was in pain. Alexandra dropped to her knees. The vision was too dreadful to watch. She didn't want him to suffer. The very thought caused aching in her heart.

"The man you love will be here with you," her mother said, "soon."

Alexandra turned her tear-streaked face towards her mother and said, "No, he won't! He can't die, you know that!"

Her mother's face filled with sympathy. "I'm so sorry you love him," she said. "But he chose his path, just as you did."

"I must go to him," Alexandra said as she wiped the tears from her face and stood.

Her mother shook her head and embraced her daughter. Sobbing, she said, "Daughter, if you leave you cannot return."

Alexandra broke from her mother's arms and said, "What?"

"You cannot return. At least, not in the flesh."

Pausing to understand her mother's words, Alexandra blinked away her new set of tears. "You mean I have to *die* to return to Eden?" she asked.

Her mother nodded. "Your place is here."

"There's no way to return?"

"Maybe, in time, you could learn how to accomplish such a miracle," her mother said. "But I know of no way."

"I don't have any time," Alexandra cried. She couldn't abandon Koneh. "Tell me how this works."

"Alejandra..." her mother said, her tone the same as Alexandra remembered from her youth. It was the same voice she used when young Alexandra was up to something naughty. "This is very important. *You* are very important!"

"I know who I am," Alexandra said. "And I'm not going to abandon my friends when I can still help them. Tell me what I need to do to open Eden."

"All you need do is touch the tree," her mother said. "The knowledge will become yours."

Alexandra stepped towards the tree, hesitant. "How does it work?"

"Those pure of soul will be allowed to enter," her mother said. "They have been waiting for quite some time."

Alexandra took another step towards the tree. "What about people who are alive? Can they come here too?"

"Yes," her mother said. "This is a crossroads of sorts. This is how He intended it to be. The pure souls may enter, though once they leave they cannot return until they have passed on."

"Same rules for the living?" she asked. "They cannot enter unless their soul is pure?"

"Correct."

Dropping to her knees, Alexandra searched her heart for the answer. How could she open Eden to only a few? What would happen to everyone else? Were they doomed for a life of pain and suffering while the moral elite enjoyed paradise? How was that fair?

"What about everyone else?" she asked.

Her mother said, "They will be reborn and given another chance when their life of sin has ended."

"How?"

"Think of it like a stream," her mother said. "The purest souls are diverted to a shimmering lake, to a place of peace and warmth. The sinners are brought back around again to flow down the stream once more. God has given us all a second chance, even those full of sin. There's just one thing left to do. Release the dam, my daughter. Release it and allow the pure of heart their reward."

Could she do it? The tree was within reach. Koneh believed in Eden, why did she have doubts? Was Eden part of the natural order of things?

Alexandra shook her head. This decision was almost too much for her. She needed time to analyze the consequences of her action or inaction. She needed *facts*! Unfortunately, her time had run short. Koneh needed her. Eden was their goal, and she had only one thing left to do. Everyone had suffered enough. The world needed Eden and Alexandra decided she wasn't going to be the one to deny paradise to mankind.

Inhaling, Alexandra touched the shimmering bark and a flood of images assaulter her consciousness. The images came so fast, Alexandra couldn't separate them. Everything jumbled together in one bright flash of light. At once she saw the gates of Eden open upon her command. People flocked to the paradise. From the silver tree, Alexandra ruled everything. However, the laws of Eden were resolute. She couldn't break them. If she left now, there was only one way to return. Then, she also saw beyond the gates of Eden. Outside, in the rocky badlands, Koneh and Erzulie suffered.

Why did the old crone want Eden destroyed? As the thought turned in her head, Alexandra saw a burning tree. The souls of Eden melted away and the Earth reclaimed the paradise into its rocky depths. No, that wasn't a path Alexandra could follow. Eden must be reopened!

Alexandra was thrown from the tree. For an instant, her wounds yelled so they could be heard, but they faded into the background as Alexandra and her mother turned to the bright light on the horizon.

"The gates are open," her mother said with awe in her words and on her face.

Alexandra felt empty. She had accomplished her task. Eden was open. Why did she feel like she made a mistake? How would the rest of the world fare while the moral elite lounged in paradise? Did it matter? Could she really stay in paradise while Koneh was on the other side? Forever apart?

"No!" Alexandra said.

Her mother turned towards her with a puzzled look on her face.

"I have opened Eden, but I cannot stay," Alexandra said. "My place isn't here. My place is with *him*. It was always with him, I just didn't realize it."

"Alejandra," her mother said, "you cannot leave. We have much work to do."

"Por favor, Mama, lo siento…"

Alexandra touched the bark of the tree again. After looking at her mother's confused face once more, she focused on the location where Koneh and Erzulie were in pain. With a flash of light, she appeared outside in the dark cold of the razor rock ravines.

Startled, the fallen angel Ael whirled and pointed at Alexandra.

"Seize her!"

Alexandra smelled the sulfurous breath of the hound before it pounced. The monster slammed her to the rocks and the world turned to black.

CHAPTER 38

Alexandra awoke in a cavern. She lifted her pounding head from the ground and waited for her eyes to adjust to the darkness.

"Alexandra..." Koneh said, his voice weak.

Several thick chains lashed Koneh to a rocky pillar in the center of the room. Erzulie lay at the far side of the chamber, silvery liquid pooling around her body. Alexandra noticed Erzulie's eyes flutter. Maybe her friend was still alive. The other fallen angel, Ael, stood near the entrance to the room. He was missing a wing and his body appeared to be crisscrossed with cuts. For the moment, he seemed to be preoccupied with something outside.

Alexandra knelt at Koneh's side. Tears formed at the corners of her eyes when she saw his broken body.

"Don't cry for me," Koneh said. "I knew this to be my fate. Tell me, what was Eden like? Have you reopened paradise?"

Alexandra nodded, but she couldn't look into his eyes. She knew, too late, that she would have preferred a quiet life with Koneh by her side.

Koneh.

In the span of a few seconds, Alexandra dreamed of what her life with Koneh could've been. They could've left Eden and all of the pain behind. Father Callahan could've married them. Erzulie would've been the maid of honor. Nicole would cry during the ceremony and catch the bouquet. Santino and Benjamin would congratulate them. Alexandra had finally found a man who excited and challenged her, a man she could love. They braved the dangers of the wasteland together, persevered, and made a difference.

Now, because they chased the dream of Eden they had doomed each other. They had sacrificed their lives to deliver hope to the entirety of mankind. Was it worth the price? Alexandra's bitterness formed into a ball in her stomach as she realized she wasn't allowed to reenter Eden. Her fate was the same as those too sinful to enter paradise.

She traced her hand along Koneh's jaw line and said, "The gates are open. You didn't fail."

Koneh closed his eyes and his mouth curled on one side into a smile. "We did the impossible, you and me."

"And now we pay the price for it," she said, frowning.

He looked into her eyes and this time she found the strength to look back. A part of her heart screamed in protest that if this was the end she wouldn't get the chance to be with him.

"*I* may be beaten, but you are not," he said, his voice weaker than before. "Don't you see? The strongest steel is forged in the most dangerous fires. This journey has molded you into something more than you were before, something more than you would be if Eden willingly answered the promise you hoped it would answer. Take that strength and use it."

Alexandra eyed Ael and whispered, "Oh, I intend to."

"I'm not dreaming," Koneh said, his eyes widened as he realized the truth of her sacrifice. Somehow, he must have known the rules of Eden. His eyes were ancient with their sorrow. "You returned for us? You shouldn't be here. You should be…"

"How could I abandon you? Erzulie?" Alexandra said. "My heart isn't in Eden…"

"No, you have a destiny. Your place is in Eden. You cannot sacrifice everything… for me…"

Alexandra shook her head. "My place is with you… Koneh, *you* are my home."

Koneh closed his eyes again and Alexandra feared he was gone. After a few moments, he said, "You found me, Alexandra. After all these years, someone rescued me from a prison of my own making. Know that you are the only light shining in my heart."

She bit her lip and turned away. The next question was difficult enough to ask. Why make it harder by looking at Koneh while she spoke? "What will they do with us?" she asked.

"They will leave me here until my bones crumble to dust. You? They will bring you to Derechi and Iblis. They will learn from you what they need to conquer Eden…"

Ael turned his attention to the quiet conversation across the room and stepped towards them. He said, "Koneh, how helpless you must feel to have your sword within your reach, yet you cannot raise yourself against your chains."

Alexandra looked. Koneh's rusty sword was propped against the wall.

"And you," Ael said as he turned his white-in-white eyes towards Alexandra. "You will tell *me* the secrets of Eden."

Desperate to stall Ael, Alexandra said, "Where are your hounds and demons?"

"This is the way of things," Ael said. "Reward is always greater when you don't have to share it with others."

"You killed them?"

"Hell has taught me many new lessons."

A plan formed in Alexandra's mind and she hoped she had the time to muster the necessary courage. Koneh and Erzulie protected Alexandra for many months in the wasteland. Now, when it mattered the most, she searched for the strength she needed to save her friends.

Exhaling and leaving a part of her forever behind, in San Antonio, she said, "Thank you for always being there for me, Koneh."

With purposefully clumsy motions, Alexandra scrambled for Koneh's sword and stood to face Ael.

"What is this?" Ael said. "The Lamb raises a sword? Do you not remember the last time you stood in my path?"

Koneh taught Alexandra that the first attack was the most important, especially if your enemy didn't know what you could do. Stepping forward, foot over foot, she maneuvered to an advantageous position. Her muscles tensed, ready for action. She glanced at Erzulie, who remained motionless, and then she allowed her tears to roll down her cheeks.

Alexandra kept her eyes on her opponent, but she tilted her head towards Koneh.

"Koneh, I should have said this a long time ago. I love you."

Ael paused, and she lunged forward. Too late, Ael reached for his weapon. Alexandra buried Koneh's sword deep into the center of Ael's chest, hoping to strike his heart. His body shook with spasms and he fell to the ground.

"I am no Lamb," she said as she twisted the blade farther into her enemy. "I am the Lion!"

The light drained from Ael's eyes and he went limp.

Alexandra fell to her knees. The world outside the cavern ceased to exist and she allowed her pain, frustration and sorrow to drain from her body. She didn't want it anymore. Koneh and Erzulie were safe. Eden was reopened. It was over.

Alexandra wiped the tears from her face and turned to Koneh. She gasped.

The chains that once held Koneh were at the base of the rock pillar. Where he stood moments ago, there was only emptiness. Dust covered the chains and a small area of the ground near the pillar. He was gone.

"No!"

"Your love was his forgiveness," Erzulie said, her voice uneven and lacking the usual singsong melody.

"Erzulie?"

"I am alive," Erzulie said, "yet, I cannot move."

"What happened?"

"Finally, after all these years, he has found peace. You gave him that."

"No, I didn't mean to…"

"Through love, all things are forgiven," Erzulie said. "The moment he knew you loved him, his sins, both past and present, were wiped clean. You brought him peace."

Stunned, Alexandra walked to the pillar and dropped to her knees. She was both devastated and relieved. She wished forgiveness for him, of course, but not until she was ready. She wasn't ready to say good-bye to him.

Alexandra recalled when she met Koneh. He protected her from a bloodthirsty mob. He was always there to shield her from this broken world's dangers. Yet, she sensed something more behind Koneh's actions and words. He cared for her. Though he said he'd abandon his mission for her, she never believed he was capable of failure. He would've found another way.

"You brought something out in me," Alexandra said, her hand on the pillar. "I just wish…" Alexandra closed her eyes, but nothing could contain her tears. "I just wish we had more time together."

Time.

Was that all that waited for them in Eden? Endless time lounging in paradise? What would Koneh think of such complacency? Alexandra imagined Koneh was a man always in motion. Be it the next frontier, the next war or the next great adventure, he lived a life of action and purpose. In the end, he was willing to sacrifice himself to secure a better future for humanity.

What would Father Richard Callahan say to her? Would he understand why she couldn't stay in Eden? Alexandra missed her adopted father. She only knew him for a brief time, but she felt connected to the priest. Time was too short in this new world.

Alexandra's tears mixed with Koneh's dust. "Good bye, my friend, my love," she said. "I'll keep your handprint on my soul. Always."

For several long moments, the wind outside the cave was the only sound. Alexandra willed the cold away from her body, which was only protected by her sports bra, fatigues, and borrowed leather jacket.

"My Lady," Erzulie said, "you must leave this place."

Alexandra allowed herself a few more moments to mourn. Then, after a deep breath, she rose from the pillar and embraced Erzulie.

"I'm so glad you're all right," Alexandra said. "I feared the worst."

"All is well," Erzulie said. "You have righted many wrongs this day."

Alexandra's tears came again. "He's gone."

"Shhh, be still."

For several long moments, she rocked in Erzulie's embrace. The presumptions about her world shattered, she found peace in the embrace of a fallen angel, a being constructed by God to serve in Heaven. Yet, Erzulie acted more human than most people Alexandra knew. Was the copy better than the original? Koneh's words crept into Alexandra's mind. Erzulie will serve her master without hesitation. At that moment, Alexandra didn't care about what the future held. She was safe in the angel's arms.

"You must go," Erzulie said.

"Why?"

"Derechi's army will be here soon. I'm not strong enough to travel, so you must go alone." Erzulie lowered her eyes. "Please forgive me for failing you. Ael was too strong for us."

Alexandra grasped Erzulie's head in her hands and said, "Listen. I'm not going anywhere, and I'm not going to lose you! Not you! Let Derechi come and try to take you from me. I will kill him with my own hands and deliver death upon his army."

Erzulie's pure white eyes searched Alexandra's face. Then Erzulie said, "I am your witness. Let it be known the Lion has shown herself."

Alexandra couldn't suppress a laugh. "Yeah, I don't know why I said that."

"It was foretold by Bishop Palusa in his altered Bible," Erzulie said. "A *Lion*, not a Lamb, will come. She is here."

"Well," Alexandra said as the cold penetrated her leather jacket. "the Lioness wishes she was somewhere warmer."

"There is nothing you cannot accomplish," Erzulie said.

Alexandra examined her wounded friend and said, "Good, then use me for support. We're leaving."

"I cannot."

"Yes you can. I'll help you."

She assisted Erzulie to her feet and propped her near the mouth of the cave.

"Oh, one sec," Alexandra said as she returned to the interior of the cavern. She approached Ael and removed Koneh's sword from the dead angel's chest. Then, she attached the heavy weapon to her belt and met Erzulie outside the cave.

"He's there, you know," Erzulie said, her eyes on the silver gates. "Your forgiveness wiped his soul clean and he will find peace."

"I know," Alexandra said. "He deserves some rest."

"I see the pain in your heart," Erzulie said. "You sacrificed your life with him so he could be in Eden. In all my years, I've only rarely witnessed such acts of love. Your love is an exceptional kind, Alexandra. Know that it doesn't die here."

"That wasn't my intention," Alexandra said, the ball of bitterness turning to regret in her stomach. "I just wanted him to know how I felt. Since I was about to attack an angel, I figured I didn't have much time left."

"You knew," Erzulie said. "Deep within yourself, you knew your love was his salvation. He knows too, I'm certain of it. He laments the sacrifice you made and his heart is broken as completely as yours. Someday you will be reunited."

The pair departed Eden and Alexandra supported Erzulie as they walked for several miles. As the first hints of orange light filtered into the black sky, they climbed a short rise to look upon Eden.

After securing her jacket and remaining belongings, Alexandra found Father Callahan's rosary amongst her meager supplies. Not sure how to best remember her fallen friends, Alexandra wrapped the rosary around the cross section of Koneh's sword. This way, she would think of them every time she drew the weapon. Alexandra decided her enemies would share her pain.

"What will you do now?" Erzulie asked.

"I don't know," Alexandra said.

"Where do you wish to go?"

Alexandra watched the silver gates of Eden sparkle in the distance. "I think I would like to return here someday," she said. "But for now, I'm glad to turn away from this place. There's too much pain here."

"They will come after you," Erzulie said. "You still hold the key."

"I know. I think I'll be ready for them next time."

Erzulie smiled. "You are the Lion. That may give them pause."

Alexandra broke her gaze from Eden and looked into the angel's eyes.

"I'm glad you're with me," Alexandra said. "You and Koneh were always there for me. I value your friendship more than you'll ever know."

"Koneh…" Erzulie said. "If I was human I would feel sadness at his passing. Should we have brought his ashes to bury them?"

Alexandra shook her head and gazed at the new, orange horizon to the north.

"We don't need his ashes," Alexandra said. "A hero has the whole world for his tomb."

Matthew C. Plourde is a cancer survivor and native New Englander. He is a husband and father of two children. His family called Vietnam "home" for a month while they adopted their son. Though writing is his passion, he currently works as a compliance consultant for large enterprise corporations. His shorter fiction has appeared on many different e-zines and he continues to write novels.

For all the latest, visit his blog:
http://matthewcplourde.wordpress.com/